Jakarta

JAKARTA

Kerry B. Collison

Sid Harta Publishers
1999

Published by:	Sid Harta Publishers for Kerry B. Collison and Asian Pacific Management Co. (S.A.) Ltd.
	Telephone: (61) (0 414) 958623
	fax: (61) 03 9560 9921
	Address: PO Box 1102 Hartwell, Victoria, Australia 3125

First published January 1998
Second Printing April 1999
Copyright © Kerry B.Collison,
Sid Harta Publishers and
Asian Pacific Management Co. Ltd. S.A, 1998

Text:	Kerry B.Collison
Cover Concept:	Guy W. Collison
Final Proof Reading:	Dr. John D. Quigley
Author's Photograph:	Courtesy of Ned Kelly and the Bundaberg News Mail, Queensland

This book is copyright. Apart from fair dealing for the purposes of private study, research, criticism or review, as permitted under the Copyright Act, no part may be reproduced by any process without the written permission of the copyright owners.

Collison, Kerry Boyd

ISBN   0 95 874 48 66

Printed in Australia
by Australian Print Group
Maryborough, Victoria.

Acknowledgements

During the considerable time spent researching material relating to nuclear power, I was most fortunate to receive the support of many who, in one way or another, assisted with my ongoing education, particularly with the subject matter contained in this novel.

I therefore wish to express my gratitude to Andrew Karam of the Ohio State University, who contributed a great deal of his valuable time to assist me to understand more about nuclear reactors and life aboard an American nuclear submarine. To Andy, thank you for your friendship and incredible support.

I wish also to thank Tim Gabruch, visiting research officer at the Uranium Institute in London, who provided me with details of Chernobyl and in-depth detail of the Nuclear Energy Club, and Richard Broinowski, Honorary Professor, Faculty of Communications, University of Canberra for his contribution in relation to the final chapters of this book.

There are others I should not forget to mention here. These include: the Information Section of the United States Seventh Fleet in Japan; the United Nations representative office in Sydney; the Information Office of the Japanese Embassy in Canberra, Australia; the representative offices of Boeing in Sydney; the British Defense Liaison Staff, Canberra; David Wiencek, Research Associate at the CDISS in Washington, D.C.; Gary Benoit, Editor of *The New American;* and Clare Booth.

To the many *The Timor Man* and *Merdeka Square* readers who have communicated their thoughts, thank you for your incredible support.

Kerry B. Collison
Melbourne

Kerry B. Collison followed a distinguished period of service as a member of the Australian Embassy in Indonesia during the turbulent Sixties followed by a successful business career spanning thirty years throughout Asia.

Recognised for his chilling predictions in relation to Asia's evolving political and economic climate and as the only Australian ever to have been personally granted citizenship by an Indonesian President, he brings unique qualifications to his historically-based vignettes and intriguing accounts of power-politics and the shadowy world of governments' clandestine activities.

The author's biographical data is avaliable on the Internet at:
http://www.sidharta.com.au

Photo of the author by Ned Kelly, published by courtesy of the Bundaberg News Mail.

Dedication

I dedicate this book, *Jakarta*,
to the memory of

Air-Vice Marshall Raden Imam Suwongso Wirjosapoetro

*Atas segala kepercayaan dan persahabatan beliau pada saya,
semasa beliau masih hidup, saya ucapkan terima kasih
serta maaf lahir dan bathin.*

*Other books
by Kerry B. Collison*

The Asian Trilogy

The Timor Man

Freedom (Merdeka) Square

Jakarta

The Fifth Season

Non-Fiction

The Leo Stach Story

"Revolusi kita, belum selesai!"

'Our revolution has yet to complete its course!'

Indonesia's founding President, Soekarno,
in his last major address to the people before
being overthrown by General Soeharto

Jakarta — Tanjung Priok Harbour Nuclear Power Plant

Contents

Map of SE Asia 12, 13
Prologue 15

Book one

1. Origins 23
2. The Salima Group 41
3. John Georgio and others 85
4. Ruswita at work 93
5. A wedding 113

Book two

6. Lim buys an American bank 121
7. Rama announcement 129
8. The Palace at work 151
9. General Seda and Lim Swee Giok 163
10. Lim and the Salima Group 181
11. Murray, Graeme, Peter 185
12. Japan's Prime Minister 201
13. Defense Intelligence Agency — USA 217
14. Australian Prime Minister 235
15. Lim and Ruswita's story 249
16. India 267
17. Islamabad 281
18. Canberra — CIA 301
19. Japan — Jakarta — Robson 323

Book three, Rama energy

Diagram of nuclear power station 340, 341
Map of Indonesia and Northern Australia .. 342, 343

20.	Ruswita and the Salima Group	345
21.	Ratna Sari, Michael in California	353
22..	The Oval Office	361
23.	General Kumar — India	375
24.	Washington — CIA and Michael	383
25.	Ratna and Michael in Jakarta	403
26.	Xanana and the Chinese Fleet	419
27.	The Bali Summit	431
28.	Bali — the countdown	447
29.	Bali and Rama	489
30.	India	509
Epilogue		517
Author's Note		521
Glossary		529

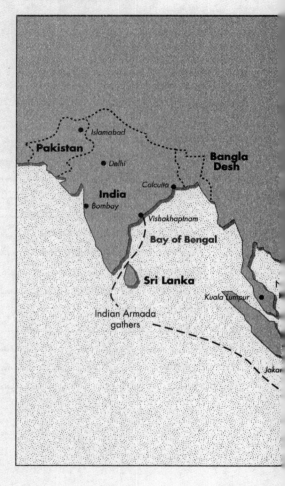

JAKARTA

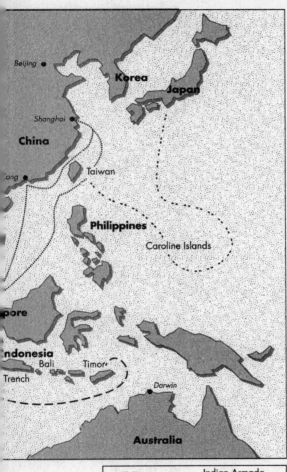

Kerry B. Collison

Prologue

*The Jakarta Stock Exchange,
the present*

'Sell Salima Jaya!' Budiman screamed hopelessly, his voice drowned in the cacophonous mix of panic trading and cries of disbelief which had prevailed since news of the disaster had reached the floor of the capital's exchange. Excruciating pain in his side caused him to catch his breath, sharply, as one of his colleagues elbowed past, waving frantically as he too attempted to off-load his client's stock in Salima Jaya Power. Budiman struggled forward, pulling against the shoulders of the others in front. *'One hundred and fifty-thousand!'* he yelled hoarsely, competing against a barrage of sellers who blocked his way, muffling his call. He lost his balance, again, and fell as the unruly mob of traders scrambled futilely to dominate the proceedings.

The floor was in total chaos as millions continued to be wiped from the value of all Salima stocks, plunging the entire market into a downward spin. In the first thirty minutes, the Jakarta Index had fallen thirty percent, while the Exchange's Chairman vacillated as to whether or not he should heed the many calls to suspend all trading, fearful that his own holdings had yet to be divested by his unscrupulous brother-in-law cum broker. He peered anxiously around the floor again, confused, resisting the temptation to leave his position and go in search of his man. Another fight erupted, resulting in a number of traders being dragged angrily away as security guards attempted to restore order. The Chairman caught a glimpse of his broker being escorted from the hall and knew, immediately, that it was too late, and that he too had been caught up in the disaster. He stared at the prominent clock and, overcome with despair, gripped the small podium's railings, his knuckles white. There was at least an hour's trading left in the day. Resigned to the possibility that he had lost everything, the Chairman saw no advantage in suspending trading and he remained stationary, a solitary, silent observer of what had surely been the most calamitous day in the Exchange's history.

On the floor below, Budiman struggled to maintain balance as the body of traders surged back in his direction, threatening to crush him as he screamed his sell order. Incredibly, it was as if the buyers could not see his mark. Budiman was lifted off his feet as the panic-driven sellers surged forward. The young Javanese trader called out loudly, certain that he would be crushed.

Amid the confusion in the Exchange, none of the frantic traders registered the shuddering beneath their feet. The unstable ground below moved, rocking the building's floating foundations for the second time that day. They were oblivious to the aftershock, an ominous signal that the threat of pending natural disaster was very, very real.

Budiman felt faint. It was as if there was no oxygen in the air. *Why won't they let me through?* he wondered, bewildered by their failure to recognise the powerful group he represented. A large *Waringan Corporation* trader's identification tag covered the area above his left breast pocket. This was the First Family's own trading company symbol. *What's wrong with them?* his mind screamed, as he was pushed and shoved, unable to maintain his balance as the other traders ignored the sell orders held tightly in his right hand. He called again, in desperation, realizing that his voice would not be heard amongst the multitude of sellers screaming over him. Then, as he felt someone rip the paper from his hand, he stumbled and was pushed, then kicked savagely from behind.

'*No!*' he called weakly, but his cry was drowned amidst the screams of others who had tripped over Budiman as he fell. Mistakenly, several traders thought they had heard a buyer call out in his direction, and this galvanised them into action. The mass of sellers surged forward, fighting, kicking and punching their way towards where they believed the only remaining buyer of Salima stocks seemed to be.

At that moment, another tremor struck, this time showering clouds of surface cement dust over the assembly. Stunned into silence, the traders waited, holding their breath. They raised their hands above their heads, anticipating the worst.

An eerie quiet enveloped the floor as the building swayed threateningly. Scrolling price indicator lights flickered, then went blank as sensitive terminals shut down, unable to cope with the inadequate power support system. And then, within moments of the volcanic surge passing, the traders' screams once again dominated the floor.

Minutes later, two of the non-government banks asked to have their shares removed from trading. Within the hour, fifteen private banks had collapsed. Most of these were majority owned by the First Family and Lim Swee Giok's Salima Jaya Group. Only moments had passed when there was a further tremor, and huge clumps of concrete were ripped from the wall of the building crushing several men to the Stock Exchange floor. It was almost as if nature, having recognised the corruption inside, had moved to punish those within. As dust settled, a solitary cry was heard and one of the traders, his legs crushed, cried out in pain. The lights blinked, again, then power failed altogether, throwing the exchange into artificial darkness.

There was a hush as traders held their breath, waiting for another after-shock. But there was none. Then, unexpectedly, there was a blinding glare of light as the automatic generators switched in, and power was restored. Within moments, the momentary blackout was forgotten, and trading recommenced with renewed panic.

'*Sell Salima Jaya Power!*' the line screamed again, competing against each other, waving their sell-notes furiously. But there were few buyers. Budiman and a number of others lay unconscious, oblivious to the disastrous events which surrounded them. Several security guards pushed their way over to where they had seen him fall, and dragged Budiman and the other bruised men to safety. The panic-driven shouting continued.

'*Salima, sell!*' a trader yelled. '*Salima Jaya sell, two million!*' he screamed, fearing that his block of two million shares would be left unacknowledged, as he waved his sell order high above the shoulders of the shorter men who were hoping to off-load another six million shares of the stock, as the market continued its incredible collapse. '*Sell at one-fifty thousand!*' the voice shrieked, offering the once blue-chip share for less than a tenth of its value when the market commenced trading that day.

'*Salima, sell!*' another frantic trader from behind yelled even louder as the pandemonium continued, '*sell three million at one hundred thousand rupiah!*' he shouted, not to be outdone by his rival.

* * * * * *

And so the tumultuous session continued. The disfavoured stocks finally bringing the entire market down more than sixty percent as rumour continued to spread of the Salima Group's disastrous accident, and of the magnitude of what had happened. Earlier, and within minutes of the first downwards trend, the Singapore market had moved into the play, followed immediately by Kuala Lumpur and Hong Kong, sending the Jakarta stocks plummeting to lows few Indonesian industrial magnates could ever have imagined. At first they hesitated out of loyalty, but soon recognised that even with their support, their old associate's company would most likely collapse. Then, they too panicked, disposing of whatever stock the buyers could absorb. When the electronic bell finally sounded, marking the end of trading, there was a hush. And in the air hung the unfamiliar smell of despair as the Jakarta Stock Market closed for the day. The Salima Group, one of Indonesia's most favoured conglomerates, had all but collapsed, precipitating the demise of at least three hundred other publicly listed companies.

* * * * * *

The panic selling had been precipitated by an abrupt announcement declaring that the Salima Jaya Power owned and operated nuclear power plant in Bali had suffered structural damage as a result of the previous day's earth tremor, and was now in imminent danger of collapse. A nuclear melt-down. Reports further claimed that mass evacuation of tourists from the densely populated Island of the Gods had already commenced. The unstable nuclear energy site had been subjected to further tremors, threatening nuclear devastation on a scale yet unknown to mankind. There would be a massive loss of life, and with that, enormous claims against the owners and operators.

JAKARTA

* * * * * *

Within hours of the disastrous trading session's close, many of Jakarta's high profile brokers, along with their military associates, quietly emptied their safes, made excuses to their families and girlfriends, then fled before the Presidential aides could comprehend what had really happened. They knew they would be blamed for the incredible financial losses the First Family had also suffered in those few short hours of Indonesia's economic Armageddon.

* * * * * *

The members of the board sat quietly, confused by their sudden change in fortunes and shocked by their chief executive's accusations. Not one amongst their number had ever heard their Chairwoman raise her voice before. This sudden outburst had only increased their feeling of foreboding as the Salima Jaya Group's matriarch stood at the end of the long, polished mahogany table, her head and shoulders silhouetted by the late afternoon sun as it continued its descent over the Sunda Straits, to the West.

'Enough!' she cried, loudly, slamming her fragile hand down hard on the table. She stood, glaring at those around the mahogany table, who were stunned with surprise at the sudden strength of the woman.

'That will be enough!' she demanded, rising slowly. One of the younger men leaped to his feet and pulled the heavy chair back, enabling her to stand. They cast their heads down in deferential silence. Their world had changed. The speed at which everything had been thrown into turmoil had left them fearing for their futures. And their lives. Suddenly, the room moved slightly, then rocked, as the upper levels of the building was whipped by the power of yet another aftershock. They all sat motionless and silent.

Less than a minute followed before nervous coughs brought the meeting back to order. They all stared towards the end of the room and waited for the small framed silhouette to speak again. And then she began.

The members of the board sat up, attentive, as she laid out the foundations for the Salima Group's future. The members sat quietly, mesmerised as *Ibu Ruswita*, their Chairwoman, outlined her plans to rebuild the Group's fortunes. There was not one amongst their number who did not realize immediately that if they refused to comply, then they would have no future at all. At least not in *that* country. In typical Asian style, accepting what had become the inevitable, they breathed deeply, silently, and listened to what the Chairwoman determined should be done. And, without exception, they knew that they would obey.

* * * * * *

Alone, having dismissed the members of her inner sanctum, Ruswita rose to her feet. The swaying sensation of the building seemed to have slowed, and she moved cautiously to the French windows which overlooked the Capital's protocol street, Jalan Thamrin. The air conditioning units had not automatically restarted and she could smell the lingering odour of *kretek* cigarette in the board room. Ruswita stared down at the small pedestrian dots barely moving along the footpaths below. She sighed, recalling the urgent communication she had received from Professor Sutomo, Chairman of BATAN, the Indonesian Atomic Energy Commission. She had listened intently as the scientist had offered his terrifying projections, projections which indicated that the loss of life could be in the millions. Perhaps even her own children could be among the victims; she had no way of finding out, as yet.

Ruswita's eyes blurred, and her mind slipped back to how it had all begun, and how her destiny had led her to this cruel predicament.

Book one

Kerry B.Collison

Chapter 1

Origins

Ruswita rested for a moment, stretched, then wiped her forehead with the back of her soapy hands. Then she crouched over the village *kali* again, taking the clothes one, by one, and rinsing them meticulously by hand to complete her washing. As she placed each item carefully into the hand-woven basket, Ruswita counted them to ensure that none were missing. Here the dark water flowed quickly and she knew that one had to be particularly careful not to slip, or lose track of the clothes spread out on the smooth, black, basalt river-rock.

Ruswita flicked at a few strands of long black hair which had worked loose from the temporary bun tied at the back of her head. One of the other women called to her friends and, at the sound of her voice, Rus glanced in the direction of the chatter, identifying the talkative young woman who had married just the week before. Rus cast another glance in the younger woman's direction, just long enough to confirm that the fourteen-year-old bride was already with child. She considered this with mixed emotions, sighed, then returned to folding her washing.

Here, on the river's banks, there were few secrets. The women gathered each morning on this side of the fast flowing stream, where the water cascaded down from the distant mountains providing life to the villagers, their fields, and the crops. During the past few years, the harvests had been exceptionally poor. But once, Rus remembered, it had all been very different.

Four years had passed since the civil war had finally ground to a halt, leaving the village almost devoid of life. The bloody and senseless holocaust had destroyed the world these simple and uneducated farmers had known, leaving little but a bitter harvest of hate and lasting discrimination. Ruswita had been most fortunate to survive those violent times considering she was of mixed extraction, a *peranakan*. Her Javanese mother had not been as fortunate. Ruswita's Chinese father had been slaughtered during the blood-bath which ensued from the general perception that all Chinese were Communist, and were therefore responsible for the violent and cruel deaths of the country's military leadership during the abortive *coup d'etat* of 1965.

When the marauding gangs had struck her village, Ruswita fled in terror, escaping through the rear of the family's simple dwelling. Terrified that she too might be killed, she did not turn back to go to her family's aid, knowing that the screams which followed were those of her mother and remaining family who had been caught, huddled together, at the entrance to their impoverished home.

The few who survived the anti-Communist blood-lettings soon discovered that their rich, fertile land had been sowed with bitter seeds indeed. Army commanders such as Sarwo Edhie embarked on genocidal missions with a determination that ultimately accounted for the deaths of hundreds of thousands of innocent villagers, many of whom were children who were not yet in their teens. The once bountiful harvests were gone. Children no longer played along the reaches of the river system, once considered their Garden of Eden. Evidence of their historical and cultural past had, in the greater part, been obliterated. Entire families, who had innocently permitted communist doctrines to infiltrate their communities, had disappeared forever.

During those fearful times, even the river boat captains refused to venture into their district, electing to terminate their journey further downstream. Their crews were terrified of the marauding gangs who, as they knew, slaughtered their enemies with incredible ferocity. Later, they saw the shocking results of the mass slaughter, when thousands of bodies washed down-stream and choked the river. Ruswita had been fortunate indeed to have been spared. As the terrifying attack on her village began, she had fled the scene, running down the river's muddy slopes, slipping and sliding in search of a safe hiding place. She plunged into the river and grasped the sides of a small timber boat behind which she hid from the marauders. There, Ruswita waited, terrified, fearful of discovery.

JAKARTA

As she clung to the side of the ancient canoe, screams and shouting continued unabated, and she closed her eyes and prayed to both the gods her parents worshipped. An hour passed, and then another, before the shivering, terrified young girl managed to summon sufficient courage to drag herself cautiously out of the muddy hiding place and crawl cautiously back up the slopes to her village. There she was greeted with scenes of absolute savagery. Mutilated bodies lay everywhere, evidence of the cruel attack. Now, as she recalled these images while bent over the very same river which had once been her temporary sanctuary, Ruswita fought to drag herself back from those moments of horror, fighting the indelible memory of seeing her mother's headless corpse.

Conscious that she had been momentarily lost in her hideous past, Ruswita looked anxiously around to see if she had been observed by the other women. Without being obvious, she watched some of the women arriving late for their daily chores along the river bank, and noted that the village chief's wife had detailed two of the other younger women to carry her household washing down to the stream. Ruswita knew that the *lurah's* wife was someone to reckon with. As the village chief's most recent acquisition, she had an unofficial position within the community which went unchallenged. The new wife was the *lurah's* fourth. That meant there would be no more opportunity for the unmarried women who might have considered themselves eligible for selection. Ruswita sighed. She really had no ambition to marry. At least, not right then. She just wanted to escape the *kampung* with its poverty and horrific memories.

* * * * * *

Early evenings, before the villagers fell into their tired and well-deserved sleep, it was customary to gather together and listen to the radio broadcast, which immediately followed their final prayers for the day. Once the village chieftain had turned the Grundig off, and was satisfied that he had disconnected his valuable radio to ensure that the leads to the car batteries were not in danger of touching, he would stand, signalling that the evening entertainment was over. Silently, the small community would then retire in preparation for another demanding day which would begin before the sun's first false rays heralded its arrival. As kerosene lanterns were extinguished and the village became quiet, Ruswita joined the others in her hut, sleeping amongst the single women on *tikar* mats, cramped together in their simple dwelling. The young woman lay on her side with her hand under her head as a pillow, permitting her thoughts to stray, enticed by the promise of sleep and images of faraway places. Each night she would close her eyes and conjure up scenes of what the cities might be like, and how she would venture into those intimidating places. Comforted by the soft sounds of the others breathing as they too slipped into their own private worlds, Ruswita lay quietly and imagined herself in a small house in some distant place, far away from the nightmares of her past, and far away from the despair, loneliness, and poverty she endured.

* * * * * *

The wait seemed interminable, and Ruswita began to lose faith that she would ever find the opportunity to escape her village. At nineteen, she was considered almost too old to be a first wife, and too young to be around the other women's husbands as long as she remain unattached. Then there was the problem of her *peranakan* extraction. Rus was the daughter of a Chinese river-trader. Her mother had been a simple Javanese woman who had resigned herself to being one of the many wives her casual husband kept along the river trading route. Resentment against the Chinese still lingered in the aftermath of the civil war and Ruswita knew that her blood-line would guarantee that she would be relegated to a less rewarding life than she deserved. Ruswita understood clearly that even if she were fortunate enough to marry within the next few years, it would be unlikely that she would live long enough to enjoy caring for her own grandchildren for, in her land of Java, very few peasant women survived to celebrate their fiftieth birthdays. Birthdays were celebrated only once, upon a child's arrival, and as most of her fellow villagers were illiterate, records were not kept as such information was passed from one generation to another merely by word of mouth.

Ruswita refused to resign herself to her unfortunate lot in life as others around her had done, accepting their roles as mothers and wives as generations of women had before them. She learned to read the new language, *Bahasa Indonesia*, from old and torn newspapers carried into the village by the river traders, and was one of the few women in her village who could understand the evening news broadcasts. It was not long before the other young women avoided her. They were envious of her achievements, and piqued that she aspired to rise above her position in the village order. Driven by the desire to achieve an even greater level of learning, Ruswita was obliged to spend considerably more time than she wished studying the *Holy Koran*, as this was the only acceptable path for a woman of such simple origins. At the age of sixteen, Rus could already read and write as well as any city child who had attended primary school. She was a bright child, and would have had little difficulty with the lessons had she been given the opportunity to attend the district elementary high school. But, because of her origins and sex, this opportunity would elude her and Rus, accepting that this as her *nasib*, her fate, went about her life, praying that her *rezeki* would change for the better.

* * * * * *

In her nineteenth year, Ruswita came to the conclusion that it was impossible for her to remain in the village any longer, and devised a plan to leave. She encouraged the attention of one of the younger men and, promising rewards well beyond what she was prepared to give, slipped away from her village with the infatuated man, leaving her place of birth forever. Ten kilometres downstream, she left the disappointed suitor and climbed aboard one of the frequent river boats used to transport produce to the shallow-water harbour on the coast. She discovered that she could survive in the coastal city, working along the roadside as a daily labourer. A month passed before she could convince one of the Chinese shopkeepers that she really was literate, and this secured a position for her, working in a dusty garment store adjacent to the main thoroughfare, and inter-city bus terminal. She worked dutifully for three months, saving sufficient to purchase a bus ticket that would take her to the nation's capital, Jakarta. Ruswita eventually boarded a bus, crammed full of people, pigs, chickens and baskets of produce, her heart filled with the promise of things to come. As she headed towards the city of dreams which had occupied her thoughts since first listening to the village radio broadcasts, Ruswita's excitement grew, confident that she had made the correct choice.

The journey was extremely demanding. Roads were broken, and in many places washed away, often requiring hours of detours around streams which no longer afforded bridges. As she travelled through the countryside, Rus felt a little apprehensive as the overladen bus ground on through the poverty-stricken towns along the coastal route, her uncertainty growing as they neared the capital, where she witnessed the thousands upon thousands of roadside dwellers camped under makeshift dwellings. Occasionally, she waved to children as they scrambled out of the bus's path, turning quickly away from the choking, cloud of dust, and black diesel smoke which followed the dilapidated vehicle. After three long days and nights, the bus finally groaned to a stop in metropolitan Jakarta, not far from the *Glodok* inter-city bus stop. Ruswita stepped down from the bus, and looked around in wonder. The spectacle was more awe-inspiring than she had ever imagined.

There were at least a hundred buses parked in the square, Some had rows of huge baskets tied to the roof, filled to overflowing with vegetables and other produce. Others, rocking and swaying over the ruts, chugged laboriously through the filthy quagmire of the square. Animals defecated where they were tied, and day-traders moved tirelessly between the maze of buses, barely able to maintain their footing while balancing their precarious shoulder-loads on long, bamboo poles. Rus removed her sandals and struggled through the mud, uncertain what to do next. She clung on to her few possessions in case she slipped and fell into the foul-smelling mud. The choking air caused her to cough, and as she did so, Rus remembered to cover her face with the end of her *selendang*.

At first, she was intimidated by the apparent chaos of the spectacle which surrounded her, but soon Ruswita's natural confidence and determination returned and she began walking quickly among the mass of people, politely enquiring about accommodations and opportunities for work. Most simply ignored her, or scoffed at her naiveté. Some of the men offered her money, and laughed when she turned from them, embarrassed. She understood clearly what their gestures meant. Ruswita felt bewildered and somewhat confused by the arrogance and obvious disdain of the city people. She had never encountered such animosity, such impolite behaviour, amongst her village-folk.

Hours passed, and Rus knew that she should try to find lodgings before nightfall. Depressed, but not discouraged, she walked away from the square. Her feet were filthy, and Rus shook her head in disgust. She had not expected that such conditions could possibly exist in the capital. Rus made her way towards a number of waiting *becak* drivers, selected one, then placed her bundle of possessions on the three-wheeled monster's narrow seat.

'Where do you want to go, *nona?*' she was asked.

'Take me to a *losmen* that is cheap,' she answered, wearily, holding ten Rupiah tightly in her hand for the driver to see. The driver grunted, lifted the rear wheel and pointed his machine away from the terminal. He pushed for momentum then climbed onto the seat, and pedalled away from the congested traffic. As he did this he was inwardly considering just how far he would take the country girl for her ten Rupiah. As they left the over-crowded square and entered the main thoroughfare connecting Glodok to the city's centre, Rus continued to cover her face to avoid not only the stench emanating from the sewerage drain running down the centre of the divided road, but also to reduce the nausea from the thick black clouds of suffocating exhaust fumes.

As they pedalled along, Rus was surprised to see continuous lines of roadside stalls selling traditional village foods, such as *durian* cakes, steamed rice wrapped in banana leaf, fried noodles, and many other dishes she had thought would not be available so far from the villages. As a familiar aroma drifted across her path, she experienced a sudden pang of loneliness and wondered, again, if she had made the right decision. Then, as the driver turned another corner, the magnificent old colonial Hotel Duta appeared, bright with coloured lights, a sight which took Ruswita's breath away. Floodlights struck the hotel's tall white walls, the luminous effect so stunning that Ruswita felt her eyes fill with tears. It was just like she had dreamed the city would be. The rows of coloured lights dancing across the evening sky made the building appear like some magic, dazzling palace. Moments later the brilliant scene disappeared from view as the *becak* turned once again, down a narrow street, and came to a halt outside what appeared to be a *losmen*. Ruswita paid the driver and, gathering up her clothes, entered the boarding house.

She paid twenty-five Rupiah to share a room with a number of other women, whose *tikar* mats had already been opened, and spread across the floor in preparation for sleep. Hungry, but concerned that she had already spent far too much for that day, Ruswita decided to skip the evening meal. She moved through the cramped quarters to the rear of the building, through a narrow passageway to the ablution block. There, she entered the primitive bathroom area, undressed, squatted on the concrete floor and peed, then rose and dipped the plastic scoop into the square shaped cement reservoir and threw the cold water between her legs. She then refilled the scoop and poured water over her head, enjoying the cool sensation. Ruswita could not remember ever missing taking a *mandi* at least twice each day before, but she had not bathed since climbing aboard the bus some three days earlier. So it was with great relief that she attacked the dirt, both real and imaginary, which had accumulated during the arduous journey from Central Java. Satisfied that she was clean, Ruswita then washed the clothes she had worn for almost four days, placed these over the outside railing, wrapped herself in a *sarong* and returned to the communal bedroom. There she unrolled her thin *tikar* and spread it carefully on the floor amongst the other women. She lay down and fell immediately into a deep, satisfying, sleep.

When Ruswita awoke early the next day, it was not until after her morning ablutions that she discovered that she had spent her first night resting in one of the city's more infamous brothels, behind *Pasar Baru*.

* * * * * *

Not three kilometers from where Ruswita had spent her first night in Jakarta, Murray Stephenson sat in his pavilion *cum* office along Jalan Tasikmalaya, examining the poorly-typed letter he'd written some hours before. As he read down through the two paged report, he corrected no less than twenty errors and sighed, knowing that this was probably the best that his secretary could do. It was impossible to expect more, he knew. There were so few secretaries available who had been trained to type, let alone take shorthand. He sighed, thinking about the number of young girls who had professed to being adequately conversant with Pitman's requirements. There hadn't been one, he'd discovered, who could take shorthand faster than he could write his damn correspondence in longhand. He stretched, leaned back, then threw the ballpen onto the teak table in disgust. If only he had a decent secretary!

Murray had been fortunate to fall on his feet, so to speak. After the coup, he left the Australian Government and returned to Indonesia to establish his own general consultancy. At first, he had been treated with suspicion by the local authorities. There was little he could do about this problem deciding that, as they had his file on record, he would just have to be circumspect about the circles in which he moved until the Indonesian authorities became comfortable with his new status. To his dismay, Murray had discovered upon his return that there were those amongst the Indonesian hierarchy who still considered him their enemy. Then there were the problems he faced relating to his limited clientele and diminishing finances. It seemed that ever since the new government had taken power and introduced its foreign investment laws, most foreign investors continued to hesitate, waiting cautiously to see whether or not it was true that the former communist country had really become receptive to Western nations investing in the near-bankrupt economy.

Murray knew that the opportunities would grow. There was an abundance of oil and, with that, he believed it was only a matter of time before a ground-swell developed, and investors began pumping millions of resource-orientated investment dollars into the formerly fragile economy. The difficulty he faced was making ends meet until he had secured enough clients to bankroll his expensive overheads.

His credentials were considered excellent by many potential investors who visited, reassured by his manner and obvious knowledge of the people and their culture. Murray was one of a small number of foreigners fluent in the Indonesian language. Before the end of his first year, he had already secured sufficient accounts to guarantee that he could remain solvent for at least another three years. Having overcome the major expense of accommodations, Murray had only to meet monthly payroll and basic living costs to make ends meet. His major client, Peter Wong, had advanced the mandatory three-year advance rental required for his premises. Murray had done everything to avoid making such an incredibly large payment but, as property could only be owned by Indonesians, and they had already been spoiled by the Embassies and other foreign legations in the capital, he had no choice but to pay the equivalent of the value of the premises in one lump sum; he knew that the landlord would then have sufficient capital to purchase another home, and most probably continue the cycle by renting out his new acquisition as well.

Then there was Coleman. Murray could not understand the speed at which the younger man's star had risen when he, with all of his connections, had to struggle to make ends meet. Murray thought about Stephen Coleman and agreed with those who remembered the story, that the former agent was indeed most fortunate to be alive. Murray had been surprised when the younger man had returned to Indonesia and elected to stay. He had been even more surprised when, in less than one year of having established himself as a competitor, the less-experienced Coleman had easily secured major contracts with the Indonesian Government. Murray admitted that he was more than a little envious of these successes, and avoided contact with his business rival. They rarely communicated. Murray thought it best, considering their common background, and the possibility that Coleman just might not be all that he appeared. The thought had crossed his mind that Coleman might still be employed by Canberra and, if this were true, it would most certainly explain how the fledgling entrepreneur had suddenly become so successful in Indonesia.

During the first few months of his return, Murray had serious doubts concerning his decision to leave the intelligence services, and the security he had enjoyed, to risk venturing out into a world of commerce which was so obviously, totally alien to everything he had known in the past. However, as he became settled and more confident, Murray discovered that there were, in fact, very few differences between these two masters. Both, he soon learned, were unforgiving towards those who made mistakes. Both, he also observed, only rewarded the winners. Others were quickly cast aside and forgotten.

Murray extracted another *Gudang Garam kretek* cigarette from the packet of ten, and placed it, absent-mindedly, in his mouth. His head ached but the strong smelling clove would soon remedy that. He reached for the stainless steel Ronson, flicked the lighter with his thumb, then inhaled the warm scented smoke deep into his lungs. He rubbed his face as if hoping this would be sufficient to wipe away the cobwebs strung across the inside of his head as a result of too many whiskies and not enough sleep. His thoughts turned to the two young women he'd left inside. Murray knew that, by now, they would have checked through everything they could find in the master bedroom. He tried to think, recalling his movements the night before and how he'd ended up with the two by himself. His mind was clouded, but he knew that it wasn't really important. Then something triggered his memory and it suddenly came to him. He'd met them at John Georgio's house. Slowly, pieces of the past evening came back and he smiled as he recalled arriving at the American's house, only to discover that Georgio had organized one of his indiscreet parties, where the women considerably outnumbered the men. It was there he remembered asking one of the local girls home, but she had insisted on bringing her friend. The rest was still hazy in his mind, but Murray could remember drinking the cheap, Italian wine John Georgio had insisted on pouring down his guests' throats.

The phone rang in the adjacent room and he knew the caller would be one of the men he'd taken with him to the party. He moaned, not really up to taking them by the hand to guide them through their appointments once again. They had insisted that he escort them down to the Directorate of Air Communications, and Murray knew that he had little choice but to attend the meeting, as the Indonesian officials would expect his presence. His secretary appeared in the doorway and signalled that the call was for him. He acknowledged this with a wave of his hand, then lifted the receiver to accept the call. Minutes later, having agreed to pick his guests up at the Intercontinental Hotel, he wandered back from the small office situated alongside his residence and went in search of aspirin. Murray knew that this was going to be one hell of a long day.

* * * * * *

John Georgio awoke with a start, and then relaxed once he remembered where he was. He was covered in sweat. He watched the overhead blades rotating slowly, wishing that he'd installed an air conditioner in his bedroom. He rebuked himself for having made the statement that he preferred ceiling fans, even though he had only done so because of monetary considerations. John knew it was vital to maintain the charade that he was financially independent, and was deeply concerned that the true circumstances relating to his financial situation remained a secret. Having declared to his friends that it was healthier to sleep with an overhead fan in preference to one of General Electric's wonderful machines, John had to put up with the sticky, uncomfortable conditions.

He lay quietly observing his surroundings. They weren't much, he thought, but at least they were his. Or at least, his to use. John quietly admonished himself. If only he could turn the clock back to when he was living the high life in the States. But he couldn't go back. He knew that foreigners in Indonesia couldn't own property, and having paid an exorbitant rent to the landlord in advance, he believed that he had probably already paid for the premises twice over. This thought made him unhappy. The owner had demanded that the rent be paid three years up front, and that amounted to most of the capital he'd borrowed from his mother back in LA. If his father discovered where the money had come from to finance his son's venture, he would have disowned him. It was not the first time in his brief career that John had, in his family's eyes, screwed up badly.

The fan moved slowly, cutting an edge though the still, lifeless air, as he thought of his mother and how she had risked his father's wrath emptying her savings to finance her son's exploits. At the time, there seemed to be little choice. Had he remained Stateside, he might not have made it at all. At least, now, his mother had the comfort of knowing that her son was a successful businessman, pioneering American investments in Indonesia.

John remained flat on his back, and laughed inwardly with self-mockery. There were few achievements for which he could claim credit. If his mother discovered the truth, she would be ashamed of her son and of what he had become. Why the hell had he embarked on an affair with a married Indonesian woman? He closed his eyes and conjured images of her face. She was, without doubt, amazingly beautiful. Probably the most beautiful woman he had ever known. When the striking woman had appeared in the lecture room on that day, and announced that she would be one of the instructors for his course, John recalled how, suddenly, he had difficulty breathing when she smiled directly at him. In that moment, John deceived himself by believing that she had smiled for him, and only him. As he lay in bed, his mind wandering, John crossed his arms and breathed deeply, remembering what had then followed.

Julianti had been employed by the United States Government as one of the language teachers for the Monterey Language Facility, where government officials were given basic instruction in the Indonesian and other languages. Julianti was contracted to assist with the Indonesian course, part time, while she lived with her husband, an Indonesian journalist, who was the representative North American correspondent for the Indonesian *Antara* news agency. Her husband's salary was meagre by American standards, and the couple found the cost of living difficult to manage. Soon after their arrival in America, Julianti discovered that in order to survive, she would have to find work to supplement her husband's income. Fortunately, within weeks, she was contracted to assist with the State Department's junior officer's course, and quickly settled down into the routine of things. Then she met John.

Although John Georgio projected himself amongst his friends as a man of the world, and one full of bravado, before meeting the attractive Asian woman, he had never been to bed with a woman. The moment John saw Julianti smile, he felt a surge of excitement as never before and they had begun their sudden and passionate affair. John had been accepted into the State Department as a junior officer in training. The United States Government had planned to send their young career officer to Indonesia upon completion of his language training but security checks had uncovered his romantic attachment to a national from the target country, and John Georgio was advised that he had been slated for a tour of Korea.

Furious with the Department's decision, but too totally engrossed with the first woman in his life, John resigned from the State Department. Julianti had told him stories of opportunities in her country and, without giving the matter too much more consideration, John announced to his family that he intended leaving for

Indonesia.

Georgio's parents were beside themselves. His parents had been born in Sicily and had migrated to America in search of a better life for themselves. They had been so proud when their son John had been accepted into university on a scholarship, and even more so when he went on to graduate with a degree in commerce. As his family attempted to come to terms with the shock of his announcement, one of their Sicilian friends initiated enquires and discovered that there was a small foreign investment company for sale in Jakarta. John's mother was only too happy to arrange the necessary funds for the acquisition. She was pleased that her youngest son had finally found a woman, and would soon be married. She could not know that Julianti was still tied to a husband who, at that time, was totally ignorant of his wife's infidelity. Less than a month later, John Georgio accompanied his mistress to Indonesia to take control of the fledgling marketing company recently licensed by the Government. After six months, the business had failed to take off and John recognized that he'd made an error in judgement, discovering that he really had no business acumen at all. Now he fervently wished he'd remained in the comfortable position he had enjoyed before being enticed into Asia by this beautiful woman.

He couldn't help blaming Julianti for the whole sorry mess. Not long after he had taken-up residence in Jakarta and arranged his affairs, Julianti's husband had come looking for them both. There had been numerous encounters and, on each occasion, the scenes had been ugly for them all. The Indonesian journalist had phoned him at home and embarrassed him in his office, screaming at the American who had stolen his wife. John had foolishly belittled the man by flaunting Julianti publicly. She had even agreed to move into his house in Menteng. So, not a month after they had returned from America, Julianti's husband decided to kill his wife's lover. He borrowed a revolver, and waited outside the small residence off Jalan Waringan, hoping to catch the man as he came out of his house.

On that Sunday John had taken Julianti for a drive to Bogor. His house guest, a fellow American who happened to somewhat resemble Georgio in build and facial features, walked out of the premises and was immediately confronted at a distance of some thirty meters by Julianti's husband, who pointed his revolver at the foreigner, and fired five times. Incredibly, he missed.

Devastated that he had failed to kill his wife's lover, he then took his own life with the remaining bullet, then and there on the street. John returned later that day to learn what had happened. The journalist's body had already been removed, and John's house guest had fled to safer accommodations. The following week, having discovered his real financial position, Julianti walked out.

As John lay reflecting on these events, he heard a horn sound outside. He rolled out of bed slowly, and looked back at the firm, brown body occupying the other side of his bed. The thought crossed his mind that he should send her on her way before leaving for his afternoon start in the office. John looked around the bedroom and decided that this would be best. His Dean Martin collection lay stacked against the wall, and he knew leaving her alone just wasn't worth the risk. He woke the girl and commenced his daily exercises, believing that this workout always impressed them. First he lifted the smaller weights, exercising his biceps and pectoral muscles. Then, standing half-naked in front of the attractive Indonesian girl, he crouched, lifted the weights, then snatched the twenty kilos up in one well-practised movement. He repeated this action while counting aloud for her to hear, finally placing the weights on the floor when he'd reached twenty lifts. John then looked at the girl and smiled.

'John, you are so strong!' she said, realizing her cue. Pipi had been told by her girlfriends that the American had a considerable ego problem and reacted well to positive comment. John expected the admiration, and she was only too pleased to make him happy. At least until she'd been paid. *'John, you look so handsome when you lift those heavy weights. You must be tired, John, no?'* Pipi had been well briefed. The constant flow of hookers had only increased their pool of knowledge regarding their American client. She knew what would happen next. The other girls had told her, laughing as they explained precisely what John would do after this, or that. He turned and drew a deep breath, filling his barrel shaped chest.

'Tired? Are you kidding? Hell, I could do this all day!' he boasted, as he bent down and pulled the weights back into position. Pipi's girlfriends had said that he would peak before thirty more pumps the second time around. They had all laughed conspiratorially, as

several of their number related similar incidents. One girl had shown the bruise marks across her chest, the result of John losing control of the weight while trying to impress her and dropping the heavy barbell across the bed. Fortunately, the soft mattress had taken most of the force, and her injury considerably less than that of the American's pride. Pipi counted as she watched the foreigner's veins swell under the exertion. She wanted to giggle but knew this would only result in his losing his temper and her foregoing the five dollars he'd promised for the night.

'*Thirty!*' he called suddenly, dropping the weights loudly to the floor. Pipi knew it was less than twenty-five but didn't care whether he cheated himself or not. It was only important to her that he did not cheat her when the time came to leave. Some of her friends had warned that he often refused to pay and then became violent. She looked around the room and saw evidence of what she believed to support this gossip. There were photographs of men dressed in military uniforms from some place called Vietnam. Pipi could read the annotation at the bottom of most of the photos of what she expected were John's friends, as he did not feature in any of these black and white images, which hung lifelessly on two of his bedroom walls. Most, she could see, had been autographed. Pipi had thought it strange, remembering the wall hangings in the other rooms, that John had not placed any of these photographs in the dining room or other entertainment areas for his other guests to see. Pipi was not to know that John had never served in the military, let alone even visited Vietnam. In fact, apart from his most inadequate appendage, he had never even held a weapon in his hand.

She clapped playfully, continuing to play the game. John smiled. He could see that she was impressed.

'*Okay, time to mandi,*' he called, heading into the en-suite to shower. '*You should join me,*' he added, strutting towards the bathroom. Pipi knew that this was not a request. She sighed silently and rolled off the bed to follow, hoping that he would not want her to do it again in the shower. As she entered the cubicle and saw John's flaccid half erection, Pipi took the soap and held the sweet scented cake between her hands while avoiding his eyes. She moved under the warm stream of water and closed her eyes. Suddenly, she felt John's hands grasp both sides of her head, and she offered no resistance as he forced her to the shower's floor. Pipi then felt John lift his body up against her face. She dropped the soap and placed her hands under his genitals. Pipi knew what was expected of her, guiding his member into her mouth, pleased that its size was nothing John would wish to brag about. Less than a minute passed when she sensed John tremble, then groan deeply. Pipi had prepared herself for what would follow, willing herself not to choke and heave as she had done earlier. Suddenly she could not continue, pulling away from John's strong grasp, unable to breathe, as her body convulsed and she dry-heaved.

'You bitch!' she heard him scream angrily, as he struck her face savagely with the heel of his palm, smashing her to the floor. Stunned, Pipi lay in shock, as she sensed him step over her prostrate form and leave the shower. She was not sure what to do next, waiting for John to return, too terrified to leave the bathroom. Minutes dragged by, and the water became cold, causing Pipi to shiver. She continued to listen for familiar sounds, but could not hear anything which would identify that John remained in the adjoining bedroom. Groggy from the blow but convinced that she could not remain where she was, Pipi rose, turned the shower off, and listened again for movement. Unsure of what might lie waiting for her in the next room, Pipi slipped the catch across, locking the bathroom door. Then she towelled herself dry, and sat on the toilet to think, while cursing her stupidity for believing her girlfriends convincing stories regarding the American.

It seemed that she had been sitting there most of the afternoon when she decided that she had no other choice but to brave it out and just leave, even if it meant confronting the man she now despised.

Aduh! she thought, *wait till I get my hands on Titi and her other friends. So much for the great time,* she remembered miserably, *he couldn't even get a full erection!* If he was still there and hit her again, Pipi decided, she would just run outside and scream. She rubbed the side of her head. Her left temple throbbed less from the vicious blow, and she knew that bruising would become apparent as the hours passed. She unlocked the bathroom door, peered into the bedroom, and was immediately relieved to discover that she was alone.

* * * * * *

John Georgio had left Pipi to cool her heels while he went out and filled in some time alone. *She would still be there when he returned,* he thought smugly, while driving the General Motors Statesman through the lunch-time traffic. He glanced down at Pipi's clothing and a smirk creased his face. Georgio had ensured that she would remain behind in his villa. He drove up and down Jalan Thamrin twice, annoyed that no one had waved to him. *Where was everybody?* he wondered petulantly. Deciding that those of any note were most probably at the Hotel Indonesia Baris Bar, he drove back up to the *Selamat Datang* statue, cut across the traffic and entered the main hotel driveway. Spotting a group of foreigners emerging from the expansive lobby-reception area, he waited until they stood within sight, then sprang out of his car and threw his keys to the surprised parking attendant.

'Leave it there!' he demanded loudly, and ran with small, almost effeminate steps up to the foyer. The affectation was not lost on the two journalists who were also heading for the Baris Lounge Bar. They had had seen it all before and veered away to avoid having to be seen talking to Georgio in public. John noticed the snub but elected to ignore the men. He disliked journalists. He believed that they had deliberately treated him with scorn as a result of his indiscretions with the wife of one of their colleagues. John entered the bar, observed that it was too early to bum a drink, waved to the cringing waiters, then left. He knew there was little point in visiting his office; he had but a few clients, and nothing was scheduled for the rest of the day. He then drove down to the Sarinah department store where, out of boredom, he harassed the staff for an hour before returning to his residence.

He parked his car inside the driveway, locked the doors and entered the house. He looked around the lonely guest room and decided that he really hated the place. Then he smiled in anticipation, visualising what was waiting for him inside. John opened the door to his bedroom and called 'Pipi', then entered, expecting the girl to be waiting anxiously for his return, as he had yet to pay her for her visit.

The smile on John Georgio's face turned instantly to anger as he discovered that Pipi had indeed departed, obviously taking whatever of his clothes she considered necessary to cover herself. She had taken his razor to everything else left hanging, reducing the clothes in his meagre wardrobe to shreds.

Chapter 2

The Salima Group

'And why should we form a kongsi with them?' Lim asked, uncrossing his skinny legs then rubbing his calf muscles to restore the blood flow. He waited for his cousin to respond.

'This man will be the next Chief of Army staff. He will unlock many doors for us.' the man replied. Lim snorted. He knew that he really had no choice. Commerce in Indonesia without the support of the military commanders was impossible. He considered the long-term ramifications of having this general in his pocket as well.

'How much will he want?' he asked, knowing it would be excessive. His cousin hesitated. He knew that Lim would balk at the request.

'Five percent,' he answered, waiting for the outburst.

'Bangsat!' Lim swore, calculating quickly, furious that he would have to agree with the general's demand to be paid an up-front fee of half a million dollars against agreeing to the Salima Group being appointed for the supply contract. *'What about our arrangements with Seda?'* he then asked, concerned that there would be a double commission. Although only a peripheral player, Seda had produced several mutually beneficial contracts through HANKAM, the Defence Department, and Lim wanted to keep that relationship alive.

'He will step back for this one. Seda's smart enough to realize that the new army chief must share in the cake. Don't worry about him. I'll set up a meeting and let him know what's going on between Salima and HANKAM.' Lim looked at the man opposite and continued to rub the back of his knees. Prematurely bald and of small frame, the multi-millionaire had the appearance of a roadside pedlar. *Who would have believed,* Lim mused, *that his association with the First Family would have precipitated his becoming the most powerful busi-*

nessman in the country?

It was only after Soeharto had assumed the mantel of President that the self-appointed leader and his team of American-educated technocrats discovered the real legacy which had been left by President Soekarno. The country was on the brink of economic disaster with a foreign debt in excess of two billion dollars. The interest on this massive debt alone exceeded Indonesia's total export revenues, and investment had all but ground to a halt.

Drastic measures were introduced to reduce the country's annual inflation of one thousand percent, and the government embarked on a program designed to entice the Chinese merchants back to the country which, the year before, had denounced their ethnic group for precipitating the events which resulted in the subsequent blood-bath. Although the Chinese were not the primary victims during the slaughter of the communists, they believed that they had been specifically targeted during the post-coup period of ethnic cleansing, and helped perpetuate the myth that so many of their number had died during the purge.

Soeharto's successful coup against the pro-Chinese Soekarno had, at first, been of considerable concern to the commercially adept race. New laws were promulgated restricting their cultural activities, moves which were strongly supported by the indigenous or *pribumi* population. A set of guidelines titled *'The Basic Policy for the Solution of the Chinese Problem'* clearly established what the New Order considered to be acceptable parameters, within which the Chinese were obliged to remain. Chinese language newspapers and schools were closed. Chinese script was prohibited in public places and the government froze diplomatic relations with China, effectively isolating the Indonesian Chinese.

But behind the scenes it was an entirely different story, and the game was played with a separate set of rules. Realizing that the country would falter without their support, the government arranged for a number of prominent Chinese *totok* to be given access to government contracts in return for their financial support. These *totok* were pure Chinese immigrants who had ventured to Indonesia, bringing with them their natural commercial abilities. Once ensconced, they soon developed their own networks and flourished, establishing important contacts with military officers who, in consideration for the *totok's* financial support, provided security to the Chinese traders.

Jakarta

* * * * * *

Lim's early life in China had not been so different from millions of others who had lived, hand to mouth, as economic refugees in their own land. His family had fled before the terror of Japanese occupation, only to suffer under the cruelty of the local war lords. Near to death from starvation, he and many of his ilk had jumped onto boats and become the first real Asian refugees to head for Australia by sea.

As the Vietnamese would discover more than thirty years later, sailing through the pirate-infested waters of the South China Sea was indeed, a considerable gamble. Indonesian, Malay and Filipino pirates waited for their easy prey, boarding the primitive vessels, killing the men and women aboard once they discovered that most of these poor peasants had nothing to offer in exchange for their lives. Lim's boat had ventured into unfamiliar waters and arrived in Java in error. At first, he and his fellow survivors were distressed that they had not reached the southern land with its abundance of gold and opportunities. Instead, he found himself in the filthy harbour of Semarang, where he hustled his way along the streets, as he had in Shanghai and other parts of China. Later in life, Lim learned not to regret the navigational error. Hungry and destitute, he undertook any task, and worked wherever an opportunity for his limited skills arose. Soon, his tireless energy guaranteed his future.

Java's Chinese traders noted his commitment to hard work and respected Lim for the incredibly long hours he laboured to make ends meet. When he had climbed off the rickety, wooden ship, he was a young, penniless man. His early endeavours, and his ready acceptance of the strange culture and people he found himself amongst, laid the foundations for his future in the Dutch Colony. The difficult conditions which prevailed upon his arrival in Java in no way daunted his spirit. He continued to work hard. It was in his blood to do so.

Once he had collected sufficient capital, Lim started his empire as a simple trader working the streets of Semarang selling peanuts and cloves. From there, he worked his way up to trading in soap and medicine which, to his good fortune, presented him with an opportunity to deal with the nationalist forces during the struggle for Independence.

Unbeknown to the freedom fighters, Lim also traded with their enemy, the Dutch. Lim remembered his first major contract with the army divisions based near Semarang. It was there he met the Lieutenant Colonel who, in later years, was to open doors which would, ultimately, provide wealth and treasures even he had never imagined possible.

There was a time, Lim recollected, when he thought he was finished. Both he and the Colonel were caught smuggling sugar, which resulted in the divisional commander being reassigned, in disgrace. He had followed the man to Bandung and maintained their relationship but, for some years, there was a financial drought as his sponsor waited for another opportunity. When it came, the gods smiled on them both.

Lim recalled receiving his first summons to the President's home. Since that day, he and his associates had never looked back. But, he also remembered, there had been a *quid pro quo* for the favours promised. Lim realized that the mutually beneficial relationship was only secure as long as the country's leadership remained intact, and in the event of imminent change, he knew he would have to be prepared to divest himself of whatever holdings he had acquired in Indonesia well in advance, or risk losing everything.

* * * * * *

Lim glanced at his cousin sitting across the ornately carved coffee table. Silently he admitted that, had they not been related, the man would not have been entrusted with the few responsibilities he had so much difficulty in overseeing. Lim wished that his two sons were older and could return to take their rightful positions at his side. He permitted his thoughts to wander momentarily as he visualised the teenagers, pleased that they would arrive that day for their summer break.

Although Lim had never attended school, he was determined that his children be given the finest education available. He had sent them to the United States where, he hoped, they would both continue their studies until graduating with a solid knowledge of the West. Lim smiled, recalling that his sons had informed him that they would fly to Amsterdam first, just to inspect the sights. Although this would add considerably to their journey, he did not care that they might be up to mischief on their way back. It was best that they get all of this out of their systems now, he believed, as once they had graduated and returned to assist their father with his growing empire there would be no room for nonsense. He would select appropriate wives for them both when the need arose.

'You will go to the airport yourself,' Lim reminded his cousin to arrange to have them met personally, and driven home from the airport.

Lim's cousin smiled and nodded while receiving his instructions. He genuinely liked the boys, wishing his own children were as bright. He accepted that he had been most fortunate, indeed, when his influential relative had arranged passage for him, aiding in his escape from China. When his ship had docked in Semarang, he was amazed at the ease with which the problem of his personal papers had been handled, and the speed with which new documents had appeared. In return, he had followed Lim unquestioningly, and was now most grateful that he'd had the wisdom to do so. Totally devoted, he had even emulated Lim and adopted the Salima name. At the time, Lim's compliance with the new regulation demanding that his race assume indigenous names had raised more than a few eyebrows within the Chinese community, as they considered the powerful *totok* exempt from having to comply due to his long-standing relationship with the President.

In 1967, Lim Swee Giok had officially changed his name to Robert Salima. Subsequent to the bloody aftermath which followed the brutal murder and mutilation of the country's military leadership, the Chinese population was encouraged to adopt indigenous names as part of a Presidential plan to reduce ethnic tension. The new President supported the concept of assimilation over integration, and the Chinese moved quickly into line, *kowtowing* to the new leadership. Lim had led the charge and was now enjoying the first fruits of his old friend's sponsorship.

As the two men sat together, sipping the cold herbal tea from miniature cups, a servant entered quietly, moved around the room unobtrusively, checked the teapot, then slipped away again to replenish the empty plate of steamed delicacies which she knew had been demolished by Lim's gluttonous cousin. Cook, and head of all things related to domestic arrangements within the Lim household, the homely servant knew that her master depended on her greatly.

She had followed Lim when he moved his business interests to the capital, taking charge of the new household and its five servants. The woman, although much the same age as her employer, was practically his mother. She doted on the man. Lim had been a widower for some years, and showed no signs of remarrying. Since both his sons had been sent to America to study, the large house seemed even more lonely than before.

The cook heard a door open, then close, and she scurried to the side door in time to observe Lim's cousin leave. When she entered, carrying a large serving of his favourite steamed cake, Lim smiled and nodded at the woman almost absent-mindedly, his thoughts preoccupied with how he would present his new proposal to the President. He was confident that he would secure the support needed for the new cement plants. His flour mills had become a reality and the Indonesian banks coffers were beginning to recover. It was time to make another move. He checked his watch, placed another cake in his mouth, scratched his stomach and rose to head for his bedroom to change in preparation for the meetings scheduled for later in the morning.

As he showered, Lim's thoughts centered on how he would handle the discussions with the consortium, and how he could maintain his majority stake in the project without using any of his own funds. By mid-morning his mind was clear of everything, except what had to be done to achieve the position he desperately needed, in relation to the project's funding.

* * * * * *

The young men shook hands with their *totok* uncle and followed him out to the waiting Mercedes. Their flight had been delayed for almost five hours as the KLM flight plan was altered to compensate for the 'no-fly' zone over India and Pakistan. Hostilities had broken out there, once again, and as both nations were armed with ground-to-air missiles, all international commercial flights were ordered away from the two warring countries. Over-flights were not permitted, and KLM, along with all other international carriers, were obliged to seek clearance to alter their flight path to the south of the sub-continent, crossing through Sri Lankan and Indonesian airspace enroute to Singapore.

Tired from their long flight and lack of sleep in Amsterdam, they were both grateful that their father was out on business when they finally arrived home, retiring immediately after they had consumed the mandatory meal prepared by the old, and doting cook. Within minutes of their heads hitting their pillows, both the teenage heirs were asleep.

* * * * * *

A small village in Pakistan

Thousands of kilometers to the north-west of where Lim Swee Giok's sons lay sleeping soundly, a youth of similar age crouched in fear as another shell exploded directly over his head. Mohammed bin Fuad screamed in fear as the air around ruptured, slamming him fiercely against the ground. *Oh, Allah, please make them stop!* he screamed, but it seemed that there was none who could hear as another explosion followed, then another, until he lay stunned, deafened by the close proximity of the strikes.

Hours passed and as shelling had long ceased, Fuad crawled painfully from under the wreckage and into the night. He did not bid his family farewell. They had all died when the savage bombardment had first commenced. Through the rubble and the acrid air thick with the stench of death, Fuad stumbled on, fighting the excruciating pain in his right arm which hung listlessly, signalling it was broken. Disorientated, scared, exhausted from the ordeal and in fear of the invading Indian forces, he willed his bleeding, unclad feet not to fail him, as he struggled away from the small resettlement village where his family and friends had died. When he fell, he crawled, dragging his tired body across the jagged earth until he reached the top of a small knoll, not two hundred meters above the ruins of his village below.

Fuad propped himself wearily against a boulder, and remained there until the heat of the morning sun drove him in search of water. When remnants of the defeated Pakistani army found his dehydrated body lying prostrate under the sun, the uncovered parts of his torso blistered by the sun, not one amongst their number believed him to be alive. As one of the raggedy soldiers turned the body over to inspect its face, he was astonished to discover that Fuad was, incredibly, still breathing. When closer examination revealed the wounded boy's broken arm, the soldier was tempted just to leave him to die, knowing that Fuad would be excluded from eating together with any others until he recovered the use of his right hand.

Against his better judgement, the Muslim soldier gave him water then tended to the badly broken arm. Having regained consciousness, Fuad joined these stragglers and followed them to the next village where he was given a bowl of mash and ordered to sit outside and eat with the dogs.

* * * * * *

Indonesia

At the close of business that same day, totally oblivious to the Hindu-Moslem conflict which would result in the creation of Bangladesh, members of the visiting Japanese banking consortium appeared satisfied that their shareholders' funds would be secure, and gave Lim the green light to proceed with his plans to construct the additional cement plants. As he stood proudly, with his sons at his side, waving at the departing bankers as they were driven away from their home, Lim smiled contentedly at the outcome of the meeting. Then a frown overtook the smile on his face as he recalled the undertakings he had given privately to each of the bank representatives.

Bangsat, he swore under his breath, totalling for the umpteenth time that day the millions he had committed in individual payments to be paid into each of the banker's Swiss numbered accounts. *So much,* he thought, sighing deeply while wishing there had been some other way. The payments would ensure his position of control in the proposed joint venture. *So much to be paid to those thieving bankers. And it wasn't even their money!* Distressed by how easily the bankers had taken his millions in exchange for their support, Lim decided to ask the President for a licence to start his own bank, wondering why he had not thought of doing so before.

JAKARTA

Six weeks later, the Ministry of Finance announced that it had issued a private banking licence to the Salima Group. The new financial institution would be known as the Asian Pacific Commercial Bank. When the bank opened its doors, even Lim could not have envisaged that his new enterprise would become one of the most powerful houses in Asia. And all he had to give away this time, for the licence, was a mere ten percent of his bank's shares.

* * * * * *

During her first months in the capital, Ruswita experienced greater hardship than she ever imagined possible. The city of her dreams, Jakarta, was nothing like she had envisaged. The filth and pollution created by uncaring city dwellers was left to accumulate along the roads, and even the city's governor, Ali Sadikin, appealed to the four million inhabitants to burn their rubbish in home made incinerators to reduce the incidence of disease. Rats as large as cats threatened those who slept outdoors, and flying cockroaches larger than a woman's hand moved through the humid evening air in search of food. Dengue, hepatitis in all of its forms, malaria and dysentery, all contributed to the high death toll of the city. Outbreaks of cholera were common, and several cases of plague were identified by World Health Organization observers.

Ruswita had moved from her first night's lodgings as soon as she discovered that, had she remained, the mamasan would have expected her to participate in the whore-house activities. Embarrassment quickly turned to anger as Ruswita hurried away from the premises, ignoring the obscenities which followed her departure. She had found other accommodations, but these were far from the city's center where she had hoped to find employment.

Day after day Ruswita walked the streets, but there were limited opportunities for one who had no experience. She even sat outside several of the embassies along with hundreds of other hopefuls, offering her services as servant labour in their foreign households. Ruswita soon discovered that this was more or less a closed shop to outsiders, as servants always endeavoured to have one of their own placed within these lucrative households whenever a vacancy appeared.

She made but one friend, Lani, a girl of sixteen whose circumstances were not dissimilar to her own. Ruswita took her younger friend with her on her rounds looking for employment, but as the opportunities for two were even more scarce than for a single applicant, Ruswita returned to her search alone. The cold realization dawned that they would soon have to beg for their food. Lani turned to the streets where, as she was still young, she could earn enough from one casual encounter to feed them both.

It bothered Ruswita that her friend had become one of the thousands of young casualties who had succumbed to prostitution in order to survive but, in typical pragmatic Javanese fashion, Ruswita continued her relationship with Lani who was delighted to share whatever she earned with her older friend.

Attracted by exaggerated stories promising employment, tens of thousands of teenage girls left their villages in search of opportunities which did not exist. Soon their numbers swelled uncontrollably, causing the Governor to declare roadside sex in the three-wheeled *becak*s illegal. His administration then encouraged the more than one hundred thousand prostitutes to move their activities out past the Patimura Cemetery, in the city's southern suburbs, and Ancol to the north. The unexpected result of this action was that the inner-city became a gathering place for the transvestite community. The governor had no difficulty in accepting this change, even agreeing to judge the first 'Queen of the Queens' beauty contest which was held at the Intercontinental Hotel Indonesia, just across the road from where the gay community normally solicited clients. And that was where Lani was arrested during a police clean-up campaign, and where she disappeared, along with many others.

Lani had been taken one hundred kilometers from the city along with some sixty other street prostitutes who had been packed into the back of an open truck, driven far enough to deter the girls from attempting to return, then unceremoniously dumped along a country road in the dark, wet night. When Lani did not return that evening, Ruswita feared that some harm must have come to her friend. Later, Rus learned of the incident from street-vendors who had witnessed the raid. Alone, and even more desperate than before, but determined not to give up hope, Ruswita moved out to the city outskirts where a floating community of itinerant workers camped.

As she walked the ten kilometers to the east, Ruswita offered a silent prayer for her young friend, hoping that Lani would not be so foolish as to return to Jakarta. Hungry, but resolute, Ruswita finally found work during her third day on a construction site in Krawang, an area designated as an industrial zone for foreign investment. The following Saturday, as Ruswita extended both her hands in the customary and subservient manner with her left hand under, and supporting her right, she received her first *gaji*.

This payment of three hundred Rupiah for six days manual work amounted to less than one American dollar and, as Ruswita folded the Monopoly-sized denominations and placed these inside her bra, she sighed, conscious of how rough the skin on her fingers had become from loading and carrying bricks around the construction site. As a treat, she paid fifteen Rupiah to one of the vendors parked outside the factory grounds for the satisfaction of sitting down and eating two slices of roughly cut bread, both of which had been spread with condensed milk, then sprinkled sparingly with colourful, minute particles of chocolate known as hundreds and thousands. The sweet, sickly combination reminded her of those special childhood moments when, on rare occasions, her father could afford to treat his children to the extravagant spread.

As she sat on the small stools provided, almost oblivious to the dust and flies and the ear-shattering sounds of bus horns as the overloaded monsters sped dangerously past, Ruswita wondered if the city children had ever experienced *kampung* life. At that moment several children ran past, screaming *'capung, capung,'* and she noticed that the boy in front was being pursued for the tasty delicacies he carried threaded on a palm stick. She laughed as the others managed to catch the child, and struggled to remove some of the roasted dragon-flies impaled on the simple skewer. Ruswita did not believe that the *capung* the children fought over would be as tasty as the ones from her village.

As Rus reminisced, she was reminded of the first time, while still very young, when she had watched the older children remove the sticky white gum from inside a Jack fruit, and smear this over the thin coconut palm sticks they carried. She also recollected trying to keep pace as the children then ran amongst the banana trees in search of the magnificently coloured dragon-flies, which darted mainly amongst the higher branches. Wistfully, she recalled how fascinated she had been as the children had taken the live insects, twisted their heads as they pulled, removing the entire stomach in one movement, before placing each catch in line on their skewers.

The tantalising images of roasted dragon-fly suddenly blurred as a siren sounded, interrupting her momentary escape. She recognized the signal calling the labourers back to work. She rose, wearily, and drifted back with the others. Ruswita spotted the children she had seen minutes before as they ran past, still yelling and screaming happily as they continued their play. She smiled as one of them ran close by, and she could see that the child clung to several of the cooked insects, with the others in hot pursuit. A pang of regret crossed her mind causing her to falter, and almost trip, as she returned to the hot, dusty conditions.

Within minutes she had all but forgotten whatever it was that had occupied her mind during her break, as she struggled to balance the two baskets of bricks she carried at each end of her well-worn shoulder-pole. Ruswita had learned early on her first day to clear her mind of everything but what she was doing, as those who dropped or damaged bricks were soon dismissed from the site.

******

Ruswita was fortunate to remain employed for three months and, as the factory walls took shape and cement render was applied, the loads of bricks which she had carried laboriously, day in and day out without complaint, were replaced by buckets of prepared cement. The palms and fingers on both hands were covered with calluses, and her nails reflected their neglect.

On the day the workmen raised the first timber trusses and placed these in line, spanning the factory's floor, Ruswita knew that her employment there would soon come to an end. She stood, unhappily, wondering what there was to celebrate as the carpenters cheered, bolting the final truss into place. A bunch of bananas was then hung from the frame, and the workers given a few minutes respite from the heat, in recognition of the landmark achievement. A *dukun* offered his blessing, then work recommenced on the last stage of the project. As the final concrete was poured, completing the factory's construction, Ruswita watched in awe as the huge packing crates which had been delivered from Tanjung Priok Harbour were lifted from the long bodied trucks, and unpacked, revealing for the first time the modern equipment intended for installation at the factory she had helped build.

Adding to the occasion, several foreigners wandered around the factory grounds, and the daily labourers ceased working, to stare at the Australians. Only a few of the workers had been that close to a foreigner before, and these had either been missionaries or Russians. Ruswita was not particularly interested in the two fair-haired men; she had seen many of these *bules* back in the city, and around the residential areas of Kebayoran Baru and Menteng when she was searching for work as a domestic. Instead, Ruswita was attracted to what was written on the side of empty crates, and stood beside one of the shipping containers engrossed, attempting to pronounce the words stencilled on the side of the huge boxes.

'That's the name of the shipping line,' a voice sounded behind, startling Ruswita. She turned instantly and found herself face to face with one of the Australians. She had no idea whatsoever of what he had said. Ruswita's face was half-covered by a dirty cloth, protecting her from the dust and cement. Only her almond-shaped eyes could be seen under the conical hat she wore to prevent the sun from burning her face and turning her skin dark brown. Embarrassed, Ruswita dropped her eyes and started to shuffle away.

'You can read?' the *tuan* asked, causing her to stop and look back at the man questioningly.

'*I am sorry, tuan, but I do not understand,*' she responded, hoping that she had not offended this man in any way. Her eyes then darted around the immediate area for help, knowing that there would be none. She heard another voice call out and knew instantly from its tone, that she was in trouble. *Why did this bule have to stop and speak to me?* she thought, distressed, as her eyes watched an Indonesian man hurry over in her direction.

'Did this girl give you trouble, *tuan*?' he asked the foreigner.

'No, no, its nothing like that,' Bill Davidson answered, lightheartedly. 'I just asked her if she could read, that's all.' He looked over at Ruswita and smiled, reassuringly.

'*The tuan asked if you could read,*' the Indonesian said, almost accusingly as Ruswita stood silently, wishing the earth would open and swallow her whole.

'Please tell the tuan that yes, I am able to read, but only our bahasa. Please also apologise that I am unable to understand his language.' As she spoke she noticed the young *tuan* tilt his head slightly as if he understood what she had said. This was translated for the Australian who, at that moment, was joined by his associate.

'What's the problem, Bill?' the other asked, his voice reflecting the authority he held as the joint venture company's general manager.

'Nothing, Neil,' he laughed, 'just a little public relations effort with this one, that's all,' he continued, nodding in Ruswita's direction. 'I was watching her trying to read what was written on the container. Thought she might speak some English, but apparently she doesn't.'

'Let it be,' the older man said, turning suddenly in the direction of a loud banging noise emanating from somewhere down behind the factory. Neil Thom walked off to see what was happening over there. They had both been in the country less than two weeks and had agreed that, if the plant was to be a success, then it would only be achieved by showing everybody just who was really in charge of the show. Davidson watched Thom stomp away, grumbling under his breath something about the place being the death of him. He turned his attention back to the woman.

'May I go now?' Ruswita asked, annoyed that they had obviously been talking about her, without knowing what she had done to attract so much attention. The interpreter ignored her, coughed and dragged a lump of phlegm from somewhere deep in his throat, leaned away from them and spat. Ruswita noticed the expression on the foreigner's face and smiled behind her face cloth. She remembered seeing tourists react with similar looks of disgust, as they attempted to negotiate Jakarta's irregular footpaths while ignoring the filthy itinerants and beggars.

'What's your name?' Davidson asked, managing another smile. There was something about this girl's eyes, Bill thought, as his gaze moved to where she stood, her feet caked in grime. He guessed that she was probably thirty to forty years old, judging from their condition.

'Ruswita,' she answered, once the interpreter explained what was said.

'How old are you, Ruswita?' she was asked. When she told the interpreter that she was already twenty and this was relayed to Davidson, she identified his look of surprise. Ruswita knew that she looked already old. She thought it rude of the foreigner to indicate that he agreed. Suddenly, bored with the confrontation, she turned to go about her business before the foreman decided that her services were no longer required. She started to leave when Davidson, to everyone's surprise, stepped forward and with a quick flick, removed her head-covering, revealing all but the lower half of her face.

'*Siapa sih!*' Ruswita snapped, alarmed by the man's actions. *Didn't this bulé know that one never touches another's head, even that of a coolie?*

'*Tuan,*' the interpreter moved to prevent a scene; what Davidson had done was unacceptable, even if the woman was a mere labourer. Her fellow countryman looked quickly at Ruswita and ever-so-lightly, shook his head at her. She glared at the foreigner, her eyes alive with hate.

'It's okay, it's okay,' the Australian called, raising his hands in submission. He was taken by surprise at her reaction, and noticed that he had drawn the attention of the other workers. They had stopped to see what had caused the altercation between one of their own and the foreigner.

'*All of you, get back to work!*' someone called sharply, sending the coolies immediately on their way.

'*Tell the tuan that I wish to leave,*' Ruswita demanded angrily, as she shook her head and released her bun with one hand, while removing her face cloth with the other. Davidson stood stunned at the transformation. She looked so young!

'Tell her it's okay,' Davidson instructed the interpreter, realizing that his actions had, for whatever reason, triggered the hostile reaction. He smiled at Ruswita who responded with an expressionless face; only her eyes reflected the animosity she felt for him. As the young woman turned and walked proudly away, he asked the interpreter the reason for her anger and was informed, politely, of his *faux pas*. Not wishing to have the local work-force off side from his first day on site, Davidson decided to take steps to remedy the blunder he had made.

The following day he instructed the interpreter to make discreet enquiries about the girl he had offended. He also asked the man to apologise privately to Ruswita in such a manner that would not diminish his authority as the operations manager, while sending a clear message to her that he had not been aware of the taboo he had broken. Davidson was pleased with the forgiving response, unaware that the interpreter, now a personal assistant, had fabricated the story himself.

In fact, when he had spoken to Ruswita, she had lashed him with a tongue even he found incredibly crude coming from such a young woman. To add to his bewilderment in handling the matter, Davidson had then insisted that steps be taken to provide ongoing employment to Ruswita, justifying his decision on the grounds that the woman could read, and might be of assistance somewhere around the office, or even in the *gudang* as a clerk checking stores.

Two months later, when the Australian-Indonesian joint venture company operation in Krawang was inaugurated, Ruswita stood proudly amongst the two hundred employees and applauded as the Governor cut the ribbon strung ceremoniously across the operation's driveway, while announcing that the P.T. Salima Jaya Products Company was open for business. It was the seventh Lim Swee Giok joint-venture company belonging to the *totok* entrepreneur's stable to be given government sanction in that one year.

* * * * * *

Earlier, she had watched as the dignitaries arrived in their splendid cars, and observed the excitement build as last minute preparations were finalized. Ruswita felt a sense of pride at belonging to something so grand and important, wishing that her parents had been alive to witness her achievement. She had been given the position of *gudang* clerk, and had spent an additional six hours each night of her own time learning many of the foreign words which were essential to her position in the store room.

Ruswita had not known why she had been given this opportunity, and her beliefs firmly told her not to question this *karma*, out of fear of negating the good fortune that had come her way. Because of her mixed background, she was often torn between following her Chinese beliefs and adhering to Javanese tradition.

Ruswita had been quite happy standing with the other employees as the official proceedings commenced, even though some of the younger men persisted in teasing her. She played the game, pretending to ignore them, until one of their number actually attempted to place his hand on her bottom. She turned and whacked the youth responsible, hard enough to demonstrate that she was not to be touched, but not so hard that she might have injured the young man. She frowned to show that she was annoyed but then turned and laughed. *After all*, she thought, *who could be angry on such an auspicious day?*

Ruswita was surprised at the brevity of the official ceremony. It seemed that none of the official party, Indonesian and foreign alike, could tolerate the extreme heat under the temporary cover erected for the occasion. She watched with the other employees as more than one hundred guests sat uncomfortably below the army tarpaulin, perspiration flowing freely from their foreheads. When the ribbon was finally cut by the Governor, there was a loud cheer. Ruswita was certain that this was more one of relief than applause in recognition of the event. The guests had then been invited to join in a traditional feast, which lay in readiness inside a section of the factory, sealed off specifically for the function.

As the thirsty gathering moved inside the factory, Ruswita and others who had been instructed to assist with the service moved away from the employees section, which had been cordoned off from the official area, and hurried into the guest area to support the catering staff. She felt privileged to have been given this additional responsibility, and was not in any way daunted nor intimidated by the close proximity of the wealthy and influential guests. As she moved quickly amongst their number, Ruswita removed empty glasses and plates, and fetched whatever she was asked, although most of the requests were totally alien to her ears. She marvelled at the capacity of the foreigners to consume alcohol, noticing proudly that none of the Indonesians she had seen present were drinking beer or the other mixtures she had so much difficulty pronouncing.

As the function progressed, Ruswita noticed also that most of the Indonesian guests had already excused themselves, and that the remaining number were mainly *bulé*, the white foreigners. She also observed that the general demeanour of these people had progressively deteriorated, becoming loud and discourteous. She was most surprised at their behaviour, having never witnessed such a gathering before.

Towards late afternoon, tired and already indifferent to what had been exciting just hours before, Ruswita was about to slip away when she noticed her general manager, Neil Thom, waving in her direction. Immediately, she hurried to where he was standing with several other foreigners, and looked to see if they required further drinks.

'Well, fellows,' she heard him say, 'do any of you require anything more?' Ruswita saw the group of men laugh, one of them said something which she did not understand, with which they all burst out laughing. Puzzled, she looked at *tuan* Neil, her general manager, confused as to what was expected of her. He said something else which only attracted more laughter. Observing that their drinks were finished, Ruswita went in search of one of the waiters. When she returned, the group were engrossed, huddled together in discussion and, as courtesy demanded, Ruswita waited for the man who had the other guests' attention, to finish speaking. He stopped, and suddenly the group broke into raucous laughter.

'Ah, you're back, my dear,' the now inebriated Thom announced, reaching for her elbow and pulling her towards the group of men. Her immediate reaction was to pull away, stepping back to permit the waiter to serve the group. She felt her face flush with embarrassment. As she looked up at the general manager, she could see that he was angry with her response. One of the other men said something which caused more laughter, but Ruswita could see from the scowl on *tuan* Thom's face that he was angry. He said something to the others, then turned to her.

'Where you work here?' he asked, attempting some form of pidgin English, believing that this would make him understood. It had worked for him in New Guinea, and he obviously believed it should also work here. Ruswita thought she understood what the question was, and replied.

'*Gudang, tuan.*'

'Oh,' Thom said, turning to the man who had offered the earlier, and offending remark. 'The *gudang!*' He paused for a moment, then muttered something to the others about waiting. Ruswita understood just the one word. She looked at her employer and became concerned that she had done something to warrant so much attention. 'I'll be back shortly,' Thom had said to his fellow conspirators, one of whom winked at Ruswita, causing her to blush. She felt frightened and looked around quickly for an excuse to escape.

'Ruswita,' she heard Thom say, 'You, *gudang*, now!' Obediently she turned, knowing that she had been told to go to her place of work. Completely confused, but greatly concerned that she had done something dreadfully wrong, Ruswita walked around the remaining guests and made her way along the factory lines, passing through the three separate stations until coming to the rear of the machinery line. She took her key and opened the door marked '*gudang*'.

Uncertain about what to do next, she waited alone expecting one of the Indonesian floor foremen to come and tell her that she had lost her job for offending the foreign guests somehow. As the minutes dragged by, the more convinced she became that she had committed some grave error, for which she would most certainly lose the only opportunity she might ever be given. She sat silently, waiting.

When the galvanised door opened and Neil Thom stepped inside Ruswita was surprised. She had expected to be dismissed by one of the senior Indonesian staff.

'Ah, there you are,' he said, the words meaningless to her as she watched, without concern, her general manager pull the bolt across the door. She stood as he approached, not understanding how she was expected to communicate with the senior foreign manager. She lowered her head and clasped her hands in submissive gesture, prepared to plead for her job. When she sensed that Thom was much nearer than she had expected, Ruswita suddenly became frightened and started to move away from his bulky figure.

In that moment, the near-drunk Australian lunged, his huge hands gripping her upper arms while his weight carried him forward, falling to the store room floor with Ruswita directly under his huge frame. It had happened so quickly she had no appreciation of what was really taking place. Her head hit the concrete floor. Simultaneously, her attacker's weight crushed the wind from her lungs as they fell heavily together to the ground. She struggled for consciousness, unable to understand why this was happening to her. She cried out for help as she slipped in and out of consciousness, but all she could sense was the foul smell of his breath as his face came into focus. Her scream was choked as Thom slammed his hand over her mouth.

He moved his weight and forced her legs apart while groping under her *batik kain*. Once his fingers touched the flimsy undergarment he tugged frantically, his excitement growing as the woman under him struggled. He pulled at the belt holding his trousers, and using his free hand pulled himself free of the clothing. Thom looked down at the helpless body underneath and grunted as he shoved himself forward.

Ruswita felt the shock of extreme pain as her attacker penetrated her body, but she could not scream. Her muscles froze in response to the unprepared entry. As the brutal rape continued, and unable to breathe with Thom's hand covering her mouth and nose, Ruswita finally succumbed to enveloping darkness, and lay motionless on the *gudang* floor.

* * * * * *

When consciousness returned, Ruswita was startled at first to discover that she was shivering with cold. Then, the memory of the attack came flooding back and she dragged herself to her knees, checking her body carefully to see how much damage had been inflicted upon her. Satisfied that she would live, she retrieved her partly torn panties and slumped to the floor crying in despair.

* * * * * *

Over the following week Ruswita continued to work in the storeroom, full of trepidation that she might still lose her position in the company. Only once during those days did she sight the man who had viciously raped her, and fortunately it was only from a distance. As that week came to a close and was followed slowly by the next, Ruswita assumed that she had been forgiven, and that her employment was secure. Then, in the third week, she was summoned by the administrative clerk up on the management floor. She sensed that she had arrived at the end of her wonderful dream, believing that she was finally to be dismissed. Instead, to her complete surprise, her fortunes changed.

JAKARTA

When Ruswita learned that she was to be moved upstairs for further training she was ecstatic with joy. At the end of her first week, following instructions to remain back to complete work given to her by her superior, she discovered why she had been promoted. Alone in the management office, and determined to complete the additional tasks she had been given, she had not thought that she might be in danger.

During the early evening Ruswita was again abruptly raped by Neil Thom. Although it lacked the viciousness of his earlier attack, Ruswita suffered the unseen bruises of helplessness and despair. She prayed that he would leave her alone, and avoided working back late even when she knew her refusal to do so was noted. For weeks she lived in fear that he would do it again. She knew that it would not be possible for her to complain. Who would believe her? And then, for reasons she could not understand, Thom never bothered her again. At the end of the following month, Ruswita knew for certain that she was pregnant.

* * * * * *

Lani entered the compound and stood in line with the other applicants. It had been less than three weeks since she had been released from the Bandung rehabilitation centre for prostitutes, and already she was considering the advantages of returning to her profession. But Lani knew that she would have to wait; the prison abortion had not gone well. It had been her second, and the ensuing infection had removed any possibility of her ever having a third pregnancy. Lani realized that she had almost died and, although the detention centre provided few creature comforts, she accepted that her time inside most probably saved her life. Unable to pay for an experienced abortionist, Lani had resorted to using the damaging and dangerous massage technique, and she had haemorrhaged badly.

Upon her release, she returned to Jakarta, deciding to at least attempt a different line of employment but, in the capital's competitive market, and without any real skills, Lani found herself working once again, as a prostitute. She applied to work as a hostess at the LCC, the military owned club built almost at the foot of the Merdeka Square Freedom monument. The manager had not thought her attractive enough, and suggested she apply to the La Paloma, just down the road. Lani was immediately employed as a hostess, and for awhile, she enjoyed working in the night-club, even though this invariably involved sleeping with the guests. At least, she had thought at the time, she was not back out on the lonely, and dangerous Jakarta streets.

Then, one night, the La Paloma was closed, and the girls all found themselves unemployed. Several of the more attractive hostesses found work elsewhere; some were fortunate enough to have foreign boyfriends who took them in, overwhelmed by the attention the young and sexually experienced girls provided, whilst others, unable to face life back on the streets, simply overdosed themselves swallowing Mandrax cocktails, or drinking straight Mortein.

Lani found work in a small club in Cikini, called Club Sixty-Nine, where the management were not so fussy about personal good looks. She had worked there for just a few months until a drug raid closed the questionable establishment, and she had nowhere to go. Arrested for vagrancy yet again, Lani was taken out of the city along with hundreds of others, and dumped, this time in the mountains, not far from the provincial city of Sukabumi. She returned to Jakarta within days, deciding to take whatever work she could find. Anything, that is, except selling herself alongside the road.

* * * * * *

She waited impatiently until her number was called, then followed the security guard into the building. The factory needed more sweepers, and Lani was desperate to establish some form of employment record without which, the government would not issue a new identification card to her. She decided to take whatever was in the offering, work for three months, then apply for the card. The government had started to crack down on the movement of people between provinces and, with her history, Lani knew that she would most probably have only one more chance to remedy her employment record with the police. She followed the guard into the factory, up the stairs, along the wooden passage-way and into the room. Lani lowered her head and waited to be spoken to.

'*What is your name?*' she was asked.

'Eri,' Lani lied, knowing that her name would simply be annotated somewhere amongst the list of hundreds of others who had applied and, as she had no identification, there was little point in using her old name. Besides, she had decided to change it anyway, not having had much luck as Lani.

'Where do you come from?' Again she answered. She wanted to smile. Undoubtedly, the other applicants were illiterate and therefore unable to even write their names, let alone complete an application form. Lani remembered that both her parents used to 'sign' their names back in their village by placing their thumbprints on whatever required their signature. She looked up at the woman who was conducting the interview. There was something familiar about her voice. She stared for a moment and then raised her hands over her mouth. It couldn't be!

'Where do you live?' Ruswita asked, and waited for the woman's response. When there was none, she looked up at the other woman and raised her eyebrows, indicating that she needed an answer. *'Where do you live?'* she repeated.

'Rus?' was all that Lani could manage. *'Rus, is that you?'* For a moment the room became quiet as Ruswita sat staring at the figure before her. She did not recognize the other person.

'How did you know my name?' Ruswita asked, almost testily. She rose and leaned forward towards the applicant, still unable to identify who she was.

'Rus,' Lani said, her face breaking into a huge smile, *'Rus, it's me, Lani!'* she cried, raising both hands to her face in excitement as she advanced on her old friend. Ruswita leaned back in surprise.

'Lani?' she gasped, stretching her neck forward without wanting to get too close to the raggedy woman. *'Really?'* she shrieked, throwing her hands out wildly, and running forward to embrace her friend. They hugged, then Ruswita stepped back and held Lani at arms' length, looking at her. She shook her head in disbelief. Rus could not accept how the young woman had aged so. Then she stepped forward once again, and held Lani tightly.

'Oh God, Rus, it's really you!' Lani cried, the tears streaming down her cheeks as they continued to hug each other. Rus remembered where they were and glanced quickly to her left, and right, to see if they had been observed. Then she turned back to her friend and held her by both hands. As she stared at the old friend who had

once sold herself to keep them both alive, an idea formed in her mind. Lani might just be the solution to her own difficult problem, one which was in danger of destroying her life, and career.

'*Lani, you can't have this job,*' she said, and before Lani's lip dropped any further she squeezed her hands and added, '*I have something much better for you.*' This was greeted by a look of uncertainty.

'*Why can't I work here?*'

'*Wait for me outside the gate. No, better still,*' Ruswita decided, '*go home now to my boarding room and wait for me. We'll talk there.*' Lani waited while Ruswita wrote her address down and, dipping into her purse, extracted ten, one hundred Rupiah notes.

'*Take this and buy some food for yourself,*' Rus said, handing the money to the destitute girl. '*Show this note to the security guard outside the main gate and tell him that I said he was to call a becak for you.*' Lani was staggered by the suddenness of events but she accepted the money and smiled.

She did as instructed, stopping on her way briefly at a roadside stall where she hungrily gulped a bowl of *bubur*, before continuing on her way with the porridge settling comfortably in her empty stomach. When she arrived home later that afternoon, Ruswita was pleased to find Lani sitting on the front steps, waiting. The landlady had refused to permit the dirty vagrant inside.

Ruswita quickly remedied that situation, making arrangements with the stern old woman to permit Lani to remain there for the time being. Reluctantly, the owner had agreed, but reminded her tenant that she would not tolerate having men visit her house. Ruswita and Lani both giggled in conspiratorial manner, Lani almost was unable to contain herself as she just could not imagine Ruswita bringing a man back to her bed. That night, however, when she learned of Ruswita's predicament, Lani held her friend close and they cried.

Ruswita was well into her fifth month. She knew that it would be impossible to hide her secret much longer. She had to make a decision, soon, or risk losing the limited security she enjoyed at the factory. Ruswita knew that it would be impossible to expect the man who had raped her to take responsibility for what he had done, although she hoped that she might just have sufficient leverage to seek at least one favour. She was determined to keep her secret from everyone except Lani, whose assistance would be vital when the baby arrived.

The following morning Ruswita gave her friend some of her clothes and several thousand Rupiah she had saved, insisting that Lani go to the markets to buy material for herself. They would sit at home together at night and sew; there was little else to do with their limited resources.

During the following days Ruswita waited for the opportunity to approach Neil Thom with her request. The general manager spent relatively little time at the factory, and his presence was rarely missed. Neil Thom believed that his role as an expatriate executive required that he visit the company's operations briefly in the mornings, after which he would congregate with his peers at The Cellar Bar, one of the few expatriate watering-holes outside the Intercontinental. Gathered there, Thom and his drinking companions would dominate the bar for the greater part of the day, often running monthly bar-tabs in excess of their own basic salaries.

As managers, they approved their own incredible personal expenditures, justifying these as necessary public relations overheads. Of course, whenever these costs were questioned by the Indonesian joint venture partners, Thom and the others would become indignant and threaten to resign, arrogantly believing that their presence was essential to the operations, as the local partners would be unable to manage such sophisticated ventures without their expertise.

It was not until Friday that Ruswita finally gathered sufficient courage, and approached Neil Thom with her request. She knew from experience that he would be anxious to leave the factory early that day as, unlike the local staff, the foreign employees were not obliged to work on Saturdays. Ruswita waited for the general manager to settle down in his office before entering and taking a cup of steaming Java Robusta with her. Thom looked up as she entered, surprised that the secretary brought coffee for him.

Privately, he had regretted what he had done to the young woman some six months before, even deluding himself that had he known she was a virgin, he would not have considered touching her. His guilt had been the reason for her advancement. Having organised her promotion, his conscience was somewhat salved. As her later behaviour towards him was devoid of any acrimony whatsoever, Thom assumed that Ruswita had put the incident behind her, and was grateful to him for the new-found security she so obviously enjoyed. He admitted that he had been surprised with the energy she displayed when attending to her duties.

The general manager was even more surprised that she had managed to become reasonably fluent in English within such a short time and, although reluctant at first to accept Ruswita as his personal secretary, Thom silently acknowledged that she had been a perfect choice. He had already lost two personal assistants, wooed away by other foreign companies desperate, as was his own company, for qualified local staff.

He watched Ruswita place the coffee to the side of the large blotting pad which occupied most of his desk, noticing that there seemed to be something different about her appearance. Thom thought that she looked healthier, somehow, then remembered that the woman was most probably eating decent food for a change, now that her salary had been increased in line with her promotion. He tried to recall how much that would be, remembering that his last secretary had been paid close to thirty dollars each month.

"Anything for me to read or sign?' he asked, lifting the coffee to his lips. He noticed Ruswita hesitate before responding. Neil Thom sipped the thick, hot coffee carefully. *Why couldn't they drink instant like civilised people?* Thom believed the traditional coffee tasted like mud. 'Well?' he prompted, placing the black, un-sweetened coffee back on the desk.

'*Tuan* Neil, I wish to speak to you please,' she blurted out, knowing that if she hesitated all would be lost. The general manager's face clouded, but she continued anyway. '*Tuan* Neil, I wish to ask for your help,' she paused, searching for the appropriate words. *Sialan!* she thought angrily, she had practised for hours and now she couldn't remember how to say it without angering him.

Neil Thom sat glaring at his secretary. He'd often wondered when she would raise what had happened. *Hadn't he done enough for the girl already?*

'*Tuan* Neil,' she started again, this time more confidently. 'I have to leave my work and return home to Java.' Thom looked at her, slightly confused. Then it dawned on him. Someone had poached her away and he was about to be stuck without a secretary for the third time in almost that many months! He looked at Ruswita, scornfully. *They always said that they had to go home to Java instead of just telling the bloody truth. Why was it that these people always confusingly referred to Java as some other place distinct from Jakarta?* He shook his head in disappointment and Ruswita immediately knew that Thom had misunderstood her request.

'*Tuan* Neil,' she tried again, 'My mother is very ill and is not expected to live more than these few months. Please, *tuan*,' she implored, 'I only wish to go home to Java to take care of her before she dies. I know that I will be gone for some time and ask that you kindly consider giving me work again, after I return.' She dropped her eyes, and sniffed, hoping this might help. 'I know that I might lose my position here but I promise to return once I have seen my mother buried.' Ruswita's convincing tears caused Thom to frown. He would need a replacement immediately.

And there was no way he could keep the position open, even if she was telling the truth. Still, he thought, there was little downside in letting her believe there would be work for her should she return. Perhaps, considering their history, it would be better for all if she didn't return. Annoyed only by the inconvenience of having to find a replacement, and knowing that none of his existing administrative staff would be qualified, Thom shrugged and looked up at Ruswita.

'Okay, Rus,' he said, almost casually, 'come back when you can.' He watched what he interpreted as gratitude sweep her face.

'*Terima kasih*,' she answered, relieved by his decision. 'I will leave after work finishes tomorrow.' As she turned to leave, Neil Thom observed her from behind, thinking that she had indeed filled out, and in all the right places. That afternoon Ruswita made arrangements with the other administrative staff, informing them all that she had been given three months leave to take care of her ailing mother. She then asked the staff if they would agree for her to take her share of the staff *arisan*, an in-house banking arrangement run by employees.

The *arisan* was not run as a lottery. The staff would contribute an identical sum from their pay, at which time all of the names of those who had not yet won, would be subject to a draw. Once an employee had won, they would be required to continue making their contributions each pay-day, until such times as all the participants had been paid. For those who won early in the year, it meant having a substantial advance against their salary. To others who were not so fortunate, they lost nothing, receiving their savings later, rather than sooner. The company accountant normally kept the records, and it was not unusual for one of the staff to request special consideration due to financial difficulty. There was not one amongst Ruswita's fellow employees who had not lost someone in their family, and so it was agreed that she could have the advance. She was popular amongst the staff, and they sympathised with her, not knowing that she was, in fact, an orphan.

Ruswita then approached her last task with considerably more confidence than she had earlier in the day. She entered Bill Davidson's office and explained that her mother was dying, and advised that she would be leaving, temporarily, to care for her. Ruswita then explained that the general manager had guaranteed her position but, sadly, he had not seen his way clear to advance her any of her salary to assist with what most probably would be difficult times for her and her family.

Davidson did not hesitate, extracting one hundred dollars from his wallet, insisting that Ruswita consider the money a loan which could be repaid whenever she was able. Ruswita dried her eyes once again, thanked the operations manager and departed, not even bothering to attend work the following day. Armed with sufficient funds, Ruswita took Lani and moved to other accommodations closer to the inner suburb of Cikini, where the hospital would admit her when the time came. Ruswita enrolled in classes to improve her knowledge of commercial English, and during this time both she and Lani devised a plan which would, in the future, accommodate both their needs.

In her seventh month of pregnancy Ruswita collapsed in pain and was immediately rushed to the Cikini Hospital. There, the Catholic missionary doctors worked to save the premature infant and, in so doing, almost lost the child's mother. Two days after the birth of her daughter, the child was registered by the hospital administration staff. Ruswita named her daughter Ratna Sari, and for the records her father was listed as having died.

The nurses were, of course, sceptical, having seen the pale-skinned infant. It was obvious to them that the young woman's child was more likely the result of an affair with one of the wealthy foreigners. How else, they all believed, could she have afforded such expensive maternity care? All agreed that the child's mother, Lani, was a most fortunate woman, having God bless her in this way. Two days after the birth, the real Lani came to the hospital as arranged, and took the pair home. As they drove the short distance to their rented rooms, Lani could not resist giggling at the prospect of being the child's mother, and how simple it had been for Ruswita to use her friend's name at the hospital for registration purposes.

The following week, satisfied that Lani understood what was expected of her, and confident that Ratna Sari would remain under her direct care, Ruswita returned to the factory and asked to be reinstated. Her timing could not have been more appropriate; her replacement had left just days before, citing the general manager's roving hands as her reason for resigning what she described as a poorly paid position. Everyone was delighted to see that Ruswita had returned, and offered their condolences at the loss of her mother. They were also relieved that she had returned to repay her debts.

As soon as her salary had been increased, Ruswita moved Lani and her daughter to a more pleasant location in Tebet, across the railway line from the elite suburb of Menteng. There, they set about establishing order in their lives, caring for each other, and bringing up the baby together.

* * * * * *

Bill Davidson could not believe how quickly his first year and a half in Jakarta had passed. As he sat in the factory office and observed the production line below, he frowned. His immediate superior, Neil Thom, had been putting the pressure on everyone lately, and Davidson could see that the joint venture partners were heading for a major dispute, if the Foreign Investment Board did not assist to settle some of the problems associated with their investment. But it was not Davidson's problem. His contract specified that his responsibilities were to oversee the production line, and maintain the equipment.

Salima Jaya Products had gone into full production expecting a return on capital in less than two years. The Indonesian joint venture partner had assured their foreign counterparts that the Foreign

Investment Board would honour the investment approvals which, *inter alia*, guaranteed protection to the fledgling company for at least three years. He knew that the Australian investment had been predicated on Indonesian undertakings to prohibit cheap imports from Taiwan.

Davidson also knew that there was more inventory of their product stacked at the additional storage facility, than the market could possibly consume. He believed that the joint venture partner's Taiwanese associates had continued to flood the Indonesian market with the identical product to the one his company manufactured under protection of the host government, and that even the tax incentives were useless against the organized dumping of product that continued to take place.

The enigma for Davidson, and his Australian masters back in Melbourne, was *why* their partner had deliberately orchestrated to defeat his own joint venture; surely, they had argued, he would understand that, in the long term, the joint venture would be far more profitable than the short term benefits of smuggling the identical product in competition with himself?

Davidson's thoughts were interrupted as Ruswita knocked, and waited outside the glass door. He beckoned for her to enter, remembering to point his hand to the ground as he waved. He removed his feet from the table, silently rebuking himself for his oversight. Davidson knew that he should never have permitted one of the staff to see him resting with his feet on the desk. It had taken him some time to become familiar with the customs, many still requiring more patience than he professed to have, or wanted to develop. It seemed that there were traps at every turn and, in his mind, assimilation seemed to be a little too one-way for his liking.

After his first blunder, Davidson went on to discover that these local idiosyncrasies and customs were almost endless, and believed that it would be overly ambitious for him to expect to understand them all. Nevertheless, he enjoyed living in the country, even if the working environment was confusing. He watched Ruswita walk in, smile, place the file on his desk and wait. The joint venture was fortunate to have her working there, he thought.

He had often wondered why she had not been tempted away by some of the recent foreign arrivals. And then, he recalled, she *had* once disappeared for several months. At the time, Thom had told him that he could kiss his hundred dollars goodbye making Davidson wish he'd not told the man about the loan he had made to Ruswita. His thoughts then returned to the documents.

'Thanks Rus,' he smiled. *Why did she always seem so distant?* 'I'll go through the file tomorrow.' She never had repaid the money he had loaned her.

'I will bring it back in the morning then,' she suggested, moving to recover the folder.

'No, leave it here.' Davidson said. 'I'll lock it away until then.' He smiled again, reassuringly. 'Goodnight, Rus.' As she turned and left his office Davidson watched her depart. As he had done so many times before, the Australian continued to marvel at the transformation that had taken place, and found it difficult to accept that this was the same woman who had stood before him in the factory yard, covered in dirt, less than two years before. He recalled, with some admiration, how quickly the transition had occurred. Ruswita had absorbed information and developed new skills with such fervour that she had soon attracted the general manager's attention.

During the factory's first two months of operation, Ruswita had moved from stores to the back-office where, within a short period, she had easily mastered the basic skills required. From there she had been moved forward into accounting. He was aware that Ruswita studied at night along with a number of other employees, and had attended the company-sponsored language lessons. The general manager had apparently seen her potential, as Ruswita was promoted to be his personal secretary. All this before the company had even celebrated its first year in Indonesia. Not that there was really anything to celebrate, Davidson thought, returning his attention to the inevitable confrontation between the partners during the first annual meeting scheduled for the following week. As production manager, he knew that he would not be invited to attend the meeting, and for that small blessing, he was pleased.

Ruswita returned to her desk, checked that all was in order, locked the general manager's office and phoned security for her transport. As the senior secretary, she was entitled to company transport, but only between the factory and where she resided in Tebet. Waving as she passed through the side employees' exit, she climbed into the company mini-bus, smiling at the security guard who had opened the vehicle's door for her. She was popular amongst the other employees, and had become a role model for many of the younger girls who discovered that they could always depend on her to listen to their problems.

The fact that Ruswita had not slept with the foreign bosses to advance to where she was did not go unnoticed although, had she done so, none of her peers would have been critical of such behaviour. Without exception, they knew that they were the fortunate ones, having secured employment with one of the foreign joint venture companies. These were tough times, and opportunities were not to be taken lightly. Ruswita had succeeded and they were pleased for her.

* * * * * *

Murray Stephenson re-read the letter and smiled. Zach and Susan had decided to tie the knot at last. He was delighted that they had caught up with each other again after Zach's tour had been completed, when he had been attached to the Defence Signals Regiment in Melbourne. It seemed that young Michael Bradshaw would have some discipline in his life after all, Murray thought, contentedly, not that Susan had done so badly without a man around the house for the greater part of eight years.

Murray looked at the enclosed snapshot and smiled again. Michael certainly had his features. He opened the top drawer of his teak desk and placed the correspondence inside. For a moment he hesitated, wondering if he should place the boy's photograph somewhere in view then, deciding against this, placed the framed photo also in the drawer, locking the contents inside. He had agreed with Susan that the boy should never know the truth. Besides, he had little security to offer a son of that age, and accepted that Zach would provide for the boy both spiritually and materially. Steve Zach was a good man; and a fine friend.

'*Telepon, Murray,*' his secretary called, then pulled a face indicating that she was not fond of the caller. Murray picked up the phone and wished that he had not dropped his guard that once, and bedded the girl. Now his secretary vetted his calls and even opened his private mail. He had wanted to pass her on to one of the new companies he represented, but she had found numerous excuses to avoid making the move.

'Hello, Fay,' he said, knowing from his secretary's expression that it would be the Australian Ambassador's personal secretary. They had dated regularly over the past few months and Murray was not displeased that she had called.

'Hello yourself. Just a quick call to let you know that I won't be over tonight. There's a stir on here and I'll be stuck sending out cables well into the night.'

'What's going on?' he asked, immediately wishing that he hadn't. They had a pact not to discuss Embassy confidential matters, knowing that to do so would only jeopardise their relationship. Fay realized just how difficult that was for Murray, considering his former association with the government, the time he had served in the Embassy and with ASIS, and his insatiable need to know whatever might affect the current investment climate. She appreciated that Murray had not been tempted to use their friendship to solicit information.

'Busy, busy, busy,' Fay said, permitting the slip to pass. Then she added, 'There's an old friend of yours coming to visit.' She knew that the tease would do the trick.

'I'm all ears,' he said, 'man or woman?'

'Eric Whitehead. Bye,' was all she had time to say before hanging up. Murray pulled the receiver away from his ear and then looked at it quizzically. He shrugged, then turned his attention to the name she had dropped. Whitehead certainly was not to be classed as one of his friends, and he was surprised that Fay would have even suggested so.

Most former agents suffered an occasional attack of paranoia, and Murray was no exception. He thought about the smooth-talking, well-groomed public relations giant and deduced that Fay must have seen an advance advice informing the intelligence boys of his arrival. Murray decided that his name must have been mentioned, for whatever reason, in that same message. His curiosity aroused, he then spent the rest of the day wondering what possible connection he could have with the CEO of Eric Whitehead and Associates' imminent visit to Indonesia.

The following morning it all became clear when he received a call from the Embassy's Political Attaché to arrange a private luncheon at his residence. Murray knew that there were few who knew that the officer holding this position in the Embassy always doubled as the ASIS Station Chief. Murray also knew who else would be present, and reminded himself to thank Fay for the warning.

* * * * * *

'Hello, there,' Whitehead extended his hand to greet Murray as he entered the residence. The white-uniformed houseboy who had escorted him onto the enclosed veranda poured an ice-tea and left the three *tuans* alone. 'It has been some time since we last met.' It was a statement of fact; Murray could still remember the precise moment. It was the evening, some six years before, when his incompetent superior, and Station Intelligence Chief, had collapsed and died not hours after being offered a position with the prominent public relations group. Murray decided not to raise the point. He had attempted to put his former association with the Australian Secret Service behind him.

He had only agreed to this luncheon with Whitehead out of curiosity. He wanted to know why his former associates had arranged for him to meet the man who provided ASIS with its commercial front in Asia. The question remained annoyingly in his mind and he knew that he had to discover the reason behind this unsolicited meeting.

'Yes,' he responded, taking the older man's hand, surprised at the firmness of his grip, 'but I don't believe we had much of a chance to talk.' He added, 'how can I be of assistance to the public relations industry?'

Whitehead smiled, enjoying the man's abrupt approach. He leaned back in the wicker chair and crossed one long leg over the other, deliberately taking his time. He withdrew a pipe, and commenced prodding the pot with a match-stick.

'Why don't we leave that until after we've eaten?' he suggested, hoping for a little more time to gauge Stephenson's current position and activities.

'Sure,' Murray replied, then turned to wave for the houseboy whom he knew would be watching them from a discreet place. The servant appeared immediately and knelt on both knees to the visitor's side, exchanged a few words, listened to the order, smiled and hurried away to prepare the whisky Murray had ordered. The men exchanged small talk until the houseboy returned with the bottle, poured a generous glass of his *tuan's* single malt whisky, and handed this to the guest.

Murray contained the smile which threatened to break through. The houseboy confirmed that the host did, indeed, keep a special bottle of single malt to one side, which he imported directly for his own needs. Murray guessed that the Embassy canteen stocks would not extend to providing such an extensive range of expensive Scotch whisky, and enjoyed his host's forced smile as he raised his glass in salute.

The meal finished, all three men returned to the pleasant patio area, waited for the servant to pour the coffees and cognac, then proceeded to the purpose of the meeting. Ten minutes later Murray was on his way back to his office, angry that the offer had been made. He had stormed out of the residence knowing that had he remained, there would have been violence.

'Well, Murray, it seems that you have not been idle in establishing yourself in the commercial sector,' Whitehead had commenced.

'We do what we can,' Murray replied, glibly. He really did not like this man, and regretted having accepted the invitation.

'Eric Whitehead and Associates wish to make you what I consider, a most generous offer, Murray,' the older man smiled generously as he spoke.

'What do I have that your organization might need, Eric?' Murray returned to the casual style he had adopted during lunch.

'The group would like to offer you the opportunity to join our ranks, so to speak,' Whitehead answered, while observing Murray's face for an indication of how the approach would be received.

'I already have a job, thanks,' Murray responded, not sarcastically, although there was an edge to his voice.

'I'm not offering you a job young Murray,' Whitehead suggested, 'I'm offering you a partnership!' Murray was struck speechless; *had he misunderstood?*

'A partnership?' he asked, incredulously.

'Yes, Murray, a partnership,' Whitehead confirmed. 'We will assume control over your existing operations, for which you would be handsomely compensated. And,' he added, 'you would be permitted to retain forty-nine percent of the Jakarta based operation.' Murray was stunned by the offer, and the man's audacity.

'What would possibly lead you to believe that I am interested in selling my company?' Murray asked, anger now evident in his voice.

'Think about it, Murray,' Whitehead suggested. 'With the support of our organization with its world-wide network, we could point a considerable number of our existing clients in the direction of a joint-Jakarta based operation. You would do extremely well from the arrangement. Hell, we'd even pay you a handsome salary!' he said, making light of the moment. Murray placed his tumbler back on the rattan table and made as if to leave.

'Wait, Murray,' their host interceded. 'There's more to it than that.' Murray looked at the ASIS Station Chief and frowned.

'I'm listening,' he said, coolly.

'We don't have the time to establish a grass roots operation in Jakarta. You are already on the ground, and know what it's all about. It might be wise of you to consider the offer, Murray, before going off half-cocked.' Murray glared at the First Secretary.

'He's right, Murray,' Whitehead added, 'as I said, you would be well compensated.'

'And,' the Secretary interrupted, enjoying his role, 'you might consider the down side.' With this, Murray had difficulty containing his anger. The statement was obviously a veiled threat.

'What down side?' he asked, glancing from one to the other. Whitehead cleared his throat, but it was their host who answered.

'Let's say you elect not to participate in the restructured company. Eric will set up office here, with or without your co-operation and, when they open their doors, without their political clout and substantial client list, yours will most probably close within six months. You would have difficulty maintaining your existing clients. Think about it.' Murray's face paled. He rose to his feet, shaking in anger.

'Mr Whitehead,' he commenced, his voice barely more than a whisper, 'Go screw yourself,' with which, he had turned and marched out, avoiding the temptation to whack their host, the First Secretary for Political Affairs across the head. And hard.

A short time later Murray stood in front of his bedroom air-conditioner unit and closed his eyes as the cool, artificial breeze washed across his face. *The bastards!* He kept repeating to himself,

JAKARTA

realizing that they could do precisely what they had threatened. Then he turned angrily and drove his fist through the wardrobe door. That night he went out alone and returned to his villa, almost paralytic from the excessive amounts of alcohol the ageing bargirls had insisted on pouring down his throat until he could no longer stand.

Then they had taken him home and put him to bed. When he was awakened the next morning by a loud banging on his bedroom door, Murray still felt drunk. Then he looked to either side of where he lay and discovered the ugly women who had spent the night in his bed. Ill as he was, Murray woke the women and told them that he would give them each five dollars if they remained inside the bedroom until dark. He didn't want his staff or others to see just how dreadful these women were. They giggled, surprised that he would want them to stay. That had never happened to them before, well, at least not for some years. Pleased with their sudden change of fortunes, they agreed. Murray showered, dressed, and walked across to his office, having locked the girls inside before leaving. He mumbled something to his houseboy who merely grinned in response. He had seen the pair when they had returned with his *tuan* in the early hours of the morning and, even in the darkness of the night, the loyal servant had shaken his head in surprise, and disappointment.

'*Telepon,*' his secretary snapped. It was bad enough that her boss was ignoring her in preference to the *bulé* woman, but this! She had managed to extract the information from the houseboy. All, that is, except the condition of the two girls.

Murray groaned and answered the phone. He struggled to clear his head as he listened to the voice at the other end of the line. He continued for some minutes, mumbling his response, then dropped the receiver heavily into its cradle. He looked up and saw the look of disgust on his secretary's face.

'*Don't start!*' he warned, rising to his feet, instantly wishing that he hadn't. His temples throbbed. '*I'm going out,*' he said, and yelled for his driver. Then he remembered the other problem.

'*Here,*' he said, throwing the bedroom key to the hostile secretary, no longer concerned with her reaction to what she would find '*Have someone fumigate my room,*' with which, he made his way outside and into his car.

Murray was at least half a block away from his office and could not, therefore, hear his secretary's screams following him down the street. As his car reversed out of the driveway, she had gone directly into his house and unlocked the door. The women inside were just as surprised as their intruder.

Murray's secretary just could not believe that he would pass her over for the two disgusting creatures who had emerged from his bedroom, demanding money he had promised each of them. Having re-locked the door, she returned to the office, opened the filing cabinet and threw the contents out into the driveway. Then she ripped the telephone cable from its socket, upended the furniture, pulled the calendar from the wall and, in one last defiant gesture, hurled the house keys over the fence into the neighbour's garden. Satisfied that there was nothing else she could do to demonstrate her anger at what Murray had done, she sat on the floor amidst the scattered mess she had created, and broke into tears.

Twenty minutes passed before she rose, wiped her face and looked around in dismay at the evidence of her tantrum. Then she sighed despondently, and went about restoring the office as best she could, knowing that Murray would most probably forgive her for the damage she had done to the company headquarters. The two women she had left locked inside the house would, however, be another matter.

* * * * * *

Krawang Industrial estate

Security opened the factory gates as his vehicle approached. Murray was surprised to see a number of metropolitan police inside the entrance and realized that this was not a good omen. As his driver jumped out and opened his door, Murray noticed also that another jeep-load of police waited close to the offices, and these were armed. He walked into the factory quickly, where he found an ashen-faced Bill Davidson sitting alone, both hands clasping his face in despair.

'Okay,' Murray started, 'tell me what happened.' The Australian joint-venture partner company was one of his clients. He received an annual retainer to act in an advisory capacity and provide additional on-ground support to the expatriate managers. This was not an unusual arrangement as Murray had several such accounts. It made sense to have access to his considerable in-country experience; there were few foreign managers with sufficient knowledge of how business was done in this country, and Murray had been engaged to provide guidance whenever called upon by the foreign partner.

'Neil has been arrested,' Davidson explained, apparently in shock. Murray waited. 'As you know, Murray, we've been having nothing but trouble with the partners here. We've got stock coming out of our ears and little support from the Salima management to rectify the problem of Taiwanese products flooding the market. We were guaranteed protection under our agreement, but this has not eventuated in any shape or form. The Salima people insisted that we were too impatient and should not antagonise the Foreign Investment Board. They have accused us of flooding the government offices with complaints, and that this has created an atmosphere in which any support for our case has gone straight out the window.'

'Why was Neil arrested?' Murray asked softly, hoping that his presence would calm the agitated production manager.

'The other day I took a call from Melbourne. To put it bluntly, Murray, they are fed up with the whole mess. Neil wasn't available at the time and so I was given the responsibility of carrying out their instructions.' Davidson paused, as if he was out of breath. He shook his head slowly. 'Melbourne were adamant that the partners have deliberately procrastinated over the market protection issue. Under the operating agreement, the technology remains the property of the foreign partner at all times, or until both parties come to some arrangement regarding our specialized tooling.' He raised his head and looked directly at Murray, knowing that he would not like what he was about to hear.

'Melbourne insisted that we remove the dies from the extrusion plant and lock these away at home until the Indonesian partners came to their senses, and met their contractual obligations as outlined in the joint venture charter.' Davidson stopped, obviously reluctant to continue.

'Go on,' Murray urged. He didn't like any of this, at all. It explained the police presence inside the factory complex.

'When Neil returned, I relayed what the Australian directors had instructed and, to my surprise, he was supportive of their action. To tell you the truth, Murray, I didn't like it, not even one iota, but I had to follow their instructions. After all, when my tour's finished here, I still have a job to return to in Australia and, from the looks of things, that won't be too far down the track.'

'Tell me exactly what happened,' Murray insisted. His mind was already racing ahead, considering their options in securing the general manager's release.

'Well, as I said, I told Neil what the Melbourne office required of us. He instructed me to remove the dies. I had little difficulty doing this as the line has been inactive for almost a week, due to the stock surplus. I told him that there was no way that I would personally take the dies out of the premises, alone. Neil got a little pissed with me and insisted that I help him load the dies into the pick-up. I did. Neil then jumped inside the cabin and drove out through the gate where the security stopped him.' Davidson shook his head again, in a disbelieving manner. 'Jesus, Murray,' he said, with a tremor in his voice, 'the bastards were waiting for us!'

'They knew?' Murray asked, his eyebrows raised in surprise. 'How?' he demanded.

'How else?' the plant operations manager replied, sarcastically. He turned his head and indicated with a nod that he blamed the person sitting calmly in the adjacent office. Murray glanced through the glass partition which separated the offices on the mezzanine floor where management and administration was housed. He turned back and looked questioningly at the other man. 'She was the one who called the police for chrissakes,' he snarled, 'and after all we've done for her,' he paused, then turned and glared in her direction as he added, 'the bitch!'

Murray was confused by the accusation. He had met Ruswita on a number of occasions and thought that Davidson might have been a little hasty in pre-judging the young woman.

'Why her?' he asked.

'Shit, Murray, she is the GM's personal assistant. She knows everything that goes on here. Mate, little Ruswita doesn't miss a bloody thing!' Davidson rubbed his hands together then scratched his head nervously. 'My guess is, she listened to the incoming call from Australia.' Murray thought about this and accepted that it may have happened that way. He knew from experience that staff often eavesdropped, acting on instructions from their Indonesian masters. He sighed.

'Have you spoken to her about this?' he asked.

'What the hell for?' Davidson snapped back.

'Good,' Murray said, 'then don't. It won't help your case, nor Neil's, to have her offside. I'll go and speak to her, then the police, to determine what can be done.' He looked back over at Ruswita who, at that very moment, had also glanced in his direction. Murray smiled, but she did not respond, dropping her eyes quickly away. This was not the reaction Murray had hoped to receive. He looked back at Davidson.

'You might as well prepare to leave for Australia, Bill, as soon as I clear it with the police.'

'But I...' Davidson started to protest but Murray cut him short.

'Can it, Bill. I'm not taking sides here, just advising you what you should do. I've seen the inside of their jails and if you stir them up any more, you might just get to look for yourself. What you both did was bloody foolish, but I guess you don't need me to tell you that now. Wait here,' he ordered, then left the rattled expatriate to consider what he'd said. Murray then went directly into Ruswita's office, knocking as he opened her door.

'*Selamat pagi, Rus,*' he said pleasantly, wishing her a good morning. Ruswita smiled but Murray could see that there was no warmth in it.

'Good morning, Mr Stephenson,' she responded, her manner cool. Murray knew that her refusal to speak Indonesian was not a good omen either. 'Are you here as the Australian representative?'

Murray was quite surprised at the woman's impertinence. Ruswita was, in his opinion, greatly exceeding her authority as the general manager's personal assistant. He tried another tack.

'Rus, I am here to help recover the situation between the Australians and their Indonesian counterparts. Would you like to tell me what happened?' he asked.

'Surely you already know from Mr Davidson?' she replied.

'Yes, he told me that he had been instructed to remove some of the machinery parts, and that the general manger attempted to remove these from the factory compound.' He hesitated, not knowing just how knowledgeable Ruswita might be regarding the terms of the joint venture. 'What they did was inconsiderate, Rus, but it was not illegal. The foreign partner continues to own that special equipment...'

'You mean the dies, Mr Stephenson,' she said, surprising Murray. 'I have received instructions from the Salima Group not to communicate with you or any of the foreign partners. I am sorry, but I must ask you to leave, as these are their instructions.'

Murray was speechless that he had been spoken to in this way. Then he realized that he really did not have any legal position to be there, as he was not directly engaged by the joint venture company. If he was to assist the foreign partners recover their position, he would have to take a softer stance.

'May I speak to Salima?' he asked, indicating the phone on her desk.

'I don't know. I cannot say.' Ruswita hesitated, looked around to see if they could be heard. 'Mr Stephenson, you should leave now,' she said, then lowered her voice and spoke quietly in Indonesian.

'I am not ungrateful Pak Murray,' she whispered, using the respectful form of his name, *'but what has happened here is very serious. Mr Salima has informed me that the factory will be temporarily closed. Do you understand that this will mean that more than two hundred people have lost their jobs today because of what the Australians did?'* Murray did understand, and silently rebuked himself for not considering the consequences of the foreign partner's actions. He sympathised immediately with the staff and workers knowing that few of their number would find other employment.

'I am sorry that this has happened, Rus. Are you sure I can't speak to Mr Salima or his assistant to see what might be done to rectify this situation?'

'No, Pak Murray, that is not possible from here. You could always try contacting him at his office, or even home perhaps. I have been instructed to remain here, along with a small maintenance and security staff while the factory is closed. Please go now before I lose my position as well,' she asked politely, and Murray nodded then left. He went down to the police to determine where the general manager had been taken, and discovered that he had been placed under house arrest. Relieved, Murray drove down to speak to him, after which he attempted to contact someone in Salima's office who might be

receptive to discussing the joint venture breakdown.

After hours of sitting, waiting patiently at the Salima Group offices, Murray was ushered in to meet with one of the senior assistants. The man's manner was officious, informing him that the group's chairman had decided to prosecute the Australians. Murray considered the statement but decided that this was but a gambit. Salima would gain nothing from having the foreign employees jailed, but the threat was there, and he knew how the directors in Melbourne must respond.

The Australian company called an urgent board meeting and decided to withdraw from their Indonesian investment, and reluctantly agreed to sell their shares in the joint venture to their Indonesian counterpart. As a matter of face, the two Australians were to be detained for three months under casual house arrest, which required only that they sleep at their accommodations. The Indonesians did not want to be responsible for feeding the expensive foreigners.

The following week both the foreign employees were secretly flown out of Indonesia, via Bali, their confiscated passports still locked in the Jakarta Metropolitan Police Chief's desk. The dies were re-installed by a Taiwanese team of engineers and, within the month, the factory re-commenced operations. Almost the same day, the Indonesian Ministry of Trade imposed a total ban on the competitive, imported, Taiwanese product. Salima's strength, and reputation continued to grow, while Murray's suffered as a result of his obvious impotence in handling the matter. He lost credibility as an astute negotiator, and several of his major accounts moved their business across to the newly established offices of Eric Whitehead and Associates.

Several months passed before Murray admitted to himself that his business was in trouble. He decided to take in a financial partner and offered his services to one of his remaining clients, an aviation investor by the name of Peter Wong. Almost immediately upon signing his new alliance with the millionaire, Murray's fortunes improved as his fellow shareholder encouraged other Chinese investors to deal through their *kongsi*, or partnership. Murray was a viable front for their Mainland Chinese capital.

The Indonesian Government might have been receptive to its own Chinese investing in its rapidly growing economy, but they still had not forgiven Mao Tse Tung's China, for the support it had given to the communists during Soekarno's presidency, and refused to restore relationships with that country or its people.

Chapter 3

John Georgio and others

John Georgio sat across the table facing his visitors, pleased that his presentation had gone so well. John considered himself the only foreigner qualified to conduct surveys and market research in Indonesia and, it was apparent from the gathering's obvious *bonhomie*, that he had the team from Pepsi Cola convinced of his credentials. They had all willingly warmed to his proposal to represent their interests throughout the country and complete a market research study on the company's behalf. The investigating team had arrived over the weekend, and John had played the role of an influential American businessman well, arranging a police escort for the first-time visitors to Indonesia from the airport to the Intercontinental Hotel. The American visitors were impressed. They had checked with the United States Embassy and established that he was the only American in Jakarta who acted as a free-lance consultant, and was licensed to conduct surveys in Indonesia.

John was ecstatic when the delegation's leader confirmed that he would be appointed to carry out their market research. Apart from oil and gas firms, American companies had been slow moving into the new market, as most were still more than a little suspicious of a country which, just six years before, had boasted the third largest Communist Party membership in the world.

John's entrepreneurial capabilities were limited primarily by his inability to really understand how to conduct business in the Asian environment. Although he was conscious of the incredible opportunities Indonesia offered to those who had the capacity to deal within the established, but unspoken commercial guidelines, John's activities were inevitably frustrated by his lack of focus. He had few friends.

Several weeks subsequent to the Pepsi-Cola team's visit John received an advance payment to commence preparing their survey. He threw himself into his work, determined to finally make his mark. And he did. John's limited knowledge of his own target market led him to make a number of dangerous assumptions. Once he had compiled his client's basic questionnaire and received approval for its implementation, John, being Catholic, decided that he would ingratiate himself with the small number of Catholic universities throughout the country by employing their students to assist with his research.

He selected five of these colleges and negotiated directly with the student bodies. John determined that a Sunday would be the most suitable time to find the average household head at home and, some eight weeks later, and on the same Sunday, two hundred Catholic university students hit the streets in their respective cities and towns, each carrying an armful of John's designated questionnaires.

Foolishly, John had inappropriately camouflaged a number of questions which amounted to a political polling of the President, and other senior government officials' popularity. He had not even been paid for this highly sensitive service. John had actually convinced himself that by doing so, the Chinese Indonesian who had made the request would be indebted to him, forever. And, perhaps, even the general for whom they were secretly canvassing the public, in order to determine his popularity. It was obvious to John that this man might be considering a challenge against Soeharto in the forthcoming Presidential elections. During the meeting with Salima's cousin, John was so overwhelmed at having been asked to carry out this favour for the important group, he failed to secure some written commitment. He was later to regret his error.

* * * * * *

In a small town in East Java, a luckless student knocked, almost arrogantly, on the front door of Colonel Suparman's house. The Moslem army officer had been asleep less than two hours, having returned to his wife and family during the early morning hours of the night before. At first, the Colonel told his wife to ignore the interruption. He had not lain with his young wife for more than

JAKARTA

two months, and was determined not to permit anything disrupt their intimate moment. Unfortunately, the persistent student continued to knock on the Colonel's door which, to his dismay, resulted in a confrontation he could never have anticipated.

'What do you want?' the Colonel had demanded. The interviewing student had no idea that the man was in the military, as the officer was clad only in a *sarong*. The young boy could not understand what it was that had angered the man.

'I am conducting a survey,' he had answered, enjoying his new-found importance.

'Survey?' the angry officer shouted, *'survey you say?'* he yelled, tearing the document from the student's hand, and commencing reading its contents. For a few minutes the Catholic youth stood silently, smugly believing that the man before him was obviously having difficulty reading the survey questions.

'This is a survey sponsored by our government to..........'

'Shut up!' the Colonel barked. *'Who gave you instructions to ask these questions?'* he demanded. Suddenly the student became confused. He had not encountered such a violent response from any other householder that morning, and felt that the man before him was behaving out of hand.

'I am part of a nation-wide survey team collecting information valuable for foreign investment,' he replied, surprised that the man was reading through the complex document. *'If you don't wish to answer the questions then I'll just go,'* he offered, worried that this one stop might cost him valuable time. He had a quota of fifty to complete before the evening.

The Colonel ignored the student, reading on through the questionnaire. Suddenly he stopped, and his eyes opened wider in surprise. Then he frowned, re-read the particular section which he'd found cleverly disguised amongst a number of unrelated questions, then looked suspiciously at the student.

'Who do you work for?' he demanded sternly. The student was annoyed with the question. He reached out to retrieve his papers when, without warning, the half-dressed man he had attempted to interview stepped forward, and grabbed him by the throat with one hand. Terrified that he had struck a madman amongst the group of houses selected for the interviews, he struggled, dropped the remainder of his papers, and attempted to break free. But his

resistance was in vain. The Colonel was considerably stronger and, within moments, the young man fell to his knees gasping for breath.

'Once more, who do you work for?' the army officer snapped, not accustomed to having such youngsters ignore his questions. He released his grip slightly as the student started to choke.

* * * * * *

While John Georgio strutted around the Hotel Indonesia swimming pool, flexing his muscles, vainly attempting to impress the ladies present, a team of investigators had already gathered in the small Javanese town to interrogate the luckless Catholic student. As John posed and smiled with his new found confidence, the young man who had innocently accepted the research assignment finally collapsed to the cell floor, unable to withstand the savage blows to his head and body.

That evening, as John Georgio stood in the doorway to his house and attempted to re-negotiate with his visitor for her time, a further twenty-eight Catholic students had already been arrested throughout East Java, and incarcerated for distributing subversive material. By the time morning arrived, and John was ready for the start of a new week, more than fifty arrests had been made, and the American consultant's activities in Indonesia were in imminent danger of coming to an abrupt end.

During the course of that week John Georgio's naïve attempt to disguise the sensitive political questions within the Pepsi Cola market research questionnaire was known throughout the country. He received two calls from intermediaries promising financial and political support, conditional that he not involve the Salima Group in any way whatsoever. Understandably, John panicked when called to attend an interview at the Indonesian Intelligence Co-ordinating Agency, BAKIN. There, he was formally served with a deportation order.

Upon returning to his villa, Georgio phoned his limited circle of friends only to discover that their recollection of any association with John had been far more casual than he had remembered. His calls and messages to the Salima Group director, who had encouraged John to compromise the questionnaire, went unanswered. Instead, he was instructed to meet covertly with one of the company's representatives, who confirmed that the Group would take care of his financial needs, suggesting that he should go to Singapore and wait until the crisis blew over, after which time he could return. Salima, according to the intermediary, had given his word. What's more, the man had revealed, John was to have the use of one of Lim's penthouses in Singapore for however long he might need to remain there. Also, there was to be financial compensation.

He was again warned that there was never to be any mention of the Salima involvement in relation to the secret survey they had commissioned. Reluctantly, John agreed, realising that seeking support to overturn his deportation order might only then be possible through the courts. Considering his financial position, and cognisant of Salima's influence within the community, he decided to make the best of the situation and gain as much mileage from his deportation order as he could. But the newspapers were determined to have his blood, and fuelled by the recent memory that one of their own had died as a result of his earlier indiscretions, branded John Georgio a pariah.

Most expatriates suddenly avoided all contact with the American, concerned that any association would be detrimental to their own activities and interests in Indonesia. Desperate, and in need of a friend, John approached the only foreigner in the city who had returned any of his calls. His name was Stephen Coleman.

* * * * * * *

In no way did it bother Coleman that his rationale for providing some support to the American had been based on the assumption that he would acquire the Pepsi account, once Georgio had departed. There were a limited number of expatriate consultants capable of providing the representation such a client would so obviously require in the event bottling plants were to proceed.

He had discussed this with General Seda, his sponsor and silent partner. At first, the powerful man had appeared intrigued with John Georgio's machinations but later, his interest visibly waned. Coleman had argued that, although there might be some who would question his judgement in maintaining any association with the American, Georgio's recommendation to the giant Stateside company might just carry some weight when it came to seeking a replacement office to represent their affairs in Indonesia. Seda finally agreed when Coleman suggested that they might then be in a position to influence Pepsi's future decision as to who might be appointed as their distributor for the mammoth market.

On several occasions, Coleman invited Georgio for lunch at The Cellar Bar, and encouraged several other foreigners present to join them. Although uncomfortable with the prospect that they would be seen associating with John, which might in turn be detrimental to their own positions, the fact that Stephen Coleman was prepared to sit with the man was good enough for them. John was relieved that he was no longer entirely alone.

Prior to his departure, and on the very evening his deportation notice had stipulated he must finally leave Indonesia, Coleman secured a written undertaking that he was to take care of John's interests until he was permitted to return. Georgio had been informed, discreetly, by the Salima intermediary, that this would most probably be no more than a few months. As John wished to maintain the Pepsi account, he offered to inform their head office that his interests continued in Indonesia, and that Stephen Coleman's organization would be overseeing Pepsi's affairs on Georgio's behalf.

Coleman personally drove John to the airport. He carried but a few pieces of luggage, truly believing that his sojourn in Singapore would not exceed that which had been promised. He had left behind what few possessions he owned, including his prized Dean Martin collection. John arrived in Singapore and caught a taxi to the Penthouse address where he discovered that the apartment was locked and unattended. He made several calls to Jakarta, but was unable to speak to anyone of authority within the Salima conglomerate. Even then it still did not dawn on him that he was, in fact, fortunate just to be alive.

Confused, he moved in with a friend from the American Embassy and waited. When the rental contract on John's Jakarta residence expired three months later, he still had not been permitted to return. It seemed that all Indonesian Embassies had been instructed not to issue a visa to John Georgio because of his subversive activities in Indonesia. John waited impatiently for the signal that he could return. He survived on handouts from others who listened to his story, and the occasional young and naïve coffee shop waitress who believed his stories of wealth and influence. Finally, as the weeks rolled into months, and months into years, John Georgio turned to the only other work which suited his temperament.

He joined with a group out of Johore Baru, providing hookers for visiting businessmen and tourists into Singapore. It would be another ten years before he was finally given a restricted visa to visit Indonesia again. During that period of exile, John Georgio tried desperately to establish himself within the Singapore community but failed, his reputation as an up-market pimp precluding him from membership of expatriate clubs and social venues. Finally, resigned to his new vocation, he set about establishing an exclusive escort service, which flourished until he was caught providing Malaysian children to a number of foreign paedophile rings. After this, and a number of other skirmishes with the law, Georgio lay low for a number of years, until returning to his old habits, supplying women to wealthy clients. It was at that time that John Georgio became a full time employee of Peter Wong, and took the first steps which would lead him back to Indonesia. And his appointment with destiny.

Kerry B. Collison

Chapter 4

Ruswita at work

Ruswita's promotion from the Krawang factory had not come as any surprise to those who had worked with her over the past two years. She had accepted responsibility with ease, and had proved that she had a calculating mind and a dedication to Salima operations. Her quantum leap from the factory to Lim's head office had been a direct result of a suggestion she had made concerning transportation of product from the factory to provincial distributors. Those who attended the meeting had frowned when Ruswita, relatively junior within the new management structure, offered her unsolicited comments.

But later, when it was discovered that her suggestion could reduce the company's reliance on individual transport carriers, she was given the credit for the recommendation that the factory use its own trucks to distribute their product into the provinces while back-loading other Salima Group produce and materials. And there were other changes implemented as a result of her uncanny ability to identify core problems and offer solutions. Within a relatively short time, news of Ruswita's sound decisions had reached Lim's ears, and he moved her directly into his head office where she continued to impress her superiors.

Ruswita discovered that her *peranakan* heritage had become a huge asset. Since she belonged to both the Chinese and *pribumi* worlds, everyone trusted her, and she soon established herself as an intelligent, no-nonsense player within the Salima Group activities. Having served Lim directly as his personal assistant for more than a year, business circles identified Ruswita as one of the select few included in the powerful tycoon's *inner sanctum*. Against all the odds, she prospered.

******

Lani continued to care for Ratna Sari as if she were her own, guarding Ruswita's daughter while remaining totally dedicated to her friend. They had become closer than sisters, their relationship further bonded by their affection for the child.

As Ratna grew, and outings together became more frequent, so did the risk of discovery. Ruswita arranged for Lani's papers to be altered, moving her companion's birthplace to her own village. Her name was also altered slightly. A hundred thousand Rupiah resolved this minor identification problem, and the official involved thought nothing of making the necessary alterations to the simple document. He had been making similar changes for years, and sometimes he wondered just who in his country had *not* altered their name. Satisfied that their relationship had been easily obscured, Ruswita concentrated on her career, knowing that her daughter was in safe and loving hands. Lani had become her widowed half-sister, and Ratna Sari was now her niece.

Ruswita's brief career had, incredibly, placed her right at *Mister Salima's* side as *kongsi* after *kongsi* grew, swelling the Salima Group coffers. She had been present when Lim had signed his ship charters with PERTAMINA, the state owned oil and gas monopoly, and also at his side in Hong Kong when he raised an additional one hundred million dollars to finance further expansion of his cement interests. It was no longer unusual for her to be seen travelling overseas with her chairman. Lim trusted her judgement implicitly.

He always insisted on her presence whenever the necessity arose for someone with her command of English, a language the Chinese *totok* had never found time to master for himself. Ruswita gave herself entirely to her career, and Lim appreciated her dedication. Slowly, his dependence on her capacity to also remove tiresome social and domestic problems grew, and even before he understood how it had happened, Lim became totally dependent on the young and vibrant woman.

******

Ruswita smiled graciously while accepting the gift. Lim Swee Giok, or *Mister Salima* as he was now known to the foreign investment community, patted her kindly on the knee and returned her smile. As Ruswita carefully unwrapped the small packet and opened the lid of the intricately carved box, Lim's eyes twinkled. He observed the expression on her face, the delicate notes of Mozart's *Elvira* capturing the moment in his private office.

She placed the magnificently crafted music-box on her lap, fighting back tears of joy as she struggled to express her thanks, but words would not flow.

Lim rose from his chair and placed his hand gently on her shoulder. Then, adding to her surprise, he bent down and kissed her on the forehead. Bewildered by the fatherly gesture, she remained still, completely at a loss for words.

Satisfied that his small gift had pleased her, Lim placed his hand inside his pocket and withdrew a small, rectangular case, and approached Ruswita once again. She looked up and smiled, then her eyes fell on the small, unwrapped box, as Lim extended his hand for her to see.

'Take it,' he offered, and was surprised that she hesitated. Ruswita *knew* that such a case could only contain a ring. She looked up, enquiringly, completely bewildered by the moment. *'Take it,'* he urged again, holding the case open for Ruswita to see the cluster of diamonds alive with brilliant, tiny beams of light. Mesmerised by the ring's beauty, Ruswita reached out as she had been taught as a child, with one hand supporting the other.

'No,' Lim said, taking her hand and pulling her gently to her feet. *'Never again, like that,'* he said softly, understanding the submissive gesture and its origins. He then removed the ring and slipped it over her finger. Ruswita held her hand, her gaze transfixed by the magnificent diamonds

There had been no indication that this might happen. Her relationship with Lim had been one of respect, and the possibility that he wanted more from her momentarily frightened her. She had never even dreamed that such an opportunity might occur; she was stunned.

Ruswita glanced at Lim, uncertain of what such a relationship would bring. She looked at the powerful figure without seeing an older man standing there before her, nor did she consider the enormous wealth and power he represented. Instead, she saw only a man for whom she had the greatest respect, a man who had provided her with the opportunity to realise something for herself when all others had deserted her. Ruswita was suddenly aware that she had been staring at Lim, and broke into an embarrassed smile. He looked at her questioningly and, without further hesitation, she took his hand in hers and nodded her acceptance.

* * * * * *

Murray looked at the calendar and sighed, observing the highlighted dates indicating the end of the Ramadan fasting month, the ninth in the Moslem calendar. His secretary had drawn heavy red rings around the four days to remind him that the office would be closed. Murray knew that he might as well close for a week, or even a fortnight, as staff always managed to find some excuse to delay their return to work. He glanced back at the calendar and observed, with another sigh, that Christmas was less than three months away. Another extended staff holiday which would run unofficially from Christmas through to the New Year. Murray smiled sardonically, conscious that Indonesians celebrated all holidays, regardless of their religious beliefs.

It had been a most eventful year, he reminisced, and one which had thrown Indonesia well into the international spotlight. Murray wondered how much damage had really been caused by the anti-Japanese riots earlier in the year, which had resulted in the destruction of some seventy buildings and hundreds of cars and buses. He knew that the figures relating to the loss of life would never be released, but his sources in government had informed Murray that at least four hundred had been killed by police and riot squads. Murray shook his head; he knew, from his ten years living amongst the Indonesians, that violence lay just below the surface of what appeared to be a tranquil society, and that sometimes even the most minor of incidents was sufficient to spark the dormant hatreds which festered there.

When the riots had occurred, Murray had been hosting a visiting group of investors. They were returning, by chance, from the Foreign Investment Board located in Cut Mutiah when their two vehicles came into contact with a crowd of demonstrators obviously bent on destruction.

Murray remembered that moment all too clearly. He had hired

two large Nissans for the occasion, and was flabbergasted when both vehicles were prevented from proceeding any further, and the occupants ordered to alight. He had gauged the crowd's mood correctly, advising his guests to do as ordered, after which Murray had then mustered the group together, and ushered them away. Murray recalled the look of terror on the foreigners' faces when the Japanese cars had then been torched by the excited rioters. Later, not unexpectedly, he sadly accepted his client's predictable decision not to invest in the politically unstable environment.

Then, as the city returned to normal, the state owned Oil and Gas monopoly, PERTAMINA, all but collapsed. Murray's *kongsi* had committed themselves heavily in the oil and gas industry, investing in supply boats to service the ever-increasing number of offshore drilling rigs, providing credit to what they believed to be a cash-rich Indonesian Government company, to enable PERTAMINA to further expand its activities even outside its charter. The *kongsi* believed it had guaranteed future goodwill by advancing millions of the shareholders' funds to directors responsible for the allocation of contracts and concession areas. Suddenly the balloon burst, revealing that PERTAMINA had accumulated debts in excess of six billion dollars. The company's directors were replaced, but not before they and their families had successfully shifted tens of millions of dollars into their offshore accounts.

Had his *kongsi* not suffered as severely as it had, Murray might have laughed at the discovery that one of the PERTAMINA directors had died, leaving more than forty million dollars in his numbered Asian Currency Unit account in Singapore. Murray knew that the man's official salary was no more than a thousand dollars per month; much of the rest had come from organisations such as his, now lost forever. He knew that the country could not possibly continue in this vein; the national debt had jumped from eight billion to more than thirty, and was still building steam.

What Murray had most difficulty with was the fact that these incredible revelations and incidents just did not seem to matter to those at the top, whose own wealth had become startlingly obvious. He wondered where, or if, it would all end, believing that political instability would demonstrably grow, as the disparity between the wealthy and poor became more apparent.

Murray's thoughts then shifted to Portugal, and the events there that had also taken place in the course of this eventful year. He had followed the bloodless *coup d'etat* which the international press had appropriately named The Captains' Revolution, and wondered how these events which had taken place on the other side of the globe might affect Indonesia. Murray endeavoured to keep himself current with world events; he understood the import of knowing what was happening outside his own sphere of activity.

As his mind wandered, his thoughts strayed to Zach and Susan. He wondered how Michael was faring at school in Washington. Zach had been promoted, and offered the opportunity to move to the United States as Australia's Defence Liaison Group co-ordinator. Susan had been supportive of what could well be Zach's last posting before retirement and had encouraged him to accept. They had called Murray from Melbourne to inform him of their plans, and departed the following month. Now, Murray knew from their recent letters, they were well settled and enjoying life in the American capital. Michael, Susan had advised, had commenced Junior High, and he was delighted that he had not lost a year in the move, as they had arrived during the commencement of the Northern Hemisphere's summer holidays.

Pleased that they all seemed to be getting along fine together, Murray glanced over at the family photograph sitting in its frame on the shelf amongst his books. It was taken outside their apartment in Washington; the ground, he noticed, was covered with snow. Murray sighed and rose to his feet. Trickles of perspiration rolled down his back. He pulled a curtain aside and peered out through the barred window into the front garden, wondering how much longer it would be before the truck arrived with fuel for his stand-by generator.

* * * * * *

Stephen Coleman climbed out of his dark, metallic blue Mercedes 450 and walked up the President Hotel steps slowly. Upon entering the foyer, he observed a rather motley group of foreigners gathered there, unshaven and obviously distressed. He walked past quickly, not wishing to become embroiled in any discussion with the familiar faces, knowing that tempers were normally short at that time of the morning, and that he would be an obvious target for their snide comments. Coleman did not have to suffer the same power difficulties which had driven these expatriates to the President Hotel.

Coleman was aware that, had he ventured into any of the larger hotels which had wisely installed auxiliary power before the extended failure had commenced, the scene would have been similar. The week before, he had witnessed a fight in progress in the Hotel Indonesia lobby where an impatient queue of foreigners had formed, waiting for their turn to use the hotel's lobby toilets. To the rear of the hotel and around the swimming pool, he had seen what would normally have passed as a most comic display of expatriate lunacy, had the water shortage not been so serious.

Foreigners formed lines there too, but to bathe, and even shave. As the swimming pool did not normally open until later in the morning, the hotel management ignored the proceedings as many of the these unfortunates had, most probably, at some time or other, been paying-guests at the Intercontinental. Coleman had been told confidentially that the power problem had arisen as a result of the new Japanese power station in Tanjung Priok Harbour. The day it had been commissioned, the aid-financed facility had failed to carry the designed load, rendering the multi-million dollar thermal power-plant unserviceable even before it could go on-line.

Coleman was relieved that his *kongsi* had not been associated with this project; it had been discovered that substantial payments had been made to officials within the PLN, the State Electric Company, and that the contractors had merely offset this cost by redesigning the project. The resulting power loss threw the capital into chaos for more than three months, and Stephen understood, and identified with, the subsequent sombre mood which persisted amongst the foreign community. He knew that their houses would not be equipped with auxiliary power, and it was unlikely that they would have hand-mechanical pumps to restore water from their wells. Without water they would be unable to shower, or flush their toilets, adding further to the discomfort of living in a sealed house without air-conditioning; this he knew from his earlier days, when serving with the Embassy. Memories of those times reminded Coleman, uncomfortably, of his humble beginnings in Jakarta.

* * * * * *

Fresh from college, Stephen Coleman had been recruited by the suave John Anderson, who headed the Australian Secret Intelligence Service, ASIS. For more than twenty years, this clandestine operation had survived with relatively little accountability other than that to the Prime Minister, through the Attorney General's office. The existence of this organisation, developed along the lines of Britain's MI-6, was only revealed to the public, twenty years after its formation, by an investigative journalist, Brian Toohey, in his exposé entitled 'Oyster'.

Stephen had been an eager recruit, and willingly underwent training in Australia. Later, when he had been seconded to the Embassy in Indonesia, he had thrown himself into his work with considerable spirit. An unsatisfactory relationship with one of the American Embassy female staff had disrupted his life, and career. He and Louise had travelled together to West Irian prior to that province's Act of Self Determination. During their stay over in Bali, and after a bitter-sweet moment together, she had decided to return to Jakarta, alone, a decision which would affect his life forever, as she had been killed when her plane crashed.

As the memory of her loss stung sharply, bringing him back to the present, the former ASIS agent was reminded that he had been most fortunate, indeed, that he too had not died at the hands of the rebels during that journey into the wilds of Irian. He had been medically evacuated to Australia where, subsequent to months of convalescence and a period of self-doubt regarding his role within the intelligence community, Coleman had resigned from ASIS and returned to Indonesia in search of some direction in life. It had been during this visit that General Seda had offered him the opportunity to work in partnership to supply the Indonesian Armed Forces with materials and weapons. The relationship had been most lucrative. Before he had turned thirty, Stephen Coleman had already set aside his first million dollars in a numbered Asian Currency Unit account, with the Standard Chartered Bank, in Singapore. What Stephen did not know however, was that his partner, General Seda, had a most secret agenda. He would discover, when it was believed that he could no longer influence the outcome, that the influential Timorese general's efforts were dedicated solely towards achieving independence for the land of his birth, East Timor.

* * * * * *

Stephen Coleman's home and office complex was located in Jalan

JAKARTA

Cik Ditiro, in Menteng, directly between the Governor's residence and that of General Hidjojo, the former Indonesian Ambassador to Australia. As the rest of the city suffered rolling power blackouts lasting days on end, Coleman's electricity was rarely cut for more than a few hours. Not that this bothered him, as General Seda had kindly arranged for an army generator, and operator, to be installed at his house.

As the lift carried Stephen to the restaurant overlooking the city centre, he acknowledged that he had been fortunate to have the influential general as his silent sponsor. Their *kongsi* had blossomed, bringing the number of companies operating within the group to almost fifteen. *Not bad for a man not yet thirty*, he thought, a little arrogantly before stepping out of the elevator where he was met by the *maître d'* and escorted to his table for breakfast. The waiters fussed as Stephen sipped his coffee and observed the traffic below.

He watched the congested traffic grind almost to a halt as buses and trucks manoeuvred their way around the undisciplined drivers entering the *Selamat Datang* roundabout. A break in the congestion permitted the flow from Imam Bonjol to join the disorder, cutting the south bound traffic altogether as drivers raced their vehicles across the circle and propped, waiting for those ahead to move again. Stephen followed a group of *becak* drivers crossing also, their steel carriages pushed courageously in front of oncoming angry drivers, unconcerned about the frightened passengers sitting up front, dangerously exposed.

'Morning, Stephen,' a voiced called, interrupting his thoughts. He turned and smiled as the other man slipped into the chair opposite and nodded to the hovering waiter. Stephen waited for the coffee to be poured and the waiter to move out of earshot before commencing the conversation.

'What's the score, David?' he asked, not wishing to waste time on pleasantries.

'It's all fixed,' the other man replied, smiling. 'I spoke to the States last night.' Stephen considered this for a moment, then nodded his head slightly with this news. It had been a long haul for all of them, dealing through intermediaries, agents, lawyers and, at one point, the American Embassy. The easy part of the entire negotiation had been the Indonesian end, Coleman thought. Their role had simply been a matter of how much and when, knowing that the Americans would be in complete charge of the project's technical aspects. The waiter returned and handed them both a breakfast menu. They ordered and then continued their discussions while waiting for their meals, ceasing to speak whenever a waiter approached to refill their coffee cups.

'When will we get delivery?' Coleman asked. 'Those dates given last week don't seem realistic.'

'The Pentagon seem to think that there will be no difficulty pushing the deal through State. Seems they have some rather excitable lobbyists working out of Houston who really want this deal to go through, Steve. Don't worry,' the American assured him, 'the squadron will be ready for delivery before the end of next year. Remember, your guys have got to find enough pilots capable of completing the conversion training. That's the only question that bothers me.' Stephen thought about the assurances given by Seda. The general believed that there would be little difficulty in having the Indonesian Airforce provide the talent required for Stateside training.

'And payment?' Coleman asked. Orchestrating the slush-fund had been the most aggravating negotiation Stephen had yet encountered. The sophisticated aircraft were to be provided under the terms of a defence aid programme; negotiating consultancy fees directly from the manufacturer had almost killed the transaction. Initially, the company had refused, citing their government's aid package as sufficient incentive for HANKAM to want to sign the order. Coleman had been furious at their naiveté. Seda had then threatened to veto the order and, for awhile, it appeared that the purchase for the two squadrons of jet fighters would not proceed, until Stephen suggested a secondary contract. This would assist the American suppliers to avoid violating their own recently introduced laws which prohibited buyer commissions.

There had been several sleepless nights as he watched the deal slowly collapse. Then, due to pressure from the oil and gas barons in Houston, negotiations recommenced. The sale would earn Coleman's *kongsi* almost five million dollars once the aircraft were delivered, and another three when the second order had been filled.

'Payment confirmed as agreed,' David said, smiling at the man across the table who would receive more money from this one transaction than any other deal in which the American had ever been involved. David had grown to admire Coleman's negotiating skills although, he admitted, there had been times when he would have been pleased to see the man give a little.

The American aircraft manufacturer's representative had been well briefed. This had included an informative meeting with the Defense Attaché at the American Embassy in Jakarta. David remembered being most impressed with the list of Coleman's accomplishments. His ability to be able to deliver a deal had become almost legendary. Or at least, this was the general perception within foreign military circles. When David had raised the question as to how Coleman had become so successful, the Defense Attaché, in turn, had shrugged his shoulders and inferred that Coleman had been just fortunate to be in the right place at the right time.

No one was aware of the relationship which existed between the company and General Seda, a relationship which had already generated millions of dollars. And now, with the two squadrons of fighters under his belt, Stephen was confident that his reputation would not suffer, particularly once word hit the street that he had been the one to broker the arms deal. The ramifications played with his mind as he sat, with growing restlessness, half-listening to the man who had delivered his *kongsi* its biggest commission ever.

He heard the American, David, waffling on concerning his company's attributes, and had difficulty concentrating. Stephen had come to the breakfast meeting solely for reassurance and, now that his contact had confirmed that their deal had been consummated, Coleman looked over in the waiter's direction, and raised his eyebrows. The bill appeared, and he signed, then rose to leave.

'David, thanks,' he said, shaking the surprised man's hand, 'but I must run. Guess you will make the necessary arrangements with the contracts?' Both men knew that, pushed by anxious clients, these would most probably be on lawyers desks even as they spoke.

'Sure, Steve,' David replied, his voice a little peeved at having been dumped so unceremoniously; he had hoped for a weekend out on Coleman's launch, having heard from the Embassy personnel that he should not miss any opportunity to visit the Thousand Islands, if invited. Stephen realized from the American's huffy tones that he had been a little brusque, and decided to offer his cruiser to the American.

'When are you leaving?' he asked, although he already knew.

Profile and other relevant information relating to the people he dealt with was already known to his office; Stephen Coleman relied heavily on General Seda, his partner. With his access to the Indonesian Intelligence Agency, they had the edge on everyone.

'Well,' the American hesitated, 'I had thought of spending a few days taking a look at the country, before climbing back on that goddamn plane and sticking my butt down for twenty hours. Guess I will take tomorrow's flight,' he said, almost pathetically. Coleman thought, *why not?*

'It would be a shame to miss seeing our beautiful islands, David,' he said, enjoying the tease. 'Would your company miss you for another four of five days, do you think?'

'Well,' David's mind raced quickly. He had envisaged a much shorter voyage, certain that he would attract too much interest from head office should he overstay. 'I could telex and tell them that we needed to tidy up a few things.' Stephen laughed as he rose, and extended his hand.

'Okay, then it's settled.'

'Will you join me for dinner tonight?' the American asked. Coleman thought about his schedule for the rest of the day, and reminded himself of the invitation he had received. One that he would be expected to attend.

'No, David, I'm sorry. There's a function I must attend.'

Stephen had not been surprised that the Salima family had placed him on their invitation list. He had conducted some business with the group in the past, and found himself looking forward to the occasion. He looked at David and decided that he deserved to be entertained. Stephen had mastered the delicate art of balancing his private life in the aggressive world of Jakarta commerce. He would invite some of the guests who attended the evening's celebrations to join them on his cruiser.

'Why don't you get yourself some shorts and sunburn cream from one of your cohorts from the U.S. Embassy, and I will have my driver pick you up tomorrow morning at six. Okay?' he smiled. Then Coleman added, 'Don't be late, Dave, the boat doesn't wait,' with which they both laughed and the Australian walked away, waving at a couple sitting on the other side of the restaurant. David watched as he disappeared behind the central columns adjacent to the lifts, wondering what would really happen if he were to be late. Then he smiled.

'Sonofabitch,' he muttered, nodding as he did so. He just *knew* that Coleman would pull the ropes and steam away leaving tardy guests behind, if for no other reason than to prove a point. David decided that he really liked the man. But he also decided to arrange a wake-up call for the next morning, not wanting to put Stephen Coleman to the test.

* * * * * *

Nyonya Seda was delighted that her husband was in such a fine mood. She watched as he placed the phone back in its cradle and laughed, slapping his hands together in childish exuberance. She was surprised, having seen his darker mood earlier in the day.

'*Mas,*' she said, caught up in the excitement, '*what is it?*' Immediately the general stopped, realizing that he was being carried away by Coleman's positive news.

'*Good news,*' he answered, his mind working quickly. *One should never disclose one's secrets,* he had decided years before, *especially to one's wife.* Seda's wife waited, sitting dutifully on the couch as she anxiously crushed a handkerchief in her hands.

'*Well, Mas, tell me,*' she implored, not really enjoying the suspense. General Seda was annoyed that he had been caught up in this game.

'*General Subroto is getting married again!*' he revealed, wondering if this would be sufficient for the woman. *Nyonya* Seda smiled and clapped her hands together with excitement at the news.

'*Who is she?*' Mrs Seda asked, smiling broadly. She had already heard the gossip weeks before and, from all reports, the girl was a *kampung* tart none of the wives could possibly accept into their homes. She knew that this was not the news that had pleased her husband so. After these many years of marriage, the secret telephone calls late into the night, and sudden departures to the Defense Department offices on Merdeka Square, she could no longer be deceived by his ploys. She bit her lip, as had become her habit over recent years. Her husband was a powerful and secretive man. Perhaps he was hiding an affair from her, she worried; perhaps he had become so bored with her that he had already arranged for a mistress to be ensconced in Tebet, the Jakarta suburb where most wealthy or influential men conducted their illicit affairs.

Nyonya Seda was afraid that it would only be a matter of time before he divorced her and took another wife. But at least he could not arbitrarily take a second wife, as many of the Moslem generals had done. She often had great difficulty when attending social engagements as most of her husband's contemporaries had remarried, some having acquired third and even fourth wives. The Sedas were Christians, and with this thought, she smiled inwardly, trusting that this would prevent him from breaking the law.

Seda glanced sideways at his wife, and decided that she would most probably have already known about Subroto's new marital arrangements. These women spent most of their days gossiping, creating more news themselves than what they heard from others. He selected a town at random, just for the sake of answering.

'Some girl from Surabaya,' he answered, feigning interest in the story he had fabricated. Seda then left the room, rubbing his stomach as he moved away, avoiding further discussion. His wife recognized this habit and sighed, knowing that her husband would most probably sit in the bathroom until he thought she would have forgotten the conversation or, having lost interest, would not pursue it. They had been through this scenario more times before than she cared to remember. She looked around the lonely, empty room, and decided to phone a friend. Moments later Seda's wife was engrossed in gossip concerning General Subroto's new flame, quoting her husband as the source.

Upstairs, in his bedroom, Seda lay on the thick quilt not caring that the servants would have clucked at his actions. It was not normally his custom to indulge in the traditional afternoon siesta; he merely used the opportunity to avoid further discussion with his wife. Coleman's call had brought the most exciting news Seda had yet received since first establishing the *kongsi* with the young Australian. As he lay there resting, Seda smiled smugly, congratulating himself on his move some years before to use the former embassy officer to consolidate his own business interests, while deflecting attention away from himself.

The general recalled how close his associate had come to being killed in Irian. Then the thought also crossed his mind that the success they had enjoyed together would never have eventuated had the faithful Umar's aim been a fraction more accurate. As quickly as these thoughts emerged he dismissed them. He had no remorse over what had happened to Coleman. Returning to the present, he cast his mind back over the intelligence meetings he had attended earlier that day. Seda did not believe that General Ali Murtopo's attempts at establishing a Fifth Column in Portuguese East Timor would achieve any great success. These efforts had been given the code name of *Operation Komodo*, and were designed to infiltrate the shaky colony in anticipation of any moves that East Timor might make towards independence.

Seda frowned, annoyed that Murtopo had jumped the gun and established subversive groups without first seeking approval from the President. As his thoughts wandered, Seda considered not attending that evening's function at the Borobudur Hotel, then decided that his absence would be noted. Besides, he thought, his eyelids becoming heavy, his wife would never forgive him if he did not escort her to what was to be the gala event of the year. He lay still, willing his body to submit to sleep.

Buried in a sound-proofed shelter below the ostentatious residence, a two hundred KVA generator's constant purr hummed faintly in the background, coaxing him to rest. Seda closed his eyes and listened to the soft vibrations, and soon drifted off into sleep.

* * * * * *

Lani sat quietly watching the child sleep. The power had only just returned and Lani opted to take advantage of the limited time she knew they would have before it was cut off again. The electric company distributed power in the most irregular, and what Lani knew to be, unfair way to the less unfortunate areas around the city. The area where they lived, Tebet, received electricity for only two hours each day, providing the suburb's inhabitants with barely sufficient time to refill their water tanks, bathe, and in the wealthier households, rest for a brief time sitting in front of their air-conditioners.

Lani stroked the side of Ratna Sari's head lovingly. It was the children who suffered most from the heat, she knew. The evening before, Lani had asked to borrow Ruswita's car and driver to provide the child with some semblance of comfort, even if it was for just a few hours. Lani had placed the young girl on the sedan's rear seat, and instructed the driver to take them along the city's by-pass roads, thereby providing Ratna with the opportunity to sleep in the air-conditioned car. Thankfully, this had been sufficient rest for the child, and Lani could see from her colour that the few hours of comfort had done her the world of good. She sighed, knowing that they would soon move to more comfortable accommodation.

Ruswita had informed Lani weeks before that she and Ratna would be moving into the main Lim household soon after her wedding. Lim had suggested that his wife's sister and niece move into one of the many rooms alongside the main house, where they would not be subjected to the stresses of power failures, and flooding. With this thought uppermost in her mind, Lani glanced at the clock and smiled, wishing that she could have attended the ceremony, or at least seen Ruswita in her gown. Lani looked down at the sleeping child she now considered her own, and stroked the soft dark hair from her face, while humming *ninabobo*, her favourite lullaby.

* * * * * *

Portuguese Timor

Xanana Soares sat cross-legged facing the two other men, listening to their words. As they spoke, Xanana nodded, agreeing to the course of action they had planned. If their people were to be free they had to move quickly before the situation became further confused. Inspired by their people's long struggle, they would now declare their independence.

At twenty, although Xanana was the youngest member of the movement's council, he was already considered leadership material, and was fifth in line to Xavier. He looked over at their President elect, Xavier do Amaral, who sat directly opposite. He was only thirty-seven. Xanana was familiar with the other organizations which had emerged during the few, short months since their colonial masters in Lisbon had announced plans for East Timor's independence. He and the other members also knew that one of these groups, APODETI, had been infiltrated by Indonesian agents who moved to dissuade their Timorese neighbours from supporting any political party not aligned with Jakarta.

JAKARTA

They had become aware that the Indonesians had mounted a campaign to undermine any efforts which might lead to Independence. Copies of intelligence they had gathered through their unsophisticated network had exposed the Indonesian operation, *Operasi Komodo*. It was apparent to the fledgeling politicians that Jakarta was determined to subvert any efforts which might create an independent state within the Indonesian archipelago.

Xanana belonged to the Timorese Social Democratic Association, the second major political party to be formed at that time. The party combined the interests of rural-based elites, with those of urbanised groups. Most of the organisation's founders lived in Dili, but they still maintained established ties with their rural origins. Their committee believed they understood precisely what the people of Timor needed. Once the first free elections had been held and they won the right to govern, Xanana's party was determined to implement literacy and agricultural programmes as their first priority.

Xanana was aware that the committee had already made overtures to both the Australian and Indonesian Governments, requesting recognition of their country's proposed independent status and suggesting that they be permitted to establish diplomatic ties. Their requests went unheeded, yet they could not understand the reasoning for this rebuff, particularly from the Australians whose soldiers had depended heavily on the Timorese people during the war against the Japanese.

They had but a few weapons. Xanana had argued against raiding the former Portuguese armouries but had finally bowed to those with more experience in these matters. Xavier had argued that there would be no need for force. East Timor, he had said, was a small bubble, floating unthreateningly within the region. Why, he had asked, should the people arm themselves?

As he sat there discussing how their party could further consolidate its position amongst the people, Xanana firmly believed that his country, having been subjected to colonisation for more than four centuries, would soon be truly free. The Captain's Revolution in Portugal had become one with their own Revolution, and the former school teacher was confident that his determined group of socialist democrats would bring prosperity to an independent people of East Timor.

The evening meeting concluded, Xanana and the others returned to their homes and families, then slept, totally oblivious to the commitments which had been signed that day in Jakarta, thousands of kilometers to their west. Commitments which would eventually bring decades of death and despair to the Timorese separatists, as Indonesia's American fighters filled East Timor's skies.

* * * * * *

Indonesian Armed Forces Academy

'Parade!' the officer in charge called loudly, dragging every syllable out slowly, for effect, *'Parade, atten....shon!'* A dramatic drum roll reverberated through the official stand, drowning the next commands as the Academy's colours were paraded. Three men then took centre stage, the soldier in the middle carrying the AKABRI colours. Another order was then heard, drifting across the parade ground towards the spectators, following which, the well-rehearsed soldiers, positioned as guards on either side of the flag, marked time, and the guard captain screamed out the order for them to halt. The long, drawn command which followed was instantly accompanied by the first note spilling forth from the military band, and the graduating class stepped out, for their final parade.

'There's Budi!' one mother cried proudly, grabbing her husband's arm excitedly.

'There's 'Man!' another pleased parent called, as the young men marched past, their eyes and heads locked on the President as he took the salute. Even before the class had completed their final march-past, the chatter from the spectators' stand could be heard by the marching cadets, and they sensed their parents' pride in their achievement. They swung their arms high, and held their weapons close. This was their day, the day they had all worked towards since the moment they first set foot inside the Armed Forces Academy.

Another command turned the column, directing them back to their original positions, where they were ordered to halt, then turn, facing their senior officers. The officer of the guard marched forward, saluted with his sword, then offered the graduating officers for inspection. There was a discernible silence, as all held their breath in anticipation of the moment they had dreamed about. The President returned the salute, then stepped down from the dais and carried out his inspection.

They knew they were 'the best and the brightest' as they remained at attention, ready for inspection by their country's leader, President Soeharto. They knew that they had been honoured, for the *Smiling General* rarely attended such ceremonies anymore. Today had been a special gift to them all, and they knew it was because of the young army officer who was also graduating in their class, Lieutenant Sujono Diryo.

When the President walked along the front file, they all knew that the *Bapak* would stop and say something to this fine, outstanding officer. There was not one amongst their number who would not have changed places with Sujono; his father had been declared a Hero of the Revolution. Sujono was tall, handsome, and obviously talented, having been among the first five in the graduating class.

The young men stood firmly fixed at attention, their eyes locked on some distant object, as their hearts and ears followed the man they had grown to love. The President stopped, his face serious, and spoke.

'*Congratulations, Lieutenant,*' he said, congratulating the young Sujono Diryo, out of tribute to the man's father.

'*Terima kasih, Bapak,*' was all Sujono could muster. Then the President continued with his inspection, the band playing softly as he walked along the lines of proud academy graduates. In the stand, tucked well behind the dais, General Nathan Seda watched the proceedings with particular interest deciding, as the President returned to take the final salute, that he would take a special interest also in the young army officer who so obviously had Palace support.

In the days that followed, during which time the young officers received their first postings, Lieutenant Sujono Diryo was disappointed to learn that he had been assigned to Army Special Duties with the Intelligence Corp. Three days after his orders had been cut, Sujono Diryo reported for duty. He had then been selected to undergo further training, after which he was instructed to report directly to his new headquarters, BAKIN, Indonesia's Central Intelligence Co-ordinating Agency. And it was there, on his first day, that he was introduced to General Nathan Seda.

Chapter 5

A wedding

More than one thousand guests attended the wedding celebration. The Hotel Borobudur had been selected for the event, as this was the only venue with the capacity to accommodate such a large number of guests. The main ballroom was suitably decorated, creating an air of festivity which spilled out into the foyer and reception, as the orchestra entertained the arriving guests. The adjoining and smaller ballroom had been utilized as an elaborate storage area, filled with more than five hundred cases of soft-drinks, beer, spirits and, of course, an adequate supply of Hennessey's XO Cognac. The Borobudur general manager had personally overseen the entire preparations. It would be, he knew, the largest gathering of Indonesia's elite Chinese community ever to congregate so publicly in Jakarta.

The hotel's staff of three thousand had worked tirelessly and, as the general manager moved through the kitchens into the servery areas ensuring that the number of staff serving food and beverages was adequate, he experienced a sense of pride at the results of months of training. He moved as inconspicuously as possible through the main ballroom into the hotel reception and lobby, to examine the continuous stream of arriving guests. As he stood overlooking the entrance and escalators, he became concerned with the apparent bottle-neck created by the swarm of guests moving through the cramped, lower foyer.

Outside, other invitees waited impatiently as the continuous line of Mercedes moved slowly forward, permitting each group to disembark directly in front of the already congested entrance. The general manager estimated that it would take an hour for the guests to file through into the main ballroom. There, they would be greeted with an opulence never before seen in Indonesia.

Westerners dressed in formal attire mingled uncomfortably with the wealthy Indonesians who, for the greater part, wore traditional dress. Many of the men had donned the comfortable long-sleeve *batik* dress shirt, while their high-heeled ladies, hair tied in magnificent buns adorned with gold filigree combs, mingled graciously around, their *kain-kebaya* combinations requiring the shortest of steps. Diamonds and precious stones added to the amazing glitter, men as well as women wore oversized rings to demonstrate their wealth. Ladies smiled insincerely at each other as they floated around the setting, hiding their envy as new dresses or jewellery were displayed, or as they identified an old flame escorting his new companion. Their whispered but cutting remarks were barely audible under the magnificent chandeliers, as the conversation rose to a deafening level.

Murray Stephenson moved amongst the other guests, stopping occasionally to speak briefly to those he knew. He regretted that Peter Wong had been unable to attend the function. Murray knew that Peter's penchant for the young ladies had most probably kept him away, although the excuse had been otherwise. He had hoped that the evening might act as a catalyst for them to identify themselves somehow with the Salima Group.

It had been more than a year since Wong had stepped in to assist salvage his company and, although the business had grown dramatically with the number of offshore Chinese investing through his *kongsi*, Murray realized that the really big money was still out of reach to him. He had been unsuccessful in developing any real access into the Salima corporate machine. Murray waved at one of the American guests, winked at the delightful girl hanging onto his arm, then turned, bumping into a familiar figure.

'Hi, Murray,' Coleman said, wiping the front of his jacket where some of the champagne had spilled.

'Sorry,' he said, waiting for Stephen Coleman to finish so that he could shake his hand. They saw little of each other, as they always moved in different commercial and social circles. Their paths had diverged. Murray admitted to himself that he had become more than a little envious of the younger man's successes, both as an entrepreneur and as a ladies man. His reputation had continued to grow, and Murray no longer doubted that Coleman had covert support from within the Indonesian Military, for to achieve what he had in such a short time would have been impossible without someone very powerful watching over his shoulder. Murray knew that, in this world of lucrative contracts, they all needed to have such a sponsor. His was Peter Wong. But who, he asked himself, was Stephen Coleman's?

'No damage,' the other man said, rolling the paper napkin he had used to dry his jacket before dropping this onto one the waiter's silver trays as it passed. 'How's business?'

'Doing just fine,' Murray responded, a little too quickly. If Coleman had noticed, he had not shown so. 'And yours?' Murray knew that he had to be friendly, even though he did not particularly like the younger man. Coleman's activities had grown and outstripped his competitors at an unbelievable pace. Murray admitted that there was a certain amount of petty rivalry amongst the foreigners endeavouring to build careers for themselves in Jakarta but, for some reason which eluded him, Coleman was just not like the others. In spite of the man's lack of commercial training, he had firmly ensconced himself within the Indonesian business community, and was sought after by many of the foreign companies keen to develop access to the Indonesian Armed Forces.

Murray had no idea how Coleman managed to do so, but it was quite apparent that he had successfully established himself as one of the major suppliers to HANKAM, accessing the many millions the Indonesian Defense Department spent on weapons and equipment. Murray shook Stephen's hand briefly, smiled at the beautiful woman who accompanied him, and spoke to her in Indonesian.

'Shouldn't talk business in front of such a beautiful lady,' he said, watching her eyes open wide in surprise. She squeezed Stephen's arm excitedly, as one would expect of a young child flattered by such comment.

'He speaks Indonesian also!' she gushed, happily, and slipped her free arm through Murray's, placing herself between the two Australians. *'I will not let either of you go,'* she declared, her bubbly behaviour spilling over causing both the men to laugh. They talked briefly before being interrupted by an announcement, which brought the assembly to a hushed silence.

'Tuan, tuan dan nyonya,' a voice called from somewhere amongst the crowd of guests, *'Gentlemen and ladies, I give you Pak Salima and*

his beautiful bride, Ruswita Salima!'

The crowd roared its approval as guests moved aside permitting the couple to enter. Murray applauded loudly along with the other guests, smiling broadly as he did so. The wedding had taken place in a private setting some hours before, permitting Lim the opportunity to return to their home where he still had unfinished business to attend to. Later, he had changed into a loose fitting *batik* for the occasion, while his wife continued to wear the white bridal gown designed especially for her wedding. There had been little change from ten thousand dollars for the magnificent garment, Murray had overheard one of the guests whisper, and he was not surprised. Ruswita looked stunning as she floated through the room accompanied by strains of Mendelssohn's *Wedding March*. Applause sounded through the ballroom as the couple moved to the centre of the hall, and waited.

'Gentlemen and ladies,' the master of ceremonies announced, *'a special song for two very special people,'* with which, the entire ballroom turned, as a deep resonant voice emanated from huge speakers placed appropriately to either side of the band.

'This is, the moment...' the singer crooned, sending the assembled guests in raptures as they identified the opening words and music to *The Hawaiian Wedding Song*. They listened as the beautiful melody filled the great ballroom, setting the most perfect mood. As light danced around the room deflected by the twin chandeliers, Ruswita and her husband moved amongst the guests, hugging and kissing until the song came to an end.

Applause filled the air once more and, in that moment, it seemed that this was the signal for the guests to commence talking again. The ambience was electric, and the moment almost too perfect as Ruswita was kissed on both cheeks by one of the President's children. It was her night, she knew, but it was her powerful husband who had commanded their respect; they had all come to pay homage to Lim, but Ruswita did not mind. She was happy.

As the band commenced playing again, General Seda and his wife stepped forward to congratulate her, and she beamed with pleasure, deliriously happy with her world. As Seda squeezed her hand lightly, and turned to move away, Ruswita felt the room move, threatening to spin. She reached for his arm for support, fearing that she was about to fall. The ballroom lights blinked once, then again, and suddenly the room was thrown into darkness. Incredibly, the packed ballroom became deathly still, instantly filled with fear.

As the twin one thousand KVA emergency stand-by generators were triggered into action, there were cries amongst the guests. Concern continued to sweep through the ballroom, causing a number of women to faint. Less than thirty seconds had passed before the generators, having achieved full power, switched across automatically and flooded the room with brilliant light. There was an audible sigh of relief, followed by cheers as guests turned to smile at each other confidently, having experienced another of the country's familiar black-outs. The band struck up once more, and the general manager breathed deeply, reassured as the music reached his ears.

Quickly, he despatched a maintenance team to correct the electrical overload problem and, half-an hour later when he was satisfied that the fault had been rectified, he instructed the generator operator to switch back to city power, as only half of the hotel lifts could operate while on emergency lighting. The engineer did so, causing but the slightest discernible flicker to occur as he threw the switch. Pleased with his equipment, he then went back to sleep in the quiet of the generator room. Two minutes later there was another jolt, stronger than the first which had triggered the initial power failure, but the guests hardly noticed the slight tremor as this time the lighting was not affected, and many of the guests were too engrossed in the celebrations.

* * * * * *

Four hundred kilometers to the east of Jakarta, nearer the earth tremor's epicentre, villages shook violently, causing roofs to collapse on those who slept inside. Walls cracked as the force rocked tiny dwellings, then toppled, as the second and more violent movement struck. More than twenty peasants died in the small hamlets during those brief minutes, but the isolated community had experienced such calamitous events before. Within days, these simple, hard-working farmers had completed their mourning, and restored their ramshackle structures. Within a week, life had all but returned to normal in the East Java *kampung,* nestled amongst the foothills of the dormant volcano known as Mount Muria.

KERRY B. COLLISON

Book two

the present

Kerry B.Collison

Chapter 6

Lim buys an American bank

Denny drove, while James continued to read through the brief again, just to be sure. As brothers, they had been closer than most; as family business associates, they had been inseparable. Together, they had left Indonesia to study in the United States, and together they had remained, building an extension to the Lim empire in the world's greatest economy, where they would eventually make their new home.

Lim's two sons from his first marriage were intelligent, assertive, and already influential young men. Both had graduated from the University of California in Los Angeles and, although their brilliance was not reflected in their academic achievements, their inherent qualities and skills soon became apparent once they flung themselves into the competitive world of banking and commerce. James, older by only one year, was by far the more aggressive of the two, and most like their father. Denny, not at all displeased with his position in life as the second child, in no way remained in his brother's shadow. He displayed much of the Lim street cunning and, as a team, the two had cut quite a path for themselves through American banking circles.

They rarely returned to Indonesia. James believed that it was their responsibility to take the Salima banking arm and develop a global strategy for their family-controlled Asian Pacific Commercial Bank. Almost a year had passed since they last visited Jakarta, when they had attended their father's wedding. The boys had been surprised when Lim had phoned to inform his sons that he was to remarry. Neither felt any animosity towards Ruswita; in fact, they had both warmed to the idea, knowing that she would remain at their father's side as his confidant and close companion. Denny had asked the obvious question during their private conversation with Lim after the wedding, and their father had assured both of his sons that their position within the family bank would always be theirs to control. James had been particularly pleased with his father's response, as the boys had discussed what Ruswita's entry into their family would mean with respect to the Lim fortunes.

They were conscious of her role within the Salima organization, and were comfortable knowing that Ruswita would not be involved in the management of the family's banking interests. Denny and James' position amounted to only thirty percent of the issued capital. Then, of course, there was the new baby, their half-brother Benny, to consider. And what would happen when he grew up.

Neither of the older boys really envisaged a future which involved Ruswita's son participating in any of the bank's activities in the United States. That was to be their personal domain and, having received such an assurance from their father, both Denny and James felt relaxed about their futures. Their shareholders were limited to immediate family and the Indonesian First Family. Their APC Bank had grown to take its place as the largest private bank in South East Asia. Lim, through his complex corporate entities both within Indonesia and offshore, owned fifty-five percent of the stock. He had given each of his two oldest sons fifteen percent each. The Indonesian First Family enjoyed ten percent of the shares, and the remaining five had been given to Ruswita to hold in trust for Benny.

Lim had agreed to an arrangement whereby James and Denny would be permitted to own control over whatever new interests they successfully developed in North America. They had given their undertaking that, as the family bank had funded their activities in the United States, the Asian Pacific Commercial Bank would be issued with forty percent of the new bank's stock. Now, having negotiated their way through the mass of bureaucracy and political hurdles which in no way had diminished their appetite for the North American financial markets, the Lim boys were close to finalizing their arrangements with the Kentucky State Governor.

'Take it easy, Denny,' James chastised his younger brother, *'he'll still be there even if we are late.'* The older of the Lim boys had every right to appear smug. Even before attaining the age of thirty, both of the American-educated Jakarta-Chinese were multi-millionaires,

thanks to their father, Lim Swee Giok and his empire in Indonesia where practically everything could be bought, acquired or fixed by coercion. In their relentless pursuit of money, the Lims had never considered their activities to be anything less than appropriate; it was the Asian way of doing business.

'We can't afford to screw up with this one, James,' Denny said, squinting, the heavily tinted glasses defying gravity, and hanging off his flat nose. *'His aide insisted that we get there on time,'* he said, worried. Although exposed to years of American influence, both still spoke to each other in the acronym-infested Jakarta dialect, with its market-place slang.

'We still have twenty minutes, take it easy,' James insisted.

They had driven from the state capital, Frankfort, heading for Lexington where their meeting could be conducted in the privacy of the senator's home. The Governor was, for obvious reasons, reluctant to be seen openly with the two young bankers. Although they had met several times, briefly, negotiations had been handled discreetly by the senator and a close, personal friend of the Governor's, who acted as his intermediary in such sensitive matters.

At first, the State Governor had been reluctant to provide the undertakings requested by the Asian businessmen. Their requests were, he believed, unreasonable. But when opinion polls had indicated that he was in danger of losing the forthcoming election, and his advisers pointed to the empty election fund coffers, he had committed himself to the Lim brothers and their future banking facilities.

Denny and James had acquired residency in the United States subsequent to their graduating from college. Neither wished to become American citizens, as this would jeopardise their positions in Indonesia. Once word had spread that the Lim family was committed to establishing their banking interests in the United States, they had been approached by several lobby groups offering their services. The dynamic Lim corporate presence had been well received, and the bankers were introduced to the influential intermediaries. When they discovered that negotiations in America were not dissimilar to those of Asia, James had laughed at the relatively insignificant sums requested to grease the Governor's political representative's palms. Denny, on the other hand, was not entirely comfortable with the arrangements.

'What do you think about the payment?' Denny asked, as he had, at least a dozen times over the past month. *'You don't think it's a little over the top?'* James turned his head and looked across at his younger and more conservative brother. He was the worrier of the two. James had spent almost an entire year setting up the deal through intermediaries and, as far as he was concerned, the payment was inconsequential in relation to the profits they would generate once their banking operation had been fully established.

'I would have agreed to pay double what they asked,' James revealed. He knew that Denny was driving too fast not because they were late, but because he wished to consummate the deal and move on. He was the impatient one of the pair.

'I'd still feel better if we'd at least had confirmation of the branch status,' Denny said, unable to restrain his heavy foot. The needle rose above seventy miles per hour, and with the new speed restrictions James knew they were certain to be noticed on the highway patrol radar.

'Slow down,' he said, his warning tone sufficient for the younger man to pay heed. Denny slowed as they entered the city's limits. Already familiar with the route, they arrived fifteen minutes later, and were met outside the white-column entrance by one of the senator's staff. The wealthy young bankers, dressed in Armani suits, were ushered through an elegantly appointed reception area, and into the influential Southerner's study.

'Glad you boys made it all in one piece,' their host drawled, indicating where they should sit as an African-American woman smiled, poured iced-tea for all three, then left as inconspicuously as she had entered. Their host offered them cigars, but both refused. Once, earlier in his career, Denny had accepted one such Havana, and had nearly choked with his first puff. He had tried the Indonesian clove cigarettes while still a youth at school, but had not taken up the habit.

'We are anxious to conclude our arrangements, Senator,' James stated, concerned that the Governor was not present. 'Will the Governor be joining us shortly?' he asked. The senior senator for the State of Kentucky sucked on the end of his cigar, exhaled slowly, smiled, then leaned forward as he spoke.

'The Governor has instructed me to finalize our, ah...,' he paused, 'arrangements.' The senator smiled again, then leaned back into his heavily lined leather chair, observing his two oriental guests. He had not had occasion to deal with Asians before meeting the Lim brothers earlier in the year, and was pleased with the relaxed way both had accepted the offer made to them. He considered the Indonesian Chinese men before him. They were half of his age and, if he could believe the report he'd received from his own financial sources before negotiations had first commenced, their wealth was such that the Lim family could most probably even make the Rothschilds look scratchy.

More than eight months had passed since the senator had been approached by an intermediary, who enquired regarding the possibility of reactivating the State banking licence which belonged to one of the failed private banks, and selling this to the Salima family group. Negotiations had not been difficult or prolonged.

He recalled that it had been an election year for the new Governor and, due to the extravagant campaign run by his political opponent, donations were desperately needed if he was to have any chance of remaining in the race. The Lim boys had been a godsend. Funds had been committed by the young Chinese and, within a week from when undertakings had been given by both parties, more than half million dollars had flowed into the campaign coffers from untraceable sources. Subsequently the Governor had won the election, and the Salima family had arrived for their pound of flesh.

Their original request had been to reinstate the bank's operating licence which, at the time of its closure, limited the institution's activities to within the municipality of Lexington. Since then, greed and opportunity had driven their demands to include other cities and, although the new Governor was not entirely disagreeable to having foreign capital flow into his state's economy, his political advisers warned of the inherent dangers in accepting campaign donations from Asian sources, concerned with the possibility that such funding might be drug-related. They had seen similar, well-heeled Asian groups arrive in other States, bringing with them their culture of drugs, terror and intimidation, and seriously advised the Governor to exercise caution when dealing with the Lim brothers.

'Do you think we will have our other licences?' James asked, assertively. He had little time for government representatives, particularly those who sold themselves for considerably less than what their counterparts in most Asian capitals might demand. The Senator sat quietly for a moment longer, then answered.

'Sure,' he said, 'but this has required substantially more lobbying than we'd first envisaged.' He paused, gauging the two young bankers, wondering how far he could push. 'An additional consideration would not be out of order,' he said. James had expected such, and was prepared, not at all offended by the man's directness.

'How much?' he had learned this from his father. There was no point in beating around the bush when dealing with corrupt officials. If one did not give them what they first asked for, experience had shown that they were sure to come back at some later date, demanding more than their original request. The senator smiled, pleased that James Salima had not been one of those evasive Asians who avoided the more direct approach.

'One hundred and fifty thousand,' he said. James noticed Denny's surprise and with a cautionary look, cut him off abruptly.

'We agree,' he responded, a little too quickly. James decided that the figure was an odd amount, and that the American, like so many other Westerners, most probably believed that all Asians bargained themselves back to some predetermined figure, fixed inflexibly in their minds. He scoffed silently at the myth, and the way occidentals thought. Although he guessed that the senator was, in fact, only looking for a hundred thousand, James believed that his hook in the Governor was even deeper now that he had acquiesced. 'And we would be delighted to be included on the Governor's guest list next fall,' he added, beaming at the statesman.

The senator's mind raced. He had the opportunity to bury an additional fifty thousand dollars without any of the Governor's inner circle ever becoming the wiser. He also knew, however, how the Governor's wife, who partnered a well-established law firm in their home state, would not care to have such people at her home. The senator decided that he would leave that problem to the Governor to resolve for himself.

'Done,' he said, much to James' satisfaction. He desperately wished to break into the Bluegrass society circles and, with the senator's assistance, they would receive the exposure necessary to promote their ongoing activities. The brothers remained just long enough to finish their cold tea, then they departed, returning to

Frankfort satisfied with the outcome of their negotiations. Neither had thought it strange that they were required to travel away from the capital to finalise their transaction with the senator. They appreciated the need for secrecy in such matters. As they drove in silence, each son considered in his own way how their family's American acquisitions might enhance their futures, and add to their already incredible wealth.

Kerry B.Collison

Chapter 7

Rama Announcement

The crowd fidgeted, impatient with the delay. The sun was partially blocked by the low pollution which hung above the Senayan Stadium. The air was still hot and humid despite the cloud, and this seemed to depress the crowd for the Armed Forces' Day celebrations.

The President was late.

An AURI officer waited nervously for the signal to alert the Halim Airforce Command that the President had arrived. The flypast had been planned to coincide with the *Bapak's* entry into the historic stadium, and it was this officer's task to co-ordinate the manoeuvre. The ambient temperature in the huge, Russian-financed complex rose exponentially as more than one hundred thousand Indonesians crowded into the stadium to enjoy the parade. The suffocating heat was stirred with the heavy smell of over-ripe *durian*. As the sewerage-like smell struggled upwards and across the grounds, the pungent aroma entered the area allocated to the foreign community, precipitating anxious looks of disapproval from those present.

Anxious ABRI generals waited in line and checked their watches surreptitiously, concerned that something might have delayed their Commander-in-Chief. He had never been this late before. The temperature continued to climb, further exacerbating their frustrating wait. Suddenly, a roar rose from the crowd signalling that the President of the Indonesian Republic had finally arrived, and those present rose to their feet. Relieved, the generals raised their hands in salute as the white-haired Javanese leader climbed from what his people had facetiously named, the *Bapak-mobile*, a special purpose vehicle designed for official occasions from which the

President could wave to the masses. The bullet-proofed limousine had been manufactured in a car assembly plant owned by the former President's son.

Leader of more than two hundred and twenty million people, leader of the largest Muslim country on the face of the earth, and recognized leader of the non-aligned nations, the Indonesian President walked confidently to his position at the centre of the covered dais, and took his place. As the former general came to attention, the crowd roared its approval, and then suddenly fell silent as the trumpeting strains of *Indonesia Raya*, the National Anthem, reverberated through the stadium. While the final stanza was played, soldiers representing the three Services left the main body of troops and marched in line carrying their regimental colour-flags towards their Commander-in-Chief.

The well-rehearsed drill was accompanied by the sounds of drumbeat, rolling through the air as the disciplined men approached the point directly below, and in front of their President, where they came to a halt, then saluted. Whispered comment passed amongst the assembled dignitaries as the President slowly climbed the dais, while waving to the one hundred thousand spectators gathered inside the stadium. Dressed in an immaculate dark blue suit, the Indonesian leader wore a white *pici* on his head instead of the more traditional black, symbolic head-dress. To some observers, this was not a good omen, as Moslem fundamentalism had grown considerably under the new President's leadership. There were a small number, however, for whom the gesture was seen as a return to the true spirit of Islamic teaching.

At the precise moment the President saluted those before him, the air suddenly filled with the roar of Raptor IF-22s as AURI fighter jets screamed across the sky above. Startled, many of the spectators panicked before realizing what was happening, clasping hands over ears as the deafening scream of jet engines pierced their surrounds. Then, as their faces turned skywards, their mouths opened in awe at the spectacle of four aircraft tearing up in a vertical climb. Suddenly, as the white trails following the aircraft turned outwards, and then towards earth, the entire assembly broke into cries of pleasure at the aerial display. As the sounds of jet engines faded, these were replaced by heavy, metallic, grinding noises entering the stadium.

JAKARTA

The crowd's faces turned towards the major entrance which had been rebuilt for the celebrations, and watched, applauding as the line of Scorpion tanks rumbled into the grounds below and came to a halt at their pre-designated positions. Following these light tanks were two surface-to-surface missiles, partially raised on their launchers, towed through the stadium by heavy-duty ancillary transports. A number of Leopard tanks then completed the spectacle, representing but a fraction of the weaponry *ABRI* had accumulated since the new President had come to office.

High up on the grandstand, above and behind where the President stood, hundreds of foreign reporters and cameramen busied themselves recording Indonesia's first public display of their missile strength. Further below, gathered in the aisles not far to the right of the Indonesian Chiefs of Staff and their ladies, foreign military attaches stood silent, lips pursed. They did not need to take photography of the weaponry before them; without exception, their own Defence Departments and intelligence gathering services all stored more information material on the Indonesian arsenal than perhaps the Indonesians had themselves. These foreign professionals were all too conscious of the fact that their host country's military leadership had been acquiring Russian and American arms on a scale not dissimilar to that of the Soekarno era.

Standing at the extreme end of the line, Colonel McMahon, the Australian Defence Attaché, watched solemnly, aware of the strike capability and range of the guided missiles before him. Even in their almost dormant state, he mused, while staring at the long silver columns, they looked most menacing. Australia had been most fortunate, he thought, that her over-populated neighbour had not seen fit to purchase any of the antiquated Soviet ICBM hardware that had become available after the collapse of Communism. On the other hand, since you could guarantee that the conventional warheads on any missile purchased from the Soviets had never been regularly tested, there was a good chance they would explode on the launch pad at any attempt at ignition. He recalled at the time how even Malaysia had rushed in to purchase the heavily discounted Russian MiGs, as these were on offer at almost half their original cost.

His thoughts returned to the missiles being paraded below, and he nodded confidently to himself, conscious of how fortunate they all were that Indonesia did not have ready access to nuclear warheads, or any suitable delivery system.

Colonel McMahon's attention turned to the amazing attendance which surrounded the military display, wondering how they managed to remain standing outside in the debilitating heat. He, along with the other foreign guests, fidgeted uneasily, sweating profusely in the humidity. Damp patches appeared behind knees and under armpits, revealing the discomfort they suffered in silence, while their Asian counterparts, more accustomed to the climate, remained relatively comfortable throughout the proceedings.

The Australian Attaché looked further down towards the President, surprised by the number of Indonesia's prominent business leaders who attended as Palace guests, privileged to be placed alongside their President. In the past, such invitations had been restricted to those in government, and foreign military representatives. Most he recognized. He leaned forward a little more to see who had moved into the two seats directly alongside the outspoken Vice President.

Earlier, as the stadium had filled, these had remained empty, giving rise to considerable speculation amongst the foreign Diplomatic Corp. As heads moved from side to side first blocking, then revealing those who had taken these seats, he raised his eyebrows in surprise, recognising the Lim couple, *Bapak* and *Ibu Salima*. He was immediately impressed, aware that the attendance of such a senior Chinese *totok* at the Armed Forces Day parade gave credence to the rumours that nothing had really changed in Indonesia - except the face of the new President at the country's helm. The military attaché leaned back into his hard uncomfortable seat. In practised movement, he inconspicuously lifted his cap and touched his forehead with a handkerchief to absorb the beads of perspiration which had formed there, while wondering how long the ceremony would last. He could see the looks of consternation amongst the other guests, whose wives had already shown signs of considerable discomfort, fanning themselves too energetically. Then, when the guests began to doubt that the parade would ever end, an announcement across the public address system courteously requested that they all take their seats for the Presidential address.

When the rustling of clothes and scraping of shoes over timber finally settled down indicating that guests and spectators were

JAKARTA

seated, the former Javanese general coughed, once, to ensure that the microphone was working; then began the annual Armed Forces' Day address.

'*Saudara, saudara,*' he commenced, then paused for effect '*People of Indonesia, members of the Armed Forces, and guests, we are here to celebrate........*' As his voice droned on in a language only a few of the foreign guests understood, an audible sigh passed through the aisles of foreign military attaches, expecting a repeat of the previous years speech which, to their dismay, had continued for more than an hour. The United States Military Attaché looked along the uncomfortable row of foreign officers to his left, catching his Canadian counterpart's eye.

He winked. The French Canadian ever so slightly shook his head in response, then surreptitiously wiped the perspiration from his moustache. As the speech continued and the ladies became restless on the hard, metal chairs, the British Ambassador's wife leaned forward, turned to her husband with an expression of apology and fainted, sliding off her seat and into the narrow aisle. Other members of the Diplomatic Corp moved quickly, relieved at having been given the perfect opportunity to leave their seats and attend to the unfortunate woman. The American Chargé d'Affaires, who had been first to come to her assistance, suddenly ceased fanning the stricken lady and listened carefully to the words which flowed from the stadium public address system. Startled, he turned to see if any of the others had heard the word *nuclear* in the presidential speech, and immediately realized that few amongst their number would have understood, or even been listening.

'*...this will involve the ongoing commitment from our Armed Forces to maintain stability as we go forward together, and build a greater future for the people of Indonesia. Members of the Development Cabinet and I have therefore decided that construction of the first five plants will begin as soon as feasibly possible, followed by seven additional plants once those in the first phase have all been commissioned. The first nuclear energy power plants will be located in Java, and Bali. They will be known as Rama I through V. Foreign participation will be invited from......*'

The acting Ambassador slipped back into his own seat and motioned towards his political counsellor to exchange seats with his wife. This activity attracted little attention from the other diplomats, who were more concerned about the duration of the

Presidential address.

'Did you get that?' the Chargé d'Affaires asked. The political secretary nodded in response. He was reasonably *au fait* with the Indonesian Language, and had noted with similar alarm that the President had announced a commitment to address the country's crippling power problems by introducing nuclear power plants. The embassy officer scanned the faces of others present. It was clear from their blank expressions that they were unaware of the announcement.

'I'd best get back to the Embassy,' the officer suggested, 'and remove my phone from its hook.' The acting Ambassador forced a smile knowing that this would not happen, but he did nod for the officer to leave. The State Department would have transcripts of the Presidential speech in Washington within the hour and, no doubt, would respond with hostile enquiries to determine why there had been no indication from their in-country sources that the Indonesians had been contemplating such a move.

He looked over his shoulder in the direction of the Japanese Ambassador and his entourage, and noticed the agitated discussion taking place. Then he glanced around for the Russian delegation and came into direct eye contact with their Ambassador, Sergei Perevozchenko whose smile suddenly broke into a grin as he watched the American's face fall with the realization that Moscow had obviously been given advance notification of the news. He returned the smile and winked, freezing the Russian's cocky display. Satisfied that would be sufficient to generate at least a little paranoia amongst their camp, the American scanned the faces of those around in search of tell-tale signs which might reflect prior knowledge of the incredible revelations in the President's speech.

He believed that the general consensus supported the view that the Indonesians would never again consider nuclear energy, having lost the initiative during the Soeharto regime when the then Minister for Technology, Habibie, had attempted to implement a similar program. World opinion had discouraged the plan and it was shelved. Now, it seemed, the plan to establish a series of plants commencing with the two most heavily populated areas of Java and Bali had been resurrected.

The President concluded his speech and the crowd roared its approval. On cue, an officer screamed loudly bringing the parade back into order, and the guests once again rose to stand. Another command was called, and the President returned their salute. Accompanied by the band's deep brass tones, the President left the podium, stepping slowly as he was escorted down to his bulletproof, glass-covered limousine. He entered and stood inside the dome, steadied himself as the vehicle moved slowly forward, then commenced waving as he was driven away. The ceremony over, crowds pushed and shoved as they too made their way from the complex, while foreign guests and other dignitaries exited through a specially designated area.

Most returned directly to their official posts where, within the hour, copies of the President's speech had been translated and read. In the course of the next few hours, urgent meetings were held in most offices throughout the diplomatic community to determine whatever ramifications there might be with respect to Indonesia's nuclear energy plans. By late afternoon, the general feeling amongst the foreign experts was that there were would be no additional military threat to its neighbours.

Before early evening had arrived, Embassies whose countries enjoyed nuclear energy were already preoccupied with preparations to offer the Indonesians whatever was necessary, from technology to finance, in their attempts to secure what would obviously become an incredibly lucrative opportunity. Lights remained burning throughout the night in the tall, Japanese Commercial Attaché's office, where representatives of Kyushu Electric Power and Shikoku Power worked together as a team. For the first time since the death of the former President, Embassies worked around the clock as communications flooded in from all over the globe. Trade Commissioners suddenly discovered that they knew little in relation to the terminology and technology associated with the production of electricity by nuclear power.

The following morning they also discovered, one and all, that they had been caught unawares yet again, when the *Jakarta Times* carried news of an overnight Palace announcement, releasing the name of the Presidential appointee selected to oversee the project's implementation, and the company which would be created for this purpose. None were surprised to read that the newspapers had already coined their own acronym for *P.T. Perusahan Pembangkit Listrik Nuclear*, the designated power company. It was referred to in the Press as PEPELIN, and before that day had come to a close, the word was on everyone's lips.

Before the public address system on Jakarta's Isitqual Mosque had again, annoyingly penetrated offices as far as Merdeka Square, calling the faithful to mid-morning prayers, more than ten foreign Trade Commissioners had placed calls requesting an appointment to call upon General Seda, the newly appointed Chairman of PEPELIN.

The race had begun.

* * * * * *

Immediately upon her return to the residence, Ruswita removed her shoes and rubbed her swollen feet. The doddering old cook, inherited from earlier days, shuffled around getting in Ruswita's way when she went to the kitchen in search of tea and biscuits.

'Where is Lani?' Rus asked, but the cook did not respond. Ruswita was certain that the woman feigned deafness, as she had often noticed that there seemed to be little wrong with her hearing whenever Lim was around. She had left her husband behind, knowing that the day's announcements would require lengthy discussions with others involved in his various *kongsis*. A younger servant entered the room to check on *Ibu Ruswita's* needs, but she merely brushed her aside, quite happy to prepare her own refreshments.

'Please call Ibu Lani,' she asked the young *pembantu*. Ruswita was firm with her staff, but never bullied them.

'Ibu Lani has gone out to the plaza, nyonya,' the house-girl advised, still hovering close by, anxious to assist her mistress. Ruswita dismissed this girl also, deciding to pour her own tea. She returned to the comfort of the lounge, placed the tea and biscuits on the coffee table, then relaxed. As she sat, rubbing her aching feet, Ruswita thought about the parade and decided that it had gone well for all, but particularly for the Salima Group. Earlier, when Lim had announced that they would attend the function, she had been caught off guard, completely surprised with his decision; it was not normally his style to be seen in public, especially in the company of the country's leadership.

As a group, Salima had to contend with the public's perception that they owned considerably more than was fact. Lim had been successful, Ruswita agreed, but did not deserve the constant attention that the International press applied to him and the family *kongsi*. Such scrutiny had not been a problem in Indonesia. The local newspapers survived, primarily because they failed to report anything which might jeopardise their licences, and it was accepted amongst Indonesian press circles that any story which referred to the wealthy conglomerate would naturally attract the President's ire because of his personal association with the multi-national group.

Other than Lim, only Ruswita was in a position to identify every asset the family had accumulated over the years. After they married, she had continued to play an active role in the *kongsi's* affairs, and held positions on each of the main boards within the group. This dedication had only strengthened her relationship with Lim, who grew to trust her judgement unreservedly. Together, they had added to the family's incredible wealth, until even they sometimes lost track of the international conglomerate's smaller subsidiaries. She knew that they owned or controlled more than one hundred companies, including cement plants, flour mills, steel factories and banks in four countries.

As the thought of their banking interests crossed Ruswita's mind, she remembered how Lim's two sons, Denny and James Salima, had almost brought down the empire with their ambitious attempt to establish themselves as players in the United States. They had both been most convincing at the time they had submitted their proposals to Lim, and subsequently secured their father's support to purchase a failing bank in the United States in order to establish a foothold in North American banking circles. Ruswita had not been too keen on the move; she believed that both the boys' judgement had been influenced by their desire to continue living the high life in America, as neither seemed ready to return and take their positions at Lim's side back in Indonesia.

Ruswita identified the problem but was not prepared to interfere with their plan, concerned that in so doing she would be accused of creating family divisions. It was already difficult enough for her. She had given birth to a son, Benny, in their first years of marriage. When he was of age, Ruswita had encouraged Benny to study in Europe, and he had done so. Lim had been supportive of the idea, satisfied that all of his sons would have a Western education. Ruswita smiled, pleased that Benny had been able to spend his summer vacation with them at home for a change. One more year, she reminded herself, and her son would be home to stay.

The logistics of caring for their sons and supporting their activities overseas had resulted in a myriad of housing acquisitions. Ruswita's own personal secretary was responsible for overseeing the accommodations and staffing for these, which included penthouses in Hong Kong, Singapore, Sydney, London and Paris, and palatial homes in Beverley Hills, the south of France, Baden-Baden and ski-lodges in Aspen and Banff Springs. Ruswita admitted to herself that she had visited some of these only once; she was too old to learn how to ski and did not particularly enjoy the cold. Besides, she felt that these homes were best utilized for the purpose they were purchased, and that her family and associates should continue to maintain as low a profile as possible. It would not do, she knew, for them to be seen too often with those who frequented their lavish estates.

Ruswita remembered the difficulty they encountered in Canada when reporters discovered the country's Finance Minister vacationing in their lodge. By chance, the Lims had visited that day, and were unable to leave out of concern that their connection with the Cabinet Minister would be pasted across the Canadian press, thereby destroying years invested in developing their existing relationship with the woman. Finally, having waited for signs that the reporters had all followed their VIP, the Lims had been obliged to sneak back to Calgary where they were weathered in and obliged to remain in the airport terminal for more than twelve hours.

Ruswita clearly understood the significance of maintaining these discreet positions. Business could never be done without such access, and she continuously monitored the *kongsi's* dealings with those in power. She knew that neither Denny nor James had developed the finesse required to maintain such relationships.

Her thoughts returned to the near fiasco both boys had been responsible for in the United States. Having convinced their father to finance their entrée into the American banking fraternity, James had openly boasted that they had greased the State Governor in order to secure approval for their acquisition. The rumour had circulated for several years, emerging as a major issue when the Governor's name was mentioned as potential presidential material for the United States. Lim had been furious and threatened to close down the entire North American operation. The young Lims practically begged their father to permit them to continue there and, as Ruswita then openly supported their request, he had acquiesced. James and Denny both realized that they owed their stepmother a considerable debt. Now, as established and respected middle-aged businessmen, who had their own families to care for, they took few risks without first clearing these through Ruswita. Until, that is, James took their American operations on a dangerous journey into the Chinese political arena.

She sat contemplating their family and business empire. Although their wealth was considered by some to border on the obscene, Ruswita had never flaunted their riches. Whenever they received valuable gifts, Ruswita would have these placed around the rambling Menteng residence, rarely conscious of the item's value or beauty. A unique painting hung on one wall behind the grand piano in the room where she now rested. Ruswita did not particularly like the flowers depicted in the painting, preferring the traditional Indonesian landscapes, which made her feel more comfortable.

When Ruswita had been advised as to the value of the painting which one of their investment agents had purchased in London, she had been furious. Her eyes moved from the Van Gogh to the piano, and she sighed. None in the family could play so much as a note, and she wondered why Lim had insisted on leaving it there.

Her thoughts turned to what the President's announcement would mean in terms of family commitments. Ruswita understood that Lim's personal participation in most of the negotiations would be essential to the company's future involvement in the capital intensive power projects. Ruswita had played a major role in the decision making process which had led to the President's decision to resurrect the project. The Salima Group had worked with those who had first proposed the grand scheme, encouraging the government to finance the programme on what was commonly known as a BOT project, a concept which provided for a consortium to Build, Operate and Transfer the finished project to state ownership once they had recovered their costs and profit. Ruswita and

Lim had spent countless evenings together discussing the plan.

In secret, Lim had orchestrated for the government to award the contracts to Salima Corporation; the company would benefit not only from the construction of the projects, but also the ongoing management, and then, finally, once the plants had been fully operational for some years, they would list these assets on the Jakarta Stock Exchange. When they believed their timing to be appropriate, the group would slowly divest all their holdings in the energy companies.

The President had been enthusiastic, and even more so when Lim offered to provide for a significant share in the company awarded the BOT contract, shares which were to be allocated to the First Family's oldest son. The President was uncomfortable with the prospects of facing another barrage from the International press concerning cronyism within his government. He insisted that the process of selection had to appear to be legitimate, and asked that Lim agree to a tender being called to satisfy public opinion. Lim had complied, committing the Salima Group's resources in raising finances to fund the ongoing project. When Lim had suggested that the budget for the entire programme would be in excess of twenty-five billion dollars, the President had visibly flinched.

The national debt, which even then the country could not service, had risen to two hundred billion. Depletion of Indonesia's oil reserves and the exponential growth in demand for electricity had placed the leader in a most unenviable position. Since accepting the mantle as the nation's new leader for his first five year term, not a day had gone by when the national grid had not gone off line somewhere in the country, throwing industry into chaos.

In his inaugural speech, the President had promised to address the nation's deteriorating infrastructure problems. Instead, he had been swayed by his former military comrades, and approved out-of-budget military acquisitions to keep pace with regional developments. As Indonesia's aggressive buying spree continued, so too did the number of major power failures. Before the end of the President's first term in office, dissent became more apparent, and rumours that a number of young officers had been arrested for petitioning their leader were being treated seriously by the investment community.

Ruswita had encouraged Lim to consider off-loading some of

their Indonesian assets until stronger leadership emerged. She had watched many of the other Chinese *kongsis* liquidating their assets and reinvesting outside of Asia. Singapore, once the darling of Indonesian traders, was no longer as attractive as it had been during the giddy days of Soeharto's regime.

She remembered how the currency traders had almost brought all of the Asian tigers to their knees and had vowed, at that time, to ensure that they would never be caught again, or at least, not as severely. Ruswita believed that ASEAN had not delivered, and that as new trade blocs emerged, so would the ASEAN ten nation dream diminish in importance as a global trading force. Ruswita had agreed with Lim's observation that ASEAN had been doomed from the start. They believed that its concept was far too inflexible for Asia, and that its exclusion of China and India, influenced by political considerations rather than economic criteria, would only create new barriers, not tear them down. The Salima Group had invested across all known political boundaries, not concerned with anything other than the pursuit of profits.

* * * * * *

Refreshed from her brief rest, Ruswita decided to take a cold *mandi* and ask Ratna if she would like to join her for lunch. She checked the tall, Dutch grandfather clock, and decided to call Ratna herself. She rose wearily, and walked though the main residence barefooted, out into the terraced area which led down to a number of disjointed accommodations. They had continued living at Lim's original residence after they married, adding rooms as necessary, until the entire land area was covered with buildings, interconnected by a number of garden walkways and terraces. At the rear of the complex there were four rooms to accommodate servants and drivers.

Lani's small apartment was located at the end of the terrace and across from a number of larger bedrooms, which were kept for visiting family and close friends. Ruswita and Lim each enjoyed their own bedrooms built on the second level, overlooking the garden walkways. He still refused to dress in anything but singlet and shorts while hovering around upstairs.

A miniature pond lay amongst *bonsai* palms, and Ruswita

stepped across to check if the servants had removed any of the goldfish from the pleasant setting. She stood there for a moment, before bending down and slowly moving her hand amongst the water lilies. Satisfied that none of the large fish had been eaten, she stood, placed her hands on her hips, and called out to Ratna. Ruswita waited for a response and, when there was none, continued through the palms carefully, until reaching Lani's rooms. Again, she paused, this time to smell the delicate jasmine's perfume, which hung softly in the air. She opened the door and entered.

The carefully decorated room made her smile once again; she and Lani had done this together, and her smile widened as a familiar toy came into view, placed alongside a photograph of Ratna's graduation ceremony from the International School.

She remembered how difficult it once was for Indonesians to access the school for foreign students. The new facilities endowed by the Salima group resolved the question of her admittance. Since graduation, Ratna had not indicated whether she wished to continue her studies, or directly commence working in one of the family companies. Ruswita sighed, moved to the buffet and lifted the teddy-bear Lani had kept since Ratna's early childhood. She placed the ageing fur against her cheek and closed her eyes, ever so briefly, and uttered a quick prayer of thanks that the baby she now called her niece, had not been lost to her. Lani had been a true friend throughout the years, and Ruswita had provided for them both. Their secret had remained intact for more than twenty years.

As she turned to leave, Ruswita heard something fall and break inside the other room. Ready to chastise whichever servant was responsible for the breakage, she walked quickly to the bedroom and opened the door.

Ruswita's face froze when confronted by the scene before her. Ratna sat upright, in bed, the sheet pulled over her naked body, barely covering her breasts. Standing alongside the bed, dressed only in his pants, was her visibly shaken son, Benny. For a moment, the only sound evident in the room was the soft hum of the air-conditioner's compressor clicking into action. Then Ruswita stepped forward angrily.

'*Get dressed!*' she hissed at Ratna. Terrified, she climbed out of the bed, disclosing her naked body. Ruswita erupted. '*You,*' she growled in her son's direction, '*Get out!*' Benny bent down, snatched his remaining clothes from the floor and fled. Ratna dressed quickly, knowing that she was in huge trouble. She pulled her jeans up and fastened them over her fine, slim waistline, then slipped a cotton tank-top over her head until it covered her ample breasts. She ran her fingers nervously through her hair.

'*Sit!*' Ruswita ordered, noticing that her hands were shaking in anger. '*How did this happen?*' she demanded, standing in the centre of the bedroom, arms crossed.

'*What is wrong, Aunty?*' Ratna cried, almost defiantly. '*Benny likes me!*' The statement drove a cold sliver through Ruswita's chest. Her eyes narrowed.

'*Did you have sex with Benny?*' she demanded to know. Ratna's eyes widered at the accusation, then the tears poured down her cheeks.

'*No,*' she answered truthfully. They had not been given the opportunity.

'*Benny is family, 'Na,*' Ruswita exclaimed, using the common abbreviation of her name. '*What could possibly have entered your heads?*' she asked, rhetorically. '*Do you understand why you should not do this with Benny?* Ratna sat sobbing, looking around for a tissue. Spotting a box, she leaned over and pulled at one angrily, the gesture causing Ruswita to scowl.

'*We are hardly even related, Aunty,*' she sobbed, defiantly, then stopped just long enough to blow her nose. '*I'm not even a close cousin,*' she said. Suddenly, Ruswita was at a loss for something to say. She hesitated, then sighed, moving closer to the bed. She felt weak and needed to sit down before her legs gave way. Moments passed before she responded to Ratna's remark.

'*It does not matter, 'Na,*' she said, the anger now gone from her voice. '*To me, you are like my own daughter, and it is enough that I forbid you to consider any such relationship with Benny. Is that clear?*' Ratna's bottom lip fell. She nodded her head, sullenly. Ruswita sat on the bed as the silence continued. She leaned over and placed her hand on the young woman's arm. Ratna pulled back, and looked away while holding the tissue to her nose. Ruswita sighed heavily, and looked at her daughter. Then she rose slowly, and moved towards the bedroom door. '*I will speak to your mother when she returns. 'Na,*' she said, her voice steady, even though she wanted to cry and take Ratna in her arms and hold her close to her chest, as a mother would. She struggled to keep the tremor from her voice. *'And in the meantime, do as I say or leave this home!'* with which, she turned and left, in search of her son Benny. Angry with Lani that she had not been there to prevent what had taken place, Ruswita knew that she had to act decisively, and what she must now do.

The following week Ratna Sari was sent to study in America, out of harm's way. Lani remained behind, as all the other mothers had done when their daughters had left to attend universities overseas. By the time her first semester had rolled around, Ratna had settled into the Salima stately home, acquired her Californian driver's licence, and knew exactly where to go for a really good time.

* * * * * *

Announcements that the country had decided to introduce nuclear power brought widespread demonstrations throughout Indonesia, but these lasted for only a few days as the Commander for the Restoration of Peace and Order sent his anti-riot troops into the streets where anti-riot centers had been established during Soeharto's regime and had proven their effectiveness in the months preceding his final presidential elections.

The President had instructed his generals to permit the demonstrations to continue, long enough to prejudice the parties opposed to his dictates. Then they had moved in, swiftly, executing the order to sweep the opposition away. Many of those detained simply disappeared. Others who had been arrested wished they'd learned from past experiences, and had remained uninvolved.

In Japan, demonstrators walked through the streets of Hiroshima and Nagasaki, carrying banners decrying the proliferation of nuclear energy plants in their own country, alerting the world once again to the dangers of radiation and the clouds of death which once claimed so many of their countrymen's lives.

In Australia, demonstrators picketed the Indonesian Embassy in Canberra, and organized crowds blocked access to the Consulates in Sydney, Melbourne, and Perth. In Darwin, Friends of the Earth joined forces with several hundred East Timorese and marched on the Consulate. When police were called to disperse the unruly demonstrators, fighting erupted and the Consulate was seized and torched by some of the extremists. In retaliation, the

British Consulate in Surabaya was stormed by militant youths by mistake, where they demanded that the terrified and confused Consul accept their letter of protest over the Darwin incident.

Opponents of the nuclear program warned of the potential disaster of locating such plants in what was considered to be a geologically unsound environment.

The Australian Government called the Indonesian Ambassador to discuss his country's announcement, and a number of meetings took place between senior cabinet ministers and the Indonesian representatives. It soon became clear that the Indonesians were determined to proceed with their plans to develop up to twelve NPPs in Java, Bali and Sumatra.

The Melbourne Age ran the headline, *Indonesia Joins Nuclear Race*, and the Sydney Morning Herald produced a series of maps showing how prevailing winds could carry radioactive dust the short distance across the Timor Sea to endanger large areas of Northern Australia. A computer simulation showing possible fallout from East Java in the event of an accident had been prepared by the Australian National University, and received widespread coverage.

New Guinea and Australia expressed alarm at the findings, which demonstrated that radio-active plume would reach both countries within a few days of any accident. Words such as Chernobyl, melt-down, China-Syndrome, Three Mile Island soon became all too familiar. By the end of the first week, most Australians were convinced that their country was in danger, and bilateral relationships between the two countries came under close scrutiny. At the beginning of the third week, the mood had changed somewhat, and Australian companies commenced looking for commercial opportunities which might be in the offing as a result of the ambitious nuclear energy scheme.

As issues closer to home slowly displaced stories relating to the earlier scare-mongering, information concerning the twenty to thirty-billion dollar project moved off the front pages and towards the sports section, until disappearing altogether as newsworthy items.

Only the Financial Review continued to run stories as, one by one, Australian companies announced that they would be forming their own consortiums to compete in the race for the lucrative contracts. Representations were made to the Indonesian Trade Counsellor, reminding him of an earlier statement in which he had stated that his country wished to maintain its good neighbour policy with its southern neighbours, and would consider submissions from countries which maintained a balanced perspective with relation to Indonesian affairs.

On the first anniversary of the President's announcement, tender documents had been completed for the first two plants. A probabilistic risk assessment secretly conducted by the Canadians had been lodged with the PEPELIN Chairman who, upon reading the startling statements contained within the highly classified document, personally had the entire file destroyed.

The first plant, *Rama I*, was to be built ten kilometers from the town of Negara, in Bali. The second Nuclear Energy Plant would be built alongside Mt Muria, some four hundred kilometers to the East of Jakarta, and would be known as *Rama II*. The remaining plants were to be constructed through Java and up to Aceh, as part of the national grid. The Chairman of PEPELIN, General Seda, advised the Press that tender documents for the first five plants would be available and ready for circulation within the following months.

* * * * * *

United States — Maryland, Camp David

The President's wife had elected not to accompany her husband once she discovered who their guests would be for the traditional late Sunday luncheon. It was not that she was in any way racist towards these people, but had acted more out of a newly acquired sense of morality. She believed that Camp David, as it had traditionally been reserved for close friends of the First Family, or visiting Heads of State, should not be used for such clandestine meetings. She lived with a growing concern that these financial thugs who used their powerful privileges to further their own vested interests would one day lead others to delve into the President's past, a past which she knew could not withstand close scrutiny. Publicity about the President's dealings with the Chinese-Indonesian bankers during his term as Governor could be extremely damaging.

James Salima sat alone with the President. He was pleased that this meeting would be conducted directly between himself, and the man whom he personally assisted into the White House. He had provided the necessary financial support to wage political war against his opponents. Although it was now time to call in the dues, James was not entirely confident that, with his new found authority, the President would remember the alliance he had struck with the Lims before leaving Kentucky for Washington.

'My father has asked that you support the transfer of technology for the *Rama* Nuclear Power Plant project. Without American participation, the tender process will become a fiasco.'

'You have my word, as agreed,' the President said, not at all uncomfortable with his commitment, as the American companies stood to gain significantly from the substantial energy programme under consideration. The technology was, as far as he was concerned, already virtually available in the public domain. Nuclear energy had been successfully developed throughout the world, and he could see no harm in giving an additional assurance to those who had provided him with the necessary support when he had most needed it. The invitation to luncheon at Camp David had been organised since meetings in this private setting were easily protected from the ever-inquisitive Press. Besides, the President knew that he might need the Lim support again, when he had completed his first term, and required funds for his re-election campaign.

It was becoming increasingly difficult for incumbents to raise campaign funds. Although he accepted that his people had bent the rules somewhat, the President had no difficulty with their behaviour, considering that his opponents were most probably being supported in a similar manner.

'There is one further matter, if I might now mention it,' James requested. The photogenic President smiled, his blue eyes masking the concern he suddenly felt as he prepared for what might follow.

'Go on,' he said, leaning back, exuding confidence. James took his time, using the opportunity to present his father's request. When he had first been summoned to discuss this issue, James had been shocked that they were to participate in what amounted to political lobbying for the Indonesian Government, and had suggested to his father that this would be most unwise considering the current climate. Lim had been adamant. His eldest son was instructed to remind the American President, if necessary, of his debt to the Salima family.

Although there were no direct commercial benefits for the Salima group arising from Indonesia's ongoing occupation of the disputed Timor territory, Lim's request was made as a gesture to the Indonesian President and the generals, whose pockets had greatly benefited from the military action. James was aware that some of those involved had cleverly reinvested their rewards in Australian based casinos, including one on Christmas Island.

'There is considerable concern in Jakarta that your Administration might take a hard line towards Indonesia's stand in relation to East Timor. I have been asked to seek your assurance that the United States will support Jakarta's position,' James revealed, hoping he had not misjudged the depth of his family's relationship with the American leader. The President mused for a few moments, then replied.

'You can tell Jakarta that the American people will remain consistent in their position over Timor, James. As long as the United States is guaranteed the same right of passage that our ships have enjoyed in the past, then there will be no change in the status quo. At least, as far as we are concerned.' The President had expected that the subject might be mentioned, and still marvelled with the frequency with which such issues were raised, not via political channels, but through powerful private lobby groups, such as the Lims. The President was annoyed that the small Asian backwater had been of considerable nuisance value to him, as it had been to his predecessors' Administrations.

The United States no longer feared Soviet intervention in the area; that bogey had been long dismissed. The concerns he and his military now faced were more focused on the growing Chinese influence in the region. There had been immeasurable resistance to continuing 'Most-Favoured' status for the militant country. China had proved itself worthy of being feared, particularly since recent disclosures revealed its capacity to deliver Intercontinental Ballistic Missiles to America's West coast. He knew that the United States, in order to maintain its forever weakening foothold in Asia, required a fresh approach to its position and alliances in that region.

JAKARTA

The Lim request would in no way conflict with already established protocols; United States Navy nuclear submarines still traversed the Ombar-Wetar Straits undetected, and he would do nothing to jeopardise this strategic position. Satisfied that both had acquitted themselves as required, the two men ate sparingly before James, understanding that he had used his allocated opportunity, departed.

That evening he caught a flight from Washington to Vancouver, then flew on to Tokyo and Beijing. Less than twenty-four hours after having sandwiches with the American President at Camp David, James Salima, aka James Lim, sat down with senior Communist Party officials in China, and laid the foundations for his bank's future co-operation to provide the People's Republic of China with even greater access to the North American market. Under a shroud of utmost secrecy, James Lim then went about making the necessary arrangements for the China Ocean Shipping Company, COSCO, China's six hundred ship global corporation, to utilise the Asian Pacific Commercial Bank's American subsidiary for all of its transactions in the United States.

* * * * * *

Subsequent negotiations would result in COSCO being awarded three significant contracts in the United States. The first, a twenty-year lease over the former Long Beach Naval Station, would be passed to the Communist Chinese shipping company, with White House approval, on the basis of a fifteen million dollar annual rental. The contract left the American public spinning; the city of Long Beach was required to allocate two hundred and thirty five million dollars to modernise the facility, whereas COSCO's lease payments would require more than sixteen years to repay these initial costs. Patrick Buchanan, one of the foremost television journalists of the time, immediately christened the former US Navy yard, *The Deng Xiaoping Memorial Naval Base*.

The second startling development was for a one hundred and forty million dollar, taxpayer-subsidised loan guarantee to a COSCO subsidiary to build ships at the Mobile shipyard in Alabama. Then, while the American people were still reeling from these revelations, the American leadership supported arrangements for a Hong Kong-based subsidiary, Hutchinson Corporation, through the Panamanian Government, to lease the 'anchor-ports' on either side of the Panama Canal, a move which granted Red China a strategic toehold in the Western Hemisphere.

Fears that Mainland China was already firmly ensconced on American shores were viewed by the United States military as a grave error on the part of the Administration. The Pentagon chiefs looked on in dismay, as COSCO's placement of companies throughout the American hemisphere became even more obvious, making it evident that the Beijing leadership had embarked on a most daring, strategic programme, one which would give its navy a distinct advantage over the United States in the future.

With the help of their new ally, Panama, COSCO acquired the Pacific port of Balboa and the Atlantic port of Cristobal, both of which flank the Panama Canal. The Charleston Daily Mail pointed out in an editorial, that COSCO's agreement to lease the ports through a Hong Kong-based subsidiary called Hutchinson Corporation was the product of some suspicious back-room negotiations:

"Panama peremptorily closed the bidding, secretly changed the rules, and simply awarded the contract to Hutchinson before the American or other firms could even know what was happening." The twenty-five year lease was to cost only twenty three million dollars a year, but the agreements granted a two-year waiver of labor laws, and veto rights over the use of abutting properties. It was also pointed out that the Hutchinson lawyer of that time, was also the head of the port authority that awarded the contract.

A notorious arms dealer was named as the employer of record for the three COSCO deals, and was observed, along with James Salima, visiting the White House for a morning coffee session with the incumbent American President.

Chapter 8

The Palace at work

The Indonesian President sat motionless listening to his Chief of Army Staff's weekly report. These sessions had always been conducted in the privacy of the President's family home, because he had never felt comfortable holding such discussions in the official residence. Besides, the meetings were always informal, and he believed that his senior officers appreciated the gesture of being received into the *Bapak's* private domain.

'*And I feel that his elevation to that position would satisfy Sumantri,*' the General said, then added with an insincere smile, '*at least, for the time being.*' The President knew precisely what General Prabowo meant, acknowledging that the competent Major General under discussion was overly ambitious, and should be closely watched in the future.

Power changed hands in Indonesia only through violence. The President knew that there were those who jealously coveted his powerful position, and that he must, as his predecessor had done before him, diligently guard against those who remained in the shadows, waiting for their own opportunity to seize control. He thought about the senior command shuffle under discussion. Prabowo had been at his side when he had assumed the mantel of President, and had his trust. Besides, they were related through marriage, and this additional bond worked to their mutual advantage.

'*What are we going to do with Arifin?*' The President asked, knowing how Prabowo felt about this man. Very few of his Cabinet were not Moslem, and he wished to prevent the growing number of Christian officers from achieving too much influence within the military. There had already been difficulties with the *Batak*

Christians in Sumatra, and that perpetual sore which he had inherited, *Timor Timur*, had provided non-Moslems in the eastern archipelago with a forum to debate their own sectarian issues.

'He is well suited for the Eastern Commander's position, but I am uneasy with that thought. If we place him anywhere else at this time, we are going to ruffle quite a number of feathers.' Prabowo knew this only too well, as he had spent weeks considering how best to reshuffle his senior command posts to reflect the strengthening of the President's, rather than his own, position. Prabowo was sensitive to the many criticisms of his leadership style, and guarded against providing too many opportunities to those who accused him of supporting cronyism within *ABRI*, the Indonesian Military. He believed that General Arifin would be a danger to their power base east of Bali, and should not be appointed to any position which might strengthen non-Muslim support.

'Why not just retire the man and send him overseas somewhere?' the President proposed. The suggested solution had often been employed in the past during other presidencies, permitting the country's leadership to dislodge powerful officers and remove them from the country by appointing them as ambassadors. Prabowo smiled. He had hoped that the *Bapak* might make this recommendation. It would be better if his leader thought of this solution as his own idea.

'That would remove the problem,' he answered, relieved that one of his own supporters would now not be dislodged by Arifin's continuing presence. The President nodded. Although he accepted the necessity of these changes, he was never at ease with the constant reshuffling of senior officers. These actions might look like indecisiveness on his part. He knew that he had yet to develop the leadership skills of Soeharto, or even those of the master orator, Soekarno, and that he had to be seen as decisive if he was ever to be accepted by the Indonesian people.

The President had been angered during those weeks of national unrest when he had been branded by the international press as a colourless and brutal leader, who was obviously determined to continue the authoritarian style of his predecessors. The President believed that he had to demonstrate, not just to the Indonesian people but the entire world, that he would not tolerate the lawless behaviour his country had been subjected to by obvious, subversive elements. He could not understand why foreign governments failed to identify the need for censorship in a country which lived precariously, with violence smouldering just below the surface. As a military commander, he had witnessed such violence in the capital. He had seen the streets erupt and hundreds perish during the riots fuelled by irresponsible vested interests groups.

The President and General Prabowo completed their discussions and the Chief of Staff took his leave, satisfied that his own powerbase had not been overly eroded. The *Bapak's* insistence that he move several of his stronger supporters into positions relatively distant from the centre of things might, he decided, bring more stability to the outlying provinces. *ABRI* had been embarrassed at its apparent inability to suppress civilian unrest in the outlying areas of Kalimantan, Irian, and Timor Timur.

Prabowo had been unable to identify the middle ground when considering the dilemma his powerful forces often faced, particularly when confronted with waging war on such minority civilian populations. He was all too conscious of world opinion in relation to the recent uprisings, and the response of his own people when so many had died during the lead-up to the last Presidential elections. Prabowo knew he was not alone in the belief that Indonesia could easily fragment into a number of smaller archipelago states, given the right set of circumstances, and he was determined to prevent such a situation from ever developing.

* * * * * *

Had the President been party to Prabowo's thoughts, he would have concurred. As a Javanese, he understood the necessity for his race maintaining rule over the other ethnic groups, and their resource rich territories. His small island of Java suffocated under the weight of more than one hundred million people, most of whom were peasants. He had attempted to rejuvenate the transmigration schemes, offering Javanese farmers fertile land and financial support on the other islands, encouraging them to move into the lesser populated areas of Kalimantan and East Indonesia. But, as his predecessor had discovered, the task was near impossible. The simple farmers would remain in their new surroundings only long enough to spend whatever they had been given, before returning to their over-populated homeland. And then there was China.

The President firmly believed that his country's Achilles heel lay in its inability to protect itself from China. He knew that his generals all concurred, that the Chinese would remain the major threat to their country's future.

As he sat considering his Presidency, the *Bapak's* thoughts turned to his family, and the image of his eldest son crossed his mind, causing him to frown. Although immensely proud of his children's achievements, he was not indifferent to the problems associated with the growing wealth his family enjoyed. He believed that many of the aspersions which had been cast were the result of rival jealousies only, and he was often bewildered by the accusatory positions taken by others who had also benefited from Indonesia's growth.

His son's most recent moves to become involved in the distribution of grain from rice field to store were, in the President's mind, highly commendable. He had listened to his son's proposal and agreed that, as rice was indeed the country's principle staple food commodity, its availability and price, should be ensured. The existing co-operative arrangement was not, his son had argued, competitive, nor was it sufficiently sophisticated to meet the requirements of efficient distribution for the twenty-first century. The President had agreed that his son should proceed to establish a monopoly over all rice production in the country, thereby guaranteeing both farmers and consumers undisrupted supply.

At first, he had been concerned that the price the new monopoly would pay the rice farmers was too low; but when his son had explained how the venture would work, the President was satisfied that the interests of all would be well served by implementing the monopoly. The retail price of grain would be raised and fixed; the wholesale floor price from the monopoly to store would increase marginally, to cover his son's establishment costs and overheads. The *Bapak* clearly understood the necessity for this and approved the higher price to the consumers. After all, he knew that only a small percentage of his people paid income tax, and the idea of this new distribution system, as an indirect means of extracting payment in lieu of a sales tax, appealed to the President.

Apart from the obvious, the other major problem with his son's venture had been in relation to the finance he required to establish the network associated with the monopoly. There had been open criticism of the project, and the President was personally offended by the suggestion that his son had been given the monopoly licence because of his relationship to the Palace. The President had instructed the Governor of the Central Bank to remove the chief executive of the government bank responsible for the scurrilous remark. The senior executive's replacement had willingly arranged for the necessary project funding, and once confirmation that the two billion dollars had been received, the new bank president's wife was appointed to the monopoly venture's expanded board. Now, it seemed, the project was experiencing difficulties again, and his son required additional funding to sustain the complicated and ambitious operation.

As he considered whom best to approach amongst his closest associates to resolve this problem, the *Bapak* knew that only the Salima Group would have the financial capacity to extricate his son from the difficulties he faced. He made a mental note to have someone summon the *totok* to discuss his son's predicament.

While the President sat deep in thought, he showed no signs that he was even aware of the constant flow of servants and family as they passed close by to his ornately carved chair, continuously checking that he was not in need of anything. Out the corner of one eye, the *Bapak* sighted his second daughter. Immediately images of her mother and the wonderful family she had given him sprang to his mind. He was particularly proud of his daughter's recent move into the world of commerce. Previously, she had been a quiet girl, living in the shadow of the other, more exuberant children. Then she married the young army officer, Sujono.

The President had been pleased with his daughter's choice, and even more pleased that his son-in-law had been promoted so rapidly over his peers. He recalled how quickly his daughter had changed, developing the confidence to venture into business as her older brothers had done. The *Bapak* willingly approved her project to place tolls on all major highways between Jakarta and Bali, and had wondered why it had not been introduced before, remembering how in past years, President Soeharto's daughter had been instrumental in introducing such measures on the capital's protocol roads.

An aide entered and stood some metres from the President,

waiting patiently until noticed. When the *Bapak* looked up and saw the Colonel standing there, he remembered it was time for his next visitor.

'Bapak,' the officer spoke softly, while standing rigidly to attention, *'Pak Seda has arrived.'* The President nodded, and the aide disappeared to his station in the adjacent room. There he would wait until summoned, knowing that it would be more than his life was worth to be caught eavesdropping on the President, and the powerful General Seda. Moments later, the tall Timorese entered, held both hands together in supplicatory manner, and bowed his head slightly in the leader's direction.

'Selamat siang,' Seda offered, entering and taking the seat across from the President, as he had on so many other occasions.

'Well, Seda,' the President began, always pleased to see this man, *'what do we have today?'* Seda smiled, prepared to move directly to the subject of their meeting. He knew that the news he had brought could only further consolidate his relationship with the Palace, and his position as the future Vice President. Choosing him would alleviate some of the problems with which the President was faced. Seda understood that a number of hopefuls had already commenced lobbying for the position which would become vacant during the President's current term in office. As Vice President, and as a Timorese, he would be perceived as offering no threat to the incumbent leader. His selection would, Seda realized, offer the President some opportunity to proceed through his term without being troubled by an ambitious deputy watching over his shoulder. Seda believed that he would be given the position, especially now, once he had delivered what the President wanted most.

'The Japanese have agreed.' Seda waited, observing the President's initial surprise, then the wide grin which spread across his leader's face. Seda had returned from Tokyo the evening before, and had deliberately delayed informing the *Bapak* until he could do so in person. The President continued to beam, extremely pleased with the news.

'You have done well, Seda,' he said, nodding at his guest, *'to tell you the truth, I did not believe that they would be interested.'* Seda smiled at the compliment.

'They have agreed to support the venture as requested. It would seem that they had been thinking along similar lines, and have committed

themselves unreservedly to the project.'

'*And funding?*' the President asked, a little impatiently as his eagerness took control. He watched the other man's eyes as he spoke. Seda had developed considerable support from both the military and civilian sectors. He had become a wealthy and influential ally to the Palace, and had been personally responsible for steering a considerable number of profitable opportunities towards the First Family's business interests. The *Bapak* trusted Seda above all others, even General Prabowo.

He had learned that Seda's judgement in the past had been exceptional, and he had grown to depend heavily on the retired general's advice. He believed that Seda was basically apolitical, and not ambitious for power. The man's wealth had attracted considerable comment, but this had not unduly concerned the President, as he was pleased that at least one of the *pribumi*, even though Seda was not Javanese, had been as successful as he.

'*The Japanese will fund the entire project,*' Nathan Seda further revealed, disguising his own satisfaction at the remarkable success he had achieved. The President pondered this information, his face showing some concern.

'*When will they make their announcement?*' he asked.

'*We discussed this at some length, and they have agreed not to do so until you have made yours,*' he replied. The President seemed pleased with this, and nodded happily again.

'*And the other matter they had proposed earlier?*' the Indonesian leader asked, dropping his voice to a conspiratorial level. It was Seda's turn to nod his head, affirming that the Japanese had agreed.

'*They have asked that I return over the next months for further discussions but, in principle, it seems that we will proceed. The Japanese wish to inspect the existing facilities in Bandung. They might wish to establish something elsewhere, something more discreet.*' The President understood this reasoning and smiled again at his guest.

'*How long would it be before completion?*' he asked. Seda looked at the *Bapak*, having anticipated this question. Very few understood that such a project took years of research and development before coming to fruition.

'*The first phase will take approximately five years,*' he said, watching the President's eyebrows move together as he started to frown. '*The Japanese may be able to run both projects concurrently and, if this is possible, then both might be realized within that period. If not, then we should expect to add anything up to an additional three years for the second phase of development.'* The President had already commenced calculating what this would mean to him, as Seda spoke. The constitution had been altered at the end of Soeharto's rule, restricting future Presidential rule to two terms, each of five years. He thought quickly, wondering how he could manipulate this ruling, as it would be necessary to do so if he was to provide continuity to the project as Head of State. The time he had spent as Acting President would not be considered as part of his term.

Seda sat quietly, confident that he knew precisely what was flowing through the other man's mind. It would make little difference to his own strategies.

'Then we should encourage the Japanese to move quickly,' the President said. He wished it had been possible to have brought others into the discussions, even the powerful Lim, but knew that secrecy was of the utmost importance to the realization of this project. He was in Seda's hands, he knew, and was momentarily beset by doubt about the powerful position his friend now occupied. He had often wondered whether Seda was simply driven by greed, or whether his aspirations lay in other directions. During the months they had discussed the proposed project, not once had Seda indicated any ulterior motive. He dismissed his concerns.

The President knew that there would be millions to be earned from the implementation of the projects, and did not deny his friend's right to his share of these funds. They had openly discussed the First Family's involvement. The *Bapak's* family companies were to be involved in all financial aspects of the project's execution, with the exception of those areas controlled directly by the Japanese. After all, they had laughed at the time, it *was* their money.

The President agreed with Seda that Indonesia's most recent military acquisitions would not protect the country from China's aggression. Both had also accepted that Beijing would eventually need to cross its borders to feed its incredible growth. *ALRI*, the Indonesian Navy, would be no match for China's fleet. His own government's military strategy had been based on the premise that China would, eventually, become their enemy. China's intercontinental ballistic missiles were of major concern.

The Indonesian Army was inadequately equipped to oppose

any such attack, and he was determined to remedy this situation. He only hoped that his decision to proceed with the Japanese had not come too late. In the future, once his army had acquired the capacity to respond to any ICBM threat, the Indonesian people would most definitely demonstrate to their northern neighbour, that they would strike back, if provoked.

The President's own military background provided him with the ability to understand such strategies. He had studied the Chinese intercontinental ballistic missile capability and, although they had only ten of any significance, his main concern had been that the Chinese had the capacity to arm these missiles with nuclear warheads, whereas the proposed Indonesian weapons would only have conventional strike capability. He had agreed to enter into the joint development of the Japanese rocket with the premise in mind, that once Indonesia had the capacity to produce such a delivery system, the real significance would be in its ability to despatch missiles armed with nuclear warheads. This threat, alone, might act as a deterrent to China, and any other ambitious neighbouring country which viewed Indonesia as an easy target.

The President appreciated how well Seda had conducted the delicate negotiations with the Japanese. He was convinced that Japan would consider their participation in the construction and operation of the new nuclear plants, as a safeguard against Indonesia's successfully secreting surplus plutonium from the operating nuclear plants, and he was prepared to permit the Japanese to continue under this allusion. There was little doubt in his mind that the Japanese would never have considered jointly developing such a delivery system if they had believed this could, at some later date, be used by the Indonesians to deliver nuclear warheads.

The President strongly supported his country's military growth, particularly in view of China's three million strong armed forces. His generals continuously reminded the Press that their overpopulated neighbour boasted more than fifteen hundred tanks and one hundred submarines of which, at least two were nuclear powered SSBN's, armed with ballistic missiles. Indonesia's Navy was no match for China's sixty destroyers and frigates, let alone its combined naval and air combat fleet of five thousand aircraft.

The President knew that it would be most unlikely that any of the other ASEAN nations would be in a position to offer resistance against a Chinese attack, placing an even greater burden on Indonesia. The President concluded that, inevitably, Indonesia would be expected to provide the necessary military umbrella to protect the ten nation association against any future Chinese aggression.

And there were other considerations which plagued the President. His country's infrastructure had degenerated as a result of fewer investments in this unprofitable area. Each year, five million new births added to the conundrum, and the national debt spiralled to alarming levels. The President realized that he would have no choice but to address these problems, and turned to the wealthier investment houses but, disappointingly, with the exception of the Salima Group, his appeals had been all but shunned. The Indonesian leader accepted that he was fortunate to have the ongoing support of the Sino-Indonesian billionaire, who had become one of Asia's wealthiest tycoons and had been directly connected with the earlier First Family.

By comparison, Seda, although wealthy, was nowhere near the *totok's* league. There were others who had also fared well from generous Palace relationships but, unfortunately for his nation's economy, most of these entrepreneurs had milked the country, then transferred their capital overseas. He looked at the man to whom he had given more power than any other, and smiled warmly. He felt he could trust this man.

'*Seda,*' he said, almost affectionately, '*enough of this, let's eat,*' with which he rose and held his arm out to his friend, and steered him into an adjoining room where several of the President's older children were seated. They recognised Seda immediately, and remained just long enough not to appear impolite, before departing to leave their father alone with his guest.

* * * * * *

That night, as Seda lay quietly, he made a mental note that he should spend more time consolidating his relationships with the Salima Group. Over the years, he had enjoyed very few opportunities to exploit the powerful *kongsi*'s hold on the Palace, and its First Family. Now, considering what had transpired with the Japanese, Seda knew that this would have to change. His star would only continue its ascent if he could devise a means to penetrate the Salima fortress, and rip the guts from those inside. For Seda was convinced, that as long as those who controlled the powerful *kongsi* continued to tighten their grip over the President, so too would his own power diminish. He *had* to find a way.

* * * * * *

Timor-Timur

'This is Leader One, on final run, do you copy?'

'Leader One, copy,' came the reply. Major Sumodjo armed the cannons and checked his altitude. It had been tricky flying. They had to tear down the valleys between the jagged mountain peaks avoiding the ground fire from the villages and then drop through the cloud at incredible speed to have any hope of identifying target areas. They hadn't taught them *that* during his training in the States.

Sumodjo belonged to 1 Squadron, based in East Java. He and his fellow pilots had been flying missions over Timor ever since the invasion had commenced, back in the days when the ageing Broncos had still belonged to 3 Squadron, and had been based in Iswahyudi, in Central Java. Their counter-insurgency squadron had been transferred back in 1989, clearing the way for the F-16s arrival.

He felt the sudden turbulence as the aircraft shuddered momentarily. He knew it would be useless looking back, as his wingman would most probably be exactly where he shouldn't be, and that would worry him even more than the rapidly approaching mountainside which had been determined as the day's target.

The American manufactured OV-10F Bronco ceased shuddering as it fell into line with the target area. All the pilot could see ahead was just more jungle. And cloud, dangerous cloud, blanketing the mountain. The crew ignored the combination laser rangefinder and target illuminator, a recently acquired modification used mainly for night targeting needs. This mission would be conducted, hopefully, with the target in full vision. Further back, an AURI Skyhawk followed, prepared to support the attack. Then, without further warning, they broke through the low cloud, sighting the target directly ahead. He didn't hesitate, squeezing the red release button at the precise moment the first village shack came into view. Bullets ripped through the air with incredible velocity during the four seconds window and, at the end of his run, the pilot released part of his load of incendiary bombs before pulling away sharply. Seconds later, the Skyhawk followed through, striking the target area with rockets. The young Javanese pilot's blood drained from his face as he pulled the powerful jet up suddenly, powering away from the hillside before any ground-fire could damage his aircraft.

The thunderous roar of jet engines was barely heard by the people below before their primitive village erupted under the impact of bombs and rocket fire. In those brief seconds, as screams were savagely cut off in mid-cry, and bodies were charred with the first fireball to rip through their compound, most of the peasants died.

There were less than five men living in the small cluster of huts, most of whom were older members of the mountain enclave. At the time the pilots delivered their deadly gifts, more than fifty women and children had been happily preparing their one meal for that day. Only two survived the unwarranted and senseless attack. One, a child of three who later died from her burns, and the other, one Xanana Soares, the self-proclaimed leader of the Revolutionary Front for an Independent Timor, who had been hiding in the remote village.

Chapter 9

General Seda and
Lim Swee Giok

Seda sat opposite Lim Swee Giok and nodded politely. Privately he was thinking that the man before him did not deserve either the power or the wealth he had amassed in so few years. Both men had built incredible fortunes in their time, although the Salima Group's wealth dwarfed even Seda's considerable assets.

'*Pak Lim,*' the former general continued, answering the Chinese *totok's* question, '*as Chairman of PEPELIN I would be in a position to guarantee that the tender decisions will favour the Salima Group. The President has already discussed this with me, and at great length. He has left it up to me as to how we provide for the First Family's interests, but I'm sure that you will have no difficulty in accommodating their needs.*' Lim knew exactly what this would be. There had not been one major contract signed over the past ten years which had not allowed for the customary ten percent payable as dues to the Palace.

What worried Lim most was the suggestion that he increase this allowance to fifteen percent, as Seda had insisted that his own consideration be calculated separately to the President's children's share.

The billionaire knew that the collective project could not absorb such obvious padding, anticipating his bankers' response, and their likely insistence that he place even more of his own capital into the new company structures which, if he could believe Seda, would undoubtedly win the tenders. He was sick of their greed. For years he had worked to build his empire, and along the way he had created many millionaires amongst the bureaucrats, military officers, and even bankers. They had stuck to his side like leeches, sucking profits from his lucrative ventures.

'*Fifteen per cent is too much,*' he said, breaking into a coughing fit.

He had not been well, and believed that the problems associated with the formation of his new energy company had contributed towards his condition. Chinese medicines and herbs had not seemed to have much effect anymore. Lim scowled, then remembered that the man before him had the President's ear, and that he should be careful when dealing with him. Lim had heard many of the stories circulating overseas as to the rewards that Seda's clandestine activities might have reaped in the past. He did not like the Timorese, but knew that there was little he could do but negotiate with him.

'Then perhaps there is another way we might resolve the problem of percentages,' Seda suggested. Lim looked at the man who might become the country's next Vice President. He knew that the rumours about him were more than idle gossip. The President had hinted directly to him during an earlier visit to the Palace that Seda was being considered. Lim knew that he now had to be careful about how he handled the delicate negotiations concerning what his circle referred to as *pungli* payments.

The Chinese abhorred the use of the word *korupsi*, as they did not consider such payments as corrupt. Instead, they had coined their own, softer terminology for these demands, without which, Lim was painfully aware, the Salima Group would never have acquired such immense wealth. It seemed that the man sitting across from him had thought his position through quite thoroughly, anticipating his reaction to the excessive *pungli* request.

'What do you have in mind?' Lim asked, struggling with another attack of coughing. Seda waited until the older man had ceased, before continuing.

'The Palace position cannot be negotiated, Pak Lim. However, I would be agreeable to having my own consideration offset against a position in the company.' Lim's surprise was evident. There had been no warning that Seda would attempt to position himself as a shareholder in the energy *kongsi*. Lim's mind raced quickly. He could not afford to have the man offside, but he also understood the inherent dangers associated with permitting an outsider access to such a substantial shareholding in his family's activities.

'That would be difficult to arrange,' Lim lied. He could not afford to have Seda so close to the centre of power. *'The bankers would be the problem,'* he added, but both men knew this not to be true. Seda

guessed that the Chinese entrepreneur had arranged his financing in much the same way as he dealt with government officials. Somewhere along the line, Seda believed Lim would have had to accommodate the bankers as well. It was common knowledge that the Asia Pacific Commercial Bank was controlled by the Salima family, and would be appointed as the major financier for the energy projects. Seda decided to try another tack.

'What if payment was made in two instalments,' he suggested, 'half when the tenders have been announced, and the balance when the first plant is commissioned?' Lim thought about this too, still unhappy with the sizeable payment he would have to find for both the President's family and Seda. He looked at the PEPELIN Chairman, and wondered if he could negotiate the man down.

'If we could make arrangements within the tender documents so that the contract values may be re-negotiated once construction has commenced, then I think the Salima Group could probably agree to a total of twelve percent.' Seda resisted the smile hiding behind his mask of politeness. He was prepared to accept the offer, knowing that he could improve his own position at a later date.

'Pak Lim, my two per cent would need to be paid up front,' he said, satisfied for the time being. Lim looked at Seda and nodded. He would build the commissions into the overall project cost knowing that, even before they commenced construction, the budget over-run would start at twelve per cent, and this man would be in a position to approve the additional costs to the government. He was not in any way concerned with the morality of how business was conducted in Indonesia. As far as he could recall, not one of the government contracts awarded since Soekarno was toppled in 1966 had been commenced without some consideration being made to the First Family and their Palace sycophants. As the projects grew in size, and the President's children reached adulthood, so too did the scale of the consultancy fees demanded.

Lim recalled when the contract for the new international airport had been awarded, and the former President's son pocketed forty million dollars for brokering the deal on behalf of the foreign contractor. But Lim knew that the *Rama* programme was very different to those other projects, and not just because of the enormous capital required to complete the plants. The investors would have to wait a minimum of five to six years before their huge investment would enjoy its first cash-flow. He clearly understood the risks in committing to the multi-billion dollar project.

Lim had decided that this would be his finest, and last, major investment in the country. He was growing older quickly, it seemed, and he planned not to spend all of his remaining years in Indonesia. Once the plants were operational, he would sell the entire structure, passing the accumulated debt to the very people who would enjoy the power generated by the *Rama* Nuclear Power Plants. The bankers would accept the Indonesian Central Bank's guarantee which Lim would extract with Presidential pressure. He knew that this would, in the future, require further payments to whoever may be in power at the time. Lim looked across at Seda, knowing it would not be him. He also accepted that it was pointless attempting to speculate about who might lead the country once the current leader had completed his two terms in office. Lim had been in Indonesia long enough to appreciate that whoever this might be, the contender's arrival on the political stage would be accompanied by the same mystique and shadowy imagery that the Indonesian people associated with *Wayang* performances.

Seda and Lim finished their discussions and parted company, each satisfied that they had done about as well for themselves as circumstances would permit. The PEPELIN Chairman visited the President, and reported most of what had transpired during his meeting with Lim.

The following week, several members of the First Family flew to Singapore and Switzerland, making arrangements with their bankers to prepare for the first *pungli* instalment from the Salima Group of companies. The Swiss bankers bowed and scraped in typical subservient manner, as the familiar faces sat before them and explained how much they expected to be deposited into their accounts. Accustomed as they were to substantial inter-bank transfers, even they were impressed when they discovered that the first transfers would exceed half of one billion dollars. And on the day the winning tenders were announced, Seda received Lim's confirmation that a similar amount had been transferred into his account, as agreed.

* * * * * *

JAKARTA

United States of America

Michael Bradshaw strolled from the tennis courts satisfied that he had acquitted himself reasonably well against his singles opponent. His doubles partner reappeared, and walked across the immaculately manicured lawn towards him. As she approached, he watched her long, purposeful stride, and well-tanned legs and he wondered what such a magnificent creature could possibly see in him.

'Great game, Michael,' she said, leaning forward to peck him on the cheek.

'That's for winning,' Ratna said, kissing him again, as she stretched, 'and that's for later,' she added, leaning closer and kissing him full on the mouth for all to see.

'Hmmn' he murmured, enjoying the softness her mouth offered. Michael then reached out to pull her closer, but Ratna resisted, pushing him back at arm's length.

'God,' she exclaimed, mock surprise on her face, 'take a shower!' Michael laughed and spun her around with a casual movement, then tapped her lightly on the bottom as they walked together towards the club house. Michael left Ratna with friends while he showered and changed. When he rejoined the group, he poured himself a long iced tea, then lay back in a deck chair, enjoying the early Spring sun.

He listened to the idle chatter, joining in whenever he felt he had some contribution to make, laughing as Ratna recounted some anecdote from life in far away Indonesia. Michael peered at Ratna through one eye, squinting in the glare, and saw that she had been observing him. He returned her smile, then lay back again, delighting in the warm sun on his skin. It was their last day together, and Michael had not objected to spending the time at the country club, knowing that there would be little opportunity to relax once he returned to Washington.

Ratna Sari continued to observe Michael as he lay outstretched, admiring his long, slim body and handsome features. She wondered how their relationship would fare once they had been separated again; she was not too keen on letting him go, alone. Ratna had indicated that she was willing to accompany him and left it at that; she was unsure what would happen if she pushed him too quickly, accepting that Michael needed at least a month to settle in to his new position, without her. Ratna understood that it might even be longer, knowing his penchant for forgetting all else once he became engrossed in his work. She had hoped that their time together in the palatial home would tempt Michael into taking that one last step, of asking her to marry him. The setting had been perfect; with the exception of the two permanent servants, the house was unoccupied and Ratna had shown that she could manage the domestic arrangements quite satisfactorily, dismissing the servants in spite of their protestations, preparing all of their meals by herself.

But Michael had seemed to be too preoccupied with his new challenge, and ignored the less than subtle hints thrown constantly his way. The possibility that he might not really love her challenged Ratna's confidence, and threatened to spoil their remaining moments together.

* * * * * *

They had first met at college. She had noticed the tall, athletic figure working its way around the track at a time when most other students had not even risen for the day. Ratna had taken to *tai chi*, and carried out her exercises alone, in the early morning hours so as to avoid the inquisitive glances of others. She had watched Michael pound his way around the deserted track and wondered who the solitary runner might be.

On another occasion, she recognized Michael playing tennis, and had stood admiring his game. It was a sport which had captivated Ratna since she had first observed it in Jakarta. It was obvious from his play that this player had followed the game for some years. She watched as Michael easily dispensed with his unfortunate opponent. When he left the court, Ratna moved directly into his field of vision, in order to attract his attention.

Michael collected his shoulder bag and glanced over at the attractive girl he had observed watching the game. He assumed she was one of the thousands of undergraduates attending college there, and turned his attention to the small group of friends who had been waiting for him to finish play. Ratna watched him join the others overlooking the courts, then walked over to where he stood and introduced herself, complimenting Michael on his game. Ratna had stood close to Michael, sending signals that were embarrassingly obvious to Michael and his friends. He was flattered; the girl's soft brown aquiline features were almost aristocratic, and her tall, slim body could have belonged to a model. When she had moved even closer, he could smell her exotic perfume.

'Hope you're available for coaching,' she said, flirting shamelessly. The other women in the group smiled at each other. Michael had that effect on most women, especially admiring undergraduates.

'Sure,' Michael grinned, deciding to play along, winking at the others, 'but I am expensive,' he had joked.

'Don't you think I could afford you?' she continued the banter, causing one of the older ladies present to cough as she suppressed a laugh. Michael gave her his best smile.

'Well, we could always find out,' he said, delighted with her attention. His friends became impatient to leave and he knew they would not be impressed should he ask her to join them. So, determined not to lose contact with the beautiful girl, he wrote down her number, promising to ring. That weekend, he had phoned and was delighted that she remembered their brief encounter. They agreed to meet. When she had insisted on picking him up from his friend's apartment, Michael had whistled when he saw the racing red Lamborghini she was driving, and regretted inferring that she was an impoverished student at their first meeting.

'Well,' he said, climbing into the passenger seat, 'I'm impressed.' Ratna laughed softly as she adjusted her sunglasses and patted him on the knee.

'Don't be,' she said, lightly, 'everyone who is anyone has one just like this in Jakarta.' Ratna went on to explain that these cars had become just another status symbol in Indonesia. When ownership of the prestige car manufacturer had passed to the Soeharto children, it had become mandatory for the rich and famous in her country to have at least one of the fabulous cars in their garages, somewhere, as a token of their support. He had barely had time to buckle-up when Ratna drove her foot to the floor, throwing the Lamborghini forward to the sound of screaming tyres.

Ratna had driven to impress, causing Michael to squirm as she pushed the needle dangerously past established speed limits. He had sat, white faced, but determined not to show his concern. When they finally arrived at the Salima residence, Michael cocked one eyebrow questioningly. Ratna enjoyed his surprise at the extent of the grounds and the magnificent residence which stood, floodlit, at the end of a long, tree-lined driveway.

'Yours?' he had asked, standing before the tall white columns and marble steps which led up to the expansive entrance.

'Aunty's,' she replied, grabbing him by the arm and running excitedly up the steps. Michael was not surprised to discover that the mansion was staffed. Two Indonesian women appeared and welcomed him as Ratna dragged him through the main reception, and through the mansion into the back garden. She laughed, childishly, pleased with the continued surprise she was causing as they came upon the delightful setting. It was as if the home had been built around an amphitheatre of natural rocks and cascading waterfalls. Incredible volumes of water poured from all around one end of the tropical garden, plummeting down through rocks until spilling over a ledge, behind which he could see the back wall of a flood-lit cave.

The grotto effect was stunning, and Michael walked slowly down the steps which led to the perfectly contoured swimming pool, as if in a dream. He stopped and turned, embarrassed, realising that he had left Ratna behind.

'Impressive, huh?' she said, skipping down the steps, two at a time. Michael watched as she removed the scarf which had been tied over her hair, and knotted it casually around the nearby railing. The moonlight caught her hair and she smiled at him again. Michael felt something warm stir inside. She was undoubtedly one of the most beautiful women he had ever seen, and he experienced a moment of uncertainty. The tantalising fragrance of her presence and the idyllic setting all caused him to shake his head in admiration.

'It's magnificent, Ratna,' was all he could say. One of the servants appeared at the top of the steps and said something totally alien to Michael's ears. He watched as Ratna offered confident instructions to the older woman then turned, pulling him to his feet.

'Swim!' she urged, pulling with great difficulty as he pretended resistance, permitting his weight to hold her slender arms powerless. 'Swim!' she said again, playfully, pretending to pout. Michael rose and followed her down to the water's edge. He stood there, hands resting in his side pockets, taking in the breathtaking setting. 'Swim!' she called once more, giggling childishly. He turned in time to catch Ratna launch herself into the pool. Michael glanced quickly to see if the servants had seen her remove her clothes and plunge into the water. Then he wondered who else might be looking down upon them from the rows of what appeared to be bedroom windows, which ran the length of the building along the second floor.

'Come in, Michael,' he heard her call, turning back just as she jumped playfully into the air revealing her breasts for him to see. He hesitated.

'What the hell,' he muttered to no one in particular as he stripped, before throwing himself into the pool quickly. When he came to the surface she was already at his side, and threw her arms around his neck, her legs turning around his waist. He watched as Ratna dipped her head forward, then quickly flicked it back, to remove the excess water on her face. Then she leaned forward and kissed him lustfully, driving her tongue deep into his mouth.

As the warmth of her kiss passed through his body Michael felt his senses react, and he broke away, embarrassed that they might be observed. Ratna flung her arms wildly as she sunk unexpectedly. She kicked against the bottom of the pool, rising back to the surface, coughing from water she had swallowed. Michael reached forward to help, but she turned and swam away, across the pool, under the waterfall and into the grotto. He knew he had to follow, concerned that she might be upset. With several powerful strokes, he too entered the man-made cave, where he found her smiling. Waiting.

Michael knew it was not necessary to speak. He moved to her and they embraced, this time his own tongue searching for hers. He felt her hand grasp him firmly and guide him towards her, as she moved firmly against his body and raised her thighs. He pulled her closer, savagely, and as he entered the warmth of her body Ratna's nails dug sharply into his back, the pain lost in the urgency of their coupling. They gripped each other fiercely, kissing, holding each other tightly, their movements gathering momentum, as they raced towards the prize which awaited them both.

Michael responded to her sensual movements, and he could

sense that she was approaching climax as her rhythm changed, driving him even harder as their bodies slapped together in the waist deep water. Suddenly, as she buried her nails even further into his back, Ratna cried out, and his knees weakened as the warm urgent flow left his body in short, frenzied, convulsions. Michael heard himself cry out also, and he groped for support as she drove her teeth deep into his right shoulder. And then, finally, they were spent, and they kissed.

For a long moment, he held her tightly, feeling a reckless passionate abandonment of caution. She raised her head and looked into his eyes, then kissed him with a tenderness he had not thought possible. Michael moved her body to the side, then placed his hands under her, to keep her afloat. Then he bent down and kissed her gently on each of her firm, pink nipples, causing her to shudder. As minutes ticked by and they began to feel the cold, Michael placed his hand around her waist, and led Ratna back through the waterfall and into the evening's soft moonlight.

* * * * * *

As they swam back across the pool, Michael saw, with some surprise, that the servants had placed two chairs and a table close to where he had stripped. Their clothes had been neatly placed on the chairs, and he could see that they had left towels and gowns for them to wear. In the centre of the table was a silver ice bucket, and what looked like champagne.

When Michael saw this, he stopped, looked at Ratna, and started laughing. She had seduced him! He climbed out of the pool and reached for her extended hands, pulling her after him. No longer concerned with the servants whom he guessed were still watching, they towelled each other, then dressed in the robes and sat at the table smiling at each other while Michael poured from the bottle of Dom Perignon. As soon as the lovers had settled down to sipping champagne, and basking in the afterglow of their sexual tryst, the servants carried dinner down from the terrace, and served the traditional dishes in silence.

Michael was concerned from their demeanour that he might have offended the two women. When they had finished serving the meal and quietly removed the dishes, he smiled broadly and

JAKARTA

thanked them both for the delightful meal. Immediately, they broke out in giggles and hurried away. Later, with the memory of their love-making still fresh in their minds, they lay alongside the pool, secure in each other's presence, listening to the evening sounds as the moon disappeared and darkness encroached upon the setting. Then they talked. Their conversation triggered childhood memories for both, as they recited tales and provided each other with personal glimpses into each others pasts. They lay quietly together, with but a few secrets remaining between them as each held back, just a little, reluctantly retaining some memories out of concern that the other might not understand. For Ratna, hers were of the most intimate nature. She knew that this was not the moment for her to purge herself of events which had led her to America. As for Michael, his recollections were far darker and more complicated than he could possibly reveal.

When the cool evening air failed to remind them of the hour, a polite cough from one of the doting servants encouraged them both to move inside. Michael followed his beautiful hostess up the stairs to her magnificent bedroom, where they shed their towels and showered, together. They were unable to resist each other's touch as the warm, pulsating jets washed over their bodies, and Michael carried Ratna, still covered with soap, into her bedroom. There, they made love again, kissing tenderly, at first, their hands stroking each other gently, softly, murmuring as their excitement grew, their passion arousing their deepest urges. They grasped frantically at each other, urged along the same sensual path which carried them both to the same sublime ending. Then, as their breathing returned to normal, Michael rolled to his side and released a long, deep, sigh.

Within minutes, Ratna and Michael had fallen asleep, the soft evening sounds lulling them as they slept, in full embrace, oblivious to the world outside.

* * * * * *

Early Californian sunshine settled softly around the pool as they sat quietly together, eating the splendid breakfast prepared by the still-giggling, and friendly servants. Together, Ratna and Michael remained beside the pool throughout the day, talking, laughing, reminiscing, and learning more of each others' secrets.

'You had to call him *the Colonel*?' she had asked, incredulously. Michael had just laughed. It was difficult to explain.

'He's really a great guy, Ratna,' he said, not really wanting to go too deeply into his past. Michael looked at her. She was so attractive, young, and vibrant sitting half-dressed before him. He accepted that he was besotted. He had never experienced such warmth before, yet a trickle of doubt challenged his feelings. 'The Colonel was more than just an officer in the Army. He was much more than that. Everywhere he went, you could just sense the respect others afforded the man.' He then fell silent for a few moments. Ratna understood that she should wait, as he seemed to be struggling with old wounds, or sad memories. When he looked up, and smiled, she could see that there was another world which occupied his mind, and knew from the expression on his face that he was not ready to share those thoughts.

'Tell me about your mother, Michael,' she asked. Immediately, Ratna noticed a change in Michael's demeanour. He leaned back, and laughed, and before he even spoke, she knew that he adored the woman.

'Well, she's still beautiful. At least to the Colonel and me,' he said. He explained that his mother had been widowed while he was still very young. As he talked, relating stories of his childhood in Australia, Ratna listened intently, sincerely interested in his early life, and how he had come to be in America. She sat quietly when he related how lonely he had felt when, as a young boy, his father had disappeared, apparently without trace.

Ratna sensed that he had tried to make light of it, but she could see the sadness in his eyes as he spoke of a childhood of uncertainty, occupied primarily by his mother, and an older woman he remembered as Grandma Muriel. There had obviously been considerable pain during his early life.

'What happened to your Grandmother, Michael, did you all leave her behind?'

'Not really,' he had answered, and again Ratna could see that he was saddened by the memory of the woman. 'Grandma Muriel was not related. The title was just a form of endearment. She was actually Murray's mother,' he had said, wistfully.

'Murray?' she asked, to induce him to continue talking to her.

She adored his voice, and the slight Australian accent which he still had.

'He was almost an uncle to me.' Ratna then noticed how animated Michael's face became. 'Christ!' he exclaimed, slapping his long, tanned legs with both hands. 'You should have seen this guy play. No matter how the club pro tried, he just continued to thrash the man.' Ratna now knew from whom Michael had learned to love tennis. She didn't mind; after all, she remembered, had he not been such a keen player, they might never have met.

'Where is he now?' she asked. She invited the answer, knowing that he was enjoying talking about the man. She suspected he might have been one of Michael's earlier role-models before the Colonel had come along.

'It might seem strange to hear,' he said, sadly, 'but I really have no idea.' This had been followed by another chasm of awkward silence, and Ratna left the table not knowing what else to do, and dived into the pool.

* * * * * *

Michael's presence had raised some of her own childhood memories of life in Indonesia, and she was not too sure that she wanted these to occupy her thoughts. Many of the images of her first years were vague. She empathised with Michael, as she too had not enjoyed the benefit of having a father around when she most desperately needed one. Her earliest, muddled recollections were those of her mother, Lani, and her mother's strong-willed sister, Aunt Ruswita.

As she recalled the two women who had both played dominating roles in her childhood and adolescence, she was reminded of how often they had seemed to be almost the one person. It was hard to think of a day when one or the other of these two women was not present.

Ratna remembered little of her early days at the *Ora Et Labora* school in Kebayoran Baru, Jakarta. The memories which had remained with her were only those of her teen years, when she attended the International School. As she remembered the years at the mixed foreign high school, Ratna inadvertently swallowed poolwater, and had a spluttering fit. Michael called out to her, but she waved back, signalling that she was fine. She leaned back once more and floated, moving her hands and legs slowly, enjoying the warm sunshine on her face. The memories flooded back, carrying her to a time when she was barely seventeen, and the first time a boy had touched her, there.

As Ratna relived those precious moments her thoughts drifted further afield to the day she had been caught, with Benny. She stopped swimming. The memory was one not worth recalling, she thought, bitterly, standing on tip-toe and running her hands across her wet face. Then she waded back to rejoin her handsome lover.

* * * * * *

Over dinner, Michael revealed how circumstances placed him at Berkeley, attending post graduate studies. Ratna learned how he had accompanied his mother and her husband, the Colonel, when his step-father had been posted to Washington. They had remained there for three years, he had explained, during which time his parents had become quite attached to living in America. At the end of his tour, the Colonel had taken early retirement when he was offered a position working as a technical consultant with the US Government. There had been no reason for them to return to Australia, and the family readily made the United States their new home. Michael disclosed, almost wistfully, that although he had taken US Citizenship he still considered himself Australian, suggesting that he might even return there one day.

As the rest of his story finally unfolded, she learned that Michael had completed his post graduate studies and was, at that time, taking a well-deserved break. When Ratna discovered that her campus tennis star had graduated *summa cum laude* in Physics more than ten years before, and had gone on to complete his PhD, she teased him. She had difficulty visualising the handsome athlete as a physicist and told him so. They laughed at her perception that all scientists looked like Einstein and were a little erratic in behaviour.

He joked about their age difference, suggesting that he was already an old man. She felt that he was fishing for a response, and Ratna had coyly explained that, as an Asian woman, she preferred mature men. Michael was surprised to discover that the beautiful creature who had been his that day was, in fact, some years older than he would have guessed. She explained that her late start at college had been her aunt's idea. Ratna did not elaborate, mentioning only that she lived in her aunt's household, and that it was in Jakarta. Michael listened, sensing that she had considerably more to tell. Ratna became quiet, as if deep in thought, then suddenly turned the conversation back to him.

Ratna learned a great deal about Michael during their afternoon, his early days in Melbourne and how his mother had raised him alone, after his father had died. She realized that she had inadvertently struck a nerve when she asked what had happened to his father, as Michael became solemn, and directed their conversation away from what was obviously still a sensitive memory. However, when she explained that her own father had died while she was still young, this seemed to draw them closer.

* * * * * *

Towards the end of that week, Ratna was convinced that she was in love. When she expressed her feelings to Michael, she was surprised, then disappointed that he had not responded as expected. Instead, he became distant, suggesting that they spend less time together. To Ratna, he seemed confused, even bewildered by their relationship, and reluctant to discuss what was bothering him. Ratna was deeply hurt by his behaviour, and by Michael's obvious change of heart. Miserable, and distracted by what had transpired between them, in the following weeks Ratna came dangerously close to failing her finals.

A stern warning ensued from her aunt in Jakarta. Ratna understood how close she had come to losing the opportunity granted to her, and re-focused on her studies, trying hard to recover lost ground. A few more weeks passed, and Michael ceased calling altogether. She was devastated.

Ratna was not alone in the world of lover's sorrow. Michael also spent the weeks feeling miserable. He accepted that he had been smitten by the beautiful, sensuous and loving young woman, but he was uncertain about the depth of his feelings; it had all happened so quickly, and he was unsure whether their relationship could stand the test of time. Michael was not prepared to sacrifice the career opportunity he had worked so hard to achieve, only to discover at some later date that the spontaneity of their relationship had been solely the result of their physical attraction for each other. He became moody and indecisive. This too, was a new experience for him.

He could not remember ever being this attracted to anyone before, and was tempted to take the plunge, risking everything. But when the final decision had to be taken, Michael refused to follow his heart. Saddened by the choice he knew would please both his mother and the Colonel, Michael packed his bags at the close of the month, and headed for Maryland, leaving Ratna behind. He had elected to take the Colonel's advice.

Michael had always respected Colonel Zach's judgement. He had been more than a father over the years; the retired war hero had become his best friend. Confused, and unable to decide which course he should take, Michael had turned to the Colonel for advice. He had been persuasive in his arguments, and Michael conceded that Zach's suggestion to see how he still felt once he had been separated from Ratna for some months had, at the time, made a great deal of sense. Pleased that he had recovered at least some of his objectivity, Michael had then re-examined his options and decided to follow the Colonel's suggestions.

For it would have been impossible for him to continue his relationship with a non-American of Asian extraction, and still expect to be cleared to the highest level of security demanded of employees working for the National Security Agency. He knew from earlier interviews how senior government frowned on such relationships, even if marriage was involved. Although the career choice had been of his own, Michael understood that the influence Zach exercised, albeit with his interests at heart, had been considerable.

The Colonel had been instrumental in arranging for his stepson's interviews and, Michael suspected, his acceptance into the NSA. They had been generous, permitting him to continue with his post-graduate studies. They continued to guide him as he was gradually absorbed into the monolithic government agency which employed many thousands of bureaucrats, intelligence officials, military personnel, and technological specialists in its global-wide operation.

His impressive academic record had guaranteed him an excellent future, and he believed that he owed it to himself, and his parents, to at least give it his best shot. After he left Ratna behind, Michael Bradshaw continued on to Fort Meade in Maryland, where he dedicated all of his energies to his new masters in what had been often, and irreverently, referred to as 'Puzzle Palace'.

Ratna completed her studies in California, then moved to Kentucky where the Lims had purchased property and acquired their first American bank. Her mother, Lani, had insisted that she make the move, sensing from their infrequent telephone conversations that Ratna should expand her horizons and, to Lani, that meant following the Lims wherever they might be.

Kerry B.Collison

Chapter 10

Lim and the Salima Group

Lim had left the meeting for Ruswita and her subordinates to finalise, as the discussions which followed would be primarily tactical. He had not been feeling well, and returned home to rest. The mounting pressures associated with the mammoth project and his declining health had contributed to his general state of lethargy. His personal doctor had insisted that he take more time to rest, warning Lim that if he failed to heed this advice, his life would be in danger

Over the years his arteries had slowly clogged under the constant onslaught of a high-fat diet. Almost everything he consumed had been fried, including his daily intake of vegetables. Although he never smoked cigarettes and rarely drank alcohol, Lim's health had deteriorated considerably over the past year, and his doctor had become increasingly concerned about his constant fatigue, and loss of appetite. The doctor had encouraged him to take Chinese herbs designed to restore energy in advancing years. Lim had even tried crushed and powdered deer's antlers and other Chinese remedies to improve his health but, sadly, these had all failed. The doctor further advised that he should return to taking mid-afternoon naps, and entrust others to carry more of his workload

Lim had listened to the advice, and asked Ruswita to play an even greater role than before. She had accepted the additional responsibilities willingly, allowing her husband the rest his body deserved. To the other senior executives responsible for implementing Lim's wishes, this seemed to be a natural progression in the chain of command. Ruswita had worked alongside her husband since the day they married, and was a most competent administrator. She clearly understood the conglomerate's activities, perhaps even more so than any other in the group, with the exclusion of Lim Swee Giok. They were, without exception, pleased that she had taken an even greater role in the multi-national's affairs. They had all worked with Ruswita over the years and understood her to be almost as shrewd as Lim in her dealings. At least, some were to whisper, relieved when alone with friends, none of the Lim boys had been recalled to take charge. Denny and James' American activities had reached the Asian Press, and those associated with the Salima group in Indonesia were apprehensive that either, or both, might be given control over the conglomerate's operations.

Denny and James seemed content to remain in North America, while the youngest son, Benny had focused most of his energies on developing the Lims' banking interests. Unlike his older brothers, Benny had concentrated on expanding the family's main financial institution, the Asia Pacific Commercial Bank, and had already successfully negotiated the branch status rights in many of the ASEAN nations. It would seem that all three of Lim's sons would become major banking entities in their own right.

Ruswita was most proud of their achievements. Her only regret was that her daughter, Ratna, still seemed to be lost in some nebulous world of her own, wandering aimlessly from one affair to another, refusing to settle down and start a family. Ruswita knew that there had been little time in their lives to spend together, and that there would always be a barrier between them as long as their secret remained intact. Sometimes, when lying awake at night, Rus would try to think of a way of telling Ratna of her true heritage, without disrupting all their lives.

Each time these thoughts entered her mind, her conclusion would be the same. Ratna must never know the secret of her birth. To reveal the truth would only bring greater pain to those involved, and perhaps even cause her daughter to despise her altogether.

* * * * * *

Ruswita was more concerned than Lim regarding the approaching tender announcements. They had discussed their position at length and, although they agreed that Seda's apparent influence over the President could represent a problem for the Salima camp, they recognized that there was little that could be done at that point in time. The only weapon the Lims had over Seda was their wealth and the ability to provide funding for the *Rama* project. They enjoyed some comfort in knowing that Seda would be unable to displace the Salima Group as they held the key to the billions of dollars required for the successful completion of the entire project.

They accepted that the tender process would be, for the most part, a mere formality. The President, if Seda was to be believed, had already decided on the tender outcome. When Lim had personally broached the important issue at his last meeting at the Palace, he had been disturbed by an apparent reluctance to discuss what was happening directly with him. He sensed that Seda had managed to manoeuvre himself into an even more powerful position than he had previously enjoyed, adding substance to the rumours of his imminent appointment to replace the current Vice President.

Lim accepted that he was already deeply financially committed to the project's success, and could now only hope that what Seda had promised would indeed eventuate. The PEPELIN Chairman had assured Lim that it was now only a matter of timing. Once the Salima Group had completed the necessary arrangements with the many international organizations involved in the project's planning, tenders, construction, financing and, ultimately, operation, the President would announce the names of the successful bidders.

Lim had managed to snare most of the likely participants through a complicated network of nominee offshore companies, and associated *kongsi*s. He felt comfortable with the contracts Salima International had put in place and, through Seda, Lim had provided the President with a final list of those consortiums associated with the Salima Group. The President's sons confirmed that they had received their first *pungli* payment, and Seda was given the green light to proceed with the winning tender announcements.

Lim's only remaining concern had been the ever-increasing role General Seda had insisted on playing in the overall implementation of the contracts. Lim accepted that the man's growing influence had earned the general a substantial slice of the pie and, as Chairman, he deserved to be well looked after. It was just the uneasy feeling the billionaire experienced whenever he spent time in Seda's company that warned him to be careful, and Lim had always heeded such gut responses over the years. They had rarely been wrong.

The ageing *totok* was disgusted with the unusual number of senior government officials who had held their hands out even before the project was off the ground. Particularly because Lim knew he would have to grease them all again, once the nuclear plants had become operational. Tired, and distressed with the thought that he no longer enjoyed the President's confidence as he had before, Lim went upstairs to his bedroom, followed by the faithful cook carrying a tray of refreshments. She placed these in his room close to the king-size bed, poured the tea, then slipped out quietly as her master commenced undressing.

Chapter 11

Murray, Graeme, Peter

Murray went through the lists again, searching for the company's facsimile number. He'd had it in front of him just moments before, now it seemed to have disappeared. Annoyed, he threw the file across the table towards John.

'See if you can find their bloody number,' Murray said, 'I'm taking a break,' with which, he rose, stretched, and strolled wearily out of the office. 'Going out for awhile,' he called to one of the secretaries who had looked up as he passed. 'Take messages. I'll be back in an hour or so.' He then walked through the maze of offices and poked his head into the Chairman's reception to let Peter Wong know that he was heading out for lunch. It was not expected of him to do so; but Murray knew that Peter always appreciated the gesture. Wong's personal secretary saw Murray and waved for him to enter.

'He won't be long, Murray, just finishing up a call now,' she said, a tone officiously. Murray looked down at the short, unattractive woman who had dedicated her life to the company. He understood why Wong trusted her explicitly. She had never married and stood loyally behind the Chairman, protecting his back, and had done so for more than thirty years. Murray attempted to drag a smile from her but was, as usual, unsuccessful. He wondered why it was that she never seemed to have empty hands. Whenever he noticed her, the woman always carried files or documents wherever she went, as if these were some permanent part of her office accoutrements.

'Hi, Murray, sorry to keep you waiting,' the frail voice was Peter Wong's, as he shuffled into the reception. 'Do you have time to talk now?' he asked, turning and heading back into his room without waiting for a response. It wasn't necessary, he was the Chairman and major shareholder. Murray, although he had become quite wealthy as a result of their relationship, still quietly referred to the man who had financed his Indonesian *kongsi* as *the Chinaman*, taking care that Peter was out of earshot when he did so.

Their relationship had become strained during recent years as Wong had grown older, and started to display signs of senility. Murray followed the *Taipan* into his elaborate office and positioned himself next to the window. He had always enjoyed this view overlooking Singapore Harbour, off Shenton Way. He looked out across the calm ocean to the south, and could clearly identify the Indonesian island of Batam. Fast ferries raced between the industrial estates there and Singapore, leaving long, white scars in their wake as they dodged the ever-present flotilla of small ships darting to and fro, evading the ever-watchful Customs.

The unobstructed view was a welcome contrast to the many months of irritating haze which had preceded the monsoonal winds that year. Indonesia's slash and burn tactics more than a thousand kilometers to the south-east, in Kalimantan, and across the Malacca Straits in Sumatra had cast a polluting smog which stretched for thousands of kilometers in all directions. Changi Airport had been closed on several occasions due to the smoke-haze, and Murray recalled the increased incidence of hospital admissions during that time as asthmatics struggled with the suffocating conditions.

Murray's stomach rumbled. He checked his watch and waited. Wong had long since given up taking his meals outside, and often forgot that others still needed to do so. Instead, he would have his secretary slip down to the basement kitchens and select an assortment of *Dim Sum*, which always included the tasty *har gao*, and *siao mai*.

'What's happening to our tender?' Wong asked, finally lowering himself into the oversized chair. Even in earlier days, when his health had permitted the Chairman to still play tennis, Murray had thought the chair to be too large for the man's gaunt frame. He noticed the absence of the poodles.

Peter had never been the same since John Georgio had inadvertently permitted one of the dogs to wander outside the building, where it had been killed by a passing motorist. Those who knew kept the secret from their Chairman knowing how he doted on the animal, and knowing how the old man would respond, if he discovered how the accident occurred. Senior staff who had been around the *Taipan* for many years knew only too well that the man had a vicious, vindictive streak. They believed the whispers that he had ordered the contract which had resulted in the death of his latest wife's lover, and had no doubt whatsoever that John Georgio would suffer a similar fate should their Chairman discover that it was the American's negligence which had cost the life of his prized poodle.

At the time, Murray had warned Georgio to disappear for a few weeks, just to be safe. Now, he had returned, and Peter had given the man the responsibility for handling the company's public relations. Murray knew that this really amounted to John looking after the Chairman's needs as discreetly as possible.

'We're just about there, Peter,' Murray answered, stifling a yawn. 'There are a few loose ends to tidy up before the end of the week but, apart from those, we're looking good.'

'What about the others?' Wong asked. Murray looked directly at the Chairman, anticipating the question. He had known Peter for many years, and expected the man to ask the obvious.

'Well, let's see,' Murray replied, settling down further into the olive green leather chair. He knew then that there would be no time for lunch. Wong would expect him to run through the entire list of registered tender applications and postulate as to how each of their competitors might fare with their submissions. He had been though this process before, and resigned himself to the tedious task of running though the information yet again. 'Westinghouse and General Electric seem to be in the driving seat as far as we can ascertain. Atomic Energy of Canada are a little short on their funding proposal, but we expect their government to step in and offer to make up the difference by offering a soft-aid package in conjunction with the bid.'

Murray continued from memory. It was not difficult, he had been working on the project for more than a year and woke up most nights with data still running though his mind. The tedious, arduous task of collecting commercial intelligence was something his earlier training and developed skills permitted him to carry out in a highly professional manner. Even so, the months of sifting through data and other material associated with the complex tendering process had consumed far too many months of his life.

It was as if he had become just another cog in the Wong machine, with few opportunities to relax. He was constantly involved in the assessment process determining where their competition might be with their own submissions. All of the principal manufacturers and operators were well known to each other. Murray knew that there were, effectively, less than a dozen firms which would qualify for consideration to construct the nuclear plants. He had spoken to them all over the months, visited plants and engineering offices, negotiated with their management and, finally, compiled a detailed report on how he perceived the tender would proceed.

His *kongsi* with Peter Wong stood a reasonable chance of winning at least one of the tenders, but Murray realized that at the end of the day, regardless of how competitive they might be, the final decision would rest with those in Indonesia whose seemingly bottomless pockets demanded attention. He had spoken to Chairman Seda on more than one occasion and, although quietly confident that his offer had been well received, Murray was still uncomfortable in his dealings with the retired general. He was not convinced that Seda had not merely used their negotiations to improve his position with other tendering parties.

They continued discussing their relationship with the American companies before Wong changed direction.

'What about the Japanese?' Wong asked. Murray nodded, and continued with his update.

'Hitachi and Toshiba are well ahead with their finance packages.'

'Yes,' Wong interrupted, 'I'd expected as much. We have to watch the Japanese, Murray, those bastards will cut the legs off their competitors, given the chance.' Murray scratched his head absentmindedly, then continued.

'Much of the information we have seems to indicate that there is a piece missing from their submissions. Our source swears that he has given us everything that's gone through, but I'm not entirely sure that he has access to everything we need.'

'Offer him more money,' Wong suggested. It had always worked in the past. Murray shook his head; greasing an un-squeaky wheel was not the way to go. He knew the source well enough to believe what he claimed.

'Not yet, Peter. Let's wait to see what else flows through before we spoil him too much.' He noticed Peter's eyes flick. Murray suspected that Wong's mind was calculating how much their informant had received, and whether they had received true value from the man. Murray was not overly concerned that his senior associate had never put much store in Murray's ongoing association with the SUBUD group until then. The government official who had provided details of competitors pre-qualifying submissions was, in fact, an active follower of the spiritualist movement. It had made Murray's task that much easier, as they could easily meet in secret within the SUBUD complex without raising suspicion.

That he used the organisation's facilities to disguise his commercial activities in no way disturbed his conscience. The movement had prospered over the years, and Murray could point to a number of investments which had been realized as a result of the secrecy which surrounded the society's activities. Murray still played an active role in promoting the movement, world-wide. It provided him with an international network of considerable substance. He looked at his inscrutable associate and wondered what insecurity caused Wong to worry about his relationship with SUBUD.

'Murray,' Wong said, interrupting what he was about to say, 'what happened to the French?' Murray frowned before answering. He had made a direct approach to represent them himself when the tenders were first announced. They had made it quite clear that they wanted nothing to do with Australians operating in Indonesia. During informal discussions with one of their executives, he had discovered that the French company had been badly burned by Stephen Coleman's sudden disappearance, and the resulting backlash from investigations into his activities relating to arms shipments into Timor.

At the time, Murray had been shocked as the rumours about Coleman emerged, some even suggesting that he was hiding somewhere in Vietnam, or Laos, and that there was a price on his head. Murray was aware that all of Coleman's business interests had been seized or closed down, fuelling speculation that he had overestimated his influence with the Palace, and had been caught somehow with his illicit arms dealing. Murray suspected that Coleman had just run foul of someone near the top of the Indonesian food chain, and had been swallowed up by his own shadowy associates, whoever they might have been.

Murray seemed to recall seeing a note from one of the secretaries some time back, mentioning that there had been a call. He had been away from the Singapore office at the time, and had not bothered to phone the number Coleman had left when he returned, as the message was already weeks old. Murray recalled that the French were not the only ones hurt when Coleman had so dramatically exited Indonesia, although there were a few who did benefit from Coleman's vanishing act. Wong's company, he knew, had acquired a fifty percent holding in one of Stephen Coleman's lucrative property developments.

Murray was aware of the arrangement as he had been responsible for introducing the deal. Now that Coleman was on the run, Murray also knew that his senior partner would take advantage of the man's demise. Murray also knew that Coleman's share in the venture had been entrusted to Wong, and that the Australian would, should he still be alive, never live to see or enjoy his holding in the property venture. If this should eventuate, it was of no concern to Murray. He had never really liked the man and, although he would personally benefit from Coleman's demise, he had no feelings one way or the other as to the morality of the outcome. Besides, he knew that Wong would never acknowledge Coleman's right to the equal shareholding he had held in trust for the man; it was not Peter's style not to take advantage of another's circumstances. Murray was in no doubt that unless he was careful in his own dealings with Wong, he could suffer a similar fate. The thought made Murray uncomfortable, and he quickly put this out of his mind, returning his thoughts to the matter at hand.

'The French are unlikely contenders, Peter. They don't have the Palace connections any more.' Murray then went on to provide more information to Wong, including his evaluations regarding potential project engineers and material suppliers. Their own *kongsi* was keen to maintain a position in the tender process, and Murray had spent considerable time in negotiations already, talking to Bechtel, Siemens, Framatome and even Larsen & Toubro in India. He was confident that their *kongsi* would most definitely be involved downstream in the nuclear projects; they had done their homework and been generous with the necessary payments required to facilitate their position.

Murray looked out through the window and wished he was on the cruise boat leaving the harbour. It had been too long since he had taken a break. He looked at Wong and wondered how the old man could continue to entertain the flow of young women that John Georgio managed to provide on call to the ageing Chairman.

'How about we catch up later, Peter,' he said, uncrossing his legs and standing. He was tired. Checking his watch he discovered that they had been talking for more than an hour. Wong merely nodded.

'Okay, Murray, see you tonight,' the old man said, catching Murray by surprise. 'Had a call from Johnny earlier. Seems he has something special for tonight's little gathering.' Wong grinned mischievously, and as he did so, Murray remembered he'd left Georgio behind to check his lists for missing communication contacts. Murray cursed under his breath, understanding then why John had slipped behind with the relatively simple tasks he'd been given.

Murray knew that the title Wong had given the American was purely to satisfy the man's ego as he was, in fact, basically the company pimp, responsible for the constant supply of Filipino starlets and Thai models through the Chairman's penthouse. Murray decided that one day he should ask some of these beautiful women just what went on in the old Chinaman's bedroom. He found it hard to believe that even if Wong consumed *all* the deer antlers in Asia these would provide sufficient impetus to maintain Wong's waning libido. Murray responded to Peter's evil grin, then returned to his own office.

'What's planned for tonight?' he asked John when he returned to his office. Georgio was on the phone and hung up the moment Murray walked in.

'Three hot babes from across the causeway,' John answered, cupping his hands under his chest. Murray doubted this, recalling some of the Johore Baru girls he'd slept with in the past. "I'm taking them up to Peter's around eight. Will you be there?' Murray thought about this and decided that frolicking around in the oversized spa might just be what he needed.

'Sure, count me in,' he said. His stomach was still sending noisy signals that he had missed another meal.

'Great!' Georgio responded, enthusiastically.

'Who else is coming?' Murray asked.

'Well,' John said, 'I could phone a couple of the Phoenix girls and drag them over if you prefer?' Murray remembered the last time these amateur hookers had entertained in Wong's penthouse. He'd caught the clap. Even with the Aids scare, none of them wore condoms. Murray knew that he'd been irresponsible with respect to his frequent, casual partners. He always carried a couple of condoms in his wallet but, since he had first arrived in Asia more than three decades before, he had often, in the heat of the moment, failed to use them.

Murray realized that he had been playing a game of sexual Russian roulette, and vowed to start using the covers in his wallet. He had overheard many an expatriate near his age boast that if they hadn't already contracted the disease, then they were not likely to do so. Murray wondered if you could catch Aids and the clap at the same time. He turned to Georgio.

'Give them a miss, John. I'll just drop in for awhile to check out the action.' Then he became serious again. 'Did you locate that number?'

'Sure, Murray,' John answered in the affirmative, and passed him the list. Murray checked the information, then nodded

'I don't need you around here, John, if you have to get on with organizing whatever for tonight,' he offered. Georgio accepted the hint and left Murray to make his calls. He rubbed his abdomen, conscious of the empty space inside and changed his mind, deciding to return to his own apartment where he would grab a quick bite and make the sensitive calls from a more secure number.

* * * * * *

The small party was in full swing by the time Murray arrived at Peter's penthouse; he had taken an afternoon nap and overslept. He punched in the security code and entered, making his way through the thickly carpeted lounge room and out onto the patio where he expected they would all be gathered. As he stepped outside, Murray was surprised to see the familiar face grinning widely from where he sat, against the pool-side bamboo bar. The small structure was covered with a thick matting of palm fibre, adding to the setting's tropical ambience. Coloured lights had been strung around the bar, and a soft, warm breeze blew across the Straits from the Indonesian islands. In the distance, well-lit ships steamed through the heavily congested waters, making their occasional deep-throated blasts.

'Well, well, well,' the man sitting against the bar called, 'John said you might not be coming.' Murray strolled over and extended his hand. Graeme Robson slipped off the bar-stool and clasped it warmly. They had known each other since the younger man first arrived in Indonesia and stayed at Murray's home during his first weeks in Jakarta. Murray had known Robson's father quite well, and had undertaken to keep an eye on the mining magnate's errant son. It had not been an easy task, although Murray now admitted that Robson had certainly come a long way since those early and boisterous times.

Graeme had dropped out in Australia, leaving his home town of Newcastle to travel the world. He never made it past Jakarta, overwhelmed by the women and their generosity. He had not found it necessary to work, as his father sent him funds regularly to keep him away from the family mining interests. Graeme had displayed a total lack of interest in working, and his idle manner had often attracted his wealthy father's wrath. Embarrassed by his son's well publicised escapades, his arrests when drunk and disorderly, and the drug experiments which had resulted in the death of an underage student, the mining entrepreneur had suggested that his son might benefit from visiting Europe.

Graeme had leapt at the offer to take some time and travel at his father's expense. Upon arriving in Jakarta, Robson went directly to Murray Stephenson's office, and offered his father's letter of introduction. Graeme then bedded down in one of Murray's spare rooms where he remained until, having placed considerable strain on their relationship, and to the older man's relief, Robson suddenly gathered his modest wardrobe one day and disappeared.

Although Murray had treated his client's son almost as a younger brother, Graeme shifted out after a few weeks, and moved in with an Indonesian Chinese woman considerably older than himself. As he had ceased communicating with his family, his father became annoyed and discontinued Graeme's monthly remittances. He had already borrowed substantial amounts from Murray, who refused further advances when Robson, short of funds, decided to renew contact. Desperate, he then borrowed from the woman with whom he lived, and she willingly advanced whatever he asked for, as she had been led to believe that they would be married. For a short time, her modest legal practice kept them both reasonably happy, until Graeme discovered even greener pastures.

Tempers had flared when Robson announced, without warning, that he was moving out. Amidst the heated domestic dispute which followed, Graeme brutally attacked the woman who had lovingly cared for him, even emptying her bank account to finance his stay in Indonesia. The police were called, and Graeme Robson fled to the mountain resort area of the Puncak, where he sought the assistance of another Australian he had met briefly through Murray. Stephen Coleman arranged for Robson to remain hidden in one of his villas, while he negotiated a peaceful settlement through one of his contacts in the Justice Department.

It had been difficult; Robson's attack had severely scarred the woman's face, and she rightfully wanted revenge. He was advised to remain in hiding, and wisely heeded the warning.

After several weeks of negotiations, Robson was permitted to leave the mountain resort and return to Jakarta, where he took up residence with the daughter of a local entrepreneur. Her father took to Graeme, relieved that his child had finally found someone who might keep her out of the foreign bars she so often frequented. Recognising another opportunity, Graeme Robson proposed, and to everyone's relief, he actually went through with the wedding. Robson senior was delighted that his son had finally accepted some responsibility in life, and had changed his errant ways. He decided to follow through with Murray's recommendations that they invest in the Indonesian mining sector, to provide his son with an opportunity to build his life, and his newly acquired family's future.

His company filed an application with the Indonesian Mines Department, and they were granted a coal concession in Kalimantan. Graeme was appointed to the joint venture board, and given a free reign to run the company. At first, it appeared that he would fail, as the rambunctious Robson had really not acquired sufficient maturity to manage the commercial enterprise given to him by his father. Murray was called in to assist, and within the year, the company turned the corner when they secured several contracts supplying coal to the government thermal power plants in Java.

Graeme had been married less than three years when he received word that his father had passed away, leaving control of his mining interests to his youngest son. Overnight, Graeme Robson became a multi-millionaire.

'John didn't mention you'd be here,' Murray said, looking around for Georgio.

'He didn't know. I only decided to fly over at the last minute. Peter's secretary brought me up to see the old man. Speaking of which, where is he?' Robson asked, turning his head and looking around the outdoor setting.

'He won't join in the tub. Peter prefers to have his action in the privacy of his own bedroom,' Murray explained, surprised that the younger man had not been to one of Wong's exclusive spa-parties before.

'Will we see him at all?' Robson asked.

'He'll come out shortly, no doubt.' Murray accepted a drink from the one domestic Peter kept on staff in his private domain. Wong had mentioned some years before that the man was an imbecile but, as he was his cousin's grandson, he kept him on. 'What brings you to Singapore on the spur of the moment then?' he asked, swirling the ice-cubes with one finger.

'Thought it was time for us to sit down and put something on paper regarding the ore supply for the plants,' Robson replied. Murray thought about this. He knew that Graeme's family company held substantial interests in mining around Kakadu in Australia. When the Federal Government had permitted the company to open what became a fourth mine in the national park, Murray remembered reading that there had been an incredible outcry. Environmentalist groups had picketed the company's head offices for weeks, retreating only when public interest had waned.

'What have you got in mind, Graeme?' he asked, although he already had a reasonable idea. Murray had checked with most of the world's uranium ore suppliers to see who had arranged representation in connection with the current tender. He had soon become familiar with how the ore companies worked, and how price variables were negotiated years in advance of any orders being delivered.

'I thought we'd have a crack at a total supply contract for the entire project,' he announced. Murray was surprised at the ambitious position Robson's Australian associates had obviously taken in respect to the *Rama* contracts.

'The competition will be stiff,' Murray suggested, not wishing to alert Robson to just how much information he and Wong had at hand.

'Sure, we'd expect nothing less, Murray,' he said. Both men turned as the sauna door came open, sending a wave of instant heat in their direction. John Georgio emerged, followed by a hot, sweaty, naked girl. Murray could see from the girl's appearance that she was not at all pleased with whatever had taken place inside. John sucked in an excessive amount of air, flexed his muscles and strutted over to the twelve-person spa, then lowered himself into the bubbling water without first showering. As he did so, the girl following stopped, coughed twice then spat on the patio floor. She looked over to her friends and shook her head in disgust, pointing her index finger into the air for them to see, then slowly bent it forward until it drooped. Robson laughed quietly.

'See John's habits haven't changed,' he remarked. Murray could not decide whether to join the others in the spa. Standing in front of his dressing-mirror earlier, he knew that he was rapidly moving into that age bracket when heart attacks were not uncommon. Still, he thought, he had worn well. Catching a glimpse of one of the nude girls as she climbed out of the tub to fetch John a drink, he was tempted, thinking that even a man in his sixties needed to feel young from time to time. When another of the nymphs displayed herself, he did not hesitate any longer. He climbed out of his clothes, threw these casually onto the plexi-glass-topped table, and walked naked to the spa. The water was not overly warm, suitably adjusted to compensate for the tropical conditions. After several minutes he felt his muscles relax with the gentle jets massaging his back and thighs. Someone splashed, disrupting his thoughts, and he opened his eyes to see who had joined them in the spa. It was Graeme Robson.

'Where did you get this lot from, John,' Robson asked, reaching for one of the girls. She did not resist as he pulled her towards him. As her body floated over his, she nestled her hand gently in his crotch and tugged playfully. Graeme Robson's attitude to extramarital romps was that of most expatriates living in Asia. Providing it was quick and clean, that's all that mattered. Even Thai wives placed condoms in their husband's pockets before bidding them farewell, and although Graeme demanded total fidelity from his wife, he saw little wrong with his own behaviour.

'JB,' was all Georgio said, using the common abbreviation for the Malaysian port of Johore Baru, situated across the causeway from Singapore. Robson turned the girl around, placing her on his lap as they sat enjoying the jets force blowing against their skin.

'Murray, what's happening with…..' Robson started, then saw the cautionary look on Stephenson's face. He nodded and changed the subject immediately, remembering that Georgio was not a member of the Wong inner sanctum. Although John provided a most valuable service to the old man, and did actually participate in the company's public relations activities, he was never given access to sensitive material. Murray looked back at the younger man and winked, while another of the girls moved alongside him and started stroking his thighs. His warning heeded, Murray stepped out of the spa and pulled the girl after him, as he walked to the sauna.

Robson watched them enter and decided to give them ten minutes before following, but Murray was back out before he had made his move. Graeme watched the older man leave the attractive Malaysian nymph standing under the patio shower, then wrap a towel around himself before settling down at the bar. Graeme climbed out and dried himself off.

'What's up, Graeme?' Murray asked.

'I had an interesting conversation with Seda today, Murray,' he spoke softly, looking back to ensure that John remained out of earshot. 'The general virtually inferred that the uranium ore contract will be handled by your *kongsi*. How did you manage that? The rest of us are still in the tender registration stage.' Murray raised his eyebrows, and waited, wondering why Robson was telling him this.

'Our group?' Murray asked, surprised that Seda had spoken of their arrangement.

'Yes, that's what he said.'

'Are you sure?'

'Well, he suggested that we speak. He knows that Australia can be very competitive, Murray. The mines in Kakadu can easily meet the *Rama* requirements, and then there is the proximity of the supply source to consider as well,' he argued.

'Did Seda say specifically that we were to talk about sourcing ore from Australia?' he asked, concerned now that too much information might have been passed to the Robson mining group in Australia. Murray knew that sometimes Indonesian officials revealed considerably more than they meant to, if for no other reason than that to improve their standing, or image with those involved in the negotiating process. He was becoming annoyed with the knowledge that Seda had held one on one discussions regarding the uranium ore contract with Robson. Then the thought struck Murray that Seda might have had similar conversations with a number of other supplier groups, including the Canadians and South Africans.

'He merely suggested that I talk to Wong, that's all,' Robson replied.

'But he never actually indicated that we would be awarded the contract, did he?'

'No, not exactly,' he answered, defensively, 'but it would make sense if he intends using his associates' shipping line for the deal. Doesn't Peter have a position in there somewhere?' he asked. Murray knew that Wong had leased the ships to the group of high-ranking military officers associated with Seda. *What was the PEPELIN Chairman up to now?*

'Sure, but that doesn't mean that Seda owes Peter any special favours,' Murray said, searching into his mind for something which might explain the strange request. 'What else did he say?'

'Not much,' Robson sounded unsure of his ground. Murray sensed that the younger man was fishing.

'Have you set anything up with Seda?' Murray asked, to the point.

'Of course not!' Robson responded, a little too quickly.

'Why not? Seems to me that you would be in a position to take advantage of the political support the Australian mines might have.'

'Sure, Murray, but I got the impression from the PEPELIN Chairman that whoever won the supply contract would be associated with Wong's *kongsi*.'

'Why would you think that?' Murray was deeply interested in what Robson had to say. If Seda had started shopping around at this late date, then they were all in danger of losing the contract. Word would leak to the suppliers and they would want to know what was really going on in Jakarta.

'Well, my guess is that he wants some Australian content. That's why I was asked to meet and discuss our position. I don't pretend to understand why, I just assumed that you guys obviously had the deal sewn up from what he said, and I decided to take a shot before you close us out.' He thought for a moment, then added: 'Whatever his reasons, Murray, perhaps you should have a rethink about taking us along on the uranium ore supply. This is a very healthy contract and I wouldn't be too happy losing it just because Peter is in bed with the South Africans.' Murray then knew that Seda had said more than Robson was letting on. Wong's *kongsi* had been very discreet regarding whom they represented in the deal. Murray had even deliberately laid a false trail, suggesting that they were representing the French and Canadians. He knew that it was imperative that he not disclose the name of his supplier. As usual, politics was playing an important role in all aspects of the decision making process.

There were still those amongst the Indonesian Military who had not forgiven President Mandela's interference in the East Timor issue during the Soeharto regime. It suddenly concerned Murray that Seda had been most receptive to the idea that the uranium Indonesia needed for the nuclear energy plants should originate from the very country which had caused so much political fallout over Timor. Murray remained casual, refusing to be baited further by the younger man.

'Look, Graeme,' he said, careful not to add credence to whatever Robson had assumed might be happening between Seda and Wong, 'I'll be in Jakarta myself sometime over the next few days. Why don't you come with me when I talk to Seda?'

'Hell, Murray, why wait? I'll take you back with me, if you wish,' he offered. Murray forced a smile. Graeme was always looking for an opportunity to invite others on his Lear Jet. Apparently he had forgotten that Peter Wong owned his own aircraft, and that Murray could avail himself of this whenever he wished.

'When are you returning?' Murray asked, as he poured himself a drink and dropped several ice cubes into the whisky.

'Not until after lunch tomorrow. I have some banking arrangements to settle in the morning.' Graeme waved at the girl he'd left in the spa. 'Why don't we set up a meet for early morning?' he asked. Murray shook his head. Unlike Indonesia, Singaporeans rarely entered their offices until mid-morning. He finished off the remaining *saté* Peter's man had placed there earlier.

'Make it around midday and I'll alert Peter. Okay?' Robson thought for a moment then nodded.

'Okay, I'll be over as close to noon as I can make it.' He lifted Murray's whisky and took a long swallow. Then he returned to the spa and the dark-eyed girl who was waiting for him. Murray watched them all play for a few more minutes, then decided to leave. He knew from experience that Peter might not emerge for some time, if at all. He dressed, said goodnight to the men, waved at the disappointed girls and returned to his own apartment.

That night, when Murray finally slipped into a fitful sleep, he dreamed that he was standing alongside a ship moored in the harbour, and that he and Graeme Robson were near exhaustion from loading the rocks stacked in mountainous piles along the length of the wharf. Each time they threw one of the rocks up and over the ships side into the cargo hold, Peter's voice cried out for them to hurry, as the ship would soon be underway. As he and Robson struggled to throw more and more rocks into the ship's hold, the mountains of uranium ore on the wharf did not diminish. Finally, they fell exhausted, unable to continue. The ship sailed away, its cargo holds empty.

In his dream he could hear a familiar noise somewhere in the background, and he struggled as his mind fought to distinguish what it was. Startled, he woke to discover it was his own phone that had been ringing. He checked his bedside clock. It was not even five o'clock. Murray moaned, then silently cursed his inconsiderate caller. He lifted the phone and mumbled his name into the mouthpiece, then listened, as a voice from his past brought him fully awake.

Chapter 12

Japan's Prime Minister

Prime Minister Hiroyuki Hata stood with both fingers stuck inside his vest as he addressed his Cabinet. Hata frowned at the group assembled before him, his piercing eyes darting around the members of the uneasy coalition government he headed. As he viewed them all, he deliberately avoided looking upon the three new Cabinet members forced upon him. All three were women. For Hiroyuki Hata, the code of *nyonin kinzei* had been broken, and he was distressed that another of the long-standing taboos regarding the exclusion of women had been removed.

'*Gentlemen,*' he commenced, clearing his throat, ignoring the women's presence, '*I need not reiterate that we are faced with a most difficult decision regarding the Indonesian opportunities.*' The Prime Minister then turned towards a window on his right and moved slowly away from the table as if leaving the discussion. The others present who had enjoyed the benefit of earlier Cabinet positions knew that this was one of Hata-san's practised mannerisms, and waited for him to continue. Others, new to the Hata-Satoh Cabinet, waited quietly without displaying any semblance of impatience. It would have been impolite.

'*We are faced with the continuing conundrum of whether or not the Japanese have the capacity to finally look forward, and accept that tomorrow's world may not have as great an American presence as it has experienced since the second half of the last century.*'

Hata glanced back over his shoulder as a reminder that he was addressing all who were present. Several of his strongest supporters shifted uneasily in their seats knowing where the conversation was heading. They had heard it all before and were still not comfortable with their leader's position.

'We have seen the decline of American military influence not just in our Asia, but also in Europe,' he continued. Hata realized that there were those who were not happy with his style of leadership but he would have to maintain his close working relationship with them until assured that their support was no longer essential to his own political survival.

'Japanese industry has followed the American thrust for more than six decades and now must consider returning to a more Japanese focused view in relation to our regional interests.' He turned, fingers still hanging from the small pockets cut into his vest. He forced a smile.

'We can no longer afford to be dragged into supporting America's political position, which we have learned from past experience translates, in reality, into economic considerations which only serve American vested interests.' Hata knew that he would have a fight on his hands; his Coalition partners had been emphatically committed to maintaining a non-nuclear proliferation policy as the mainstay of their political platform. He refused to look at the three women who, to his dismay held the balance of power in the Diet. Desperate for power, Hata had accepted that he would have to make concessions during the course of his tenure as Prime Minister, and his party's term in government. He could still not bring himself to any direct negotiations with the group. Instead, Hata had relegated his Junior Minister for Women's Affairs to handle all negotiations with the trio. He removed one hand from his inside coat and pointed somewhere into the air.

'We have arrived at the cross-roads; it is time for us to select the path which will be most beneficial for the Japanese people.' He then returned his finger to the more familiar position, and looked over his shoulder through the window. He could barely see the buildings across the park. Pollution had also been high on the political agenda during the election campaign. Japan was choking on itself, he thought, himself a firm supporter of an even greater nuclear energy program than that he had inherited from his predecessor.

Although Japan had long before made energy conservation a national priority, domestic energy demand had grown by more than twenty percent over the past ten years. In that period of time, the Japanese Government had embarked on an ambitious programme to increase its nuclear power generation plants, as it depended on foreign sources for more than seventy-five percent of its energy needs. As a relatively junior member of earlier Cabinets, he had clearly understood that Japan would have to remove this dependency. As an industrialised nation, they had little choice if they wished to continue to compete against the rapidly developing economies of China and other Asian nations. Although Japan had become an economic superpower, its defence forces were totally adequate.

For years following the Second World War the Americans had prevented his people from re-arming, using propaganda to convince the new generation that to do so would only convince the world that Japan had not changed its ways. Earlier Diets had, he recalled, placed a ceiling on defense spending of one percent of his country's Gross National Product. It had been impossible, with such a restrictive amount of funding, to maintain any real military force. Hata knew that this had been orchestrated by the United States to permit them to maintain their own presence in Asia, thereby enhancing their trade opportunities and political influence over the region. He was pleased when, finally, subsequent Prime Ministers had been encouraged by the Diet to increase this spending which resulted, towards the close of the twentieth century, in Japan becoming the third largest military spender in dollar terms, worldwide, even surpassing Great Britain, Germany and France. Hata also remembered how the American newspapers had pointed to Japan's growing militarism, alerting alarmists to question his country's intentions. He was pleased, at the time, that this did not prevent the Japanese Government from continuing to fund Mitsubishi and Fujitsu, the appointed manufacturers for Japan's recently developed sea-based Anti Ballistic Missile system, which had been developed as a counter-measure to defend his country against a potential North Korean missile attack.

He had been disappointed that the Americans had been successful with their military lobbying, securing the bulk of Japan's defense spending for United States-manufactured weapons. Joint Defense projects, he knew, were rarely cost effective, and he believed that Japan would always be disadvantaged in such contracts. He remembered reading in one of the defense reports how four Japanese-built F-15s had cost fifty percent more to produce than in the States. Had it not been for Japan's insistence that the Pentagon buy a substantial number of the M-1 tanks back from Japanese plants, then these would have been considerably more than the five million dollars each had cost his people to produce for their own military.

Hata did not trust the Americans; the defense pact signed before the turn of the century cleared the way for his country to play an even greater role in respect to regional defense considerations, but the guidelines were typically restrictive. Hata had scoffed when the Japanese Government of that time had entered into the agreement, which committed Japan to United States security strategies in the Asia-Pacific region, including the Korean Peninsula. Loose interpretations describing the pact had suggested to Japan's neighbours that his people would re-arm and fill any vacuum created by the ongoing American withdrawal from the Far East. There had been considerable resistance from the ASEAN nations and, as expected, from China, who viewed the move as another provocative step initiated by the United States to prevent China's reunion with Taiwan.

There were even many of his own citizens, he knew, who totally opposed Japan's move to rebuild its defense forces. It was Hata's view that Japan had little choice but to move towards establishing itself, once again, as a dominant military power. He scorned those around him who suffered from political myopia; these would be the first, he believed, to come running should Japan be threatened. Hata believed that defense spending should be at least doubled to recover from the years of American dependence. Japan could not boast about its defense forces; the Japanese Navy had only twenty-five submarines, less than seventy destroyers and a handful of Mine Warfare ships and auxiliary craft. If Japan were attacked at that moment, Hata knew that his country would be in grave danger without the American presence. Japan's strength, if it had any, lay in its airforce. Rotary wing and combat aircraft totalled one thousand aircraft; but Hata believed that these would only be of value for a limited period should his country come under attack.

As Prime Minister, he accepted responsibility for Japan's re-armament, even if this required that he manipulate the system to achieve these goals. Hata staunchly believed that Japan had little choice but to enter the nuclear age if his people were to survive the twenty-first century.

At first, there had been considerable resistance in his country towards increased nuclear power production. It had been difficult to educate the people. Hata had always been aware that the issue was as an extremely sensitive one for the Japanese. Although none of his own family had died in either Hiroshima or Nagasaki, he had known many who had lost someone.

There was a cancer of fear and ignorance evident in Japan which was greater than any disease resulting from the two atomic bombs of 1945. The Japanese were always going to be reluctant to see the perpetrators of this devastation as benefactors but American raw materials were needed if Japan was to advance. Hata had the support of many of his colleagues in Cabinet, and Industry, for they clearly understood that Japan's future would lie in its ability to maintain an uninterrupted supply of raw materials and fuel.

Japan had few natural resources and had become overly dependent on fossil fuels. The Japanese forecasts had frightened some of the old guard into action. When they finally understood that the world's supply of petroleum was expected to run out in forty-five years time, and that natural gas would follow in less than twenty years after that, the cry had been to return to coal. The problem of pollution was suddenly forgotten as the country faced rolling strikes and street demonstrations advocating a return to mining coal. It almost brought the shaky government down.

Hata had not been the first leader to realize that his country's dependence on coal and oil had to end. But he had been the first to risk his political career on confronting the issues. First, as a leading spokesman for his Party, and then, for a short time as Opposition Leader before becoming Prime Minister, Hata had persisted in supporting the accelerated growth of the nuclear power industry in Japan. Finally, his country proudly boasted seventy-five plants.

Japan's jealous neighbours had become unsettled as their own economies had fought to survive, alarming the rest of the world by claiming that Japan's fast breeder reactors had a sinister, and more secret agenda than the Japanese would admit to. For a time, ignorance had reigned supreme, precipitating calls for trade embargoes against his country. World opinion moved to believe that because Japan based its nuclear power program on reprocessed plutonium, the country was perceived as planning to develop nuclear weapons.

One of his Ministers coughed politely, breaking through his

reverie, and he snapped back into action.

'...*and we have to look to our future, a future when Japan could no longer rely on an American presence to maintain regional stability. It is therefore imperative that we protect Japan's interests by consolidating our position in those resource rich countries requiring development capital.*'

'*Hata-san,*' a voice called, immediately attracting looks of surprise from the others present. '*Hata-san, would you kindly tell us what it is that you wish to propose?*' The men present were struck speechless that one of the women, Aki-san, had brazenly interrupted their Prime Minister's discourse. Hata turned and looked directly at the leader of his Coalition group and nodded in perfunctory fashion. There was an almost audible intake of air as those who knew their leader best, noticed the change in his demeanour. They watched as he stared at the insolent woman. The men waited anxiously, their eyes surreptitiously moving from their leader to the woman.

Didn't she know that it was customary to wait until he had finished? Had she no manners? Will Hata sacrifice Coalition unity now to save face?

'*Aki-san,*' Hata commenced, moving closer to the table and standing directly across from where the women sat. Hata had been against giving any of the women positions in his Cabinet. At first, he had refused; *it was unheard of,* he had argued, *having any woman in his Party's Cabinet, let alone three!* Now he found himself faced with the possibility of entertaining general discussion with their leader, in front of his colleagues.

'*Aki-san,*' he continued, '*our country must consider taking positive action which will reduce the number of pollution related deaths amongst our young and elderly.*' Hata had anticipated there would be objection at some point along the way, and had prepared for the moment. He had been surprised that it had come so quickly. In an earlier government, Hata had served in a capacity which had required him to be abreast of the health problems associated with Japan's industrial pollution. He had been disturbed to discover the number of children and elderly people whose deaths could be directly attributed to the country's pollution nightmare.

Influenced by the facts before him, Hata had decided then, that if he were ever given the opportunity to reduce the country's dependency on coal and other high carbon fuels, he would do so. But his political experience dictated that he approach the issue in a tangential way - the Japanese way. Hata had decided that Japan should demonstrate to its people how harmless yet beneficial nuclear energy continued to be. He aimed to completely remove his country's dependence on gas and fossil fuels within the coming decade. It was, he knew, a most ambitious plan.

But Hata also had secret hopes for Japan's re-emergence as a military power, knowing that in the course of the next fifty years most of the world's natural fuels would disappear, and that only those countries with the capacity to survive with nuclear energy would continue to develop. Hata also realized that his country would need to be able to protect its sovereignty as neighbouring countries looked enviously at their successes.

He was aware how useless it would be to attempt to explain that there were more than five hundred such plants operating safely in countries such as the United Kingdom, France, and the United States, as three generations after the *Enola Gay* had dropped her bombs, the Japanese still lived in fear of the two words *nuclear*, and *American*. Hata knew that he would have to lead the way, accepting that he may not live to see the results of the seeds he had planted, knowing that his strategy would require years, even decades, of dedication from all involved.

'I am looking for your support to have the Coalition Government fund a Japanese investment in Indonesia, Aki-san,' he said, surprising all but two in the Cabinet. There was a hushed silence as they waited for their Prime Minister to continue. Instead, Aki spoke first.

'Then what is all this subterfuge about, Hata-san?' she asked, at which several of the Hata Cabinet went into near apoplectic fits. Aki-san's two supporters paled. This was much more than they had bargained for. *Was Aki-san mad?*

'Please remember where we are!' one of Hata's older members admonished, shaking his head at the woman's rude behaviour.

'Aki-san, you must apologise to Hata-san!' another demanded. Hata stood staring at the woman, his face taut with visible anger. Inside, forces prevented him from displaying his displeasure. He continued the game, moving in skilfully, laying a sticky return path which would entrap his opponent. If, in the future, the unpredictable did occur and there was political fallout as a result of his strategies, Hata was confident that his Party could always cast the blame onto

the inexperienced women. Hata raised his hand to silence his fellow Party members. He had to appear to be generous.

'Aki-san, would you support our Government's decision to build, own and operate a series of nuclear power plants in Indonesia which would provide, not only considerable immediate benefits to our construction companies, but also long term, down-stream opportunities for the Japanese people?' Hata left his statement hanging in the air. The male Cabinet members sat staring at their leader, then slowly turned to the woman he had addressed. None present had ever seen such discussion in the Cabinet room before.

'May I ask what the status of these plants will be upon completion, Hata-san?'

The Prime Minister paused, knowing that the time had come to play his first cards.

'First, I must have your assurance that what transpires here today will remain within these walls, as the Indonesians have insisted that secrecy is of the utmost importance,' he commenced, the gravity in his voice reflecting the seriousness of what he was about to reveal. Without exception, those present bowed their heads, agreeing to his request. He looked around the Cabinet, hesitating for effect, then spoke with a clarity that surprised even those who had known Hata longest.

'We have been asked by the Indonesians to assist them to develop Fast Breeder Reactors similar to our own.' He paused again, observing that those at the far end of the room had leaned forward to hear him more clearly. He deliberately lowered his voice, even further.

'The Indonesians wish to develop a Fast Breeder Reactor for the production of plutonium.' He looked around the room.

'If we agree, then we will be responsible for providing the Indonesians with a means to produce sufficient plutonium which, if unfavourably applied, could launch that country into the nuclear race. This particular reactor would be developed in parallel with eleven other reactors which, in time, will form part of a national electric power grid from Bali to North Sumatra.' The room remained silent. Everyone present considered the extreme significance of what had been said. A small voice broke through the silence.

'Why would we want to do such a thing?' Aki asked. The men present looked from her to their Prime Minister. They too wished to know but were pleased that it had been she who had asked the

question. Hata nodded, indicating that he thought the question fair.

'Because Indonesia is the world's largest Moslem nation. Because the Moslem nations control most of the world's oil and natural gas outside of Russia, and could use that economic weapon as they have in the past, to extract whatever they believe is important to their survival. And last, because if we say no, the Russians will say yes.' Hata stared coldly at Aki, and challenged her to accept total responsibility for her Party's position.

'Would you believe that the Japanese people would be forgiving if we were to cast them back to the dark years in the Seventies, when the price of oil doubled, then tripled, nearly crippling our industries?' Hata asked, his voice dropping, forcing those at the end of the room to lean forward to hear.

It seemed that minutes had passed before Aki spoke, and in so doing, she rose in respect and bowed with dignity towards her Prime Minister. There was an audible *'aah'* heard from the men, pleased with her change in attitude.

'Hata-san, I would support such a proposal, of course.' Aki had been confused by the suggestion that she might not support such an idea. It was preposterous that any present should consider that she was not supportive of all Japanese industry. Japan had been partners in several such ventures over the past years, including the Koreas. Her objection would only have been to the introduction of more enrichment facilities into Japan itself. Her political platform had been based on environmental issues; she would not support any further expansion of the nuclear industry in her country.

Aki had no qualms about her country's owning and operating plants which might be harmful to others; she only drew the line at having such facilities operating in her own country. She had committed her party to maintaining the moratorium on further expansion of the industry in Japan. It was all over. Aki had been cleverly manipulated by the more experienced politician.

The Prime Minister offered a conciliatory bow in her direction as a gesture of his appreciation, followed by which the room filled with another, and more audible sigh of relief. There would be debate on the Diet floor, of course, but few present would be told the extent of Japan's commitment to the Indonesians. Other and less relevant information would, over a period of time, be deliberately leaked into the public domain. The Prime Minister considered this consequential to his long-term plans.

Hata smiled. Once the Japanese people discovered that they had participated in the successful operation of Fast Breeder Plants in Indonesia for some years, he believed that public acceptance to the next steps would be inevitable, as these were essential to Japan's survival. Hata stood at the end of the highly polished redwood table, a gift from a grateful American Senator whose constituency had re-elected the man as a result of Japanese manufacturing commitments made to his State. He then passed the floor to his Deputy and sat, deep in thought, considering his success.

As Hata looked down past the line of faithful politicians sitting quietly, while listening to his Finance Minister read his boring statistics, the Prime Minister observed Aki staring down at her lap. Convinced that she no longer represented any potential impediment to his government's plans, Hata ignored the Ministerial notes as they were read, considering instead which of the three major Japanese companies he would have his trusted intermediary approach to discuss the government's financial support in relation to the Indonesian project. His thoughts then moved to how he and his Defense Minister would need to disguise the undertaking they were about to give the Indonesian President, to secretly convert the Japanese Civilian H-3B rocket technology to produce a military version to serve the defense needs of both countries. Hata had been thrilled, some years before, when Japan had enjoyed considerable success with its H2-A rocket programme, which had then led into the current generation of sophisticated rockets. Japan had cleverly committed itself to the development of a range of rockets which would be used to launch his country's satellites, moving away from the dependency on American and French launch facilities.

Negotiations had already been completed. Japan would provide Indonesia with the technology and necessary funding. The H-3B had already proved successful in its civilian applications and the conversion to military use, although not overly complicated, necessitated complete secrecy. In the event their purpose be exposed, both countries could easily maintain that the joint venture had been initiated at the request of the Indonesians to advance their own technology, which would enable the Indonesians to launch their own satellites in the future. Mitsubishi's Heavy Industry company had produced Japan's first major indigenously designed expendable cryogenic-fuelled engine, known as the LE-7A. Its successor, the LE-9, would be used to propel the military version of the H-3B. The development and testing would take place in Indonesia.

In so doing, Hata believed that he had legally circumvented the requirements of his own country's nuclear charter, which stated that its people were not to possess, produce or introduce, nuclear weapons into its territory, while advancing Japan's interests for the future. A future in which Japan's role in world affairs would be considerably stronger than it enjoyed today.

* * * * * *

Jakarta

The main auditorium was crammed beyond its designed capacity, causing many to stand outside the side doors while those inside cursed the loss of cool air as it escaped through the open exits. The noise level fell noticeably as several officials walked up onto the dais, and tested the public address system, only to rise again when they left the area once satisfied that all was in order. A large, black security case stood ominously at the centre of the platform. Those present expected that this contained the confidential winning tender documents.

The hall was designed to accommodate one thousand guests however, on that day, more than fifteen hundred had packed the auditorium to witness the tender draw. As the hour approached, a solitary figure appeared, and coughed as he tapped the microphone, before requesting those present to stand. They complied, and a line of officials all wearing the traditional black *pici* on their heads, filed onto the dais, took their positions and waited, hands crossed subserviently in front.

Moments later, a tall, gaunt-faced Indonesian strolled to the center of the raised platform and stood to attention. The national anthem, *Indonesia Raya* commenced, accompanied by an audible groan from a group of foreigners towards the back of the hall.

Finally, after some tiring minutes had passed, the anthem finished and the Chairman, General (retired) Seda, spoke briefly before moving to one side to permit his deputy to commence with the formal tender announcement ceremony.

Television cameras whirred softly as cameramen jostled for better positions, and hundreds of flash-lights blinded all present. The official ceremony was relayed by RCTI, which had established itself as a private monopoly in the television broadcasting industry some years before. As Professor Ali Mochtar ceremoniously unlocked the security case, viewers around the world watched the proceedings with mixed emotions, via the Indonesian *Palapa* satellite system.

There was a hushed silence as an envelope was handed to Chairman Seda, and he broke the seal. Seda smiled, stepped over to the microphones, and commenced by thanking his deputy. Enjoying the moment, he then read the results of the tender submissions for all to hear.

'*Rama I,*' he started, lifting his head as he spoke to the audience, '*the winning tenderer is The Bhakti Corporation!*' There was a roar from someone in the middle of the assembly, as the American joint-venture partners who had signed with the Bhakti Group burst into cheers. The Chairman waited for the hall to recover before continuing. He looked down into the sea of anxious faces.

'*Rama III,*' he continued, '*The Harapan Group!*' There was a muted cheer as the surprised French executive almost choked with the news that his company's partner had won.

'*Rama IV,*' Seda called, as he looked down into the front row and identified Murray Stephenson. '*Rama IV*', he repeated again, '*The Bhakti Corporation*', and the hall erupted once again as the American syndicate screamed out in excitement.

'*And, finally,*' he announced, anticipating the looks of surprise on the sea of faces below, as they realized that something was wrong, for he had not mentioned *Rama II*, '*to complete the first phase, Rama V.*' Representatives looked at each other then back at the general, to see if he hadn't made a mistake. The Chairman paused again, then looked directly down at Murray. '*Rama V has been awarded to The Nasihat Group.*'

Murray smiled and nodded in the retired general's direction. He didn't need to throw himself wildly into the air with excitement.

JAKARTA

He had known for some months that his group would be awarded *Rama V*. He was, however, just as surprised as everyone else present that something had happened to the number two plant. Company representatives who had spent considerable time and, in some instances, millions of dollars in the preparation of the tender documents stood waiting, confused by the omission.

'*Saudara-saudara,*' Seda called, but the Indonesians, who had been interpreting for their foreign counterparts, were engrossed in their own conversations trying to explain that there had no announcement regarding the *Rama II* bid. Annoyed, Seda tapped the microphone several times to silence the hall.

'*My friends,*' he tried again, '*there is an additional announcement of considerable relevance to these proceedings.*' He then paused, waiting for those below to learn what he had said. Slowly, the room settled down and he continued.

'*I have here, in my hand, a statement which the President of Indonesia has asked me to read. Would you all kindly remain while I accommodate our President.*' Seda then removed another envelope, this one from inside his suit. He opened the document, first ensuring that he had the attention of those present, and that the television cameras were still rolling.

'*To the people of Indonesia and guests who have attended the official awards ceremony for the Indonesian Rama Nuclear Power Plant Programme, may Allah look upon you all and smile.*

'*Citizens and guests. I have asked my friend, General Seda, Chairman of PEPELIN, to read you my message. I believe that it is appropriate that the announcement you will shortly hear is made on the very occasion that commences the process which will establish Indonesia as a responsible world citizen, a citizen concerned about the rapid depletion of world energy resources. As no doubt most of you are aware, Indonesia is the third richest country in the world in terms of natural resources. It would be irresponsible of us to assume that these resources will always be available to us, such as gas to provide fertilisers for our farmers, oil to fuel our transport and coal to feed our hungry power plants.*

'*It should not come as a surprise then, that the Indonesian leadership wishes to strive for a future when, once these resources are no longer available to our people, our great nation will not be dependant on others for its survival. We have limited uranium deposits in Kalimantan. We are unable to yet determine whether these might be sufficient in the years* to come, to feed the nuclear reactors currently planned as part of the Rama NPP Programme.

'In consequence, the Indonesian Government wishes to announce, that it has finalized negotiations with the Japanese Government for the construction of what is known as a Fast Breeder Plant for the production of plutonium.' Seda stopped, and signalled for water. No one spoke as they all waited for the Chairman to continue. As the interpreters caught up with the speech, adding to the silence, looks of amazement swept across the faces of all present. Seda continued.

'Nuclear fuel recycling reduces the consumption of uranium resources and eases the environmental burden of radioactive waste disposal, since the uranium and plutonium recovered from spent fuel would otherwise have to be discarded.' Seda paused for a few moments, certain that the Indonesians would be having considerable difficulty passing this information on to their foreign colleagues as the technical terms were alien to most of his fellow countrymen.

'Indonesia has committed itself to nuclear fuel recycling in order to secure a stable long-term supply of energy, and promoting the use of plutonium constitutes an essential part of this programme. According to international experts in this field, it is estimated that the world's supply of uranium will run out within seventy years.

'This project will be known as Rama II, and will have a capacity of 1,500 MW, making it one of the largest plants in the world. It will be located near Mt Muria, in Java. As it was considered that premature release to the public of the terms and conditions relating to this project would not serve the Indonesian national interest, maintaining complete secrecy was imperative. The Indonesian Government wishes to assure the International Community that it does not have a secret agenda. Our reasons for selecting Japan as our partner in this special project are numerous, amongst which, is Japan's commitment to peace, and as the world's only nation to have known the horrors of nuclear devastation, the Japanese people are strongly committed to nuclear disarmament, as we, ourselves are.

'In closing, I trust that the Indonesian people will be proud of their country's achievements, and continue to pray for Allah's blessings to guide us forward. Terima kasih'.

The silence continued only as long as it took for the foreign community to understand what had been said, before conversations erupted throughout the hall. Seda had not finished, but realizing

JAKARTA

the impact the President's statement was having on those present, he did not mind. He had played a major role in the Japanese-Indonesian negotiations. All had agreed that it would not be in either country's interests to reveal that the remaining seven NPPs would, in the not too distant future, all be built by the Japanese; and these would all be Fast Breeder Reactors.

'Terima kasih, gentlemen and ladies, that concludes the official announcement of the winning names of those companies which will build and operate the first five Nuclear Power Plants in Indonesia. May God bless this project and smile upon us all.'

The crowd rose as Seda left the podium, quickly followed by the other members of his team. Reporters called out questions but they were ignored. Unable to obtain further information regarding the surprise announcement, they turned to interview the foreigners present, hoping that they would comment on the President's message. Others attempted to interview the winning company representatives, but these had already moved away from the main body, pushing their way though their competitors ranks as insincere words of congratulations followed their exit. Murray exited along with the others, wishing to avoid the feeding frenzy of journalists in search of interview possibilities.

There was not one of the Salima Group present. They had been instructed not to attend. There had been no need, as the results were already known to Lim and Ruswita. Other than the President, General Seda was the only other living person who was aware that the Salima Group controlled each of the winning corporations. And there was little doubt in his mind that they would want to be heavily involved in the Fast Breeder Plant as well, although to what extent, Seda knew, would depend mainly on the Japanese, the President, and their clandestine project.

Kerry B. Collison

Chapter 13

Defense Intelligence Agency — USA

The Director for Scientific and Technical Intelligence finished reading the report and called for his assistant to remove the document, instructing her to return the material by safe-hand delivery to its originators. Across the file's cover, large bold letters indicated that this would be the National Security Agency, the NSA. The classification of Top Secret had been stamped in fire-engine red on both covers, and also above the heading of every document contained in the sensitive file. He then instructed his secretary to bring Michael Bradshaw into his office.

The communications intelligence (COMINT) activities of the United States are the responsibility of the NSA, which was created in 1952 under President Truman. Unlike other such bureaucratic births, the NSA arrived in silence, smothered in secrecy. It was given a mandate to listen to and decode all foreign communications of interest to the security of the United States. It has also used its power in many ways to slow the spread of publicly available cryptography, to prevent the country's enemies from employing encryption methods too strong for the NSA to break.

The Defense Intelligence Agency, or DIA, although also a gatherer of intelligence, has operations vastly different from other agencies because it is a designated Combat Support Agency and the senior military intelligence component of the American intelligence community. Although considered the new boy on the block, the Agency was established as recently as 1961, and the director was conscious of the rivalries which had grown between other intelligence agencies and the DIA since its creation. The DIA and NSA had rarely become embroiled in such rivalries, as neither organisation's charter actually encroached on the other.

The DIA director was a US Army officer, as were the heads of the other directorates. They all reported to the three-star general who led the massive organization, which employed thousands of civilians alongside their military counterparts. DIA employees could be found on every military base, in all American Embassies, in Maryland and working on the Missile and Space Intelligence Center in Alabama, or where the bulk of the staff were based, at the Defense Intelligence Center on Bolling Air Force Base in Washington. This was where Michael Bradshaw spent most of his time.

* * * * * *

At eighteen, Michael had graduated from high school and started college. For a while, he seemed to drift, plagued by a restlessness which interfered with his studies. Against his mother's wishes, but supported by his step-father, Zach, Michael enlisted in the United States Navy, where he remained for three years. During that time he travelled extensively but eventually, realising that the opportunity might not come round again, he decided to continue his formal education.

When he turned twenty-three, Michael applied for, and was accepted into the commissioning program, which resulted in his returning to college. He remained there until completing his undergraduate degree, achieving honours, and was immediately accepted for Naval post-graduate study. In his twenty-sixth year, Michael completed his Masters degree in Science, and returned to the fleet as an officer. He spent time onboard the nuclear submarine, *USS Plunger*, travelling the world's deepest ocean trenches.

Michael enjoyed his time on SSN 595 as a submariner. He remained in the service until he had completed his active duty obligations, and then returned to college to complete his PhD. At thirty-five Michael was snapped up by the American Government and given extensive training with the NSA. After several years he decided that, although intelligence gathering and interpretation was an exciting enough role, he wished to be more active on the gathering side, which resulted in his being accepted into the DIA. There, Michael's background experience was utilized by the Agency in its efforts to keep tabs on foreign government nuclear development programmes, which required an in-depth understanding not

JAKARTA

only of nuclear armaments, nuclear power plants and their applications, but also a keen sense of what was building politically in specified target areas.

His investigations often necessitated disguising his true vocation, and Michael travelled regularly, under the guise of an inspector from the International Atomic Energy Agency. This was not so unusual, he discovered, as the IAEA appreciated any feedback resulting from interdepartmental exchange.

'Great report, Michael,' the Director beamed, 'seems that your time in Meade wasn't wasted.' Michael smiled at the compliment. He knew that his earlier training with the NSA would have contributed to the ease he now experienced in executing his missions.

'Does that mean I can have some of that time off you promised me?' he tried, knowing that it would be unlikely that they would cut him loose for the month he'd requested. To Michael, it seemed that the DIA's demands on his time were endless.

'Good try, Michael, good try,' the Director responded. He hadn't had time off himself for more than a year. He looked at his intelligence analyst, recognising that Michael Bradshaw was perhaps one of the more gregarious agents on his team. The director had considered Michael's penchant for country clubs and other socially active venues as a negative, until realizing that the man's natural ability to mix at all levels could be used to the Department's advantage. He had considered Michael's extra-curricular activities and decided to support his exposure, using this to further enhance his cover while roaming the world's trouble spots.

'Hope you haven't made any plans for this weekend,' the director said, knowing that it would be most unusual for the younger man to be at loose ends. Michael waited for the punch-line. He'd grown accustomed to surrendering his weekends to the Agency.

'Well,' he started, 'thought I might manage to get a few sets in sometime. I've almost forgotten how to hold a racquet.' The Director knew this not to be true. He had had the recent misfortune to partner against the younger man during one of the rare office social functions.

'I want you to jump on a flight for Tokyo. Go and see our man at the Embassy, and see if you can develop some feel for what the Indonesians are up to.' Michael had read the classified memo regarding their announcement to build a fast breeder reactor in conjunction with the Japanese.

'I think it would be judicious to spend some time visiting several of the Japanese plants. I'll arrange for the IAEA to provide the usual assistance. I want your face known over there, Michael, and I want you to try and establish rapport with some of the Japanese who would obviously be in a position within their nuclear industry, to offer some further insight into the Indonesian-Nippon venture.' He looked across at Michael, his face solemn.

'I don't have to tell you that the Pentagon views the relationship in the most negative way. We should expect to have them on our backs over the next few years while construction is under way, and then some.' Michael understood how superpowers always felt threatened when others moved to join their exclusive nuclear club.

They discussed the parameters of his mission further, and forty-eight hours later Michael arrived in Tokyo, where he quickly established his bona-fides and went about developing a strategy which would accommodate his government's future needs. If the Japanese intention was to assist the Indonesians to disguise the production of excess plutonium, this would require the assistance of at least one of the senior Japanese nuclear engineers or physicists involved in the Indonesian project.

* * * * * *

Japan

Tired from the long flight, and annoyed that he had not taken the train from the airport in lieu of the taxi service, he paid the two-hundred-and-fifty-dollar fare and checked into the Hilton Hotel. He showered and, as he then felt reasonably refreshed, caught a cab down to the Ginza where he planned to wander around just long enough for his body clock to readjust itself.

Michael Bradshaw enjoyed his visits to Asia, particularly Japan, where he found the unique blend of Western and Asian cultures quite refreshing. As he wandered around the well-lit night-club strip, he smiled as he observed swarms of chauffeur-driven limousines depositing executives outside their favourite clubs, and reminded himself that he had perhaps selected the worst night of the week to go wandering around the Ginza streets. He remembered being told during an earlier visit that it was customary for executives to leave their wives at home, and go drinking together with their friends on Monday nights.

Michael remained in the area until midnight, witnessing the evening come to an end for the weekly revellers. Hordes of drunken Japanese men, having been dragged from the clutches of hostesses, struggled back onto the streets where they sang loudly. Some collapsed on the footpaths while others swayed in the evening air, the expressions on their faces reflecting the nausea which always preceded a violent vomiting attack. The remainder generally carried on enjoying themselves until their transport arrived to take them back to their wives and families.

Tokyo, for Michael, had always been a contradiction of cultures. Protocol dictated every movement, yet Western and other influences were evident as parallel layers. It had been necessary that he study the land, its people and culture, and although he had not attempted to learn the language, Michael had acquired enough of the basics to assist him with the required courtesies.

The next morning, refreshed and anxious to start, Michael caught a taxi to the American Embassy where he was ushered upstairs for his appointment with the DIA liaison officer, Derek Parkes, who had prepared additional information for Michael's Japan brief.

'What do you think of the schedule?' the Defense Intelligence Agency representative asked. He had prepared a draft programme in advance, and sent this to Washington prior to Michael's departure.

'I think I'll need a little more flexibility, Derek. Maybe we should cut out some of the smaller plants. It would be unlikely that the sort of people we are looking for would be working in the more junior positions,' he replied.

'Okay, then,' Parkes agreed, 'which ones?' His own knowledge of the Japanese nuclear power industry had taken a quantum leap over the past fortnight, having been instructed by the Director to prepare the ground for Bradshaw's visit.

'Let's eliminate all secondary power plants to start,' Michael suggested. 'I'd prefer to target the main stations in the energy producing companies, as it is more likely that the senior engineers will be selected from these locations.'

'All right, what's that leave us with?' Parkes asked, ready to make the necessary alterations to his copy.

'I'd like to visit Hokkaido if it can be arranged. There are two new plants nearing completion, and these might just be the last we'll see for awhile. Seems that the ruling Japanese Coalition is nervous about further developing their nuclear industry.'

'Will these be the Hokkaido Electric Power Company plants?' Parkes asked.

'No,' Michael advised, 'the Tokyo Electric Power Company owns both of these. The Hokkaido Company plants are fully operational.' Michael thought for a moment, then added, 'but it wouldn't hurt to have a quick inspection of either one of theirs as well.'

'Okay,' the liaison officer responded, ticking at his own list, 'what else?'

'I want to visit Kyushu. There are two plants there of interest to us. We'll inform both the Kyushu Electric Power Company and Shikoku that the IAEA inspection will take place towards the end of next week. Then I'll be able to drop in at the Chubu station at Hamaoka on my return leg.' The men remained discussing Michael's itinerary until he was satisfied that they had selected the most appropriate locations, then they broke for lunch.

That evening, having refused his associate's invitation to dine out, Michael remained in his room, finalizing his notes in preparation for the commencement of his journey through the Japanese nuclear plants. Early the following morning, he visited the first of these, the Japan Atomic Power Company's plant just fifty kilometers from Tokyo city.

* * * * * *

Michael's notes showed the rapid development of the Japanese nuclear industry from their humble beginnings to the current number of seventy-five operational plants, with several still nearing completion.

Japan had already achieved the position of being the world's fourth largest producer of nuclear power, after the United States, France, and Russia. But, even with these impressive advances, Japan's energy supply structure remained extremely fragile, as the country still depended on foreign fuel sources for seventy-five percent of its needs, most of which was petroleum. Michael understood the political, economic and social considerations relating to nuclear power use in this country, and sympathised with the general public's perception of the dangers relating to the production of power from nuclear sources.

There had always been mixed reactions in Japan to the country's continued expansion of its nuclear plants, particularly as Japan was a forerunner in the promotion of plutonium for nuclear power generation.

He identified the reasoning for disquiet amongst those who understood the production of nuclear power, and the complex questions raised as a result of Japan's insistence that they pursue a policy of using plutonium. At a time when the world community was struggling with the problem of disposing of the enriched uranium that had been left over after the former Soviet nuclear arsenal had been dismantled, the question had been raised time and again, whether it was necessary for Japan to press ahead with development of fast breeder reactors to breed plutonium.

Michael knew that the quantity of enriched uranium that had become available from scrapping the former Soviet arsenal had, in the main, already been consumed by world demand. He also understood that the development of fast breeder reactors was necessary to ensure long-term supply of nuclear energy resources. Although France and the United Kingdom had changed direction with relation to their policy of promoting this type of reactor, he believed that both nations would continue to jointly develop a new-generation series which would incorporate even more safeguards to allay public fears.

Michael considered the proposed Indonesian plants, and decided that their government had been clever in its decision to incorporate the production of drinking water, as well as power. He knew that Indonesia suffered acutely from pollution of the country's coastal underground reservoirs, particularly on the islands of Java and Bali. He also believed that the production of drinking water, although relevant, acted to distract public opinion away from the fact that the first Java plant, currently under joint construction with the Japanese, could easily be utilised to disguise the excess production of plutonium for weapon's use. If this were to be, then Michael agreed with the American intelligence community's conclusion, that the Indonesians would also have to be planning to develop a delivery system for the future.

Similar questions had arisen when Japan first announced its intentions to use plutonium produced from its own plants. It was now his task to search for information channels which might provide answers to the question as to whether Indonesia's future use of plutonium would eventually lead to the development of nuclear weapons. As a signatory to the Nuclear Non-Proliferation Treaty, Indonesia had already stated that this would not be so; however, signs now indicated the contrary, and Michael, along with a team of others in the field, were given the responsibility of searching for information which might provide answers to Indonesia's motives in developing the *Rama II* Fast Breeder Reactor plant in Java.

During discussions with others in the DIA, Michael had pointed out that, although it was true that Indonesia did not possess a high level of technological expertise in the field of nuclear energy, there was most certainly an abundance of such resources available from the former Soviet Empire. Building a nuclear bomb posed little problem for those with the experience and specialized knowledge.

Technicians with the ability to develop nuclear weaponry could be easily sourced from any of a number of former Soviet satellite nations, and Michael had suggested that, if United States intelligence agencies could concentrate on targeting former Eastern Bloc nationals moving into Indonesia, then they might have a greater chance of discovering what the Indonesians might really be planning. The DIA director had agreed, and later mentioned this to his counterpart in the CIA.

* * * * * *

Washington

At the conclusion of his three weeks' inspection tour, which had taken him through the majority of the Japanese nuclear power plants, Michael had short-listed three names from those he had met in the course of his visit. He carried this information back to Washington and placed his report on the DIA director's desk.

When he had finished reading through Michael's submission, the director had the three names cross-referenced with the other

JAKARTA

Agencies for a more detailed investigation of these potential resources. The Japanese nuclear engineers were subjected to a full CIA and NSA check, and when the information had been collated and returned to the DIA, the director smiled as he drew a circle high-lighting the third name on the list. This person would be their conduit to gather information concerning the Japanese-Indonesian venture.

The Intelligence Chief tapped the man's photograph attached to the report. There would be little difficulty in recruiting the man, he knew. His eyes searched for the incriminating photograph buried amongst a number of others, and attached to the text of the second page. He extracted the damning evidence from the folder, and flipped through the pages. The director snorted in disgust, and wondered just how deeply they could hook the man. And what the Japanese Prime Minister might say if he became aware of his brother-in-law's deviant behaviour.

* * * * * *

Japan

Colonel Sujono Diryo closed his eyes as the warm sensation flowed through his body, cleansing his mind of the day's pressures. The soft, scrubbing motion relaxed his tense back muscles, and Sujono grunted with pleasure as the woman's expert hands worked their magic.

'*Sujono-san is pleased?*' she asked, continuing with the therapeutic, but gentle kneading around his lower-back. It had been troubling him for some time. He grunted, and the geisha girl accepted this as approval of her experienced technique. She continued in silence, allowing time for her honourable guest to completely relax. The girl pushed Sujono's head and shoulders slightly forward, as her hands worked their way expertly over his body. When she thought the water had lost some of its temperature, she nodded to the other geisha waiting patiently, silently, in the corner, and more hot water was added. Bubbles of soap rose with the heat, and she stopped, momentarily, to brush some of the suds away from Sujono-san's face.

She sat, her legs to either side of Sujono's, massaging his back, enjoying the warmth of the hot tub, and pleased that her regular guest had returned.

When he had missed his Friday appointments three weeks in a row, she had assumed that the Colonel had moved his business elsewhere. It had happened many times before with other clients. She leaned forward so her tiny breasts gently touched Sujono's back, recalling from earlier visits that this would arouse him, then moved the sponge around to his firm abdomen, and rubbed softly.

Sujono groaned with contentment, delighted that he had been able to return in time for the pleasurable bath, and the geisha's attention. He had recently been recalled to Jakarta, where he had remained for some weeks attending briefings of the greatest importance to his country's future defense. When the coded instruction had first arrived, he had suspected that his tour of duty as Defense Attaché had been cut short, at his wife's instigation.

It had not been easy for him, married to the President's second youngest daughter. She had joined him in Japan for no more than a few months before fabricating a number of excuses to return home to Jakarta. There she had busied herself with her enterprises, their prolonged absences from each other's company further endangering their childless marriage. Gossip plagued their relationship, but Sujono remained content to be married to her, accepting that he owed his rapid promotion to his association with the First Family. He had returned to *HANKAM* more than a little dispirited at having to leave Japan. Sujono enjoyed the people and their traditions. But even more so, he enjoyed their doting women.

Sujono had not been surprised to discover upon his return to Indonesia that his orders had been issued directly by the Palace. Before even visiting his wife, Colonel Sujono had been instructed to proceed to General Seda's home, where he spent several hours being briefed by his influential sponsor. Sujono accepted that his early career involvement with the powerful Seda had not, in any way, harmed his position within the military.

It was during Sujono's time as the general's *aide-de-camp* that he had met the President's daughter. He had risen to Lieutenant Colonel within months of their marriage, but had not received any further promotion since his posting to Japan. Sujono knew that he was being punished for his wife's failure to bear children, and resigned himself to the possibility that divorce might just be an option for them both.

'*You have been selected for this assignment on my recommendations, Jono,*' General Seda had informed him. '*If you discredit yourself in any way, then you also discredit me.*' He remembered the feeling of disbelief he had experienced when Seda had revealed details of the rocket development negotiations with the Japanese Military. Sujono had been sworn to secrecy and, in less than subtle terms, threatened. He had resented being reminded of the consequences should the project be compromised in any way, but accepted that secrecy would be paramount for the successful realization of the programme. Sujono had then given the necessary undertakings, as demanded. Later, when he sat with Seda and the President at the *Istana*, he listened intently as the *Bapak* reiterated the importance of secrecy, and he had given his solemn oath to the President that he would strive to maintain the project's integrity and dedicate himself to the joint Japanese-Indonesian defense co-operation.

'*You have been given a great responsibility, Jono,*' The President had told him, solemnly. Sujono remembered wondering if his father-in-law was aware of his daughter's marital difficulties. He had decided that this would be most unlikely, considering his summons to the Palace. '*You have also been given a position of trust which I know you will respect, not just as an ABRI officer, but also as a member of this family. You have a great tradition to maintain, Jono. You must always remember that you carry the name of one of Indonesia's most respected heroes.*'

Sujono remembered how his eyes had misted over, when the *Bapak Presiden* had then spoken so highly of Sujono's father. He had very few recollections of the general; the one memory which had remained with him throughout the years was that of their last moments together, when his father had herded his family into a bedroom and locked the door behind for their safety, before confronting the murderous communists who waited downstairs.

As the President reminisced, Sujono remembered his mother holding his small hands tightly, as the general was laid to rest at the heroes cemetery in Kalibata, on Armed Forces Day in 1965.

As the son of a Hero of the Revolution, it was only natural that he should follow in his father's footsteps. Sujono entered the Academy, and excelled. Upon graduation, he had been assigned to the Intelligence Corps, and was posted to the Indonesian Intelligence

Co-ordinating Agency, *BAKIN,* where he was soon identified for his diligence and dedication. General Seda had selected him as his personal assistant, following which, his marriage into the First Family advanced his career beyond his wildest expectations.

Within the span of a few short years, Sujono's friends witnessed a transformation in his attitude and demeanour, but were not surprised to learn of his accelerated promotion to Lieutenant Colonel. He had then been posted to Japan, where he quickly adapted to his new environment, becoming fluent in the language during his first year at the Indonesian Embassy. His wife had become bored, and longed for her own culture. At first, she had taken a few short trips back to Jakarta. When the first year had slowly passed, and then the second, they found that their marriage had all but become one of convenience to them both. Sujono knew that she still loved him but he felt little for her in return. He was, however, astute enough to realize the career consequences should they separate, or even divorce.

At first, there had not been a great deal for Sujono to do in Japan, as there was little defense co-operation between the two countries. The Japanese Home Affairs and Defense Ministries had few secrets to hide, and he had been given *carte blanche* to roam Japan on tours, building his knowledge of the people and their culture. With less than six months of his tour remaining, he had been recalled.

It was then that Sujono had discovered that his future would be considerably brighter than he had grown to believe. He had returned to Japan, filled with a new confidence, knowing that the secrets he now held would guarantee his future, with or without the President's insecure daughter at his side.

* * * * * *

Sujono decided that he'd had enough, climbed out of the tub and walked to the shower. The geisha followed, washing any remaining soap from his firm, brown, athletic body, before leading him into another, but smaller, delightfully scented room. There they made love in a mechanical fashion, as they had done so many times in the past.

Colonel Sujono Diryo smiled as his geisha bowed formally, her face devoid of all emotion which might indicate her satisfaction with the envelope he had earlier filled with Yen and placed in her kimono pocket. He assured the young woman that he would return at the scheduled time the following week, and departed, mentally refreshed and physically satisfied.

As he walked from the geisha house and crossed the road to hail a taxi, Sujono was too distant to hear the rapid whirr of an automatic Pentax Z-1p's zoom capture his exit from the well known address. As the Indonesian Intelligence Colonel disappeared from view, the American photographer unscrewed the telephoto lens from the camera, placed his equipment back inside the brown leather case he carried, then returned to the United States Embassy. Within hours, Colonel Sujono Diryo's photograph lay on the DIA director's table in Washington.

* * * * * *

Indonesia — Bandung Research and Development Center

When the President had first summoned Professor Mohammed Subroto to the Palace and broached the subject of Indonesia's opportunity to join with the Japanese to develop a multi-purpose rocket, the gentle academic had smiled and prepared to leave, wondering why the country's leader had played such an inconsiderate hoax on an old man. When he realized that the President was indeed serious, Subroto was so overwhelmed, he was speechless.

It had always been his dream that Indonesia would one day direct some of its resources towards the development of its own space industry. Some years before, when the then Minister for Research and Industry, Doctor Habibie, had played a prominent role in the development of Indonesian aeronautical and science sectors, Professor Subroto had believed that he and the others who had waited patiently for so many years might finally be given the opportunity to participate in the development of Indonesia's own satellite industry, launching these from within the Republic. But he and his close associates were to be disappointed. Instead of allocating resources to provide opportunities to the country's talented pool of scientists, most of whom were United States trained, resources were re-directed into uneconomic aircraft production programmes in Bandung, which added little to the country's prestige when these programmes were eventually terminated.

Subroto recalled, that during the mid-nineteen-seventies, when Indonesia had contracted for the Hughes Corporation to launch the first of the *Palapa* satellite series, he had been devastated to discover that the entire *Palapa* technology had been retained by the Americans. He had watched, unhappily, as only the more menial aspects of the programme were contracted to local companies, such as the erection of the many communication towers necessary for satellite positioning control. Subroto had been deeply annoyed by the appointment of foreign companies to manufacture these towers and other equipment overseas when he was confident that these could have been produced locally. Subroto realized that many would benefit financially from this and similar contracts, but it would not be the citizens of Indonesia.

The professor had visited one of the tower construction sites and recalled how shocked he had been to discover the number of foreign riggers employed to erect the relatively simple structure. He was informed, confidentially, by one of the Indonesian observers that the local company, Communications Service, had acted merely as a front for the expensive foreign labour contractor and that its founder, Stephen Coleman, had pocketed considerable profits at the expense of local competitors.

Professor Subroto had been disillusioned for years by his country's lack of direction and leadership. He was convinced that Indonesia had sufficient resources to develop its own aeronautical and space technologies, and could call upon a number of qualified Indonesian technical experts to assist implement such a programme. He believed that his country's leadership had deliberately been misled by the West who, in his opinion, feared the possibility of yet another developing, or Third World country emerging to demand their place as a member of the exclusive Nuclear Club.

When the opportunity was granted, the professor had happily accepted the position to head the Indonesian team, as the senior counterpart to the Japanese technical party. When he learned that future plutonium stocks were to be derived from excess production in the *Rama II* plant, he had simply smiled, pleased that so much thought had gone into planning the project's long-term needs.

JAKARTA

The fact that the surplus plutonium was to be secretly stored in the reconstructed under-ground shafts only strengthened his resolve and commitment to his country's defense strategies.

The joint development rocket was to be based on the successful Japanese civilian rocket programme which had already been utilized to launch a number of Japanese satellites over the past years. Professor Subroto understood that the final product would be used not only for Indonesia's own satellite launch programme, but also for military purposes. The possibility that he might, in future years, be considered the founding father of Indonesia's rocket industry, carried great store when Subroto was first introduced to the project.

He pledged his total support to the President, and accepted that there would be those who might accuse him of hypocrisy once they discovered that he had played an instrumental role in developing Indonesia's first Intercontinental Ballistic Missile delivery system. Acting on the President's suggestion, the missiles were to be appropriately named the *Pedoman* Series, which they all agreed would be sufficient deterrent against any future Chinese aggression.

* * * * * *

In determining Indonesia's needs, Subroto had been instructed to work with the Japanese to develop a delivery system which would place Beijing within range of an Indonesian launch. The professor knew that an intermediary range missile might suffice, as his country had the advantage of being able to establish launch sites more than one thousand kilometers to the north of Jakarta and closer to any of the selected Chinese targets. However, with the recent developments in the South China Sea, the professor, in response to suggestions from the Military, agreed that Indonesia should plan to develop a delivery system which would be compatible in basic design, with the launch rockets required for future satellite requirements.

The Indonesian development team was faced with three main factors which would influence the effectiveness of their ballistic missile. These were range, accuracy and the size and type of the missile's warhead. After several weeks of discussions with the Indonesian Military leadership, it was decided that the *Pedoman* missiles be designed as a three-stage ICBM, with a range of eight thousand kilometers. This, they all agreed, would be sufficient to keep any aggressor at bay.

As for accuracy, Subroto agreed that the Japanese advanced computer-controlled guidance systems, used in the H-3B experimental series, would most likely be appropriate for the *Pedoman* as well. He had also recommended to the President that the Indonesian ICBM be designed to carry only a single nuclear warhead similar to that of the French Intermediate Range Ballistic Missiles and the Chinese ICBMs. They had all agreed that in the interests of disguising their intentions from the Japanese, a conventional warhead would be also be designed as the designated missile's explosive.

* * * * * *

The Chairman of the Indonesian Nuclear Energy Company, PEPELIN, General Seda, assumed charge of the overall project. Prior to his appointment, Professor Subroto had never met the retired general and was surprised to discover that Nathan Seda was conversant with even the technical aspects of the joint development project. When the scientist was advised that *BAKIN* would be responsible for all security and the vetting of staff, he had not objected.

Subroto calmly accepted the introduction of security controls, which, although he considered extreme, were highly effective. These measures had resulted in regular visits by high-ranking *BAKIN* officers, whose intimidating interviews bordered on interrogations. The professor complained that he found these unannounced security checks to be disruptive, but bowed to the PEPELIN Chairman's insistence that these were necessary in the interests of national security. Although he totally supported the measures introduced to safeguard against possible security leaks, Professor Subroto had become increasingly concerned with the tactics of one man in particular, Umar, who had been given total freedom of movement throughout the Centre.

The Professor's most senior assistant was Doctor Sunarko, a well-respected Javanese physicist who had studied in the United States and Japan, and was conversant with the Japanese H-2 and H-3B rocket designs. Sunarko had also spent four years working with the Hughes Corporation in America, and had been responsible for many of the innovative changes that had been introduced into the final *Palapa B* series satellites during the past decade.

Sunarko had complained to the professor that the senior security officer, Umar, had followed him several times from the research centre into Bandung, and kept him under surveillance the entire time. Although such behaviour was considered unusual, there was little that Subroto could do about the matter, except speak to the man. Following his brief discussions with Umar, Professor Subroto had been surprised to receive a call from General Seda within the hour and immediately wished he had not been as critical of Umar as he had.

The PEPELIN Chairman had not minced words, making it quite clear that the security officer had explicit instructions directly from the President to ensure that none of the research centre's staff compromised the project in any way, even if this meant taking steps which might, under other circumstances, be considered excessive. The professor clearly understood the underlying threat and Umar's real role within the security team. Later, he spoke at some length with Sunarko, urging him and others on his team to disassociate themselves from anyone who might be considered a security threat to the highly secret project.

As the following months passed, members of the professor's research and development team threw themselves into their work, often not leaving the centre for weeks at a stretch. When Sunarko did finally take one of the jeeps into Bandung for a break, he was followed. And, some weeks later, when he left the Centre during the dead of night and drove along the dangerous, un-surfaced clay roads that wound through the mountains before joining the Bandung highway, he was also followed. The next day Umar reported to Seda what he had seen, and even the General had expressed surprise when he learned that the foolish Doctor Sunarko had paid a visit to the Australian's residence in Jakarta.

KERRY B.COLLISON

Chapter 14

The Australian Prime Minister

They all stood as the Prime Minister entered the room, accompanied by Professor Ian Hyde. The Australian leader motioned for the members of his Cabinet to be seated, and indicated for his guest to sit at his side. Although the country had become a republic, it still basically followed the Commonwealth system of government, providing its citizens with both an identity separate from England and a Westminster form of representation. What had been previously designated Governor General had merely been supplanted by a change in nomenclature. The Australian President, not unlike those of Singapore and India, was simply the Head of State. He was not involved in the day-to-day running of the country's affairs, and his attendance was most certainly, not required at this meeting.

'Gentlemen, as you know, I have called this session in order that we might obtain a clearer understanding of what is happening in relation to the Indonesian announcement concerning their Nuclear Power Plant programme. I asked Professor Hyde here, with whom many of you are already familiar, to address this meeting to assist those amongst us who have little knowledge or understanding as to what these developments in Indonesia might mean to us and the Australian people. Professor?' the Prime Minister then passed the meeting over to Ian Hyde.

'Thank you Prime Minister. Good afternoon everyone,' he began, looking around the room, recognising some familiar faces. Those he had not had the opportunity to meet in person he recognized from the media interviews all had given at one time or another.

'Firstly, it is my intention to brief you in laymen's terms on what the announcement will mean in terms of nuclear power capacity, costs, timings and other relevant data. Then, I would prefer that you ask questions and address those issues which are obviously foremost in your minds, such as what risks there might be to Australia, and the opportunity for the Indonesians to produce plutonium for other than use in their reactors.' The professor took a crumpled handkerchief from his trousers pocket and dabbed at his dry nose out of habit before commencing. He spoke without notes.

'It appears that the Indonesians intend addressing their electrical power problems by embarking on what most of us believe to be a quite incredible path, to produce power from nuclear energy when, in fact, they still have sufficient alternative resources available. However, we will come to that later.' He looked around the table.

'The Indonesian announcement advised that they intend building twelve power plants, and that these will be constructed in two stages.' He paused, and wiped at his nose again.

'The first phase will consist of five plants, one of which will be located in Bali, while the others will be spread throughout Java. The Indonesians have called this, the *Rama Project*. I am not sure how familiar you might all be with the *Ramayana*, although its relevance is not important to what we are to discuss; it may be of interest that *Rama* was one of the more prominent figures from that lengthy story. Considering the nature of the project, I would have expected that *Kalki* might have been a more appropriate name.' This was lost on those present, they having never heard of the mythical spirit of destructive power. The professor continued.

'The Indonesians have quite cleverly decided to use the nuclear generating plants in a dual role. A proportion of the energy will be dedicated to the production of pure drinking water through a desalination process. The remaining power produced will be dedicated to electrical needs for those Indonesian people fortunate enough to be living within the proposed grid. *Rama I*, and I am now quoting directly from the Indonesian Ministry of Home Affairs, will be located in Bali, and will produce one thousand megawatts of electrical power and two hundred thousand cubic meters of drinking water, daily.' He observed by the looks on the faces of some that they were suitably impressed by the scale of the operation.

'The Bali plant will be amongst the biggest in the world, and will, for a reasonable time, or until the island's people fully develop into major electrical consumers similar to that of Western standards, produce sufficient power to accommodate the entire island. The drinking water will obviously be a major bonus to their tourism industry, considering the number of visitors who regularly fall ill as a result of drinking contaminated ground water there.' Hyde then paused again, reminded that even he had fallen dreadfully ill during a holiday he had taken in Bali some years before.

'*Rama's III, IV and V*, are not dissimilar to *Rama I*, in so much as these are all what is commonly known as PWR's, or Pressurised Water Reactors. These systems are considered to be more reliable than BWR's, or Boiling Water Reactors, which are favoured by the Russians and Eastern Bloc nations. These plants are approximately the same capacity as *Rama I*, and will also produce drinking water for the thirsty one hundred millions living on Java.' Someone coughed, and he hesitated, permitting the senator responsible the opportunity to finish before he continued.

'As many of you would have read, Java is suffering from another water shortage, due not so much to drought, but as a result of water tables being polluted as salt water moves in to replace the shallow ground water which, I might add, continues to be consumed at an alarming rate by the island's coastal dwellers. Sewerage has also filtered down into the water systems, polluting ground water even further in those areas with high population densities. In short, most of the island of Java.

'The Indonesian Government's tender information release indicates that *Ramas VI to XII*, will be offered for bidding over the next few years. The first five plants are to be constructed, as near as is practical, simultaneously, and the nuclear plants are being offered to foreign and domestic investors on the basis of what is commonly known as a BOT project. This terminology refers to Build, Operate then Transfer of projects by investors, and has become quite popular in Asia as a means of funding infrastructure developments.

'In the United States, such projects would normally require up to fifteen years to develop, due to the number of government agencies and other bodies which oversee the construction and operation of nuclear plants. In authoritarian regimes such as one would find in Asia, this development schedule could be reduced dramatically, perhaps to as little as four or five years. The actual construction requires only two to three years. The rest lies in preparation, and commissioning.' Professor Hyde then paused, collecting his thoughts.

'What is of real interest, is the fact that the Indonesians have also announced a government-to-government joint venture with the Japanese, to construct and operate what is known as an LMFBR.' He smiled at the frowns around the table.

'*Rama II* will be a Liquid Metal, Fast Breeder Reactor,' he said, pausing again for effect, 'and it is this plant which will be used by the Indonesians and Japanese to produce considerable amounts of plutonium, both economically and efficiently.' He looked at the stony faces around the table. They were already aware that the second plant would be capable of producing plutonium, as the Australian Press had talked of nothing else ever since the announcement had been first made.

'The Indonesians have advised that *Rama II* will produce both power and drinking water, as do the other plants. They have stated categorically that the purpose of this plant is primarily for those purposes, and that the additional production of plutonium is supposedly part of their forward thinking to the time when there will be very little uranium left to mine.' He rested for a moment, then offered the opportunity for questions. The Prime Minister was first.

'How much will these plants cost, and are they economically viable considering the life of each plant and the cost of power production?' Hyde fielded the question. He had discussed this with the man before the meeting had commenced, suggesting that the Prime Minister lead with these, as this would assist Hyde to introduce the basic description of the plants so that the others could more easily comprehend how a typical nuclear plant might operate.

'Nuclear Power Plants, or NPPs, have a life of some twenty-five years. The American experience indicates that NPP electricity still costs marginally more than Thermal Power Plants, or TPPs. According to the Worldwatch Institute, new NPPs in the States are producing power for around twelve cents per kilowatt hour, while natural gas plants come in at around seven to nine cents. It is true that NPPs require huge initial capital investments. Financing such projects from their own resources would not have been a viable option. That is why these will all be fully financed on the basis of BOT.'

'Why would they embark on such an ambitious programme considering their extensive coal deposits?' The question was asked by the Defense Minister. 'Would it not be more advantageous for them to upgrade their existing plants?'

'I would be the first to agree that retrofitting existing coal-fired plants with high-tech desulfurization and denitrification technologies, or switching their existing coal-fired plants to cleaner burning fuels like natural gas which, by the way, the Indonesians have in great abundance, would reduce environmental impact and increase combustion efficiency. But, unfortunately, there are stronger political issues at play here, stronger than environmental considerations, I fear.'

'Will they be able to produce an atomic bomb?' the Immigration Minister asked, knowing that this was highly possible. He had read the report in the Canberra Times over the weekend, and thought that perhaps Australia should be considering its own Nuclear Power Plant be upgraded to do more than just produce isotopes for medicine. The controversy surrounding the proposed three hundred million dollar expenditure for rehabilitating the Lucas Heights reactor in Sydney was a continuing irritation to him.

'The short answer is, yes. Providing they are able to collect sufficient plutonium without discovery, then it would be relatively simple for them to do so.' The room was gravely hushed at the thought that their nearest neighbour would have such a weapon. 'Of course, they would still have to develop a delivery system for such a weapon to be of any real use.' The Defense Minister's mind turned to reports he had read concerning the number of missiles which had been trotted out for the Presidential announcement during their Armed Forces' Day parade. He wondered how difficult it would be to exchange the conventional warheads for nuclear, and whether there was anything in the Indonesian weapons' arsenal which they were yet to disclose. The Minister realized that, with the collapse of the Soviet Empire, nuclear weaponry had been made available for sale to countries such as Indonesia and other developing nations which would otherwise have had no opportunity to advance their countries to nuclear capability status.

'Getting back to these reactors, Professor, how much uranium would they consume annually in terms of dollars?' Several other ministers turned to look at the junior cabinet minister from the State of Northern Territory.

'Whoever wins the supply contract could expect something in the order of almost two million tonnes of product. That would earn around sixty to seventy million dollars. Once all twelve reactors were in operation, this figure would more than double.'

'Professor Hyde, I must apologise, but I'm still a little confused as to how this all works.' The statement came from the Minister for Ethnic Affairs; others in the room were relieved that the question had been asked. Professor Hyde admired the woman for admitting she had not understood.

'Not all uranium is fissile, that is, able to be split or divided. Most uranium ore extracted from the earth contains less than one per cent of Uranium 235, the rest being approximately ninety-nine percent Uranium 238. Uranium 235 is the only element found in nature which is fissile. When its nucleus is hit by a subatomic particle, a neutron, it splits into two fragments. In this fission process, a large amount of energy is released and more neutrons are produced.' He paused and smiled at the woman who had asked the question.

'I'm fine, so far, thanks Professor,' she said.

'Okay, then,' he restarted, 'energy is released, and more neutrons are produced. These can be used to split further U-235 nuclei and set up a chain reaction. A nuclear reactor is simply a means of controlling the chain reaction and converting the energy produced into heat and, subsequently, into electricity.' He paused, and when he was certain that she had understood, continued.

'The proportion of fissile isotopes can be increased by fuel enrichment. Now, this is very important. There are two man-made fissile elements, plutonium Pu-239, which is produced from the U-238, and the other being U-233, which is produced from thorium. The three elements U-235, U-233 and Pu-239 are the basic fuels for nuclear reactors.' Professor Hyde then rested, knowing that this would have been too much already for most of those present.

'Sorry, again, Professor, but what is a Fast Breeder Reactor again?' she asked.

'Humn,' he started, biding his time. He was judging how to

JAKARTA

explain simply without seeming to patronise his audience.

'World-wide there are only a limited number of fast-breeder reactors. The FBR is not a thermal reactor...it has no moderator for control purposes. Fission takes place in the core and produces heat, which is then carried away by, let's say, liquid sodium, such as I would expect the Japanese might introduce for *Rama II*. This heat is contained within a large pool and exchanges its heat with a second intermediate circuit of liquid sodium. This, in turns, transfers the heat from the sodium pool to steam generators where the heat is transferred again, to water, creating steam to drive the engine.' Hyde stopped and looked around the table, knowing that many of their number would not have followed.

'It's okay, thanks Professor, we can always ask questions later,' the Prime Minister intervened. Hyde nodded thankfully, then continued.

'All right, then. Because the core contains no moderator, the fission neutrons are not slowed down and retain fast speeds. The core consists of a mixture of U-235, Pu-239 and U-238, contained within a blanket of more U-238. The incineration of plutonium in the core is inevitable; the choice as to whether or not to produce plutonium within the blanket is optional. What you need to understand is, once the fast reactor has been launched, it becomes self-sufficient and may produce excess plutonium. This is why it is given the appellation of "breeder".' He could see from a number of faces that they had clearly not understood. He looked for a simple analogy.

'Lord Marshall of Goring once described the process in this manner.' He looked at the Prime Minister who smiled and, pleased with the supportive response, continued. 'Imagine a group of castaways on a beach, trying to keep warm. We will assume that they collected a small supply of wood, most of which was wet, having been washed up by the sea. They knew that they could burn the available dry wood, and that would be that. Or, if they were to place the wet timber around the fire, building a blanket so to speak then, as the dry wood burned, keeping them warm, it would also dry out the wetter material, providing an ongoing source of fuel. In this way, the castaways could keep their fire burning in perpetuity.' Satisfied that they understood, he continued, once again.

'I have given you a simple analogy to the operation of the fast breeder reactor. The fire of dry wood is analogous to the incinerated plutonium in the core. The drying out of the wet wood is analogous to the production from the U-238 blanket. The wet timber is analogous to U-238, both of which would be useless waste products unless used in this manner. The process of building up the blanket of wet wood, extracting dry wood from this and throwing the dry timber onto the fire, are exactly analogous to the fast reactor fuel cycle.'

Ian Hyde could see from their expressions that most of them understood.

'Professor Hyde,' one minister called, raising his hand slightly, 'I'm Timothy Garbutt, Minister for Resources.' The senior minister paused, looked at the Minister for Defense, then plunged straight in with his question.

'If we were to assume the worst case scenario, uhm,' he paused again, knowing that he would have trouble later with some of the members who were committed Asiaphiles, 'what, no,.. how long would it be before the Indonesians would be in a position to have produced sufficient weapons' grade plutonium to threaten their neighbouring countries?' Hyde looked at the man and sympathised with his difficult portfolio.

'Assuming they could go on-line in five years, they could have sufficient stockpiles within that year.'

Someone shuffled papers nervously and this could be heard in the ensuing silence. They were, one and all, speechless with this revelation that Indonesia could, conceivably, join the nuclear club before the end of the decade. One of those present coughed nervously.

'And what are the probabilities that the Indonesians could deliver such a weapon?' the West Australian Minister for Mining's deep baritone voice filled the room. All present turned to look at the professor, who merely shook his head.

'Your are asking the wrong man here, I'm afraid.' Then he turned to the man sitting on his left. 'Your Defense experts could help you with that one, Prime Minister,' with which, the Prime Minister looked over in the direction of the Joint Chief of Staff who had been invited to attend in an observer capacity. Lieutenant General Sharpe rose in response.

'If I may, Prime Minister,' he began. 'Correct me if I am wrong,

Professor Hyde, but I think it is important here that we understand, first of all, that all nuclear reactors produce plutonium. A breeder reactor is simply designed to do it more efficiently.' He sighed. The Australian Military had spent more than three decades building solid relationships with the Indonesians, and he could only remember one government over those years which had reached out to Australia's nearest neighbour and established real rapport.

'Firstly, we should not jump to conclusions here. The Japanese have been awarded the contract for *Rama II*. That, alone, should give us a certain amount of confidence as there is no way that the Japanese Constitution would permit them to be involved with the production of plutonium for other than peaceful purposes.' He looked at the faces he had come to despise. Politicians' faces. They had been obstructionist and self-serving throughout his career, and he wished, sometimes, that Australia could be governed in a manner not dissimilar to that of Singapore - or even Indonesia.

'Secondly,' he said, his anger not evident, 'any plant that reprocesses fuel will have the opportunity to separate plutonium. It is chemically difficult because plutonium and uranium have similar chemistries, even though the procedure is well known. Hell,' he said, hoping to allay fears that the Indonesians one purpose in life was to attack Australia, 'you can even down-load this information off the Internet.' He wanted to shake his head in disgust, but refrained. 'Should the Indonesians feel the need to make a bomb, we would not be able to prevent this from happening, but to do so, they would have to be much more clever than one would expect.' The general looked directly at the Prime Minister, and again the thought flashed through his mind that he wished Australia had a similar covenant to Indonesia, and America, prohibiting such people from governing for more than two terms.

'If the Indonesians wished to enrich their own reactor fuel and divert this to some sort of clandestine uranium enrichment plant to make sufficient weapons' grade U-235, then they would have to be far more devious than you or I. They would require a substantial number of additional facilities. If it was their intention to produce a uranium weapon, they would require secret facilities out of view of the American spy-satellites, just to start. Then, if they decided on a plutonium bomb, they would require a fuel reprocessing facility and a place to hide the plutonium. This would not be easy. Again, the satellites would identify any such 'hot' spot immediately it was established unless, of course, they buried this deep inside a mine shaft somewhere. Then, having camouflaged all of these clandestine activities, they would have to successfully hide whatever else they were doing from the IAEA.' When he saw blank looks, he explained.

'That is the International Atomic Energy Agency, which is responsible for maintaining a close watch on such operations.' He turned to the man who headed the table.

'Prime Minister, in order for the Indonesians to succeed if they were, and I must stress that I don't believe that they are, planning to produce a nuclear device, they would have to withdraw from the non-proliferation treaty and the IAEA in order to do so. Should this happen, then, and only then, would we be concerned as to their intentions.' The general had successfully avoided the question. There were but a few among those present who had knowledge of the secret Indonesian installations nearing completion in Bandung. He then returned to his seat, feeling suddenly uncomfortably hot.

'Professor Hyde, how would you see the Indonesian NPPs impacting on Australia in the event that one of them was to go supercritical, and collapse, or meltdown?' This had been asked by the Minister for Science and Technology. The professor had been expecting this question, and was prepared.

'There is always the danger that the uninformed public will view all new technology with suspicion. It is a fact, unfortunately, that the greater majority throughout the world perceive nuclear energy only in some distorted apocalyptic manner. Nuclear Power Plants are necessary if we are to save our limited reserves of fossil fuels for more beneficial uses. As for coal, this too has a finite life. Within one hundred years we will survive only with solar and nuclear energy as the earth's resources would, by then, have been stripped of most of its fossil fuels. It may very well be that we will be able to generate power from new, and yet undiscovered or undeveloped forms of energy, such as from sea water. Unfortunately, that race is yet to begin. As for your question, I am not attempting to avoid it, just qualifying my answer.' He removed his handkerchief once again, and wiped his face.

'Indonesia is geologically unstable. We all know that from the constant reports of volcanic activity and the frequent number of earth tremors registered each year. I do agree that more time should have been allocated in determining the most suitable locations for the individual plants. We may feel some consolation knowing that the Japanese are involved in at least one of these plants, and that the Americans are responsible for the project in Bali, and another in Java. However, I do wish to emphasise that I believe the Indonesians are in too much of a hurry to construct these plants and bring them on line. There are inherent dangers involved; the Americans and Russians will support this. Although the Three Mile Island disaster shocked America at the time, the United States still leads the world in nuclear energy plants, boasting well over one hundred operating NPPs throughout the country. No, I wish to state that I believe in nuclear energy production of electricity, but stress that no one, I repeat no one, should charge into the development of such systems as quickly as the Indonesians have.'

'I'm sorry, Professor, but could you give us some indication of what might happen if one of these plants was to meltdown? I believe that was the question asked.' The Prime Minister looked sharply at his Minister for Education who had spoken, and reminded himself that had she not maintained such strong political support from within the Party, he would never have entertained having her on the Front Bench in Parliament.

'If I were to extrapolate the number of possibilities relating to the cause and effect of a meltdown, madam, we would be here for weeks.' Professor Hyde was visibly annoyed with the woman. 'Simply put, there are nowhere near the number of dangers that the general public believe exist with such events. There are containment shells built specifically as additional measures to ensure the public's safety. I could go on, forever, but I won't. There will always be an element within the community which will feed off such ridiculous clichés as the *China Syndrome*, or such nonsense. Yes, there are intrinsic dangers with these plants. Yes, people have died as a result of Chernobyl. No, I do not believe that the *Rama* plants are a danger to Australia, principally because the Japanese are going to build the Fast Breeder Plant in Java, and the French and Americans will oversee the development of the others.' He paused again before adding, 'but I would be most concerned had Soviet technology and training methodology been considered for any of these plants. Fortunately, this is not the case.'

'I am sorry to push, Professor,' she insisted, 'but are you saying that if either of these plants suffered, say, some sort of explosion or whatever as a result of geologically unstable ground, that we would all be safe?' Professor Hyde glared at the woman, his annoyance now more visible.

'A cloud of radio-active dust would cause casualties within a radius of some fifty kilometres. Should weather conditions be unfavourable at the time of any such accident occurring, then this area would increase proportionately to wind velocity, the terrain surrounding the accident and, of course, the extent of the explosion itself. This would most likely result in an increase in radio-activity in most parts of Australia. I should add, however, that I would not expect the increase in radio-activity levels to be of any paramount danger to our population.'

'My god!' she responded. 'No danger to Australians, you say?'

'That's correct, madam,' he replied. 'We should not confuse a meltdown with that of a nuclear bomb detonation. There is no mushroom cloud, no loud bang, so to speak. There would be, however, lethal increases in radiation levels in immediate areas surrounding such an incident.'

'Would there be any warning?' another asked. Hyde could see that his audience had pre-conceived ideas as to affects of such an accident, believing that such a meltdown would inevitably wipe out most of Australia.

'No, not much,' was all he said. The group then fell silent, and he knew that they were attempting to visualize what might happen should a meltdown occur. He had received a similar reaction from most audiences he had addressed on this topic, and never ceased to be surprised at how intelligent people focused only on the potential disaster aspects of nuclear energy, and not the benefits. As there were no further questions, the Prime Minister thanked the professor, who then departed, leaving for his home in Sydney.

* * * * * *

As he sat comfortably sipping the fine Chardonnay served during the flight, Professor Hyde thought about the meeting and decided that it had gone reasonably well. That is, with the exception

JAKARTA

of the persistent woman. He sighed, as earlier tension all but disappeared. Relaxed by the alcohol, his thoughts drifted as the Fokker started its descent over the Blue Mountains, and he watched the city's fringe dwellers' homes appear below. The scene was reminiscent of homes and pastures he had visited many years before.

It had been during the months following the disastrous incident in Russia, when a design flaw had caused the reactor to trip, and then explode. The images of what he had found in that accident's aftermath triggered the professor's thoughts, and he experienced a sense of relief that the location of Indonesia's nuclear plants were far enough away to minimise the effects of any potential fallout to Australia. As the memory of Chernobyl returned to cloud his mind, he reflected on the number who had died of acute radiation sickness subsequent to the disaster, and a sense of foreboding concerning Indonesia passed through his mind.

Images of those who had not died within the first days, yet wished they had, flashed through his thoughts. He remembered the brave men and women of Chernobyl, as death painfully approached, the radiation causing extreme damage to brain and gut, knowing that even if they survived the first days, within weeks they would die as the sickness penetrated bone marrow and vital organs. He looked out the window at the congested clumps of homes, and again felt saddened by what had happened to the Russians.

That evening, alone in his study, Professor Ian Hyde sat re-studying the ramifications of such a meltdown occurring in the densely populated provinces of Java and Bali and discovered, to his horror, that the Chernobyl model he had used projected casualty numbers he could never have imagined possible. Later, as he lay awake, unable to sleep, the scientist uttered a short prayer of thanks that the nuclear power plants being built along known geological faults to Australia's north were not being constructed with Russian technology.

Chapter 15

Lim and Ruswita's story

Ruswita breathed deeply, identifying the pungent odour of *durian*.

'*Sumi, send one of the servants over to the village. I can't stand it anymore, let's fill our stomachs while we have the villa to ourselves.*' Sumi laughed, Ibu Ruswita's passion for the vile-smelling fruit was often the topic of office gossip back in Jakarta.

'*I'll go myself,*' Ruswita's personal assistant offered, '*are you all right, alone for a few minutes?*' Ruswita smiled at her concern. These days, she wouldn't dream of travelling without the woman at her side. Sumi had been a godsend at a time Ruswita had been desperate for a competent aide she could trust. Now, Ruswita could steal away for a few hours, sometimes even an entire day, knowing that her able assistant would provide the necessary buffer against the irritation of incessant telephone calls.

When Sumi went in search of the delicate tasting fruit, Ruswita stretched out, enjoying the fresh mountain air. She watched a bird fly overhead, and she suddenly realized that she could not remember the last time she had seen any birds flying around Jakarta.

The capital had become a major Asian commercial hub, and now suffered the consequences of unchecked growth as urban sprawl encroached on outlying villages and the poor were driven even further from the densely populated city centre. Ruswita sighed, remembering when the drive up to the Salima mountain retreat in *Cimacan*, just over the *Puncak Pass*, would take little more than an hour. Now she considered herself fortunate if their driver could manage the distance in less than two. Whenever possible, she avoided city driving, preferring her husband's routine of conducting business from their home. Especially during the wet season.

All but a privileged few of Jakarta's twelve million inhabitants had no choice but to put up with being trapped for hours in the inadequate transport system as flood waters from the tropical downpours inundated the major thoroughfares surrounding the central business district.

Children's playful cries drifted across from the *kampung* reminding Ruswita to call the older boys, and enquire as to how Lim's grandchildren were getting along. The boys' marriages had resulted in a sudden explosion of numbers in the Salima family, with over-zealous wives openly competing with each other for their father-in-law's favours. Rus thought about the growing family wistfully, as neither Benny nor Ratna had started their own. The thought of Ratna, gallivanting around the world without her husband, deeply distressed her.

Ratna and she still spoke frequently, Rus learning what was happening in the young woman's life during calls from the most exotic places around the globe. Ruswita had made arrangements for Ratna, providing her with funds to maintain her independence. Her daughter still called her 'Aunty', and both Lani and Rus were determined to maintain the charade, as Lim still was not aware of the true circumstances relating to Ratna's birth.

Often Ruswita had wished that she had disclosed their relationship to Lim, as this was the one secret which she had kept from him. Sometimes she wondered how he would have reacted, had she informed him prior to their marrying. But what was the good of such speculation? She had lied to her husband, and now needed to maintain that secret.

For a moment, Rus thought about her old friend, Lani, concerned that she had become noticeably distant over the past year. When they discovered Ratna had recently divorced, Ruswita had been most surprised at Lani's insistence that she go to take care of her. Of course, this had been out of the question. Lani was still very much a *kampung* girl at heart, and Rus was certain that her daughter would probably be embarrassed. Lani had never travelled, and it was most likely that she would only add to Ratna's burdens during her difficult times should she suddenly decide to visit.

Ruswita missed her children, and found that the Salima empire consumed far more of her time than she could ever have imagined. Escaping to their weekend villa nestled amongst the hills had become a rare treat for her, and Rus was amazed that, for once, she did not feel guilty at having left business unattended back in Jakarta.

They had driven up during the early morning hours, before the city's congested arterial roads could block her escape. Ruswita was so delightfully relaxed she was tempted to phone home and inform the household that she would not return until evening. Since her husband had become ill, Ruswita made a point of trying to be home before Lim rose from his afternoon nap. It was her custom to take tea in the afternoon when at home, where Lim would find her sitting, reading reports, when he shuffled out of his room and into the upstairs lounge.

The thought reminded her that she should soon be leaving, deciding to do so once she had indulged herself with the tasty *durian*. She smiled. Her husband refused to have the fruit anywhere near their house, and Ruswita graciously confined her habit of eating the smelly but delicious *durian* only when in the mountains, and away from his sensitive sense of smell. Lim never complained whenever Ruswita slipped away quietly by herself. He understood the demands made on their lives, and knew that she would always be there for him, if needed.

* * * * * *

Lani's attention was distracted by the clock's chimes. She had been looking out through the lounge bay-windows for some time, expecting to see the security open the gate for Ruswita's Mercedes. Instead, she had spied the housekeeper gossiping to someone standing outside the entrance, their forms hidden behind the tall, reinforced pillars.

Lani was most concerned that Ruswita had not returned, knowing that it was not like her to be tardy. She chewed a finger-nail absentmindedly, then looked down at the row of poorly manicured stubs. Ruswita had often scolded her for it but she could not break the habit, which had followed her since childhood. Then she noticed that she had spilt some tea on her *kebaya* and hurried to her quarters at the rear of the mansion to change her blouse. When she returned to renew her vigil, Lani observed that security had closed the front gates, and that whoever had been talking to the cook had left. Lani continued to watch, waiting there by the window, patiently, hoping that Rus would return soon. Rus had asked Lani if she had wanted to accompany them for the day, but Lani had refused, not entirely happy with the patronising manner Ruswita's personal assistant often displayed towards her.

She stood, her mind wandering, thinking about Ratna's last call from overseas. Lani had not been there when the call was made, and was visibly distressed at having missed the opportunity to speak to her. Although Ruswita had relayed her discussions with Ratna, it was not the same as speaking directly to Ratna by herself. It had already been far too long since she had visited, and she missed the young woman, dreadfully.

Lani recognized that she had been grinding her teeth, and stopped. She knew the reason for her depression. She had not spoken to her adopted daughter for more than two months. Even then, it was Ruswita who had taken the call, and she spoke to Ratna for what seemed like hours before Lani was given the brief opportunity to talk to her.

Sometimes she felt that life had been most unfair; she had raised Ratna Sari as her own daughter, and now considered it only appropriate that she should think of the beautiful young woman as her own child. Her thoughts turned to Ruswita, and a twinge of regret passed quickly though her. They had once been so very close. Then Rus had married the wealthy man and begun sleeping upstairs and, slowly, everything had changed. Lani had virtually become just another of the household dependants. It was not that she was ungrateful, although she did feel that Ruswita might have treated her a little differently, and given her more say with regards to their daughter.

An hour passed. Agitated by her friend's unusually late return. Lani decided to refresh the afternoon tray she had prepared and left upstairs earlier for Ruswita. Lani knew that she would expect the customary lukewarm Chinese tea to be waiting for her. She uncrossed her arms and turned to attend to this chore, almost bumping into the old housekeeper who had, at that moment, walked silently up behind her.

'Get out of my way!' Lani snapped, startled by her presence. She disliked the meddling old woman immensely, and could not understand why Lim had not let her go years before, when she had

become too old to manage the kitchen by herself. Her duties had been changed from cooking to light housekeeping, even though there were others whose responsibility it was to clean and wash for the Lim family and guests. The housekeeper stood her ground, her mouth open wide as if to speak but the words would not come.

'*What is it?*' Lani asked angrily, her curiosity aroused by the woman's strange appearance. The housekeeper's eyes were open wide, as if in surprise. She couldn't speak. Instead, she turned her head and looked over her shoulder towards the staircase. Lani frowned, followed her gaze, then looked back at the panic-stricken woman. Instantly, she knew that something was terribly wrong.

'*Oh no!*' Lani cried, fearing the worst, and hurried up the stairs, leaving the stricken housekeeper alone.

* * * * * *

As she waited for her assistant to bring the *durian* Ruswita listened to the village children's voices. She remembered earlier days when she too played along the village dirt tracks, climbed mango trees, and squatted in the dirt with the others playing *kelereng*, her tiny, clumsy hands unable to flick the stone marbles. She smiled, revisiting her childhood days, remembering the smell of *pisang goreng*, whenever her mother served deep-fried banana, and other tantalising village-food aromas.

Neither Ratna nor Benny had been exposed to this simple way of life and, sometimes when reflecting on her early youth, Ruswita regretted that her children had not experienced what life could be like without the benefit of money. She knew that Benny would follow in his father's footsteps, as he had already displayed the Lim street-cunning in his dealings. The older boys were, surprisingly, quite different from their father. Both had been influenced by their extended stays in the West, and it was apparent to Ruswita that they were no longer comfortable living in Indonesia. As she considered Denny and James, she became concerned with their American commitments, and some of the difficulties spawned from their banking activities.

Some aspects of their American operations remained unclear to Ruswita, but she could certainly read a profit and loss sheet and she was well aware that Lim's sons were hiding the greater part of whatever they had been up to in the United States. Ruswita had become concerned, at first, when she discovered that a number of Lim's international subsidiaries which were controlled by the two older boys, had been actively investing in the Peoples' Republic of China. The Lim family had substantial interests in the Republic of China, and she knew that should the Taiwanese discover their cross-border vested interests there would be problems.

As the conglomerate had grown, so did the need for Lim Swee Giok to divest himself of day-to-day control over his empire. He was growing old, and his punishing childhood years living from hand to mouth in China had left their legacy. Lim no longer had the strength to oversee his empire. He entrusted Ruswita to maintain vigilance over all they owned, and asked his two oldest sons to assume control with her, in Jakarta. They had both blatantly refused.

Lim wanted desperately for them to return, leaving their American interests in the hands of capable managers. Still, they had cited pressing financial obligations in the United States which dictated that they remain. Ruswita interceded, urging Denny and James to consider their father's needs. They were both required at home now, she explained, as their father's health had deteriorated dramatically over the past months. Finally, Denny had phoned and explained that they could not return at that time, and begged Ruswita to understand. There were problems, Denny had explained, and these would grow to damaging proportions if they did not remain to resolve the bank's difficulties. Ruswita was then obliged to assume even more responsibility for the complex operations, as her husband remained at home, only occasionally holding court with some of his closest business associates. He no longer visited the Palace; slowly, he seemed to lose interest with what was happening within the Lim empire.

Ruswita managed, alone, and even enjoyed overseeing most of the *kongsi* activities, although she wished at times that the Salima Group had never involved itself with the massive undertakings associated with the *Rama* nuclear project. Ruswita was concerned with their financial exposure in the four privately operated plants. Whenever she attempted to discuss these with Denny and James, they appeared distant, as if the investments were not as dear to their lives as one would have thought. Difficult as it was, Ruswita persevered, finally coming to grips with the ongoing problems associated with the plant's construction cost blow-outs, management difficulties and government interference.

First ground had been broken two years before, and construction was well under way. Ruswita had not visited the sites, nor did she encourage visible involvement by any of those close to the Salima family, as these projects had attracted considerable controversy. The Salima Group supplied most of the materials for the plants' construction. Cement, steel, engineering services, heavy equipment, cranes and even on-site catering was, in one way or another, controlled by the Lim group of companies.

The Mt Muria plant had been different, and Ruswita believed that only the PEPELIN Chairman would understand why this had come about. Lim had been outraged when he discovered that Seda managed to divert most of the contracts relating to the Japanese fast breeder reactor plant away from the Salima organisation to one which had very little substance but was, Lim suspected, closely associated with the greedy Chairman. Infuriated, Lim had gone directly to the President and been shocked to discover that the *Bapak* supported Seda's intrusion into what Lim perceived to be Salima domain. He had even approached the Japanese directly and, for the first time since he could remember, his *kongsi* had been excluded entirely from the supply of cement, steel and other materials he had dominated for decades.

It was at this time that Lim's health had suffered some deterioration, and he kept more to himself, often wandering around their home, still dressed in singlet and shorts, like some peasant recluse.

Ruswita had sensed that Seda had somehow broken through their monopolies because of the growing tide of anti Chinese sentiment, fuelled by those jealous of their achievements. There had been rumblings even from the floor of the Indonesian Parliament, and she firmly believed that this had originated with the former President's children, whose permanent representation in both Houses had been a bitter legacy indeed for the Indonesian people.

Ruswita remembered how Lim had attempted to maintain close relationships with the former powerful family members, but they had become a substantial financial liability, one which the Lim group could no longer support. Ruswita recalled that at least four of the former President's children, and grandchildren, all held seats in Parliament, from where they attempted to regain some of the power their family had lost when their father had passed away.

Ruswita had not been surprised that Salima then also lost the military materials supply contract for the aeronautical research and development plant being constructed in Bandung. When she had been informed that Seda's associates had been appointed as sole contractors, Ruswita knew that it was time for the Salima Group to reassess its position in Indonesia. She spoke to Lim about her concerns, but he was adamant that they would not liquidate their energy assets until the power plants had been in operation for at least two years, citing the potential for publicly listing the company as his reason.

As a result of their difficult financial position, he had finally agreed to selling a minority stake in the Salima Group company, before which the energy assets and those related to all off-shore subsidiaries, and his control in the Asian Pacific Commercial Bank, were protected. Several months later, the market fought to purchase the first Lim-associated shares, when forty percent of the company which owned and operated cement plants, steel mills, property and a myriad of other investments within Indonesia, was sold through the Jakarta Stock Exchange. The company had changed its name prior to the public listing, and became known as P.T. Salima Jaya Corporation. Within hours of the shares being offered to the public, the company's value doubled. Capital raised by selling almost half of the Indonesian assets was immediately channelled through the family bank, APCB, which was then used to relieve a considerable part of the debt accumulated in the Salima energy investment sector.

Their exposure in relation to the financing of the first four plants was not limited. Lim had insisted on maintaining a majority interest through their off-shore holdings, and had heavily committed cash-flow from existing investments to accommodate the foreign banks. Ruswita was aware that their projected accumulated debt at the time of completion of all four *Rama* NPPs, would exceed ten billion dollars due to extensive redesign and cost over-runs. She had examined the latest cost estimates just days before, and had been distressed to learn that each plant could easily exceed three and a half billion dollars, almost double the original estimates.

Ruswita understood clearly that the foreign partners associated with each plant would not suffer financially. They had been clever, entering into cost-plus contracts and, as they held the key to management, there was little that could be done to re-negotiate their positions.

Even the uranium supply contracts had caused concern when the Australian suppliers experienced difficulty with environmentalists. Ruswita had been further alarmed when disputes over land and mineral rights had been challenged by the Aboriginal people, who had been given rights over the Kakadu National Park, and insisted on assuming control over the mines. She had immediately contacted other suppliers, and was shocked to discover that the world demand had already accounted for most of the available ore, including that from the Vaal Reefs South African mines. Salima technicians confirmed that changing suppliers would not alleviate the problems, as the lead times required for uranium conversion, enrichment and fuel manufacture was in the order of two years.

Finally, she received personal assurances from the Australian company's major shareholder, Graeme Robson, that they would be able to meet the supply deadline. Ruswita was satisfied with this undertaking, or had been until she discovered that Robson's activities somehow had become enmeshed with her rival, Seda. She became suspicious and had Robson's activities in Indonesia monitored.

When Ruswita received confirmation that it was Robson who had been sourcing alternative material supplies for the *Rama II* plant's construction, she became even more suspicious of their relationship.

Prior to the contracts being awarded, the Salima Group had entered into an arrangement with Peter Wong, using one of his companies as the vehicle to control *Rama V*. Ruswita had learned that Wong's junior partner was the same foreigner whom she had come into contact with many, many years before. She had phoned Murray Stephenson and was pleased to find that he had returned to Jakarta, to act as a liaison consultant for Wong's company, the *Nasihat Corporation*. As she rested quietly, waiting for Sumi to return with the promised fruit, Ruswita recalled the meeting she had with the Australian.

* * * * * *

At first, Ruswita had not recognized him, for she remembered

Murray as he had been, more than twenty years before, in the joint venture factory, where she had been employed as the foreign general manager's personal secretary. His once fair hair had thinned, exposing ugly, red blotches on his scalp, and his roguish face now featured wrinkled, sun-damaged skin.

'Thank you for the lunch, Rus,' Murray had said, as she escorted him from the dining room into the congested lounge. He had been most surprised at having been invited, and even more so to find that he was to be the only guest. They had eaten and engaged in light conversation through the meal, and it was time now to reveal the reason for the meeting.

'Murray, I have invited you here to discuss a matter which *Pak Lim* and I believe you might be in a position to assist with,' she had started. Murray looked intrigued by the statement. 'We have not been prying into your business, but by accident we have discovered that you are quite friendly with those involved in the materials supply contract for *Rama II*.' She paused for effect.

'*Pak Lim* has been very concerned regarding the loss of this contract, but is more concerned that we might have difficulty with future supplies of uranium ore from Australia.' Murray frowned, he was obviously wondering where their conversation was heading.

'As any disruption in supply, for whatever reason, could also be of major concern to Peter Wong, through our *kongsi* with the *Nasihat Group* and *Rama V*, we were, therefore, hoping that you might be in a position to explore the relationship which exists between this fellow Robson and General Seda.' Ruswita had observed her guest closely, trying to determine whether he was aware of any association.

'Why the concern?' he had asked.

'Robson's group has controlling interest in the uranium mines which are under contract to supply all four NPPs we are building. It's no secret that Seda has managed, as Chairman of PEPELIN, to firmly ensconce himself amongst those who were awarded the lucrative supply contract for the Japanese plant. The Salima Group is becoming concerned that as Seda makes further gains in these areas he might also decide to become involved with the supply of uranium fuel from its source.' Ruswita knew that she would not have to explain that the Lim group was moving to avoid a situation in which they could be held to ransom over the enriched uranium supply contract.

'Why would Seda wish to do so?' he had asked, 'and if he did, how would you expect him to go about this?'

'Well, Murray,' she had replied, 'that's what we were hoping you might be able to assist us determine for ourselves. If Seda wishes to raise the stakes and acquire an influence over the Australian mining operation, would it not be reasonable to expect that Robson, whose company owns control over the extraction process, might just accommodate the general?' She could see that he was considering what she had said.

'I will do what I can, Ruswita, but no guarantees. I don't see as much of Graeme as I used to, but I will make a point of raising the issue with him,' he had promised.

'I don't know how you might do this, Murray, as Robson's association with Seda seems to have grown considerably. His company has acquired a number of lucrative contracts other than the Japanese plant including the cement and steel for the Bandung research and development project which, I am told, is substantial.' Ruswita could see his surprise, knowing, as would the Jakarta business community, that Lim had controlled most of the government contracts to date, and that it was most unusual for the Palace not to have intervened on his behalf. Ruswita did not feel the necessity to further explain how Seda had consolidated his position with the First Family, and what this might mean to her own *kongsi* and its position in Indonesia.

By the time their luncheon meeting had come to a close, she had received an undertaking from Murray that he would assist. Ruswita remembered feeling that there was more to this man than he showed, and hoped that she had not made an error of judgement in seeking his assistance regarding Lim's concerns.

* * * * * *

A voice called, bringing Ruswita back to the present, and she looked to see Sumi returning, followed by one of their servants carrying several *durian*, which had been tied together. Minutes later, Ruswita sat on the porch, tearing the flesh from inside the fruit with her fingers, laughing as she did so, while relating stories of her youth.

Well into the feast, they heard the phone ringing, and her personal assistant hurried inside to answer the phone. Ruswita finished eating the remaining flesh, and, as Sumi returned, laughingly held the finished fruit up for her to see. But her dedicated assistant didn't respond. Ruswita was startled by the younger woman's expression, and a cold fear gripped her heart as she searched Sumi's face for some indication as to what was wrong.

'*Sumi?*' she asked, suddenly dreading her answer.

'*Ibu Rus,*' she stammered, resisting the temptation to break into tears. '*Ibu Lani wishes to talk to you, urgently.*' Ruswita's first reaction was one of annoyance. It was not unlike Lani to phone, just for the sake of it. The thought crossed her mind that Lani might be sulking again. She hurried to the phone.

'*Lani, what is it?*' she snapped, immediately wishing she hadn't. Lani was crying.

'*It's Pak Lim, Rus,*' Lani said, '*it's Pak Lim!*' she sobbed, uncontrollably. Ruswita became engulfed with fear.

'*What is it, for God's sake Lani, what has happened?*'

'*Pak Lim is dead, Rus, he's dead!*' she cried, her voice choking. For a moment the shock did not register, and Ruswita stood quite still. Rocked by the cold realization of her husband's sudden death, she dropped the phone, and felt her knees become weak. Sumi ran to her side, placed her arm around the older woman's waist, and assisted her to a cane chair. For a moment, she was not sure that Ruswita would not faint. Then, she recovered her composure and breathed deeply, nodded that she would be all right, and patted her assistant's hand in gratitude.

'*Call the driver, Sumi,*' she said, softly, and her assistant obeyed, hurrying away to do as instructed. It was not until they were more than half way down the mountain, speeding around the dangerous curves, that Ruswita realized that she hadn't asked Lani what had happened. The Mercedes sped down the mountain side, bypassed Bogor, and raced along the Jagorawi Highway. Sumi glanced at her employer, and placed her hand in Ruswita's. She observed that there were no tears. These, she knew, would come later. Thankfully, they missed most of the midday traffic congestion, as they continued through the sprawling city's outskirts, then along the ring-road and into Menteng.

JAKARTA

When they arrived, the driver had barely brought their vehicle to a standstill when Ruswita flung the heavy door open and hurried inside, past the familiar form of the Lim family doctor. His eyes dropped in deference as Ruswita brushed by; there was nothing he could do. Lani had been waiting anxiously for their return and, as Ruswita appeared, she raced up to her, and flung her arms around her friend's neck, still sobbing uncontrollably.

'*He's dead, Rus,*' she cried, '*he's dead!*' Ruswita unlocked Lani's arms from around her body and pushed her gently aside. The old housekeeper stood wringing her hands, looking nervously upstairs. Rus placed her hand on the old woman's shoulder as she walked past her to the stairs leading up to the private bedrooms she shared with Lim.

She entered the second storey quarters, passing slowly through the common lounge and study area, where they had spent most of their lives together. They no longer shared the same bed, or the same room. This was not a question of love, simply a necessary arrangement they had both accepted due to their age difference and the pressure of their lives.

She could see directly into Lim's bedroom, as the door had been left open. Ruswita inhaled deeply, then walked towards the unmade bed, her hands shaking slightly as Lim's body came into view. She moved to his side and stared at her dead husband.

She placed her hand gently on his outstretched arm, noticing how cold his skin felt. Ruswita wondered if she should cover his body, but instead, she leaned over and closed his staring, lifeless eyes. Alone with the man who had given her more than most people could ever dream of, she closed her eyes to steady herself, wishing that she had not left him alone that day.

Ruswita still could not bring herself to accept that he was gone. In death, Lim's emaciated form in no way reflected the enormous power the man had wielded, or his incredible wealth. She remained at his side for several minutes, praying, then Ruswita removed his clothing and redressed the body.

After some time had passed, she called downstairs for the doctor. When he entered their quarters, Ruswita could see that the man was genuinely saddened by her husband's death.

'*I am terribly sorry, Rus,*' he said, taking her by both hands and sitting her down slowly, '*but there is something that you must know.*'

Ruswita looked up into the doctor's eyes and immediately felt fear clutch at her heart. She looked away momentarily, then across at the still form of her husband, Lim.

'*What is it?*' she asked, pulling her hands away from the man's grip.

'*I don't really know how to begin, Rus,*' he answered, then sighed. He sat on the edge of the bed, partially blocking the dead man's corpse from Ruswita's view. Then he dropped his bombshell.

Ruswita sat silently, almost in disbelief, listening to his shocking revelation. She asked several questions and was stunned by his answers. As her heart filled with rage at the betrayal, her anger displaced her sorrow, filling her with hate. Questions flooded her mind and she could find no answers. *Where were the servants when he had died?* She remained with the doctor, discussing what had taken place just hours before, somewhere in this room. They looked around, together, but could find no evidence to support the doctor's conclusions.

The old housekeeper had found Lim unconscious on the bedroom floor. It was her practice to waken the master from his afternoon rest. She had called the doctor, immediately, not knowing that Lim had already been dead for some minutes when she first discovered his body. She had called Lani and the security and, while waiting for the doctor to arrive, they had placed their stricken master on his bed. It was then that the servants understood that Lim was indeed dead. Lani had placed her call to the mountain resort, and the doctor had arrived shortly thereafter. At first, he thought that Lim had died of a stroke, but upon further examination, he knew otherwise.

Once the circumstances surrounding her husband's death had become clear to Ruswita, she solicited the doctor's assistance, knowing what she must then do.

Ruswita knew that she would have to move quickly, to prevent the inevitable panic which would follow amongst the Chinese community once word spread. She begged the doctor not to communicate with anyone, not even family. Salima's future was at stake, and Ruswita realized that they were in danger of losing it all, especially if others overreacted and commenced liquidating their assets in Indonesia.

They talked quietly, together, until the doctor reluctantly agreed to her requests and left her to make the necessary arrangements. Then she called Sumi to join her upstairs, and issued instructions as to what she must then do before alerting the others in the family. Her assistant understood, and went immediately to the phones to carry out Ruswita's orders.

Ruswita then went down to speak to the servants and security staff, ordering them to remain inside the grounds until instructed otherwise

Lani looked at her friend questioningly, but Ruswita ignored her, returning upstairs where she too spent the following hour making urgent calls, overseas, in preparation for the selling spree she knew would take place the moment news of Lim's death reached the markets. Ruswita realized that this would be their real test, and hoped that she could count on their foreign bankers not to call in their notes.

There was no doubt that the Chinese community would wait to see which way their bankers would move before they too decided whether to liquidate assets. Ruswita was gambling that their friends would support the market, that they would survive the inevitable roller-coaster ride the Salima Group shares would experience before, hopefully, settling once again.

But she also knew that all of this was only possible as long as she had the confidence of the market, and that if the cause of Lim's death became known, then there would not be a single Chinese investor who would not immediately move to divest themselves of not only their Salima stock, but their own assets as well, creating a massive outward flow of capital from the Indonesian market. She believed she had no choice but to disguise the fact that Lim had been murdered. The Chinese would believe that if the powerful tycoon with his Palace connections had not been safe, then who in this city of Jakarta was?

Satisfied that she had done all that she possibly could, Ruswita settled down to wait for the doctor to return with a copy of the death certificate he had agreed to endorse, showing that her husband had passed away comfortably in his sleep.

* * * * * *

When news finally broke regarding Lim Swee Giok's death,

Salima shares and those associated with the conglomerate suffered a sharp fall, tearing more than twenty percent off the stocks' values. There had been only one major seller, and his name was whispered amongst the traders as they went about filling his sell orders.

As the stocks plummeted, the Asian Pacific Commercial Bank stepped in and started buying its associated stock. At the close of the morning session, the shares had regained half of their losses, and when it was announced that Salima's major shareholders were buying their own stock and had called an extraordinary meeting of shareholders without notice, the market interpreted this as one of confidence, that the family were demonstrating their support for Lim's widow, and closed the afternoon session with an overall gain for the day.

* * * * * *

The board meeting had gone as she had expected. The others really had little choice but to follow, she knew, initiating the call for the extraordinary meeting of the few major shareholders.

As she continued to gaze down through the double-glazed windows from the penthouse in the building which now effectively belonged to her, she smiled. But not in mirth. Ruswita thought about the meeting which had just taken place and the ease with which she had managed to totally emasculate those who had attended, knowing that none would ever have expected to see her take control of the company's board meeting, let alone chair the event. But that was behind her, she thought, and life would be different now she had taken charge.

Ruswita stood, gazing out through the windows. Below, she could see the bogged traffic fighting its way slowly along Jalan Jenderal Sudirman. She glared directly across the divided thoroughfare at the building opposite, not one hundred metres away. It housed the enemy. Her enemy. And she knew in her heart that he had been the one responsible for her husband's death. Ruswita turned away from the view and walked through the lavishly decorated board-room wondering what she could do about Seda, and how she could prevent his charge upon her family holdings. He had shown his hand by attempting to drive the stock down, confirming Ruswita's suspicions that it had been Seda who had paid the assassin responsible for poisoning Lim.

Kerry B.Collison

Chapter 16

India

Vijay Rakesh believed that he was a good leader. Certainly, he mused, judging from public opinion polls he was obviously not the most popular Prime Minister India had ever had. The new millennium had not improved his people's lot; if it was not enough that his country already suffered from drought, now there was the phenomenon of *El Niño* to contend with. As he gazed down the empty hall over the magnificent Canadian Oak table, a gift to the new independent nation from Viceroy Mountbatten in 1947 which, only minutes before, had been covered with reports and submissions, Prime Minister Vijay uncoupled his hands and placed these firmly on the table, then rose slowly using the structure as support. His body had become even more frail over the past days. Vijay attempted to ignore the constant pain which had accompanied him for months, hoping that his scheduled operation would successfully remove the problem.

Slowly, he dragged his feet the length of the room until reaching the window which overlooked the square. He noticed that the glass had not been cleaned and thought to himself, how it could be, that in a country of one billion people one still can not find someone to clean the Prime Minister's windows? He raised his left hand and slowly rubbed against the glass in a clockwise motion, his thoughts wandering as the pain-killers interfered with his normally clear mind. He became momentarily mesmerised by his menial task. A wave of depression suddenly descended, causing him to cease what he was doing. Vijay Rakesh turned slowly, painfully, and dragged himself back to the head of the table where he lowered himself, carefully, back into the impossibly heavy chair, then stared into space.

The diagnosis had been confirmed. The doctors had informed him that it would now be only a matter of time unless he agreed to surgery. They had urged that he step down and permit someone younger and stronger to take control of India's leadership, but he had refused. Then they had challenged him and still he had refused, determined to remain on as long as his spirit did not fail him; he would hold on to prevent the political hyenas and jackals from attacking prematurely, and would resist those who sought to accelerate the inevitable.

His face twisted in agony as excruciating pain pierced his lower abdomen. These attacks were becoming more frequent, and more severe. Vijay Rakesh's fingers located the pills the doctors had prescribed, and slipped two more into his mouth. The mixture of aspirin and morphine hydrochloride entered his bloodstream, and he waited for the spasm to subside.

After what seemed an eternity, his breathing returned to normal and he looked down towards the window once again; he knew that outside, few amongst the city's swelling population would bother to cast a second glance at the huge and distorted red sun, as it squatted on the horizon. Vijay remained sitting alone, thinking nostalgically of his youth, and the snow-clad mountains in the north. Then, as he began to feel more comfortable, his mind turned once again the to terrible dilemma which haunted India.

Many of his countrymen were starving. India could no longer feed its people. And they, in turn, refused to listen. The population continued to grow to staggering levels, adding two million new mouths to the economy each month.

Following the announcement that India had finally passed China as the world's largest population, India had celebrated. On that day, Vijay had stood, feeling nothing but despair, waving from his balcony as the crowds cheered, celebrating their own demise. India's population exceeded one billion. As everyone else celebrated, he had felt nothing but outrage for the Malthusian outcome.

During his term in office, he had been unable to initiate steps to curb the exponential growth in the population. Vijay had called upon the country's religious, academic and social leaders to act, before it was too late. But he had been ignored. Political, racial and religious dogma prevented his government from achieving any form of consensus necessary for them to succeed. His every attempt had been frustrated by rivalry and ignorance.

As millions of Indians perished across the land, there seemed to be no acceptable solution to remedy the problems of over-population, and drought. Vijay had appealed to his old friend, Dr Imran Malhotra, who had offered the services of the Centre of Strategic Studies to assist in developing strategies to address India's problems. Such matters had come before India's National Security Council but, to his dismay, since being established in 1990, the Council had met only twice in its first ten years. After that, the ineffective NSC had been considered something of a joke.

Vijay had been shocked with the Centre's projections in relation to the number of Indian children who would die from malnutrition and starvation. And this was before the country had been severely affected by *El Niño*. The Prime Minister had spent numerous hours discussing the problems with Imran, whose sympathetic ear understood the vastness of India's conundrum. India needed food, desperately.

There were simply too many people living on what had become arid land. Vijay instructed Imran to prepare a report, for his eyes only, offering alternative solutions to overcome India's dilemma. Understanding the urgency involved, Imran Malhotra dedicated most of the Centre's activities towards producing his study. He personally acted as censor for the project, trusting none with the collective information until he had presented this to the Prime Minister in its final form.

When Dr Malhotra handed the report to his dear and respected friend, there were tears in his eyes. It would appear that their country was on a most dangerous course, one which would undoubtedly result in an apocalyptic end for the people of India. Malhotra had then guided his Prime Minister along the path neither wished to take. He believed that the gravity of their country's situation demanded a bold solution. For Imran Malhotra, there was really no choice. India was starving. India needed more fertile land for its people.

Accepting the gravity of the decision he must make, Vijay had decided to proceed with Malhotra's ambitious strategy. He believed he had little choice, justifying that the number of lives his country could lose in any short term confrontation would be relatively insignificant when considered in respect to the gains India would make. He called a meeting of those closest to him, to seek their support.

At first, his colleagues were horrified that Vijay had even entertained what one of their number referred to as India's Doomsday Plan. The Prime Minister had solicited the President's support, and it was he who had finally persuaded the others that, for India, there were really no viable alternatives but to embark on an immediate path of regional expansionism. India needed to secure more fertile ground to provide for its people. The alternatives were obvious. The Centre's Director, Dr Imran Malhotra had explained that, within five years, India could well implode politically as a result of famine and its growing inability to feed its millions. To do nothing would be to invite revolt against its central government.

Those present clearly understood the ramifications of what they had heard. India's borders could then easily be overrun in the northeast by China and there was little doubt that old animosities would drive the Moslems back across from Pakistan and into Kashmir. Following these successes, India's northern provinces would most probably be occupied. The audacious plan soon gained acceptance, paving the way for Vijay to order its secret implementation.

A list was prepared of those whose support would be essential to the project's success. One by one, Vijay called each of these to his home for private consultations, where he swore them to secrecy, demanding that only he, as Prime Minister, would have absolute authority over the implementation of the plan. The last to be called was Admiral Krishna Gopal, the only member of the Armed Forces to be taken into the Prime Minister's confidence.

India's Navy had always enjoyed preferential treatment whenever budgets were prepared. Over the latter part of the twentieth century, it had become one of the largest navies in the world. Vijay was not concerned that the Admiral was the only military representative to be briefed, as the other services would not be required during the initial phases. Gopal had been one of his government's strongest military supporters, unlike the Army leadership, which had never identified with any of his policies. With an understanding of urgency, the plan was then put into action, Imran Malhotra acting as co-ordinator. Meanwhile his friend, the Prime Minister, underwent urgent surgery.

* * * * * *

JAKARTA

On the ninth of May, Admiral Krishna Gopal returned from China and went directly to visit the Prime Minister in the hospital, carrying the Chinese Chairman's personal undertaking that they would support India's inclusion as a permanent member of the United Nation's Security Council. This would bring the number of member nations to twenty. With the addition of Japan, Germany, South Africa and Brazil to the existing number of permanent seats, India's inclusion would bring the expanded total to ten, and all with the right of veto.

On the sixth of November, the General Assembly moved to vote, and although Indonesia had substantial support from fellow ASEAN nations and other Moslem countries, the seat was narrowly won by India.

Three weeks later, China's Navy sailed into the Spratly Islands, having further consolidated its position in the Paracel Island Group, and claimed sovereignty over the rich undeveloped oil and gas fields which surrounded the islands. Vietnam's ageing IL-28s and MIG-23 fighters turned back to their base in Vung Tau when confronted by the superior force. Within the month, China had also boldly taken control of Natuna Island and, without so much as one shot being fired, Indonesia lost possession of one of the world's largest known gas fields.

* * * * * *

China

Since the middle of 1993, China had been a net importer of oil, and her dependence on crude imports had doubled over the previous decade as a result of increased demand for motor vehicle transport and electric power. Her neighbours had few reserves of any consequence, and China had become vulnerable to the safe supply of oil from her suppliers, Iran and Iraq.

Indonesia immediately invoked the earlier international agreement guaranteeing its sovereignty over all sea-lanes within the Indonesian archipelago. China reacted as expected, and ordered ten *Jianghu* class frigates, and thirty-seven *Huangfeng* missile ships from bases in Zhanijiang, Aoemen (formerly known as Macao) and Xianggang (old Hong Kong) into the area it now controlled. Within days, the naval build-up added two *Anshan* and eight *Luda* class destroyers. Out of sight, but lying within striking distance of all ASEAN capitals with their Intermediary Range Ballistic Missiles, four *Han*-class SSNs patrolled the South China Sea, determined to prevent disruption to China's oil supplies from the Middle East. China immediately demanded the right to freedom of navigation of all international waterways for those ships carrying the Chinese flag. Beijing argued that Indonesia had no legitimate basis on which to maintain her claim over the Natuna gas deposits, and the entire region shook, as China made its presence felt in the volatile Asian arena.

An emergency session of the Security Council was called, during which Japan moved that China be censured over its aggressive and illegal annexation of the disputed territories and its military expedition into Indonesian waters. As a permanent member of the Council, India vetoed the call. In doing so, the former adversaries declared their hand, and the world watched with growing apprehension as it witnessed the birth of a new, and powerful alliance between the world's two largest populations. And the rest of Asia leaned back in shock, and trembled.

* * * * * *

Jakarta

General Nathan Seda remained dedicated to the cause to which he had committed his life. He continued to secretly implement his ambitious plans for an Independent East Timor, and would remain loyal to its realization until his death. When the last reports of yet another cleansing operation had been whispered to him in private, he had struggled to maintain his composure, knowing that time was running out. But he continued with his plans, adapting them to suit, rearranging them whenever required, patiently yet impatiently, reworking his strategies until he was satisfied that he had finally developed a plan which would work.

Seda realized that he might not be given another such opportunity. While there was still considerable resistance to Indonesia's occupation of his homeland, he believed that he should commit all of his resources to this one, final effort. He might soon be too old to continue with the struggle.

Seda had little comfort from the knowledge that the East Timorese refugees living in Darwin were growing fat from lying around in Australia, while their fellow-countrymen continued to be subjugated by the Indonesian forces. Although he found their position untenable, particularly that of Xanana Soares whom Seda considered something of an interloper, he knew that he would require their support if his operation was to succeed.

He clearly understood why the United Nations had been powerless to enforce its recommendations for the reinstatement of the former colony's independence; monthly reports which flowed across his desk indicated that Australian business would benefit greatly from the joint Indonesian-Australian oil and gas ventures in the Timor Sea. This is why he specifically targeted the offshore production platforms, and exploration rigs, in his initial concept. Seda knew that the incumbent Vice President would step down in less than eighteen months. The President had promised Seda this position, and he had agreed to accept the high profile office, once he had returned from Australia as its Ambassador. But Seda had done so only to disguise his real intentions. He used word of the imminent appointment to consolidate his powerful position, and assist with the implementation of his strategies.

The fortune he had amassed had been ear-marked to finance his complicated plans, and Seda was convinced that he would be successful. The riots leading up to his appointment, the attacks on oil production centres around the Timor Sea and the landings in Darwin and Western Australia had all been thought through in detail.

He had never been concerned that the Indonesian Military machine might offer more resistance than he was prepared to challenge; the United Nations, Australia, and the United States would support his move once they discovered that an independent Timor would be in their national interests. Seda had helped develop the nuclear power plant programme; and in so doing, had used the funding he had derived from this project to finance his ambitious, and perhaps final attempt to secure East Timor's freedom. He had received more than half a billion dollars from the Salima Group, but Seda knew that he would need every penny to finance his brilliantly conceived operation to achieve independent status for his people. He acknowledged that it would be impossible for him to become President of Indonesia; that was reserved purely for those of Javanese stock. There was no other solution; he would become President of an independent East Timor instead.

Seda smiled when he considered the incredible financial drain Indonesia had committed itself to with the *Rama* Nuclear Power Plant energy programme. Recalling his initial discussions with the billionaire, Lim, Seda had thought it would have been much more difficult to extract such large amounts from the Chinese *totok*. Instead, Seda had been surprised when Lim had undertaken to pay the incredible commission for his part in assigning the winning tender to the Salima Group. Unwittingly, Lim had financed the greater part of Seda's dream.

Although his own wealth was already considerable, Nathan Seda had been delighted with the windfall. That, and the knowledge that Indonesia would be encumbered with an incredible debt, one which would take several generations to repay.

As for the Japanese H-3B rocket development programme, Seda had used this perfectly as a distraction, knowing that such a project would be impossible to keep secret. He expected that the Americans would attempt to pressure the Japanese into withdrawing from the joint development programme once the Bandung experimental research centre's true purpose had been discovered. Should this eventuate, it did not overly concern him that the Indonesians would need to find a substitute nation to continue with the programme's development. By then, Seda believed he would have already succeeded in his mission.

Should international pressure fail to influence Indonesia's position concerning their rocket development programme, Seda expected that the threat of Indonesia possessing such a delivery system could only enhance East Timor's right to possess similar weaponry. In this world of ever-changing political alliances, he was certain that an independent Timor would have little difficulty in identifying a sponsor willing to contribute funds and technology to assist the development of similar weaponry for the strategically positioned island nation.

The retired General was convinced that East Timor would be in a position to maintain the integrity of its sovereign status, even in the shadow of its giant Moslem neighbour.

JAKARTA

Seda thought about the complicated structure that had been put into place to ensure secrecy with the Bandung project. The mountains surrounding Bandung had long been renowned for the number of mining shafts which had been put down during the Dutch colonial times. It had not been difficult for him to acquire such a location, one which encompassed a defunct gold exploration operation. As the land already belonged to the government through the Ministry of Mines, possession had been easily transferred to the newly created research organization.

The Japanese had provided funding and technical expertise, while Seda's team accepted responsibility for the project's construction. The installation was to be maintained as a secret defense research centre and, while the general public would be informed of its existence, they would not be aware of the centre's secret activities.

The facility had been designed with a dual function, the first being the joint development of a missile delivery system designed and funded by the Japanese in conjunction with Tokyo's existing H-3B programme. The second, and far more sinister purpose would be the utilisation of the deep mining shafts to store excess plutonium, which would later be generated from the *Rama II* nuclear power plant's operations.

Seda had easily convinced the President that the Japanese would not be required to know the purpose of the secondary and underground installation. A plausible story for the secret bunker could be easily concocted should the need arise. Besides, Seda knew that it would be impossible for *Rama II* to commence producing fissionable material before he had firmly ensconced himself as President of East Timor and armed his people. Seda believed that it was necessary for Indonesia to be nuclear armed. Without this threat, an independent East Timor would never be able to justify securing similar weaponry. The thought of realizing his dream provided Seda with a moment for reflection. He had worked tirelessly to achieve his ambition.

As his mind wandered back over the past years, Stephen Coleman's face flashed across his mind and, for a brief moment, he was surprised to discover that he experienced a sense of sadness over his former associate's demise. In some perverse way, Seda accepted that Coleman had been mainly responsible for many of the financial successes he then enjoyed.

When the most recent East Timorese rebellion had failed, Seda had all but lost hope. The slaughter had been even worse than those during the first years of occupation. He had been devastated by the results. Investigations had been thorough, and Seda knew he must remove any possibility of his relationship with Coleman being discovered before his position was compromised. Stephen Coleman had to go. Nathan Seda had ordered his execution, and his trusted servant, Umar, had willingly accepted the mission.

Frustratingly, Coleman sensed what was happening, and had disappeared completely in spite of Umar's best efforts to track him down. Umar had followed his quarry's trail through most of Asia. When more than five years had passed, and Coleman had still not made any effort to seek compensation for the assets he had left behind, Seda believed that the man who had been responsible for creating their *kongsi's* first millions, had simply disappeared, and might even be dead. He would have felt easier had there been some evidence reflecting Coleman's status, one way or the other, and could only hope that his former associate was, in fact, gone forever.

Seda thought about Umar's service over the years, and agreed that the man he had found incarcerated in the Magelang Detention Centre, just months after the 1965 coup, had certainly served his new master with unprecedented dedication. Seda had already decided to take Umar with him to Australia; the success of his mission depended heavily on the former Communist army officer.

He then considered the other officers on whom he might rely; Sujono Diryo, Seda knew, could most certainly not be included amongst these. He had sensed that the younger man might also have his ambitious eyes on the Vice Presidency and, in Seda's opinion, that would be a major political error for the unprepared, and relatively inexperienced officer to make.

Being married into the President's family would not necessarily guarantee Sujono support from the other generals. As this, and other thoughts passed through his mind, Seda became troubled by his former protégé, Major General Sujono Diryo, and wondered whether or not he should consider having Umar arrange for the rising star's early retirement from the Vice Presidential race.

* * * * * *

JAKARTA

Murray Stephenson disliked attending meetings in the Kuningan building. He knew that there would always be those amongst the foreign community who would misconstrue the purpose of his visits to the Australian Embassy and, in consequence, he avoided going there even to have his passport extended.

He sat opposite the grey-haired director and could not find any reason to be civil to the man. When he had been involved with the Australian Secret Intelligence Service, this was the man who had deliberately set out to destroy his career. Murray wasn't even sure that Anderson had not been responsible for many of the events which had clouded his last weeks in the Service. Although Murray despised the man, he acknowledged that ASIS still played an important role in maintaining his country's security; and it was for this reason, and no other, that Murray had decided to meet with the director.

'We all appreciate what you have done, Murray,' Anderson had said. Murray knew this not to be true. The man obviously had no heart; he wanted to ask what had happened to Stephen Coleman but thought better of it. He had not been involved for more than twenty years, and wondered how Anderson had managed to remain in power, considering his age.

'Sure,' was all he said, rising to leave. He left the documents lying on the table. They would be of no use to him any more. Anderson extended his hand but the gesture was ignored. Murray left them then, hoping that what he had done would prevent what could have developed into a major threat to the Australian people.

He had protected his source - not out of respect for Ruswita so much, but because he knew to do so would be prudent, considering his financial dependency on Peter Wong and Wong's obvious relationship with Lim's widow. He wished, sometimes, that he had never become involved in the *Rama* projects, but Murray, like so many others, had been caught up in the intricate, financial web that had been so cleverly woven by Lim, and he accepted that there was no immediate escape.

The knowledge he had so recently acquired had acted as a warning to him also. Murray's instinct told him that there was a major move afoot, and he was frustrated by his feeling of impotency, knowing that he was familiar with all the players and yet had no idea what the game plan might be.

Kerry B. Collison

******

United States of America — Washington

Victor Lombardo had been serving in the American Congress for more than ten years, representing his home State of New York. He reflected on the mechanics of politics, never ceasing to be amazed at the intricate system which had provided the comfortable life-style he now enjoyed.

The Congressman finished drafting his speech for the next session, then leaned back in the leather chair to consider the consequences of his plea for Indonesia's Most Favoured Nation status to be revoked. Lombardo was confident that he had sufficient numbers to push his motion through should he still find this necessary. Politics was all about power, he knew; and power was about money.

Lombardo then reflected on his meeting of the evening before with the two Asian bankers, and the insulting offer they had made. When he had checked the contents of the envelope and discovered what value they had placed upon his services, Lombardo had thrown this back at the Lim brothers, and suggested that they reconsider just what they were asking of him. He had expected that they return with another offer and, when this did not eventuate, Lombardo decided to give them a taste of the stick he carried in Congress. He would call for the dismantling of Indonesia's MFN status, and see how quickly they then returned to discourage him from proceeding. His demand would be mentioned in the following morning's press, and the Congressman reminded himself to call in the appropriate favours to ensure that this would occur as planned. Then, when the Lims were sufficiently concerned that their country might be in danger of losing the MFN status which, he knew, would cost the Salima conglomerate dearly, he would re-negotiate his position. Providing the two wealthy Chinese bankers met his price, he would then permit opposition debate to convince him to withdraw his motion, and everyone would be satisfied.

He leaned forward, made another note on the draft speech, then lay back in his chair as he visualised how he would spend the two hundred thousand dollars he expected the Lims would pay.

UNITED STATES OF AMERICA

Congressional Record

INDONESIA'S MOST-FAVORED NATION STATUS
(House of Representatives) [EXCERPT] [Page: J 4221]

The SPEAKER pro tempore. Under a previous order of the House, the gentleman from New York [Mr Lombardo] is recognized for five minutes.

Mr LOMBARDO, Mr Speaker, during the course of the following weeks, Members of this august house will be obliged to consider a great deal of information, while subjected to an unprecedented lobbying effort from both sides of the issue, which will then eventuate in their casting what could very well be one of the most critical votes ever to be taken in this Congress.

I refer to the vote on further extending most-favored-trade status to the Republic of Indonesia. The results of this vote, Mr Speaker, will demonstrate to the world where American priorities lie and will, most probably, be closely watched by our other Asian trading partners with respect to how they too might be treated during subsequent reviews regarding MFN status.

There will, no doubt, be those amongst this Congress who might well consider that the debate regarding Indonesia's MFN status extension is nothing more than an attempt, by those of us who are opposed to such an extension, to be obstructive in terms of global trade. Let me assure you, Mr Speaker, that this is far from the truth. There are more than 160 nations which enjoy MFN status in one form or another. Of these, only Indonesia and China have emerged as the nations which continually flout the considerations extended by this United States of America. In reality, the Indonesian MFN debate is about human rights. It is about Indonesia's refusal to abide by the decisions taken by the United Nations in respect to their occupation of East Timor. A vote in favor of Most Favored Nation status for Indonesia, is a vote, Mr Speaker, to condone that country's illegal occupation of another country. [EXCERPT]

KERRY B. COLLISON

Chapter 17

Islamabad

Mohammed Ali bin Fuad searched the skies for planes. It had become a habit, one he had acquired as a youth. He spotted two aircraft which he judged had just entered into their holding patterns, then he turned back downwind to watch the ageing Boeing 747 land. The screaming sound of runway concrete ripping into rubber struck his ears as the aircraft touched down heavily, leaving visible puffs of burning tyre-smoke in its tracks.

Fuad turned to his team and shouted above the high-pitched jet engines as decibels exceeded acceptable levels, then adjusted his headphones to deaden the noise. The ground engineer team waited, pensively, until the aircraft turned into the hard-standing apron area. Fuad moved out quickly and stood directly in line with the huge aircraft, guiding the pilot towards the allocated parking bay.

The service team swung into action as the aircraft braked to a halt, co-ordinating ground handling as they had been trained. Fuad stepped forward, plugged his communication lead into the aircraft's ground system and spoke to the pilot. Minutes passed before the doors were released from inside the cabin, permitting the final connection to be made as the passenger steps clicked into place. An hour later, as he observed the jumbo-jet depart, Fuad knew he would not be needed again until the following day. He completed his ground engineering report, lodged this with the station manager, then left the terminal building for home.

The bus dropped him off on the outskirts of Islamabad, where he lived in a small cluster of low-cost houses constructed for airport employees and their families. Fuad lived alone; he had never married, and at his age, had decided that it might already be too late to do so. Fuad's life was now relatively simple in comparison to his earlier years, when each new day brought life-threatening challenges, and all that he possessed were the torn rags on his back.

He entered his compact quarters and observed that his clothes had been washed and folded, and a note advising how much he owed the woman next door. He placed the clothes in the wardrobe and then showered before lying down on the narrow, hard timber-framed bed to sleep. As he lay there, resting, Fuad remembered how long it had taken him to accustom himself to city living conditions, and the uncomfortably soft beds people used there. When he was first taken to the swelling metropolis, Fuad had preferred to sleep on the hard, cement, store-room floor, behind the kitchen in his benefactor's home.

He thought about the people who had accepted him into their household and provided food and shelter at a time when refugees, such as he, had swamped Islamabad by the hundreds of thousands. Haunting memories of those times had not grown dim over the years. Instead, Fuad accepted these reminders of just how cruel life had been under the Hindus. As a child, his family had been driven from their own country, India, and forced to live in the arid regions of Pakistan where the heat was so severe, trees shed their leaves to preserve moisture during the day and birds flew only at night.

Then, when he had barely entered his teens, his former countrymen had crossed the border and commenced a campaign of ethnic cleansing which drove Moslems even deeper into Pakistan. His family had died during such an attack. Had it not been for a band of retreating resistance fighters, he too would have died in the desert. They had taken him with them, providing Fuad with water and *chanai*, the peasant's hamper.

As he lay on his back, resting, Fuad's thoughts carried him back to the long trek he and the others had made. Moving from village to village, living on the most meagre of rations, the armed band continued their retreat until they were no longer threatened by aerial attack. He sometimes still woke in the quiet of night, finding himself screaming aloud in his sleep as memories of the helicopter gun-ship attacks intruded on his dreams.

It was months before Fuad ended up in Islamabad. He had just followed the others, as he had nowhere else to go. The soldier who had saved his life when his village had been destroyed continued

JAKARTA

to care for him by taking him into his modest home and providing food and shelter. The brief and bitter war had ended with India gloating over its victory, and before Fuad had even arrived in the city life had already returned to normal.

* * * * * *

He had worked alongside the demobilised soldier, learning what he could of the man's mechanical skills. He learned to read. Before his twentieth birthday, Fuad's knowledge of engines had guaranteed him permanent employment with the government and, when the opportunity arose, he joined the army. There he received specialist training, and was placed in Pakistan's elite mobile ground defense corps. When hostilities broke out between India and Pakistan again, Fuad found himself out in the desert defending his adopted country against the land of his birth.

The fighting continued for seventeen days, during which time his unit had accounted for three Indian Mi-25 Russian gun-ships which had penetrated deep into Pakistani territory. The war had ended as had others between the two countries, with tens of thousands dead and no clear resolution.

When Fuad's unit had returned to Islamabad, he had been decorated for his efforts in shooting down the enemy gun-ships. His photograph had been placed in the capital's newspapers and, for a brief time, Fuad was treated as a hero. Then, along with many others, he was de-mobbed.

He was fortunate to find work at the airport. There, his dedication and skill attracted the attention of his superiors, and Fuad was given assistance to attend evening courses where he further enhanced his empiric skills, learning mechanical theory and even English which, he had discovered, was essential to his work at the airport. As the years had passed, Fuad consolidated his position at the airport by accepting a position with one of the foreign airline companies which required its own native speaking engineers. He had been given an excellent salary, and was taken to the United States where he underwent intensive conversion training on the United American fleet. By the time Fuad had reached his fortieth birthday, he had been appointed first assistant ground engineer for the airline's Islamabad services.

As he lay thinking about his career, Fuad reminded himself to check with the station manager regarding final confirmation of his posting. He had been informed that he was on a short list, and had been recommended for an overseas assignment. His six-month tour with the United American ground handling team in California had whetted his appetite for travel; that, and the incredibly generous allowances paid to staff while away from their home stations.

It was during his training there that Fuad had been surprised to discover the number of airline staff involved with the illegal import of drugs. Once, during an undercarriage inspection, he came across a two kilo package of white powder which he knew, instantly, from his time on the streets of Islamabad, was heroin. He had been tempted to remove the shipment and try and sell it himself, but realised that without contacts this would have been dangerous

Unbeknown to Fuad, he had been observed inspecting the shipment, and was later approached by the ground crewman responsible for its recovery. Fuad was offered five hundred dollars to remain silent. He willingly accepted the money and became friendly with the American engineer. As their friendship developed, Fuad even helped recover some shipments, when asked. By the time he had completed his time in Los Angeles, Fuad didn't want to leave.

He cherished his short stay, and wished he could remain. Fuad discussed this with his friend, who embellished the penalties associated with illegal entry, as he did not want Fuad being picked up as an illegal immigrant and possibly revealing whatever he had learned about the illicit drug activities around the airport. Fuad then decided that he would look for another way to return to America but, after several years back in the Pakistani capital, he acknowledged, sadly, that his dream would never materialise.

He wanted desperately to leave Pakistan and its bitter memories. There were a limited number of choices for those with Fuad's engineering expertise, and one of those included Bombay. He had thought of what he would say should the company offer to send him to India. Fuad frowned, discovering that this thought had caused him to bite through the soft flesh of his lower lip. No, he decided, even if it might mean that he would never again be offered the opportunity to travel away from Pakistan, he would most certainly refuse.

The hate he felt for the Hindus had all but consumed him during his younger years, and Fuad accepted that his feelings could never be any different. The memory of his parents' broken bodies lying under the rubble which had been their home could never fade. Disturbed that he had permitted his latent anger to spoil his rest, Fuad attempted to erase the past from his mind by conjuring up images of other things, but failed. An hour passed, then another. Finally he gave up altogether, dressed, and went out in search of something to eat.

On Friday, as he was preparing for the mid-morning prayers, Fuad was called into the station manager's office and asked if he would accept a two-year assignment as the company's senior ground-handling engineer in the Philippines. Fuad was overwhelmed by the opportunity, and eagerly accepted the promotion. He had often seen Filipino stewardesses when their flights had transited Islamabad, and smiled at the thought of living amongst such beautiful women. And, he remembered, some of them were also of the Moslem faith.

A month passed before Fuad arrived in Manila. He settled down to his work, and soon discovered the similarities between working in Los Angeles and his new station. Before he had celebrated his first year as the United American Airline senior ground engineer, Fuad was making ten times as much money from moving heroin as he was from his salary. And that was when he attracted the attention of the Drug Enforcement Agency, whose agents had been monitoring staff employed by airlines which flew between the United States and Asia.

Three months later, Fuad was arrested and interrogated by American agents seconded to the Filipino Bureau.

They decided that he could be far more useful working for the DEA than being incarcerated in some filthy local prison. He was offered the opportunity to avoid imprisonment of fifteen years, and Fuad leaped at the offer. Fuad then commenced reporting on a regular basis to the in-country DEA agent, knowing that his dream of ever returning to America was then an impossibility.

His file was sent to Washington, from where it was distributed to all United States defense and intelligence agencies. Within the month, his records had been amended to include his service records and other information gleaned from data collected by the American Embassy in Pakistan. It was then that he came to the attention of the United States Defense Intelligence Agency analysts, at Bolling Airforce Base in Washington and the world's most powerful covert agency, the CIA.

* * * * * *

China — Beijing

China's paramount leader sat transfixed, listening to his Admiral's discourse on regional naval strengths, and the unopposed annexation of the southern islands the Indonesians referred to as Natuna. He was most pleased with the results of the first expedition, and particularly satisfied that there had not been any interference from the United States forces, particularly its Seventh Fleet stationed in Japan.

The Chairman clearly understood the economic realities which confronted his nation. China's economic growth continued to be stifled by its inability to satisfy the country's insatiable demands for more fuel, and he had personally accepted responsibility to resolve this national dilemma. Foreign investments had doubled, then later tripled, once the West had been satisfied with China's handling of Hong Kong and the former colony's intellectuals. But the Chairman knew that the solution to China's difficulties would not be found in the slow transfer of technology from either the Russians, or the West. Instead, he had strongly supported the small dedicated group which had proposed a more lateral approach to China's quest for current technology, while maintaining its military growth and supremacy along the tens of thousands of kilometers representing China's borders.

As China's entire southern economic development belt scrambled for its share of infrastructure dollars, so too did the demand for greater fuel supplies grow. From Shanghai down through Guangzhou and across to Chongging, China's more liberal south had leaped forward at an incredible rate as these provinces continued to enjoy unparalleled, industrialised growth. Oil imports had dangerously exceeded all previous economic forecasts, and the Chairman had encountered few difficulties in obtaining support to remedy China's predicament.

Of the dozen or so nations which shared borders with his

country few, with the exclusion of the Russian states, produced sufficient fuel for themselves. So occupying these countries was not considered a viable option. He knew that any attempt to occupy Siberia would be met with an immediate, and most probably nuclear, response from Moscow and that isolated territory's other allies.

To the south, the rich oil and gas fields of the South China Sea offered a solution only to China's immediate problems. Later, they would need to look further afield to accommodate the country's incredible thirst for fuel and the funding necessary to accommodate this burdensome need. He believed that there could only be one solution to resolve these financial considerations, and that lay in China's acquisition of Taiwan, with its hundreds of billions in gold and dollar reserves.

The Chairman had stated the obvious to his political and military supporters. China needed to secure its lines of supply from the Middle East while developing a strategy which would deliver control over the substantial oil and gas reserves to the south. The implementation of his programme would, however, require that the United States of America be rendered powerless to intercede in any regional conflict which arose out of China's expansionist moves. The United States, they had been reminded by a senior strategist, had considerable economic interests to protect by remaining on a friendly footing with the world's third largest state.

The economist had emphasized that American trade with Asia had grown to half a trillion dollars and accounted for more than five million jobs in North America. The United States, he had gone on to say, had invested more than one hundred billion in Asia, while their Oriental counterparts had reciprocated by placing almost double that amount in American investments.

The Chairman's strategic advisers had pointed out that the United States was losing its military foothold in Asia. With the exception of Guam and Japan, which often played host to the Seventh Fleet and permitted the Americans to maintain a small contingent of troops and combat aircraft, the United States military presence had all but disappeared from the region.

The subsequent Party Congress had unanimously supported an increased military budget, one which would expand China's Navy and ensure the suppression of any civilian unrest which might occur along the borders. What surprised most China-watchers was the sudden shift Beijing made towards developing closer ties with the United States, believing that the two countries were entering a new era of friendship and co-operation. A goodwill visit had soon followed, during which time the American public discounted newspaper reports from one journalist who had overheard China's powerful Peoples' Liberation Army warlord, General Chi, comment that his country had already perfected a missile delivery system which could easily dispatch a nuclear warhead to Los Angeles.

In the wake of fading public indignation over the Long Beach affair, when China had successfully taken control over the former naval base for China's COSCO fleet, three Chinese warships, including two destroyers, were permitted to dock at the North Island Naval Air Station in San Diego Bay for a five-day 'goodwill tour'. North Americans welcomed the visit with unprecedented complacency, accepting visiting Red Chinese Vice Admiral Wang Yongguo's statement, that: *"Although China and America are far away from each other, we believe our countries can be linked by the Pacific Ocean."*

In just one year, the Chairman's skilful diplomatic measures had all but erased memory of the chilly confrontation between the two countries just twelve months earlier, when US carriers were sent to the Taiwan Strait in response to his country's efforts to intimidate the so-called Free Chinese during their presidential elections. Since then, due to substantial diplomatic inroads being achieved by his emissaries, the Chairman was delighted to observe that the American President had become far more deferential to China's concerns.

The Chairman's thoughts turned to the two young men most responsible for delivering the Americans to China. Although the paramount leader clearly understood what really motivated the Lim brothers, he could not help but believe that they were also driven by their Chinese heritage. The two bankers had been instrumental in providing the key which opened the door directly into the White House, and delivered not only the Alabama shipping facilities and the Long Beach naval yards to China, but also control over the anchor ports situated at both entrances to the Panama Canal. Now, given that the time was rapidly approaching for China to make its move, the United States would consider its position very carefully before interfering with his country's ultimate goals.

The Chairman recalled that world opinion had turned against his country during their early attempts to gain a foothold in the United States and Panama. Those responsible for jeopardising his country's dreams had been severely dealt with, and he had warned those who might be tempted to emulate their misguided colleagues that he would not tolerate such disastrous results. Because of a few, China's entire American strategy had almost been destroyed.

The Chairman frowned with the recollection of how a COSCO crew had been discovered secretly off-loading a shipment of two thousand AK-47 rifles in Oakland. Accusations of deliberate attempts to establish a Chinese Fifth Column in the United States had covered front pages for weeks. Then, as the issue started to fade away, the Chairman was infuriated when claims were made that China had permitted its shipping line, COSCO, to develop lines of supply within North America for heroin distribution. Then the US newspapers leaked stories claiming that more than four hundred Chinese businessmen were under federal investigation for espionage, suggesting that many of these were also COSCO associated.

Other articles claimed, irresponsibly he had thought at the time, that according to the United States Defense Intelligence Agency, China had increased its North American intelligence operations to the point where the DIA, and other American agencies, had been overwhelmed by the sheer number of China-related cases. In order to prevent any further deterioration in China-American relationships, his government had moved quickly, and once again the Lim brothers became involved in assisting China shore-up its relations with the United States. It had taken considerable lobbying and substantial funds to change American opinion, but inside one year they had succeeded in achieving this goal, during which time COSCO's underground activities reached an all time high.

The Chinese shipping company flouted every law in the land, and went virtually unchallenged. Its access to the American nation's largest container port, conveniently located near several sensitive defense research facilities, proved a windfall for their clandestine activities. Through the Lim's banking arms in Kentucky, they were able to purchase many of the Pentagon's high-tech surplus military parts then ship them back to China, hiding these in seagoing containers under tons of metal scrap.

Then, without warning, COSCO's ships were raided by the United States Secret Service. Among the items seized were fully operational encryption devices, submarine propulsion parts, radar systems, electron tubes for the Patriot guided missiles, and even F-117A Stealth fighter parts. Many of these parts which had been sold as 'surplus' were, they discovered, brand new.

The Chairman was aware of his country's intelligence agencies' dedicated efforts to secure technology from the Americans and had, in fact, condoned the measures, knowing that acquisition of such high-tech information and materials would assist China to drastically reduce its own research and development costs. His country's emergence as a mega economic power had, without doubt, paralysed its neighbouring countries with fear.

The Chairman then changed his country's strategy, moving the pressure back onto the Americans. When the British press disclosed that they had confirmation of China's ability to deliver a twenty-kiloton yield nuclear warhead to United States shores, and postulated a future which would include a Chinese inspired Armageddon, United States defense officials reconsidered their country's position, once again, in relation to the Republic of China.

The week following the disclosures made in the London tabloids, the Chinese Minister for the Interior had openly sought the immediate removal, and execution, of the engineer identified as responsible for the leaks. Photographs of his country's newly developed DF-31 Intercontinental Ballistic Missile, and technical data which suggested that this would be the missile used against American shores, had been deliberately leaked. Orders were given for the engineer involved in the ruse to be secretly moved to another research and development centre, where he could continue with his valuable work, and a common thief had then been executed in his place.

World attention was once again focused on China. Amnesty International highlighted past atrocities, and isolated intellectual groups demanded greater representation. The Chairman refused to accommodate requests for further political reforms, and ignored suggestions that China's Human Rights record was at an all time low. He firmly believed that there was no role for Western ideologies in the authoritarian state; China had entered the twenty-first century and demanded its place within the greater structure of the new global society.

The Chairman was an ardent historian; he firmly believed that, as China had once dominated the East, it would soon do so again. He admired the great Mao Tse Tung, revelling in the many stories of how Mao had kept the super-powers at each others' throats. As a young man, he had studied the Great Chairman's tactics and philosophies. As an older and wiser politician, he had learned that the wisdom of Mao was not necessarily appropriate for a nation which needed desperately to climb out of its economic quagmire. Although he had also respected Mao's political position in relation to India, the Chairman believed that China, in the new millennium, needed to have these people as allies.

He reflected on their historical relationships. Under Nehru, India had begun its slow crawl forward, and was admired by the West, and this relationship had continued until the Indian Prime Minister, during his state visit to America, had sided with Mao Tse Tung when Chiang Kai Shek's nationalists were defeated, and fled to Taiwan. As a Chinese, the Chairman would always thank Nehru for insisting that Mao's new China be given the vacant United Nation's seat and his refusal to condemn China over its anti-West stance. The Chairman knew from history that Nehru envisaged an Asia controlled by the two great powers, and mistakenly trusted Mao's loyalty. When Nehru had emerged as the self-proclaimed leader of the non-aligned nations, Mao simply sent Chou En Lai to the Bandung Conference as a token gesture of his support.

The Chairman reflected on the 1962 Chinese invasion of Tibet and North-east India, challenging Nehru's strength. Although India had appealed to the Americans for support, none had eventuated. As a staunch Mao supporter, the Chairman could not understand, at the time, why Mao then had withdrawn Chinese troops from the thousands of square kilometres already seized. The self-proclaimed and one-sided alliance between the two nations dissipated as quickly as it had appeared. India and China had immediately become border enemies. Now, as China's new absolute leader, the Chairman had been given the opportunity to use India once again and, in so doing, guarantee China's future lines of supply and natural rights within the region.

The Chairman had given his final approval for the rapprochement offered by China's natural enemies, understanding that the common denominator which tied New Delhi to Beijing would be their strength in controlling the seas. United, he believed, the world's two largest populations would soon dominate Asia. Once China had consolidated its position, he would review the alliance created with India. The Chairman sanctioned the bold move to send the South Sea Fleet across the South China Sea into Indonesia's undefended northern islands of Natuna. China's sea-lane access needed to be protected, above all else. Power, fuel, electricity: these were the driving forces which required that China move quickly, to feed its hungry millions.

The well-informed Chairman was familiar with most recent developments in technology. He also knew that, with China's annual growth ballooning into the double digits, even the ambitious nuclear power programme would never keep pace with his country's incredible demand for electricity. He had been one of the first to endorse the additional expenditures required for the advancement of their nuclear power industry, although he realized just how time consuming this new approach would be. He had clearly understood that, even with the development of a hundred new plants, these would generate but a fraction of his country's demands. The few NPPs already scheduled for construction would not even provide sufficient electricity for a city the size of Shanghai, let alone the entire southern region where factories remained working, demanding even more power, day in and day out, twenty-four hours each day.

His country's ambitious plans for expanding nuclear electricity generation had been severely curtailed by those nations which controlled the flow of uranium ore. The Chairman recognised that China's deposits of this precious ore were insignificant in terms of the nation's needs. Even the China National Nuclear Corporation, with its three hundred thousand employees, had been unable to resolve the question of China's self-sufficiency. Production centres, such as the Lantian mine in Shaanxi Province, contributed little towards satisfying domestic demand. He believed that there could be only one solution. China desperately needed to acquire its own natural energy sources, and in so doing, protect its existing lines of supply from the Middle East. *If only China had Australia's uranium ore reserves and Indonesia's oil!*

* * * * * *

The paramount leader of more than one billion Chinese finished listening to the Admiral's report, then dismissed his senior officer. He sat, contemplating China's immediate future and its relationship with India. The world's two largest populations, supported by two of the largest navies. *Who,* he thought, *could possibly prevent the successful implementation of their strategies?*

* * * * * *

Indonesia — Bandung Research and Development Center

Doctor Sunarko slipped away earlier than usual, feigning family illness. He drove down the slippery mountain road slowly, worried that the earlier rain might have dislodged part of the unstable cuttings which sliced precariously through to the lush, volcanic, rain-sodden soil. He braked entering a corner and the Toyota's wheels refused to steer, threatening to send the four-wheel drive crashing over the embankment into the river two hundred meters below. At the last moment, the vehicle corrected itself, and Sunarko braked again, his heart thumping dangerously.

His fear could not be altogether attributed to his poor driving skills; he was scared. Earlier, he had observed the Research Center's security officer watching him closely. Sunarko feared discovery, and now believed that this had happened, otherwise he would not have come under scrutiny from the security chief, Umar.

Lightning cracked to his right, causing him to catch his breath. Within moments, his vision was blurred as the thunderstorm released thrashing rain, carried by turbulent, mountain winds. He braked and swerved, again. Without warning, another deafening crack of lightning struck nearby, and Sunarko stomped heavily on the brake pedal, sliding to a halt. Shaking uncontrollably, he then buried his head between his arms, gripping the jeep's wheel. Then the engine died.

Suddenly, he couldn't breathe and, fumbling for his inhaler, discovered that he had left it behind, which increased the severity of his asthma attack. Sunarko struggled for air, but it was as if his airways were blocked. Within seconds, he felt his body slipping away, losing consciousness. His head slid slowly across and against the driver's door and, in that moment, he noticed another flash reflected by his exterior off-side rear-vision mirror. His last thoughts were that Umar had followed him and that he was surely going to die! He heard the other vehicle brake, then a door slammed shut, followed moments later by a fist banging on the side of his jeep.

'Are you all right?' he heard someone call, the man's voice barely audible. Sunarko cringed, not wishing to look outside into the dark, rain-swept night. Suddenly, the door was jerked open, and Sunarko shrank back, waiting for whatever might follow.

'Don't hurt me!' he cried out, covering his head with his arms.

'I'm not going to hurt you,' he heard the man call loudly, his voice partially drowned by another loud thunder clap. He looked at the stranger standing in the torrential downpour, and identified the figure as that of a foreigner.

'Who..are..you?' he asked, choking as he fought to breathe. He felt the man's strong hands grip him firmly, then pull him away from the driver's seat. Sunarko no longer cared if he was going to die; he just wanted to be able to breathe. He experienced the slight nausea associated with his loss of oxygen and panicked, trying to suck air into his lungs.

'Hold on, Mas,' the voice said, but Sunarko just let go, and slumped forward unconscious. Murray Stephenson grunted, pulled the engineer from the Jeep, and carried him with great difficulty back to his own vehicle. He leaned the Indonesian aerospace engineer against his car, opened the rear door, and dropped him onto the rear seat. Then he returned to the Jeep, turned the wheel to unlock the steering, and knocked the Japanese machine out of gear.

He watched the Jeep crawl to the side of the road, then dip its nose forward, before sliding down the steep embankment, and Murray cursed those who had arranged for him to meet with this engineer out in the mountains. He turned, then slogged his way through the thick, sticky clay, becoming totally drenched before reaching his vehicle. Once inside and behind the wheel, he dragged his filthy, mud-caked boots off, and threw these angrily onto the passenger's floor. Murray looked over to the rear seat and could see that Sunarko's system had closed down, putting him safely to sleep. Then he released the hand-brake and drove carefully around the mountain into Bandung.

* * * * * *

Umar swore loudly, then kicked the side of the Jeep's flat tyre. He looked down the muddy road, his eyes following the vehicle's lights to the next bend in the mountainous road. He had lost sight of Sunarko more than five minutes before, and knew that it would be hopeless attempting to catch him once he had changed the wheel.

He tugged at his coat's collar as rain stung his face and neck, driven by the gusty, mountain winds. Then he set about unlocking the spare wheel while considering what his next actions should be. Umar dragged his heavy boots through the mud, and stood at the rear of the Jeep unscrewing the bolts attached to the spare while contemplating his quarry, Sunarko. He knew that the man was up to something; he had followed him several times before and was convinced that the senior technician from the secret research and development facility was communicating with someone from outside. He had set out to follow Sunarko, hoping to discover who it might be that was so interested in the Bandung project.

Ten minutes passed before Umar could follow. He knew that it would be most unlikely that he could catch up with the other man, considering the weather and the dangerous road. Umar decided to return to the research centre and wait for a later opportunity to trap Sunarko. Then the thought struck him that he may not be given that chance, as he would soon leave for Australia to accompany *Bapak Seda* as his security chief.

Umar's face twisted in what some might believe to be a smile, as he recalled his first meeting with the General in the dungeons of the Semarang detention centre, where he had been imprisoned, interrogated, and brutally beaten regarding his role in the Communist Party's abortive *coup d'etat*. He accepted that Seda had saved his life, in exchange for which, Umar had agreed to follow the powerful intelligence officer unquestioningly. And he had for more than three decades, even when this loyalty sometimes required that he act as the general's personal executioner. He had been well rewarded. The former communist officer had discussed his retirement with the general; Seda had agreed that Umar would be relieved of his commitments once they had returned from the general's brief tour as Ambassador to Australia.

As he drove carefully back to the well-guarded facility, Umar smiled at the thought of his leaving Java to spend the next years in Australia amongst the likes of Stephen Coleman. The image of the general's former associate flashed through his mind, and Umar scowled, remembering how close he had come to killing the man the first time, more than thirty years before, when the Australian had visited the jungles of Irian, and stepped into his sights. Umar had fired, believing he had killed the foreigner, only to discover later that he had merely wounded the man.

Umar had been confused when General Seda later invited this man to enter into partnership when he returned to Jakarta. Even then, Umar believed that Coleman would always be a danger to them both. When Seda had issued instructions to kill his partner, the Australian had escaped, fleeing overseas. Umar and Coleman had barely missed each other in the Philippines and, later, in Phnom Penh. Umar had spent more than two years searching for his quarry to no avail. Finally Umar decided that someone else must have completed his task for him, as Coleman had simply vanished.

As he turned into the research centre's driveway and flashed his lights, two security guards stepped out into the rain, saluted, then opened the heavy gates. Umar drove through and returned to his quarters, thoughts of Stephen Coleman already washed from his mind.

* * * * * *

Jakarta

Geoffrey Thistlethwaites in no way reflected the image of what Hollywood traditionally promoted as a typical, flamboyant, handsome, and daring intelligence agent. His communications company, P.T. Communications Ready-Serve, had started out as a front for the confusing number of Australian intelligence agencies which had inundated the Jakarta capital over the past thirty years, but his company had actually developed into a *bona fide* operation, embarrassing his masters in Canberra. There were no less than five such listening posts in Jakarta attributed to the Australian intelligence agencies, most of which came into being after the press exposed the clandestine activities of Eric Whitehead and Associates' operations throughout Asia, resulting in the prominent public relations executive decision to resign from the public company and enjoy his forced retirement.

GT, as his friends called him, was a simple communications conduit who received and passed information in consideration of a modest, and often overdue, retainer. On this day, he took the taped interview and went down to the Embassy in Kuningan. There, under the subterfuge of meeting with the Defence Attaché, GT surrendered the tape to the First Secretary, Political, and returned to his workshop office in Cilandak. Not two hours had passed before the tape's contents had been encoded, despatched, and received at the relevant destination in Canberra, where the desk officer identified the highly sensitive coding, and passed the message directly to his superior. An hour later, the contents of Sunarko's interview were known to the Australian Attorney General.

* * * * * *

India — Army Northern Command

Undisturbed by the heat, General Rahul Kumar stood, almost majestically, his right arm hand prepared to snap his salute as the approaching column of soldiers responded to the command, 'eyes right!'. Standing behind, and slightly to one side of the Chief of Army Staff, was the Officer Commanding for India's largest military command, recently boosted to include three infantry divisions. As the soldiers marched past on parade, General Kumar recognized that these troops represented India's first line of defense in the event that his country was attacked by any of her aggressive neighbours.

General Kumar realized that it was highly probable that the young men proudly marching past before him would see action at least once during their military careers. The last confrontation with Pakistan had ended, as before, with an Indian victory. Although many years had passed since India and China had fought along each other's borders, he firmly believed that he would live to see hostilities break out between the two countries again. As he gazed proudly at the columns passing before him, Rahul Kumar was reminded of the graduation parade he had attended as a young officer, and the exhilarating speech the Officer Commanding had given, stoking the fires of patriotism in their young hearts. He could still recall most of what the general had said, and how he had attempted to follow this advice throughout his military career.

* * * * * *

Rahul Kumar had graduated from the Indian Army Officers' Academy at the age of twenty-two. From the very beginning of his career he had displayed those qualities which would result in his meteoric rise through the Army's ranks, becoming Colonel before his thirty-fifth birthday. His parents had been very proud; particularly his father, a retired major who had served under the British Raj, and had been responsible for instilling discipline in his son almost from the time Rahul had taken his first steps. He admired his father, and sorely wished he had survived to witness his graduation, but this was not to be. Kumar's father had been killed in one of the frequent border skirmishes with Pakistan the very month his son was to graduate.

Rahul had always enjoyed the many opportunities he had received to advance his career, including an extended visit to England, where he attended the Royal College of Defence Studies in London. Upon his return, Rahul Kumar was confirmed in the rank of Major General. Mainly because of his military acumen, but also due to the fact that Kumar had remained apolitical throughout his military career, he was appointed as India's most senior army officer. Admired by his fellow officers, but disliked by his counterparts in the country's navy and airforce, General Rahul Kumar had experienced few difficulties in establishing himself as India's foremost military officer.

It was unfortunate for the country that Kumar had never developed the desire to accommodate those who led India's political parties, often coming into confrontation with politicians whose acts of political expediency, in the general's mind, blatantly undermined India's position as a leading power. Then, when he refused to publicly support the incumbent Prime Minister's policies, Rahul experienced his first real concerns for his future. Those closest to him advised caution, and suggested that he settle his differences with the influential politician. He refused, and from that moment the army was relegated to a secondary position behind the Indian navy, particularly when it came to budgetary considerations. Kumar and his fellow officers were angered by the preferential treatment shown to the navy, particularly when it became obvious that Admiral Gopal, Admiral of the Fleet, also enjoyed a personal relationship with the Prime Minister, Vijay Rakesh. It was then that General Rahul Kumar first turned his attention to the United States, fostering ties with that country's representatives in New Delhi. Before too long, his open support for closer defense ties with the United States became a political embarrassment for the Rakesh Administration, and Kumar was summoned to the Prime Minister's office, where he was severely admonished for so openly promoting defense co-operation with the Americans. His behaviour, Vijay Rakesh had suggested, was in contradiction with India's policy of non-alignment. When Kumar had pointed out that the government had already established this precedent by publicly identifying itself with both the former Soviet and Western Powers, the meeting deteriorated rapidly, with both powerful men accusing the other of attempting to lead India in the wrong direction.

Within days, their animosity towards each other spilled over into the public domain, and General Kumar struggled to maintain his position as the Indian army's Chief. It was only due to the intervention of others that both men finally stepped back from their most public dispute, distancing themselves from each other as they continued to carry out their duties. Kumar managed to hold onto his powerful position, actually improving his level of support within the army. However, he did discontinue his open affiliation with the Americans, realizing that this could be used to undermine his position with the Indian military establishment, and his control of one of the world's largest armies which consisted of no less than one and a half million soldiers.

* * * * * *

As the highly polished trombones punched their harsh notes

through the stifling morning air, Kumar recognized that the parade was nearing its end, and turned his thoughts to the ceremony. When the final column had passed by followed by the band, General Rahul Kumar dropped his salute, turned to the Officer Commanding and smiled, congratulating his loyal friend on his Command's fine performance, not knowing that in the not too distant future, he would call upon this officer to consider an Indian army presence beyond their country's borders.

Chapter 18

Canberra — CIA

Harold Goldstein had been in Australia for more than two years, and longed to return to the States. The Aussie environment had not been up to his expectations, nor had the potential for him to improve his standing within the Agency. Nothing ever seemed to happen in Australia. Stranded in the middle of nowhere, he had enjoyed very little of his time in the country which boasted great beaches, barbecues and scantily clad women. For Harry, his appointment to the American Embassy in the Australian Capital had been a great disappointment. He went over the weekly report again, and yawned with boredom. Then he turned his attention to a copy of the New York Times, and observed from the date that he was reading last week's news, again.

'Morning, Harry,' a voice intoned, the southern drawl easily identified as that of his senior field agent, Ian Chalmers. Goldstein looked up, smiled at his visitor and offered him the only chair in his office.

'What's up?' he asked. The CIA officer rarely appeared in his office before lunch. Goldstein, whose official position was Political Attaché, expected Chalmers was looking for someone to make up a fourth for some golfing appointment.

'Something's on the boil, Harry,' the agent reported, handing a brief report to his station chief. 'Seems there's been some activity in one of the listed safe-houses. Thought we should take a closer look.' The Station Chief looked through the notes, examined the black and white enlargements, the dropped them back onto his desk. He would be surprised if anything of any real importance was to occur in this sleepy Capital.

'Who is it?' he asked. Chalmers turned the file around and placed his finger directly on the man's face.

'His name is Coleman. Stephen Coleman. He used to be with ASIS until the early seventies. Then he disappeared, there's....' Goldstein was suddenly alert, and picked the file back up again, staring at the photograph.

'Well I'll be...' he said, staring the photograph. The other man was surprised by his Chief's reaction.

'Do you know this guy?' Chalmers asked, responding to Goldstein's grin.

'Shit, Ian, this arsehole has been missing for years!' he laughed, shaking his head as he re-examined the photographs. He picked the other snaps up, looked at these, then dropped them back onto his desk. 'Where did you say these were taken?'

'Just down the road,' he answered, surprised with the reaction this brought.

'Jesus H Christ!' he exploded, 'Are you sure?' Chalmers was taken aback by the response. He picked the file back up again and read directly from the report.

'Stephen Coleman arrived at the safe-house at approximately sixteen hundred hours yesterday, the sixteenth of August. He was observed, and photographed, entering the old Soviet-listed residence. Since its use was compromised back in the early eighties, the Australians took control over the address. ASIO used it for some of their domestic needs, but there hasn't been much of any significance to report on the address. Until now, that is,' he added. Chalmers felt that perhaps he should have been able to identify the man Goldstein had recognized in the photograph, but he had no recollection of anyone named Coleman listed in the current CIA lists. He looked over at the Station Chief who was deep in thought.

'Who do we have watching the address?' Goldstein asked.

'No one at the moment,' Chalmers replied, knowing that this would not be the answer his superior would want to hear. 'But I can get someone onto it ASAP, if that's what you want.' He waited for instructions, even more curious than before. Later, he would go back into the computer and search for more information, sensing that he should have already known who this man was.

'Get someone down there, or have someone lock the place down until I have spoken to Langley,' Goldstein ordered sharply, surprising his subordinate even more.

JAKARTA

'You got it,' Chalmers replied, waiting for more. Goldstein looked over at him.

'Do it now, Ian,' was all he said, wondering what had brought this ghost from the past into play. His number two nodded, rose, then left the room without anything further passing between the two men.

* * * * * *

Prime Minister's Offices

'I don't like it, I tell you, I don't like it at all.' The statement was made by the rotund Leader of the Opposition as the bipartisan discussion continued. It was not often that political parties in Opposition were asked to attend government meetings involving defense-related issues.

'Well, Bill,' the Prime Minister said, now convinced that it had been an error to invite his political foe to the discussions, 'none of us do. What we have to achieve here today, is for us all to reach consensus and send a clear message to the Indonesians that we refuse to be threatened, and that this message is from *all* the people of Australia.' Jack William Evans searched the faces of his Cabinet members and wondered how many of his own team would attempt to make political mileage out of the volatile situation.

As Prime Minister, he had called the urgent meeting to discuss Indonesia's growing dispute with Australia, which had been suddenly brought to a head by unprovoked attacks on Australian oil rigs operating in the Timor Sea. These had followed a break-down in negotiations over the Timor Shelf production rights, throwing the many concessions there into dispute. Arbitration had been attempted, but the Indonesians had refused any other venue but in their own country. Jakarta had denied any knowledge of the terrorist action, claiming that pirates had also burned villages in some of Indonesia's less populated areas in the eastern archipelago.

The Prime Minister knew that he had to avoid any further escalation at all costs. Indonesia's military build-up had outstripped Australian capability, creating an alarming gap between the two countries' defence capabilities. The former Soviet Mediterranean Fleet, which Indonesia had purchased and then mothballed, had been refitted. Jakarta had purchased American nuclear submarines which had also been taken out of mothballs and sold to the Indonesians under their United States Joint Defense Aid Program. Now, the *'Kalki IV'*, formerly the *USS Plunger*, carried Indonesian crews, and joined their American counterparts as they transited the Ombar-Wetar Straits off Timor, undetected.

Indonesia's ongoing defense build-up had been of concern to him for some time. When he last examined the country's Order of Battle which listed Indonesia's military equipment, he had been shocked to discover that her forces had more than doubled during the past four years.

The Prime Minister had read that ALRI's Eastern Command had stationed a further four corvettes and ten Soviet *Osa* class missile patrol craft around Irian Jaya, and did not believe for one moment that this strategic repositioning of its naval forces was in any way related to the recent Free Papua Movement uprising in Indonesian New Guinea. The Indonesian Air Force, AURI, had mysteriously acquired a further squadron of F-22 Raptors and, according to intelligence reports, had planned to base these on Natuna Island prior to China's annexation of the island. His concern now was with the most recent Defense Intelligence Report, which confirmed that these aircraft would be stationed at the rehabilitated Kupang airstrip within tactical striking range of Australia's north.

The Australian leader feared that his country's inability to defend itself against the threat from the north might tempt its Asian neighbours to test their resolve. Since Federation, Australian leaders had argued that the country's fundamental security interests lay in maintaining its alliances with the United States and the British Commonwealth. He knew, as had those who had gone before him, that Australia's limited military resources could never withstand any serious attempt to attack, or even invade the country. Australia's four guided missile destroyers, eight guided missile frigates, six *Collins* class submarines and a handful of support ships would be no match against such superior forces.

Faced with growing regional instability, he was not entirely convinced that the United States would support either Indonesia or Australia should any confrontation develop between the two countries.

Australian intelligence sources had been unable to provide evidence that the Indonesian Military was actually responsible for the recent and provocative action directed against Australian interests in the Indonesian Republic. His Cabinet had supported the position of further discussion with Jakarta before seeking the support of the United States Government. He had known for some time that the Indonesian leadership was in danger of swinging further to the right, and understood the problems their President faced, with China's threatening posturing along Indonesia's northern and unprotected coastline. The Australian leader had been greatly disturbed by the growing number of reports of armed piracy along the sea-lanes, and the possibility that these were directed at further destabilising Indonesian-Australian relations.

The Prime Minister had been further concerned when Australian shipping reported incidents of Indonesian naval vessels deliberately interfering with their passage through recognized international shipping lanes. These provocative steps aimed at intimidating Australian business had resulted in reciprocal action being taken by Australian waterside workers against Indonesian shipping.

There had been further riots directed at the Australian Embassy in Jakarta, and business interests there had revealed that they had been threatened with sanctions should Australia continue to disregard Indonesia's claim over East Timor.

The Prime Minister decided that this was pure sabre-rattling in preparation for the forthcoming United Nations vote as to whether a UN-sponsored plebiscite should be held in the former Portuguese colony. He was aware that the motion might just have sufficient support to be passed. He had discussed this with his Foreign Minister, and both had agreed that the Indonesians were demonstrating their displeasure at the increased Australian public support for the annexed province's independence movement.

It appeared that both countries were being dragged uncontrollably towards a political abyss by an emerging, and more militant, Indonesian leadership.

'I warned you Jack, but you wouldn't listen,' the Opposition Leader accused. 'You played softball with those bastards and now they're going to run all over us.' He turned and snarled at the Foreign Minister. 'And Lord only knows what *you* have probably promised them.' He looked back at the Prime Minister, believing that had the roles been reversed, this situation would never have developed.

'Don't you think it's time that we showed the Australian people some real leadership?' he challenged, caustically, 'Don't you think they're scared out there?' he asked, rhetorically, pointing his stubby finger through the air.

'You're not on the floor of the House, now, Bill,' the Treasurer snorted, as he moved his seat backwards and forwards, playing with the swivel.

'You're bloody right, I'm not!' he barked, his temper rising to the bait. 'Jack, let's at least do something to show the Indonesians that we mean business,' he pleaded, frustrated by the inaction.

'We have warned Australian tourists of the dangers of travelling to Indonesia, particularly Bali,' the Attorney General advised. 'Short of restricting flights, there's very little we can do to prevent Australians continuing to travel into those areas.'

'Gentlemen, I wish to remind you that we have inherited some of this mess from our friend here's predecessors.' The Opposition Leader bristled.

'Not that old.....' but was cut off by the Defense Minister before he lost the floor.

'I believe that much of what we are experiencing has its roots further back than the Timor Shelf agreements.' He paused, and raised a sheet of paper from the table. 'The Indonesians have always been suspicious of our support in relation to the Timor question. It is difficult for an authoritarian regime such as theirs to understand that we do not, unfortunately, have the same controls over our press as they do in Indonesia. Every time something appears in our newspapers which offends Jakarta there is a backlash.

'The very fact that we provide material support to East Timorese refugees in our country is considered not on its humanitarian merits, but as a distinct move by Australia to provoke the Indonesians. Hell, if we can be objective, they have a reasonable case when you consider the number of refugees this country has accepted from East Timor. And,' he said, looking directly at the Opposition Leader, 'those bastards in Darwin have actually formed their own government in exile!'

'Surely no one takes Xanana Soares seriously?' someone asked.

'Serious enough for the Indonesian Ambassador to raise the issue during his last meeting with our Department,' the Foreign

JAKARTA

Minister claimed.

Almost without exception, those present wished that Gough Whitlam had taken the initiative in 1975 while still Prime Minister, and accepted Indonesia's urging to send troops into East Timor, or *Tim-Tim* as it later became known.

The current Prime Minister had been a young back-bencher at the time, and had called for Australia's intervention in Timor, citing East Timorese requests for Australian troops to be sent. He had not understood why Whitlam had procrastinated at the time; it could easily have been a *fait accompli* as both the Indonesians and the East Timorese supported an Australian presence.

When the Australian, New Zealand and British journalist teams from Australia's television Channels Seven and Nine were executed by Indonesian soldiers, he had been the first to shout 'shame' at the lack of leadership shown at the time. Looking back, he now realized that had Australia not bowed to American pressure, Timor could just as easily have become an Australian territory, providing the bridge into Asia that so many of his contemporaries had dreamed about over the years. Now, he knew, it was far too late.

'Look, gentlemen,' the Prime Minister intervened, 'what it all boils down to is whether or not we tell the Indonesians that we are prepared to take action over these attacks, and before we do that, is the Australian public prepared to suffer the consequences?' The Minister for Trade shook his head in disagreement.

'We currently enjoy a surplus in trade with Indonesia of approximately one billion dollars each year. That could disappear, or worse, our five billion dollars in trade with Indonesia might disappear altogether. We should all think very seriously about issuing any statement which might be perceived by Jakarta as a threat. They have nothing to lose.'

'Nothing to lose?' the overweight leader cried. 'What a load of crap! The bloody Indons sell us more than three billion dollars worth of product every year,' he challenged, throwing his arms wide as he did so. Prime Minister Evans sighed. He knew that they would not be able to agree on a joint statement which would satisfy everyone.

'This decision will not require a vote, gentlemen,' he said, 'but I do require your assurances that we are all in agreement that whatever message is sent to the Indonesians, it must appear to be representative of all the Australian people, and not just the voice of one political faction.' He turned to his opponent in the House. 'Bill?'

The Leader of the Opposition shook his head. 'I'd not be happy with anything less than a demand that they honour their agreements, and either provide protection to our rigs or permit our own defence forces to enter the disputed areas.' The Prime Minister thought about this then nodded.

'Okay, let's give it a shot,' he decided, ignoring the unhappy faces of his own Party members. His opponent did not bother to smile, knowing that in politics things were never what they seemed, and today's pact could just as easily become the basis for tomorrow's dispute.

'Prime Minister, will you be attending the reception being held at the Indonesian Embassy to mark their Independence Day celebrations? Ambassador Seda has suggested that it might be an opportunity to demonstrate to the people of both countries that our relationships are not as strained as the press would have everyone believe. Also, we might remember that reliable information would have it that he is slated for the Vice President's position when he returns to Jakarta.' It was the Foreign Minister who asked. His leader looked at the man in surprise, wondering how he had been lumbered with such an inadequate figure.

'No, I don't believe that we should demonstrate anything of the kind. In fact, I don't want any of my colleagues so much as showing their faces anywhere near the Indonesian Embassy until we see some response from them regarding the issues at hand.' Several of those present had received invitations, and would now have to explain to their wives that they would not be attending what had been promoted as the social event of the year for Canberra. The meeting came to a close and all but the Prime Minister and his Attorney General departed.

* * * * * *

'Why didn't you tell them about the Japanese H-3B missile venture?' the Attorney General asked.

'Shit, Doug,' Jack Evans snorted, 'then it wouldn't be a secret anymore, would it?' The other man shrugged his shoulders.

'What are we going to do about it?' he asked.

JAKARTA

'Do about it?' the leader repeated. 'Nothing,' he said, 'nothing at all.'

'Are you certain about this?' the Attorney General pressed, although he privately admitted that he wasn't confident that the information would not leak, even from his own department. The Prime Minister just shook his head.

'Doug, there isn't a goddamn thing we could do, even if we wanted to,' he said.

'What about telling the Americans what we know?' The information revealing the Japanese arrangements to jointly develop a military version of the H-3B had been obtained by ASIS agents operating in Indonesia, and they were yet to share this recent intelligence with their American counterparts.

'I would doubt if the Americans didn't already know and are keeping the information to themselves, as usual.' Then: 'Their own political interests no longer run in parallel with ours, Doug, you know that. Not that I am entirely certain they ever did,' he added.

'I'm very uneasy with regards to their lack of open support for Australia on the Indonesian issue. Do you really believe that they would still come to our defence if we were confronted with the possibility of an Indonesian attack?' he asked, suspecting that they would not.

'Their interests have changed. Nothing's been the same since the Soviet collapse. But look on the brighter side, Jack,' the Attorney General said light-heartedly, 'if all else fails and our economy takes another slide, we could probably ask the Americans for Most Favoured Nation status.' The Australian leader attempted a smile in response, but instead frowned at the prospect of going to the voters with the economy stagnating as it had throughout his government's term in office. Unemployment had reached twelve percent, and the Australian dollar had fallen to new lows, just below the Singapore dollar.

'What do you think the Indonesians are really up to, Doug?' he asked. The politician thought that the Prime Minister looked exhausted. None of them had enjoyed a full night's rest for months.

'Well, I would have to agree with Anderson's conclusions.' He knew that Jack Evans, as had earlier Prime Ministers, trusted this man's opinions even more than those in his Cabinet. Anderson had served successive administrations loyally through the years, and yet, his was one of the least known faces amongst the multitude of Canberra bureaucrats.

Although well past mandatory retirement, Anderson still headed the Australian Secret Intelligence Service and reported directly to the Attorney General. 'He's worried, and with good cause, that Indonesia might start to fragment and break up. Anderson supports the position that ASEAN, as a geopolitical block, has failed miserably. Now that three of the member nations have withdrawn and entered into their own agreements with India and China, the original concept of a ten-nation trade block has required considerable review. As for the sea-lane dispute, well,' he paused, scratching the side of his head, 'Indonesia's attempt to police international oil shipping through its sea-lanes has been condemned even by some of its ASEAN partners.'

'And rightly so,' Evans interrupted.

'There had always been a certain amount of smugness around the Jakarta camp in the past, with relation to China's relative distance from their country, or at least that was the situation until Beijing annexed Natuna Island. The Indonesians had always intended that ASEAN represent not just a trade bloc against Chinese economic expansion, but also a buffer against any military threat. Indonesia viewed those ASEAN partners which shared borders with China as a long-term military barrier, but failed to recognize the possibility that these smaller countries with struggling economies, could just as easily become perfect satellites for China's ultimate expansion. As for Indonesia's domestic problems, these have been exacerbated by the ongoing corruption and cronyism apparent throughout all levels of government. Half of the main arterial roads now have tolls, and these are owned, predictably enough, by the President's family.'

'But that has never been a problem before,' the Prime Minister suggested, 'at most, whenever these stories appeared in the international press there was little evidence that the Indonesian people would not continue to accept the status quo.'

'Sure, but only because the government introduced those brutal riot squads we saw hitting the streets during the last demonstrations, and the controls exercised over what may or may not be placed in print. Their greed, unbelievably, has exceeded even that of their predecessors. Latest reports indicate that the First Family is even considering assuming monopoly control over all rice production. Do you remember when Tommy Suharto grabbed the Indonesian clove industry, throwing it into chaos? In the end, the farmers' own co-operative had to bail the President's son out of his half a billion dollar fiasco, and at their own expense. It's a disgrace; but one that has continued ever since Soekarno lost power to the so called New Order.'

'Anderson suggests that the Javanese are slowly losing control,' he continued, 'and are over-compensating by encouraging a swing to the more radical fundamentalist Moslem groups. This is not the first time in the country's history the Jakarta establishment has been challenged by minority groups.' He rested, swallowed from the glass which had been placed there before the meeting had commenced, then looked at his political associate.

'The way I see it, Jack, the Indonesians are confused by what is happening, particularly China's threatening naval build-up to their north. They, like us, are heavily outnumbered by the Chinese. Now that they are being squeezed by their giant neighbour, there may just be sufficient paranoia floating around Jakarta for their leadership to misconstrue Australia's motives in relation to the Timor issue. Their disappointment over losing Natuna Island is obvious, however the lack of international support, particularly from the Americans, came as quite a shock.' He uncrossed his legs and leaned back in the leather chair to stretch.

'The Indonesians were naïve to believe that the Americans would do more than shake their fists at China. US investment in both countries is impressive, but at the end of the day, China is more important to them. Even the Brits have been able to take advantage of the sea-lane disputes. Most of China's oil is still being carried through Indonesian waters by British ships. God, Jack,' he said, shaking his head in admiration, 'it's a little like Vietnam all over again, only on a much grander scale.'

The Prime Minister knew that the Attorney General was referring to another time when British ships entered North Vietnamese harbours, providing materials and supplies to the Communists, while Australian and other allied troops fought against the very same people being supplied by their Commonwealth partner. It was about that time, he remembered, that he learned the true meaning of political expediency. He listened as his knowledgeable associate continued.

'Beijing has been very clever. First, they demonstrated to the world that they are good guys by permitting Hong Kong to continue, virtually as it did prior to the British hand-over. Remember, Jack, we discussed this at the time? It was obvious, even then, that China would permit business to continue as usual, but only until such time as it managed to snare Taiwan as well. Hell, who wouldn't? Taiwan's reserves are double those of Japan and still growing. They must be really pissed off that they still haven't been able to take Taiwan. But given time, I'm sure they will.'

'Do you think the Indonesians believe that China might start chipping away at their more isolated provinces?' Evans asked.

'Now wouldn't that be something?' he replied. 'We sit here worrying that the Indons might invade Australia, and they sit up there worrying that the Chinese will do the same to them. Yes, I believe that Jakarta is more than a little paranoid concerning China, and rightly so. After all, they did swoop down and knock off their Natuna gas fields.' He then thought for a moment.

'It's quite possible that the Indonesians are going to do exactly that to us in the North-west, Jack,' he said, solemnly. 'They might not be that naïve after all. Let's assume that they believe it possible to take control over all the Timor Shelf production and extraction. We certainly could not prevent them to any great degree. A handful of *Collins* class submarines won't go a hell of a long way against the Indonesian fleet. What if the Indonesians already believe that they might have tacit approval from the Americans to do so? After all, the States did little when the Chinese took Natuna, and maybe Jakarta believes that the precedent will continue, only this time it will be in their favour.'

'It might be an opportune time for a quick visit to Washington.'

'Don't know how much that would achieve right now, Jack, but I guess you could give it a try.' The Attorney-General rose and walked around to restore circulation in his legs.

'If they agree, why don't we hit them with the H-3B developments at the same time? It has to be obvious to them as well that the Indonesians and Japanese will soon have their own missile delivery systems. Then, of course, it won't be too long before they'll have their first reactors on line in Bali and Java. Before you know it, Jack, the bastards will be nuclear armed with a Japanese-sponsored delivery system.' The Prime Minister nodded. They had been through this before with the Chiefs-of-Staff at Defence. All present had agreed that it would be unwise to panic the Australian public further. The Prime Minister had taken it upon himself not to reveal the information to the rest of his Cabinet colleagues. He would do so, however, when he considered it more appropriate.

'I'll sleep on it, Doug,' he said, wearily, rising to his feet slowly, 'given the chance.'

Both men smiled. They had been surviving on less than a few hours each night since the trouble had started. The Attorney-General left a few minutes later and returned to his own office, leaving his old friend alone to decide in which direction he should move, to counter the Indonesian threat.

* * * * * *

Coleman and the ASIS Chief had talked throughout the day, breaking only for a light meal.

Anderson had produced convincing evidence proving that Seda was involved in a most dangerous game, one he apparently played successfully for more than three decades. Seda's secret agenda had never been detected by his fellow generals or any of the others who had worked side by side with him. Slowly, step by step, Anderson laid the whole picture out before the disbelieving Coleman. Much of the earlier information he already knew, as this had been the core of their discussions some years before when the intelligence chief had provided the most amazing detail of Seda's bold initiatives for East Timor.

Coleman also remembered at that time he had been given an ultimatum, which he had unwisely ignored. In retrospect, had he listened and co-operated when the demand had been made then maybe, just maybe, he would have come out of the whole mess in much better financial shape. Still, he thought, as he listened to the detailed exposition from the well-informed bureaucrat, he had not done too badly. At least, up to now.

Twice Anderson made the point that Coleman was fortunate to have left Indonesia when he had, as it was most likely that he would have been killed by General Seda had he obstinately remained.

'Seda couldn't afford to have you eliminated until he was certain that you had not left any incriminating evidence behind somewhere. Seda was reasonably confident that you hadn't, but he was not quite ready to take that risk. His world was disintegrating, what with the failed uprising in Timor and the seizure of most of the weaponry which had been stockpiled across on Pulau Kambing. You had been party to those shipments, Stephen,' Anderson had said, almost accusingly. Coleman was then surprised when Anderson revealed that ASIS had actually made attempts on General Seda's life and, on both occasions, had failed.

'There must be a number of agents who could do the job for you without the necessity for all of this,' Coleman said, waving his arm around the maximum security cells buried below the Department of Defence, where he had been held incognito by Anderson's security. Stephen Coleman had been picked up in Hong Kong by an ASIS team and flown back to Australia. He had not been given the opportunity to call his lawyer; that recourse, he knew, would not be made available to him. It went with the territory. Even for former agents. Stephen did not need to be reminded that, having signed the Official Secrets Act, he had forgone all rights to be treated as an ordinary citizen.

Anderson looked at the man whom he had once considered one of the best in the business. Coleman had not aged well. He had gained weight, his hair had thinned, and there were obvious signs that he had given the booze a bashing over the years. The intelligence chief tried to recall how long it had been since he had first recruited Stephen. It was difficult to believe that the man before him now could have been the same young, enthusiastic agent, of some twenty-five years before. Anderson tried to recall how long it had been since they had last met; he knew it had to be almost five years, but looking at his former protégé, he had difficulty accepting this. He thought about Stephen's question as to why he had not selected one of his other agents for the task before them.

'Firstly, none of our current operatives are as familiar with Seda's voice as you are. This is essential to the timing of the detonation. We don't want others being exposed, and need to contain the effect to minimise casualties. Your responsibility is to detonate the small charge once you identify his voice. We'll talk more about the operational side later.' He then paused, examining Stephen's almost blank expression. 'Another reason why we have decided not to use current agents is that, frankly speaking Stephen, operatives today just don't seem to have the same commitment anymore. Not that you were particularly outstanding in that area yourself in later years,' Anderson suggested, referring to Coleman's sudden exit from the Service years before. 'Also,' he added, 'we would never be sure that we could guarantee their silence.' Coleman's face immediately turned to stone. Anderson moved quickly to calm his fears.

'Obviously, Stephen, you'll be taken care of in the appropriate manner. You will need to disappear as you have done before except, this time, we will provide you with reasonable cover. That would be another identity, and travel documents should it become necessary.' He hesitated, then continued. 'I personally don't believe it will come to that. You don't need funds, from what I hear, so you will just have to be satisfied that we will consider your slate as being wiped clean, after which we will thank you quietly for your participation, and ask that you go back to whatever you were doing before this bloody mess required our intervention. Okay?'

It took a further two meetings before Coleman finally agreed to accept the assignment. Coleman had remained stubbornly adamant that he would not be Seda's executioner until Anderson, in desperation, lied, suggesting that the woman Stephen had loved, and lost, so many years before in Bali, had actually died as a result of an attempt by Seda on Stephen's life gone wrong. This was enough. Coleman had then agreed to participate in the deadly sanction against the Indonesian Ambassador.

* * * * * *

Indonesian Embassy, Canberra
17 August — Indonesian Independence Day

Ambassador Seda was not entirely displeased with the news report in the so-called objective press. He had become used to such biased reporting very early in his career.

He sat drinking his coffee while skimming through the pages, stopping to read only those articles which commented on his address to the Press Club luncheon. Some of the stories were inaccurate and slightly derogatory, several exaggerated the answers he had given in response to questions on Timor even suggesting that he had responded with an air of arrogance. Seda was not irritated by the remark. He had deliberately answered in provocative fashion, hoping to ruffle the feathers of the press.

As it turned out, the result was positive and in no way did he consider any of the articles to be detrimental to his real cause. As he expected, the majority of the stories came out in support of a United Nations resolution to provide the people of Timor-Timur with the opportunity to vote on the question of Indonesia's annexation and their right to self-determination.

He was pleased that most editorial comment challenged the Government of Australia over the Indonesian Government's refusal to withdraw from the former colony. This was the result he had set out to achieve, to prime the Australian public and prepare them mentally for the next frightening events so that their future response would lead to more than just feelings of indignation towards the Indonesian people.

Seda's plans called for a much stronger response. One which would drag both countries to the brink of outright war well before Indonesia had finally developed its own nuclear capability. His years of planning for an independent nation would finally become a reality. And he would be its leader. With these ambitious thoughts foremost in his mind, he went about his duties, anxious for the evening's festivities to commence.

* * * * * *

Umar Suharjo was satisfied that the van would be safe parked hard up against the sliding door which led into the armoury. He had set about rebuilding the room adjacent to the Embassy's registry immediately upon his taking up post as the Indonesian Embassy Security Attaché. His diplomatic status had provided the means for him to move equipment and weapons in and out of Australia, without question. During the four months since his arrival in Canberra, he had completed the tasks given him by Seda, and he now waited eagerly for the signal to proceed.

The specially designed and rebuilt van was ready. Inside, Umar had stacked layer upon layer of plastic lined bags filled with ammonium nitrate around an open drum of diesel oil. Before the van was moved, he planned to re-attach the container's lid for the relatively short journey planned. The Australian Parliament was a few kilometers from where the van now stood in readiness, its deadly cargo including a number of hydrogen canisters which Umar intended would act as a 'kicker' to increase the impact of the bomb. He knew that the extra ingredient would give the explosives far more cutting power allowing it to cut through the Australian Parliament's thick walls.

While other members of the staff prepared to assemble in the foyer, Umar re-entered the chancery and slipped surreptitiously through the registry. He crossed the room and unlocked the armoury access door. Umar wished to check that the surplus containers of pentaerythoritol tetranitrate (PETN) stored there would not block his access from outside, and that the double-locks had engaged when he had closed the sliding door earlier. Satisfied that all was in order, he re-locked the armoury and went upstairs to check that the Ambassador's private rooms were still secure; and to check on Seda's earlier guest who had been left upstairs, alone.

* * * * * *

Chalmers raised his binoculars again and refocused, noting that there was still nothing unusual happening in the former Soviet residence. He then returned his attention to the Indonesian Embassy, impressed with the lighting display. He logged the time, then concentrated once again on the safe-house occupied by Stephen Coleman.

* * * * * *

Umar observed that the visitor had left when he arrived at Seda's rooms. He completed his security check and, noticing the elegant briefcase left there earlier by the Ambassador's visitor, he picked it up and was immediately surprised at its weight. The leather briefcase was much heavier than he had expected. He examined it for a few moments and, unable to ascertain what it contained, decided that he would lock it away until he had either located the missing visitor or had discussed the situation with Seda.

Umar Suharjo mumbled *'sialan'* as he caught his knee on the side of the desk.

Back in his room at the safe-house, Stephen Coleman was waiting for the sound of a voice - Seda's voice. On hearing Umar cry out in pain as he struck his knee, Stephen panicked and his sweaty hands squeezed the small, luminous button, sending the dedicated frequency transmission through the airwaves.

Coleman tensed. He waited for the distant explosion.

Nothing happened. He tried again, Another malfunction! A feeling of incredible disbelief swept over him and he slammed this fist hard down on the table accidentally knocking the remote control to the floor. He cursed as he had never cursed before.

Coleman pulled the heavy curtains back angrily and stared across at the brilliantly lit building surrounded by hundreds of limousines belonging to the elite of Canberra's society enjoying themselves inside. Waves of disappointment flooded through his tired body, and he kicked angrily at the broken mechanism lying on the floor.

They had failed!

* * * * * *

Umar rode the lift down to the lobby and, wishing to avoid the multitude of guests now crowding every corner of the Residence and Embassy gardens, he slipped unnoticed into the empty registry. He looked around and, identifying the switch he sought, turned the lights on in the adjacent room. Inside, he could hear the guests clapping as the Indonesian melody came to an end. Outside, in the magnificently decorated garden, most of one thousand guests clapped as the Indonesian Ambassador, General (retired) Nathan Seda, stood in front of the military band and raised his hands over his head, clenching them together in appreciation. The conductor then waited, his body half-turned observing his Ambassador, poised for the signal.

As the General nodded, the baton waved delicately in the air, and immediately the handsome Menadonese drummer commenced his roll calling all present to attention. The guests rose to their feet as the band started the Indonesian national anthem.

Umar moved to open the metal doors leading to the arsenal of weapons hidden there. He nonchalantly dropped the briefcase containing the plastique explosive casually into the corner.

The sensitive mechanism, which was unable to receive the earlier signal, immediately reacted to this excessively rough handling. As the deadly package hit the floor an eight-centimetre detonator activated causing the highly brisant RDX plastique to explode. The primary and secondary explosions came within a milli-second of each other as the C-4 exploded, firstly with the surplus containers of PETN, and then directly through the walls into the remaining pentaerythoritol tetranitrate which had been prepared inside the van to detonate the packed ammonium nitrate after the vehicle was later positioned under the nation's Parliament.

The first shock-wave pushed through into the parked truck and ignited its deadly cargo activating all of the contributing components which would rock the political world.

The first to die was Umar.

In that moment, an enormous burst of energy erupted through the assembly, turning the entire area into one massive fireball of destruction.

Figures danced momentarily before disintegrating into heaps of lifeless flesh and bone. The roar had ripped through the guests, hurling musical instruments into the maelstrom of human carnage, decapitating a bandsman. Then, for an immeasurable moment, there was silence.

A shrill cry pierced the quiet, then a cacophony of screams emphasized the full horror of the blasts. And amongst it all, General Nathan Seda, Ambassador Extraordinary and Plenipotentiary, future Vice President of Indonesia, lay dead.

* * * * * *

Chalmers lifted himself back off the floor, checking as he did so for injuries. Still suffering from shock, he sat, disorientated, wondering what in the hell had happened. Then he remembered, and moved clumsily towards his viewing station.

At first, he was unaware that the window had disappeared, destroyed by the thunderous blast which had ripped through the suburb of Yarralumla. He could smell the acrid smoke in the air and fumbled to focus his binoculars on the scene. He was overawed by the spectacle which greeted him. Chalmer's face felt wet, and he wiped it, unconsciously, with the back of his sleeve. In the dark, he could not see that this was blood, the result of splintered glass which had showered his body when the window had imploded.

Engrossed in the spectacle across the street, Chalmers almost missed the car as it pulled up outside Coleman's address. He had heard the horn, and it was only by chance that he noticed the sedan's arrival. Still suffering from slight concussion, Chalmers turned his attention back to the safe-house and readjusted the binoculars.

When he saw Coleman hurry from the house, he realized that he had been caught, flat-footed. He searched around his darkened room, found the pair of night-glasses, and rushed down to his own vehicle. He gave the sedan a cursory inspection for damage, then drove away in pursuit of the *Ford Taurus Ghia*, and the man he had been instructed to keep under surveillance.

* * * * * *

Director Anderson glanced at the rear-vision mirror once more before steering the Ford into the steady stream of traffic. He drove carefully, not wishing to attract attention.

'Is he dead?' the ASIS chief asked Coleman. Occasional shadows flashed across Stephen Coleman's face as he sat, silently, still suffering shock at the extent of the explosion. Nobody could have survived that blast, he thought.

'Yes,' was all he said. There was no point in explaining that the detonation had not taken place as planned; he knew that all Anderson would be interested in was whether Seda had been killed. Coleman wanted to scream out loudly but could not. He felt entirely drained of all energy.

They drove on in silence, Anderson back-tracking several times as he continued to guard against being followed. And compromised. Finally, they pulled into the Government forrestry reserve amongst the pines. In the distance they could see the blaze which continued to burn around what was once the Indonesian Embassy. They sat in silence, observing the extent of the bomb's destructive power. Smoke billowed into the sky, and the warning sirens of fire engines and other emergency services filled the night.

JAKARTA

Anderson placed his gloved hand on Stephen Coleman's, who continued to stare at the horrific scene believing he was responsible. Suddenly, the moon broke loose through cloud and cast an eerie glow of its own across the smoke-filled sky.

Anderson's hands moved again, lifting the cold, steel barrel to within touch of Coleman's head. In the moment that Stephen Coleman's eyes registered shock at the betrayal, Anderson squeezed the trigger gently, and a bullet burst from the handgun.

* * * * * *

'Mother of God!' Chalmers uttered, automatically crossing himself with one free hand. He remained crouched off the side of the road, and waited. The agent had been fortunate to observe his quarry's car doubling back to avoid being followed. This had given him the opportunity to follow, which he did, maintaining surveillance at a safe distance.

Chalmers had driven after Coleman, pulling back from time to time to avoid detection. When the Ford had taken the observation point road, he pulled back even further, permitting those in front to believe that they were not in any danger of discovery. At the top of the hill, Chalmers parked his car to the side of the road, and covered the remaining distance on foot.

Coleman and another man seemed content to remain sitting in their vehicle, watching the fireworks below. He moved closer, hoping to identify who the driver might be. Then, without any warning, he heard the shot, and caught the brief flash as Coleman's head snapped to one side.

He watched the unfamiliar figure move away from the scene. Chalmers waited until certain that Anderson would not return, then slipped through the darkness, over to where the other car was parked. There, he discovered the body of Stephen Coleman, as it lay slumped forward in the front, a bullet hole evident in the side of his head.

KERRY B. COLLISON

Chapter 19

Japan — Jakarta — Robson

Prime Minister Hirohuki Hata accepted the rebuke with an outward display of calm, while inwardly his inner emotions ripped at his vitals as surely as any traditional *sepuku* sword might have done.

He knew he would have to resign. There could be no other choice. Should the photographs be displayed publicly in the press, his family's shame would be intolerable. Hirohuki Hata continued to look down at the floor, the burden of his family's disgrace almost too great. Slowly, he forced his eyes back to the table where the damning evidence lay spread, as if challenging Hata to examine their content again. The selection of black and white photographs all too graphically displayed his brother-in-law's deviant sexual behaviour.

The Prime Minister could not be certain of who had been responsible for capturing his wife's younger brother in these compromising situations. The evidence had been sent to his Coalition partner, Aki-san. Hirohuki Hata had granted the woman the private interview she had requested, during which Aki-san had handed him the opened contents, then waited for his response.

He might have been able to live with the shame of his brother-in-law's disgusting acts, but Hata knew there was no chance he would survive any disclosure of his government's involvement in the H-3B rocket Research and Development center in Bandung, Indonesia. A brief summary of the secret installation's objectives had been attached to the photographs.

He had been requested to provide an undertaking to his coalition partner, Aki-san, that the project would be discontinued immediately, failing which, she had threatened to go public with the entire contents contained in the damaging dispatch. His career had been ruined, and with that, Japan's future role as a military power had been reduced to one of continuing subservience to others.

* * * * * *

In the weeks following Ambassador Seda's death, the Japanese Government announced that, due to domestic economic considerations and as a result of reviewing its own development needs, Japanese involvement in the construction and funding of nuclear power plants outside of Japan had been temporarily halted. No further information was made available to the press. Prime Minister Hiroyuki Hata resigned, and the coalition went to the polls under a cloud of accusations of being expansionist, and lost the election.

This outcome, coupled with the believable rumours which had passed through the halls of the Japanese Diet, caused the *Rama II* project to falter. Several months were to pass before the newly elected Japanese leader learned of his former opponent's clandestine redirection of government funds, which had been used to finance the ongoing development of a military version of the Japanese H-3B missile. All dialogue with the Indonesian President, the Bandung Research and Development Centre and the Japanese Government, in relation to the production of a prototype delivery system, was discontinued. Japan immediately repatriated its scientists and engineers, destroying whatever technology was left behind.

* * * * * *

Indonesia

The Indonesian President had signed the decree appointing his son-in-law, Major General Sujono Diryo, as the new Chairman of PEPELIN, simultaneous with the announcement of Seda's selection as Ambassador to Australia, some months prior to the former general's departure for Canberra.

Within hours of the Palace press release, Sujono's office had been inundated with requests for interviews, and official appointments. Amongst these was a petition from the company president responsible for the future supplies of uranium ore from Australia,

JAKARTA

Graeme Robson. When news of Seda's death reached Indonesia, mourning was brief. The powerful general's sudden demise had created unbelievable opportunities for others.

* * * * * *

'I am in a position to offer financing, as well,' Robson had suggested. He was pleased so far with the way negotiations were proceeding. Not unlike the rest of the community involved with the construction and development of the nuclear power plants, Robson had been more than a little nervous when the President's son-in-law was appointed to the influential position. Seda's appointment to Canberra had come as some surprise to the investment community, but his death had been an even greater shock.

'How long would it be before construction could re-commence?' Sujono asked, knowing that the President was most anxious to restore the *Rama II* project's schedule as quickly as feasibly possible. The Japanese had left his country in a difficult situation. Having withdrawn from the fast breeder plant joint venture, Sujono's first major task as Chairman had been to secure a replacement partner. Following Seda's death, Sujono found himself floundering in a sea of intrigue and financial disaster.

It seemed that everywhere he turned for support to locate a substitute investor to replace the Japanese, doors remained closed. He was not to know that the United States Government had moved quickly, undermining any overtures made by the Indonesian PEPELIN Chairman for finance and technical expertise which might result in the resurrection of the *Rama II* project. General Sujono soon became desperate, concerned that the President might have him removed from the powerful position.

Robson's approach had been most fortuitous. Not only was the man's group already involved in the downstream provision of uranium ore, he had totally committed his group to the completion of the *Rama II* project. It would seem to Sujono, that in the absence of other contenders, he would have little other choice but to deal with the Robson *kongsi*.

'*Why are you using Russian technology to complete the plant. Surely it would be more prudent to engage another Japanese firm, having started with their engineers?*' Sujono asked.

325

'*Pak* Sujono,' Robson continued in English, wishing he was more fluent in *Bahasa Indonesia*, 'we canvassed the Japanese engineering and power firms. Seems that their government has placed an unofficial ban on working outside Japan for the immediate future. We also tried the French and British, but they too don't seem overly anxious to pick up from where the Japanese left off. Also, we spoke to the Canadian and American firms, but it seems that they would only be interested in participating if the IAEA were given inspection rights upon completion. That left us with the Russians. There is nothing wrong with their technology, *Pak* Sujono,' Robson argued. In fact, he had little experience in the field, viewing the project entirely for the profits it would generate and the subsequent political gain he expected to enjoy from his involvement.

'Are you certain that the Russians will be able to re-commence quickly and complete the project within the original schedule?' asked Sujono sceptically. It had been several months since any real work had been carried out at the Mt Muria site.

'I guarantee it, *Pak*,' Robson replied. He was desperate to secure the contract. This would be the first major negotiation he had concluded without his corporate consultants' participation. When word spread, he knew that none would believe he had managed to put this deal together by himself. Graeme was reasonably astute, but even he admitted that without his late father's substantial wealth to support his ventures in Indonesia, and Murray Stephenson's considerable contributions of time and advice during his first years in Jakarta, he might still be living off a monthly remittance in a remote village somewhere.

'And you agree that your company will, in no way, have any role in the management and ongoing operation once the project has been completed?' the PEPELIN Chairman asked, again. Unlike the other nuclear plants which had been tied to the principles of Build, Operate, and Transfer, *Rama II*, in the interests of secrecy, would not be managed by any other than an Indonesian military board. All technicians involved in the day-to-day running of the nuclear plant would be Indonesians selected by Sujono for their trustworthiness and, of course, technical skills.

'The Russians will continue with whatever training programmes are needed. You will also be required to establish who, amongst the Indonesian technicians, should be sent for training overseas as soon as practical, *Pak*,' Robson suggested.

'*And your company is quite comfortable with the financing package we have requested?*' Sujono enquired, quite surprised that the funding had not really been an issue with this consortium.

'We will fund the project, as agreed, *Pak* Sujono. Our bankers will provide whatever finance is required based on our involvement, and they have offered us terms based on our capacity to repay within twelve months from completion of the turn-key project.' Robson was excited, and had difficulty hiding his eagerness.

He would, as already agreed, pledge his group assets and future cash flows to the foreign banks, and they would provide the balance of the funding required to complete the entire project. There had been no other way to arrange the complicated financing package, primarily because the completed plant could not be offered as security for the bridging loan. The Japanese had already expended more than half of the estimated completion cost, and had agreed to a government-to-government, thirty-year soft-loan package covering repayment of their investment up to when they withdrew.

Robson needed to find close to one billion dollars to complete the project. The syndicated bank loan would provide these funds on the basis that repayment would occur within three years or twelve months after construction had been completed and the plant commissioned, whichever of these events came first. Robson had, as majority shareholder in the company founded by his father, pledged future cash-flows generated in Australia and Indonesia, primarily from coal and uranium ore sales

He believed he understood the risks and, although there had been considerable opposition within his own corporate management, Robson had insisted on assuming the project's debt. He firmly believed that there was no way the project could fail. His executives had expressed concern regarding the company's exposure during the construction period. This remained a problem as none of the major insurance firms were interested, deterred by the project's history and location.

'*There is another matter that needs to be discussed,*' Sujono suggested. He had BAKIN investigate Robson well before inviting him back for the second round of discussions. The intelligence agency had reported on the Australian's commercial activities. There was no doubt in Sujono's mind that Robson would have, somewhere along the line while conducting business in Indonesia, paid the necessary dues for whatever licences he had acquired. Robson had expected to be approached by an intermediary, and was surprised that the Chairman had gone directly to the heart of the matter, himself.

'I believe I understand already, *Pak* Sujono,' Robson said. 'As my group will be directly responsible for all materials and equipment supply, we would be most indebted for any assistance you might offer to facilitate the implementation of our contract.' He then waited for a response, having opened the door for the Chairman.

'*As you know, I speak for others, Mas Graeme,*' Sujono lied, assuming, correctly that Robson would believe this to be true, considering Sujono's Palace connections. '*There will be a consideration set aside for those who will provide the final authorisation for your group to proceed.*' He was pleased to see that Robson nodded, affirmatively.

'*Pak* Sujono,' Robson interrupted, knowing how difficult these moments could be. He had been present when Murray Stephenson negotiated the coal contracts for his father's company some years before. In those days, he remembered, payments were broken down into a number of isolated arrangements, and the percentages were nowhere near as crippling as they had become in the current business climate.

'The bankers have set aside a fund of five per cent, based on the remaining construction expenditures.' He then waited for a response, watching as Sujono's brain switched into high gear, calculating how much this might represent.

It was a formidable amount, Robson knew, but one which was necessary if he were to secure the contract. It made little difference, as this figure would simply be added to the project's final cost, included as some fictitious consultant's fee, and the Indonesian Government would end up paying the graft themselves. This was how business was done in the country, and Robson knew that every company operating in the Republic would have, at one time or another, participated in making such provision for senior government officials.

During the initial construction stage, and while the Japanese had still been in control of the overall project, Robson had already negotiated an arrangement with Sujono's predecessor, the late

Nathan Seda. Cement, reinforcing-steel for concrete, and a substantial percentage of other materials had been directed through Robson's offshore corporate structure to facilitate payments to the PEPELIN Chairman and, if what he said could be believed, the First Family. Robson knew that Seda's manipulations had put the powerful Salima shareholders offside; however, in his mind, the substantial profits generated by the relationship had compensated for any downside or political fallout.

'I believe that the fee you suggested is too low, Mas,' Sujono implied. 'I am confident that you would be appointed as the project's contractor if I could report that the consideration was, say, ten per cent?' Robson listened to the influential general, taking his time to ensure that he had understood exactly what the man had said in his native tongue.

Major General Sujono Diryo was not a greedy man. He had expected Robson to have understood that this figure was the standard rate for such a project. He observed the foreigner for a few moments, deciding from the uncomfortable look on the man's unhappy face that he might have gone too far.

'I'm sure we can handle that, *Pak* Sujono,' Robson unhappily agreed. The general showed no reaction to Robson's acceptance to pay what would most probably amount to more than one hundred million dollars. 'If you would provide me with the details, I will make the necessary arrangements,' Robson advised. He knew that these would most probably be given the same day contracts were signed, and the project officially awarded.

Satisfied that their undertakings were clear to each other, they parted company. Robson raced back to his office, barely unable to restrain his excitement, confident that his group had secured the nuclear energy and desalinisation plant's construction project. Upon arriving at his office along Jalan Jenderal Sudirman, Graeme Robson phoned his bankers immediately, and arranged to meet with them in Singapore the following day. He then instructed his secretary to warn his personal pilot of his departure details. He phoned through to Singapore to instruct John Georgio to arrange something special for his visit, as he wished to ensure that his bankers enjoyed the pleasures Graeme knew Georgio would be able to provide, even at such short notice.

When Sujono reported his decision to award the contract to Robson's group, and that he had received an undertaking that *Rama*

II would be completed on schedule, the President had reacted most favourably. Sujono informed his father-in-law also, that he had arranged for a small consultancy fee to be paid into the family coffers.

The President approved of Sujono's actions, although he was somewhat disappointed when he discovered the size of the fee. He then suggested that Sujono have the five per cent paid directly into the dedicated account in Switzerland. Sujono politely agreed, and contracts for *Rama II* were prepared and executed within the month. Less than six weeks were to pass before Major General Sujono Diryo also secured an undertaking from the President of Iraq, to provide the advanced rocket technology they had been given by their supporters in Beijing. Ironically, before the end of that year, the Bandung Research and Development Centre had secured plans through their Moslem brothers in the Middle East, which would permit them to duplicate an advanced version of the Red Chinese three-stage rocket Beijing affectionately referred to as *The Long March* missile.

* * * * * *

Australia — Ulladulla Harbour, New South Wales

Few amongst the local fisherman paid much heed to the trawler as it prepared to leave the jetty. Most crews from the Ulladulla trawling fleet had already returned to their homes, those remaining went about finishing off outstanding chores in preparation for the following day.

The small ship's engines throbbed as the captain idled back, checking his instrumentation one final time as he prepared to leave. Satisfied that all was in order, he nodded to another man who then released the thick ropes restraining the trawler, and jumped on board as the ship moved slowly away from the jetty and headed out to sea.

The two-man crew navigated north, towards Sydney, their course taking them directly past the state capital, and further along the coastline where they would take on fuel and supplies before continuing on to Queensland's Great Barrier Reef. There, in the

JAKARTA

Whitsunday Islands, they would alter course and sail for Port Moresby in New Guinea where, for the second time, they would replenish their fuel and food stores before heading off to Guam. Once in the safety of the American territory, they would off-load their precious cargo then sail on to the Philippines, where they would remain for several months before returning to Australia.

Neither of the two men were at all concerned that they had not caught any fish; the vessel belonged to the American Government, and both sailors were experienced field agents belonging to the United States Central Intelligence Agency.

* * * * * *

Darwin

Xanana Soares slapped at the bothersome flies, then scratched his head. It was hot. Even hotter than Dili, he remembered. He looked at his visitor and wondered how much longer he must wait before the Indian Government advanced further funds in support of his government in exile.

Otelo Ramalho had arranged their first meeting. Xanana recalled his surprise at the time, as his people had never expected assistance from this quarter. And, he remembered, it had been most timely. Support for their cause had dwindled as most nations accepted the reality of Indonesia's occupation of his country, East Timor.

'You will be able to travel, then?' his visitor asked. Xanana nodded.

'I have asked the authorities for a passport, and it seems that this will not be a problem,' he replied. Xanana Soares was not ungrateful to the Australian people for the sanctuary provided to him and the many thousands of his fellow refugees. He had not been amongst the first to flee the island, electing to remain and fight against the Indonesian troops which had crossed into his country some thirty years before, towards the end of 1975, and occupied the former Portuguese colony. It was not until the Indonesians officially annexed his country that Xanana and his comrades realized that they had been betrayed by the Portuguese Government.

Formerly known as the Timor Social Democratic Association,

the Party's charter, and name was now the East Timor Liberation Front, and under this banner Xanana and his colleagues prepared a programme to build the new nation. They had waited for more than a year before their reformed party, Fretelin, declared East Timor an independent nation. Nine days later, on the seventh of December, 1975 Indonesia had invaded his country. Although the United Nations called on Indonesia to withdraw its armed forces from Timor, the toothless tiger's demands were ignored.

Xanana remembered the bloody fighting and the years of terror which followed. At first, his resistance movement managed to hold its own against the much greater forces, their spirits lifting with each call of the United Nations for Indonesia to withdraw; but the Indonesian troops had remained, and Jakarta had sent its planes, provided by the American Government, to rain death upon the Timorese villages. Then, as Xanana and the others fled into the mountains to regroup, leaving thousands of their dead behind, the Indonesian Government initiated a campaign of terror against his people.

His restless nights were still occupied with dreams of times of unimaginable terror; of times when entire villages had been destroyed and tens of thousands of simple farmers annihilated by the brutal, invading forces; of times when Indonesian soldiers rounded up innocent, frightened children, and forced girls who had not yet entered puberty into prostitution to service the hungry soldiers. Branded rebels and separatists, Xanana and his freedom fighters continued to wage war on the invaders.

Jakarta responded by initiating a forced sterilisation programme thoughout the villages. But the worst was yet to come. Determined to eradicate all signs of resistance, and provide an embarrassed world the opportunity to move on, the United States Government arranged for the delivery of sixteen A-4 counter insurgency bombers to be delivered to Jakarta. These, along with the Bronco OV-10 jets, accounted for the deaths of thousands of innocent women and children as the deadly aircraft commenced strafing missions over East Timorese villages. Then, it seemed, the entire world had turned against his people.

The British jumped on the band-wagon, selling eight Hawk ground-attack aircraft to the Indonesian Air Force, and the Australian Government provided the forum for Australian companies to negotiate the substantial oil and gas deposit concessions with

JAKARTA

their Indonesian counterparts.

Xanana followed his countryman Nicolau Lobato, faithfully, as the newly elected Fretelin President led his poorly equipped band against the superior Indonesian forces. Weeks rolled slowly into months, and then into years. When Xanana heard that Australia had given *de facto* recognition to Indonesia's occupation of his country, he believed that the Australian people would, one day, regret their act of betrayal. Soon, his resistance movement would all but collapse. His only contact with the outside world had been by radio.

He remembered cheering along with the others in their secluded camp, when they heard news broadcasting the United Nations vote calling for the withdrawal of Indonesian troops and the right for self-determination to be exercised in East Timor. Jakarta responded by doubling its troops, destroying all of that season's crops, and slaughtering fifteen thousand more villagers. Soon Xanana was to witness the deaths of children as they starved, and listen to terrified women speak of their ordeals at the hands of the Indonesian soldiers.

Almost three years to the day after his country had been invaded, Xanana's spirits fell even further when they lost their only means of communicating with the Timorese people. Two weeks after Radio Maubere ceased transmitting, Fretelin's President, Nicolau Lobato, was shot and killed by the enemy.

Xanana had remained hiding in the mountains. He knew that Indonesian soldiers had received instructions from Jakarta not to take political prisoners. As each year passed, his enemy pressed further and further into the most remote mountain areas, annihilating entire villages they suspected of harbouring resistance fighters. Soon there were few left to carry on the fight. The rebels had run out of weapons.

Four years after the invasion, Indonesia still had not conquered his country, nor had it broken its spirit. The United Nations General Assembly passed a resolution condemning the Indonesian occupation, and called again for an act of self-determination. This call would also go unheeded.

Xanana had finally decided to carry his fight overseas and left his home behind when he and sixty others sailed the short distance to Australia, where they knew they would be well cared for. They sailed to Darwin, where they were immediately interned by the authorities, as unauthorised arrivals, and subsequently processed and placed in one of the many camps the Australian Government maintained under its refugee programme.

After some months had passed, Xanana was given his freedom and permitted to remain in Australia. He was, however, warned not to create mischief, threatened with deportation to an Indonesian jail in the event that he did not comply.

Xanana had exploited his position within the refugee community, and established a quasi government-in-exile. He assembled a team from amongst those he considered most qualified, and set about organizing the Timorese community in Australia to provide support for his dream of an Independent East Timor. He received substantial support from the international press, and financial assistance from the many Timorese in Australia. He established contact with representatives within the United Nations and the Portuguese Government, and continued the struggle for recognition of their demands. As the years passed slowly, Xanana came to realize that their cause would never receive the support it deserved, as there were just too many economic and political barriers and vested interest groups which thwarted the Timorese wherever they turned.

He had always wondered why the American Government had been so supportive of the Soeharto military dictatorship; then he discovered how strategically important East Timor's seas were to United States nuclear submarines. They could reduce sailing time by more than a week by transiting undetected through the Ombar-Wetar Straits just north of his land. Xanana learned a great deal over those years, and became philosophical regarding his dreams when he realized that his host country, Australia, continued to benefit from ignoring the plight of those he had left behind.

Whenever he strolled around Darwin Harbour and noted the increased activity, Xanana came to understand that economic considerations drove Australia's desire to maintain peaceful relationships with its giant northern neighbour. When he read that Australia and Indonesia would reap many billions of dollars in revenue from the very area which surrounded East Timor, he finally accepted that he would never live to see freedom for his people.

And then he received his first visit from the Indian Chargé d'Affaires.

* * * * * *

Xanana had been pleasantly surprised to discover how knowledgeable his guest had been regarding Timor's history and its people. As the day progressed and they continued to discuss East Timor's position, Xanana was impressed with the diplomat's response to his request for financial support. Before departing that day, he had received a commitment from his visitor to provide a donation to establish a special fund for the Timorese refugees. Within the week, and true to his word, the Chargé d'Affaires informed Xanana that his government had agreed to deposit two hundred thousand dollars towards this cause.

Xanana Soares, self-proclaimed President-in-exile, was ecstatic over the donation. He had understood the diplomat's request that India not be identified as the source, and the reasoning behind this request. Immediately, Xanana went about further consolidating his position amongst his fellow countrymen, using the fund to lift his movement's profile, and dispersing some of the money to those he considered most in need.

It was then that Xanana received an invitation to visit New Delhi, which he willingly accepted. Once again, the Chargé had suggested discretion in relation to the proposed journey.

The diplomat pointed out that the Australian Government would not be pleased about the Indian Government extending such an invitation, and further suggested that Xanana not divulge his travel arrangements to anyone. Xanana had not been entirely satisfied with this request, hoping to use his visit to gain some additional press. Finally, he accepted the diplomat's advice, acknowledging that the purpose for the unofficial visit was to assist the Timorese to further their cause for Independence. That had been sufficient to convince Xanana to adhere to the request and respect the need for secrecy surrounding the invitation. He made application for an Australian passport, which was granted on the basis that he had already become a naturalised citizen the year before.

'Will Otelo be joining us in India?' he had asked. Otelo Ramalho was responsible for the unofficial East Timor Embassy in Canberra. There was, in fact, no Embassy at all. The Australian Government, bowing to public pressure, had resisted administrative calls to remove the small hut which had been illegally erected on a vacant block of ground directly across the road from the Indonesian Embassy. This had been an embarrassment to the government and, ironically, although the butt of many a joke from passers-by, the small structure became identified with the East Timor Independence Movement. Xanana was indebted to Otelo for his introduction to the Indian High Commission.

'No, Otelo will not be joining you, Xanana. It is of the utmost importance that he know nothing of your journey,' the official had insisted. The following week Xanana left Darwin and flew to Singapore, where he changed flights then continued on to Delhi. Upon arrival, Xanana was whisked hurriedly away, and taken to a government guest house where he remained, *incommunicado*, for more than a week.

At first, he had been disappointed that he would not been allowed to move around freely. It was almost as if he had been placed under protective custody, as if his hosts were embarrassed by his presence. But when he was informed that he would meet with the Prime Minister briefly before lunch the next day, Xanana panicked, fearing he would have little to say to the powerful leader.

The following day, while he was being escorted through the stark, white-washed building, Xanana refused to believe that this modest building could possibly be the office of India's Prime Minister. Bewildered by the subterfuge surrounding his visit, he was finally introduced to the man who led a nation of more than one billion people. When he left the meeting, an hour later, Xanana was no longer confused about the reasons for secrecy. He was driven back to the guest house, the content of his incredible discussion with the Prime Minister still buzzing in his brain.

The Indian Government had offered to support his cause by granting official recognition to his government-in-exile. This meant that he would have a powerful ally to provide a protective military umbrella over East Timor from its aggressive neighbours. India would enter into a twenty-five year Defence and Economic Development Agreement with his government, and establish a formal naval presence in Timor, similar to that which the Americans had achieved years before in Subic Bay in the Philippines. Together, their countries would exploit Timor's oil and gas which would then belong to the independent state, and India would station its ships within East Timor's territorial waters to ensure the new nation's sovereignty over these and the Ombar-Wetar Straits.

Xanana had been promised his own war chest of ten million

dollars. He knew that this was insignificant in terms of power to purchase weapons, but what it represented was confirmation of India's commitment to his country. He had unhesitatingly accepted the terms offered by the Indian Prime Minister. Following this, all that was required of him was his attendance at several briefings over the following days, before returning to Australia where he would wait, until called.

* * * * * *

On the twenty-eighth of November, in recognition of Fretelin's declaration of Independence on that date decades before, the Republic of South Africa sponsored a resolution in the United Nations General Assembly which called for an immediate withdrawal of Indonesian troops from East Timor, and for recognition of Xanana Soares as the rightful head of state for the Republic of East Timor.

The resolution was carried by eighty-nine votes in favour, ten against, with only thirty-six abstentions, including Australia and the United States. India and China had led the charge and, as support swept across the floor of the chamber, the Indonesian Ambassador to the United Nations stormed out.

* * * * * *

Xanana Soares gathered his possessions in Darwin and moved to Canberra where he went about soliciting further support and establishing an official base of operations for the *Fretelin* cause. His Australian citizenship was brought into question on the floor of Parliament House, which resulted in a screaming match when a Democrat pointed out that, some years before, a Cambodian First Prime Minister appointed to Prince Ranariddh's former post was also an Australian citizen. The following week, Xanana flew to Singapore and took possession of the first two of his ten million dollars, and placed this in a numbered account with the Hong Kong Bank.

Indonesia reacted as expected, by moving additional troops into the area. In recognition of Australia's lack of support, the Indonesian Ambassador to Australia, Major General Sudarsono, left his temporary quarters and drove to the Foreign Affairs building where he formally handed notification to the Minister that Indonesian sea-lanes would forthwith be closed to Australian shipping until further notice.

United States satellite coverage, identifying an Indonesian military build-up in close proximity to the Timor Shelf oil and gas fields, was passed to counterparts in Australian Defence. Within days, tension between the two neighbouring countries spilled over, erupting once again into street violence and demonstrations in both nations' capitals.

Book three

Rama Energy

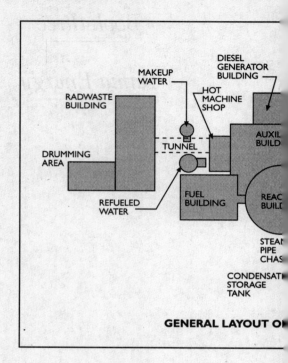

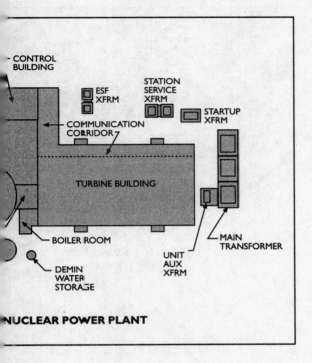

JAKARTA

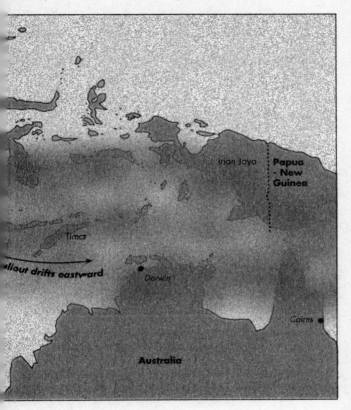

Kerry B. Collison

Chapter 20

Ruswita and the Salima Group

Vijay Rakesh winced with pain, and felt saddened that he might not last long enough to witness even the first step in the realization of Malhotra's strategy.

'The South African President has agreed,' he said, trying to disguise his discomfort. The medications no longer worked. He knew he would soon die. The thought of the State funeral and subsequent funeral pyre suddenly seemed appealing. Vijay was terribly tired.

'Vijay, why don't you rest,' Gopal said. 'Leave the implementation to those around you. There is little left that you can do.'

'We must push ahead with the Summit,' Vijay insisted. Malhotra's suggestion had been well received by all. Considering the regional conflicts, the timing was perfect for such a gathering of leaders to resolve their differences.

'Now that the South Africans are co-sponsoring the call, it will most surely happen, Vijay,' Gopal said, kindly. The three men had been close friends for many years, and shared the same ideals.

'And what about Imran's suggestion to involve those people in New Guinea?' Vijay asked. Admiral Gopal had played a major role in approaching the Government of New Guinea to suggest a goodwill visit by the Indian Navy. This would be essential in order to disguise the presence of such a large number of ships proceeding through the area.

'Port Moresby has agreed, Vijay. All seems to be in order.'

'Then, all we must do now is wait to see if the Indonesians take the bait,' the Indian Prime Minister suggested. Admiral Gopal grinned.

'I am sure they will jump at the opportunity to host a regional peace summit. Otherwise they might just be seen as being indifferent to settling their differences.'

'At least we have the Chinese supporting our strategy,' Vijay said, wincing again. Gopal could see that his friend was in severe pain and decided he must soon leave the Prime Minister to rest.

Rising to his feet he said, 'Yes, we have the Chinese, Vijay, and they, in turn, have the Americans to contend with.' Vijay Rakesh forced a grim smile and nodded.

'Do you think they will betray us?' the Prime Minister asked, knowing that everything depended on their support.

'No, Vijay,' Gopal said, 'they can't afford to do so. At least, not yet,' he added. 'I must go now and leave you to rest. I will come back tomorrow.' He moved closer and touched Vijay's arm, the gesture being rewarded with another smile. The admiral then left his ailing leader alone. As he walked down the corridor he reflected that they were on the verge of taking their country on a daring voyage into the future, one which would hopefully place food in the mouths of their starving millions.

* * * * * *

JAKARTA

Ruswita waved the servant away impatiently, returning her attention to the papers before her. She checked the covering overview letter which had been prepared by her son, Benny, saw that he had extended the period for amortisation over the most recent plants to come on line, and looked for the referenced explanatory notes to see why. Satisfied that he perhaps now knew more than she with regard to financing, Ruswita closed the final document and removed her glasses. She was weary from the demands placed upon her as Chairwoman. She glanced up at the framed photograph hanging on the opposite wall and smiled at Lim's face. It was one of the few photos he had actually posed for, as he had always feared ridicule because of his appearance.

Rus rubbed her eyes then placed her bifocals back on her nose to read the opened letter lying to the side of her official correspondence. It was from Ratna, and was addressed to *'Ibu Lani dan Dear Aunty Rus'*. She finished reading the letter and placed this back inside the envelope for Lani to read later. Rus thought about her daughter and her wasted life, saddened by the news of her divorce. She looked over at the clock and made a note to phone Ratna when it was appropriate, remembering to make allowance for the time difference between Jakarta and California.

Ruswita could not understand what Ratna really wanted out of life. She had always been restless, and lacked motivation to do anything which might involve the company's activities. She could virtually have had her choice of careers, Rus thought, and been given a solid start with any of the Salima companies which then spanned global trade and commerce, from timber concessions to banking, mining and shipping and, of course now, power generation.

Ruswita turned her attention back to the nuclear power plants under the Salima Group control. *Rama I* had been commissioned three months before, while *Ramas III, IV and V* had all come in under time four to five months earlier, earning considerable bonuses for the group. She had attended the official opening ceremony for *Rama I* in Bali, but delegated the other functions to Lim's oldest sons, who reluctantly flew from the United States specifically for the occasion.

She thought about these young men, who were already making a mark of their own, and wished that they would settle down in Indonesia and assume some of the burdensome responsibilities she carried. Her youngest son, Benny, had also taken to banking. He had been appointed President of the Asian Pacific Commercial Bank, which their family still controlled. She remembered that he had commenced negotiations to establish operational branches in India and the Middle East and, she thought miserably, this would lead to his spending more time away from her, also.

Ruswita missed her husband. Her busy life had not eased the loneliness she felt. It was not until she assumed control over the group's activities that Ruswita realized just how active Lim had been, and how unobtrusively he had conducted his business affairs. She brushed the memory of his sudden demise away as quickly as it had entered her thoughts, knowing how painful such recollections were. When Lim had been murdered, she had never been able to confirm her suspicions about how he had been poisoned, but she knew who had been responsible. She knew too that one or more of her staff must have been engaged to carry out the murder. Unable to discover which of her servants had betrayed their master, she had systematically removed them all from her household, including the old housekeeper, and replaced them with staff from other residences she owned.

The doctor had been of great service to her, taking care of the necessary arrangements through to the burial. Ruswita had insisted that only immediate family attend the small service, after which Lim's body had been cremated. She had lied to their surprised children, stating that Lim had once discussed such arrangements, and had specifically requested that his body be treated so. For weeks, flower arrangements had continued to arrive, reflecting his power and popularity around the world. Then, with his funeral behind her, Ruswita had turned her attention to their company's activities, and taken control.

Then, before she had been given the opportunity to strike at the man who she believed to have ordered her husband's death, Seda was already dead.

Many had agreed with her that Seda's appointment as ambassador was most bewildering. They all were aware of his considerable power, wealth, and influence over the President. Why then, had he removed himself from the very seat of Indonesian power and taken a lesser position? She had heard the rumours that he was being considered for appointment as Vice President at the time of his death. Ruswita did not believe that this would have eventuated. Seda had collected powerful enemies in his time, most of whom, she remembered, moved quickly to fill the vacuum created by his death.

The vultures had swooped, tearing at the flesh of his company structure, until the inner workings of Seda's entire operation had been exposed. Those closest to the President assumed many of the roles Seda had skilfully taken for himself. Supply companies changed hands within days and, once the military were satisfied that his widow had been adequately provided for, they absorbed the rest, distributing contracts and projects among themselves before others had any chance.

Ruswita had been asked to visit the President's home to discuss the *Rama II* plant after the Japanese Government had withdrawn from the project, citing domestic political pressures.

JAKARTA

When they withdrew, the project had been more than half completed. She had pledged her support to the First Family, but refused to provide any funding for the project. The government banks were also reluctant to provide loan capital to the new corporate entity established to assume control over the plant, until the President personally insisted that the Central Bank guarantee the project. It was then that Jakarta business circles discovered that Seda's original contract had been assumed by the President's youngest daughter and the Robson *kongsi*. The Jakarta rumour-mill fed off the relationship which existed between the new PEPELIN Chairman, Major General Sujono Diryo, and his wife, the President's second daughter.

Now, Ruswita's sources confirmed that construction of the Fast Breeder Reactor plant was nearing completion, and that *Rama II* would most probably be on line within six months. There had been disturbing rumours about the plant's safety, and concerns that the rush to complete the project might compromise established safety procedures. Ruswita's *kongsi* did not even bid for the ongoing supply contract, suspecting that the government's project management team would be unable to meet their financial undertakings. As a major shareholder in the largest private Indonesian bank, Ruswita knew the value of the government's Central Bank guarantee, and hoped that none would ever have reason to call upon it.

She was surprised that Robson still managed to keep his foot in the door somehow, pledging his assets to gain a position in the plant's construction, providing Indian cement, Vietnamese steel reinforcing-bars and whatever else he could lay his hands on through credit. As his name came to mind, Ruswita remembered how close the Salima plants had come to losing its uranium supplies from Australia.

When the President had unwisely invoked Indonesia's sovereignty over its sea-lanes in retaliation for what he perceived to be disloyalty over the United Nations vote, Ruswita had sent her own emissaries directly down to speak to the respective Chiefs of Staff, warning them that the Australian uranium, or yellowcake supplies, could not so easily be replaced just at a whim. When they had learned that the *Rama Project* could be delayed for years, the ruling generals had approached their stubborn President and requested that he withdraw his edict. Amazingly, he refused. Then, General

Sujono and his wife also appealed to the President, explaining how *Rama II's* commissioning would be delayed indefinitely, should ore supplies be disrupted at this late date.

She remembered how he had shaken his fist in Soekarno style, then publicly forgiven the Australians for the inappropriate position they had taken at the time. Shipping had returned to some semblance of normality, although tensions still ran high thoughout the region.

Ruswita had smiled when the new Chairman of PEPELIN had been appointed prior to Seda's departure for Australia. The international press had enjoyed a field day, crying nepotism, when General Sujono was appointed to the position. She knew that the young general would be a very wealthy man before the remaining seven power plants had gone out for tender, and even richer once these had been brought on-line. She didn't mind. Lim had taught her how to handle such situations, encouraging her to accept that payments only guaranteed contracts, not loyalty.

Ruswita knew for certain from their family bank that the First Family's wealth had grown close to two billion dollars over the nine years the former general had held office. She believed this to be a modest amount for one who occupied the presidential seat. Lim, she recalled fondly, often laughed privately about those who had become President over the powerful economy, as their children squandered millions of Indonesian banks' funds on their misadventures and were rarely called to account over their debts. Lim had warned her to be cautious when dealing with these children, as most were inept when it came to monetary matters. Not that it really mattered to the First Family, Lim had joked, revealing the billions which successive Presidents had moved overseas into numbered accounts. After all, the Lim bank had been instrumental in arranging most of these transactions.

Ruswita planned to emulate the First Family's desire to hold their assets outside the country. She would divest Salima of its burdensome exposure with the energy plants, but not in accordance with Lim's original plans. Ruswita decided not to wait until they had been operating for the two years her late husband had suggested. The Salima Jaya company, whose shares had already been listed before Lim's death, had enjoyed the confidence of the stock market investors, and Ruswita had decided that it was time to consolidate the family's holdings by retiring as much debt as she could. She knew that this would mean floating the energy company well before cash-flows had been proven, but she no longer considered these projections to be relevant, as the Asian markets were operating at a level considerably higher than most had forecast. Ruswita decided to take advantage of renewed investment confidence and list the company, Salima Jaya Power and Energy, as soon as she had amalgamated all of their energy interests. Ruswita expected that they would be ready to float the entire operation off through the Jakarta Stock Exchange before the end of the year. Benny had provided her with projections as to what they could expect from the sale of these assets, and Ruswita had not even blinked when she saw the final figure of twenty billion dollars. They would still retain their banking interests and a token position in the energy company.

Divesting themselves of these assets would be met with public approval, as Ruswita expected the indigenous investment houses would have a field day fighting over positions in the proposed share-float, considering the conglomerate's successful cement plants, flour mills and other major operating assets. The remaining shares in the family flagship, Salima Jaya Corporation, would then be sold through the Stock Exchange as soon as the market had absorbed the energy company's shares. Her son, Benny, had estimated that their total cash assets would then exceed fifty billion dollars, not including the Asian Pacific Commercial Bank's net asset worth. The only outstanding issue, she mused confidently, would be how to incorporate the *Rama II* power production into the Salima Jaya Power and Energy stable. She understood from her son, Benny, how the nuclear power plant's construction had been financed; their family bank had picked up all the outstanding notes relating to the project. Ruswita knew that she would require Palace support to instruct the government banks, and superannuation fund managers, to commit to advance positions for her public float.

A voice outside reminded Ruswita that she was expecting a visitor. She opened a drawer to the desk, slipped the file inside, and moved into the next room to receive her guest, smiling as she entered the room to greet the recently appointed Vice President. The handsome Javanese general rose and returned her smile.

'Good morning, Ibu Salima,' he greeted, gently squeezing her extended hand.

'Selamat siang, General Sujono,' Ruswita said, warmly, as she welcomed the President's son-in-law.

Chapter 21

*Ratna Sari, Michael
in California*

Ratna lay back and breathed slowly as the sun reappeared from behind the cloud. She looked across at the man resting alongside, and admitted that she had not been this happy for years. Then she wondered what might have happened, had chance not taken her to the country club on that day, a month before. As she lay there soaking up the sun's warmth, Ratna smiled, recalling how their paths had crossed during the tournament.

******

Ratna had been enjoying the tennis when someone walked up alongside her and coughed politely. She turned, lifting her sunglasses to see who had practically coughed into her ear, and Michael grinned sheepishly then merely said, 'hello'.

For a fleeting moment she remained startled, then her mouth opened in surprise as recognition flooded her face. He leaned forward and kissed her on both cheeks, and smiled, the faint and tantalizing suggestion of Issey Miyaki gently arousing his senses. Immediately, memories of their affair came flooding back as she stood, smiling, and suddenly it was as if they had never parted. Ratna's instincts reacted accordingly, noticing the other women's admiring glances as the tall, handsome man stood close to her. She was suddenly excited by how well Michael looked. His skin was heavily tanned and his hair fairer than before, signs that he had spent considerable time outdoors.

'I see you haven't lost your fascination for tennis,' she said, referring to their first meeting years before. She placed her hand gently on his arm. Suddenly, It was just like old times.

'And I see you're still trying to pick up handsome young men at these events,' Michael responded. He looked at her with obvious delight and Ratna could see that he was smitten all over again.

'My, my,' she teased, 'who suggested that you were handsome?' Michael laughed, relieved. 'Come,' she ordered, commanding Michael in a familiar way. Ratna slipped her arm through his, and led him outside onto the veranda overlooking the tennis courts, where they sat and talked, occasionally looking down at the players as the competition continued.

* * * * * *

Ratna laughingly related her experiences over the past few years while Michael listened. She had shed her tomboyish manner and grown into a beautiful, sophisticated woman. Ratna explained that she had married and divorced all in one year, returning to the States once the lawyers had finalised the property settlement. Ratna did not appear bitter in any way, nor did she appear saddened by what had taken place.

'You're staring again,' she said, wondering what was going through his thoughts.

'Let's get out of here,' Michael suggested, and when she nodded he called for the check and they left, unnoticed in the crowd which had gathered at the country club. As they walked outside he sighed, wishing he had hired a rental and not caught a cab out to the club. A deep metallic purple Lamborghini appeared, and Michael did not express surprise when the attendant passed the keys to Ratna.

'I'll drive,' she smiled, squeezing into the car. Michael hesitated, then followed, climbing into the expensive sports car. He buckled up immediately and, remembering how heavy footed Ratna had been in the past, braced himself for the ride. Instead, he was pleasantly surprised when Ratna did not stamp on the gas pedal as had been her habit when they first met and fell in love, but drove away from the club in a most sedate manner.

'Thanks, Ratna.' Michael said, sincerely. She turned to look at his face and laughed.

'What ever do you mean?' she responded, suddenly kicking the accelerator down, recklessly. Michael looked at her imploringly.

'Oh,' she said, mischievously, 'you mean that, back there?' Again she laughed, but seeing the concern on his face, slowed the car, bringing its speed back within acceptable limits. 'Last week I was called to order by the club president. Seems that I could lose my parking privileges if caught speeding through the grounds again.'

Michael shook his head sadly.

They drove up the old coast road and parked overlooking the ocean. There, they sat and talked though the afternoon until the cool sea breeze became too chilly for them to remain. Michael took the keys and drove them both back into the city. He did not seem comfortable sitting in the passenger seat along the winding, dangerous stretches, and Ratna had surrendered the keys without comment. He drove directly to his hotel and parked in the driveway, then turned and looked at Ratna questioningly. She climbed out of the car as he moved around to take her hand, and lead her inside.

'No, Michael,' she said, removing the car keys gently from his hand. 'It's too soon.' She looked up into his eyes and smiled, then raised her mouth to his and kissed him gently.

During the afternoon, Ratna had considered how she might react when he inevitably invited her to stay. There had never been any doubt in her mind that he would ask, and she wanted desperately to spend the night with Michael. But the memory of what had transpired between them before was still on her mind. She had to be sure that he would not disappear again, once they had tumbled into bed together. 'Perhaps, when you return,' she promised.

'Okay, that's fine, Ratna. There's no pressure,' he said, but she could sense his disappointment.

'Thanks, Michael,' she responded, then looked up into his eyes. 'When will I hear from you again?'

'I'll be gone for about a week. I promise to phone then, okay?'

'That's fine, Michael, you do that.'

Michael had explained that he would be leaving the following morning, but would be back within the week. Ratna felt he seemed a little vague about what he was doing, and was not entirely convinced that he was telling her the truth. She asked if there was someone currently in his life, and Michael had assured her that there was no one. Ratna was uncomfortable with his reply, and had difficulty accepting it as true. Michael was a handsome fellow, and would be considered a fine catch. It was unlikely that he had not already found someone, and settled down.

Michael squeezed her hand, again promising to phone. They parted company, and Ratna returned to the Salima mansion. As the days passed without a phone call, she became despondent, fearing that he had passed fleetingly through her life again, never to return. At the end of the week, she was convinced that he had lied. Then, suddenly, he was there, standing outside the mansion, his handsome face all smiles. Ratna flung herself around his neck, and laughed, kissing him as he playfully struggled to hold her at bay. Michael had returned, as promised, and they then spent the following, wonderful weeks, totally engrossed in each other. And for Ratna, it was a matter of falling in love all over again.

* * * * * *

Now, she knew, the strength of their relationship was about to be really tested, as Michael was to leave her, again. Ratna reached over and pulled the sun-bleached hair on Michael's forearm, bringing him instantly awake. He had dozed off under the warm sun.

'As it's our last night, what do you say we go home now and lock ourselves in?' she suggested, hoping he would agree.

'Sounds fine to me,' Michael answered, sitting up and taking a quick gulp of the iced tea. It was lukewarm; surprised, he checked his wristwatch and discovered he had dozed off for almost half an hour. He rose, grabbed his gym-bag and took Ratna by the hand. Promising to catch-up when Michael next visited, they left the others and drove back to the palatial estate. Ratna left the Lamborghini directly in front of the house, knowing that it would be safe. They strolled leisurely up the steps and through the mansion, then down to their favourite setting. Michael strolled over lazily and activated the outside spa's pumps, then turned to see Ratna standing naked, reaching up to roll her long, black, shiny hair into a bun.

'You're staring, again,' she laughed, unashamedly, and Michael immediately felt the heat rising in his loins. He knew he couldn't get enough of her, remembering the passionate hours they had spent together in her room upstairs. Michael stripped, and slipped into the bubbling spa as Ratna walked gracefully towards him. As she stepped into the water, her eyes seemed to convey that she was as anxious as he, to make love. Michael reached out and pulled her towards him slowly, turning her onto her back, then kissing her, impatiently. She responded, taking him in her hand and stroking him gently, until he was fully aroused. Then suddenly, Ratna pulled away, climbed out of the spa and ran to the pool, and propped.

'The servants will be watching,' she teased, then threw herself into the pool and swam towards the grotto. Michael didn't hesitate. The old women who had guarded this house had probably seen worse, he thought, scrambling after his woman. He hit the water hard, winced, then swam over to where she waited behind the waterfall.

He dived under the cascading water, coming to the surface where she sat, perched on the rock-pool's edge like some golden mermaid. Droplets of water clung to her body, and she posed sensually, opening then closing her legs. Michael moved in closer, lowering his head until his face touched her firm abdomen. He kissed her skin softly, and then again, as Ratna moaned and grasped his head with her hands, begging him not to stop. Michael tickled her with his tongue, and, as she cried out once more, he placed his hands around her slender waist, and leaned her gently on her side.

As she lay outstretched along the narrow ledge, he leaned over her breasts placed his warm mouth over her erect nipples, and teased her generously. Then, he rolled out of the water, and moved to dominate her body with his. Gently, lovingly, he parted her legs and stroked softly. Ratna said something which he could not understand, and moaned once more as he mounted her body and filled her completely with his. They moved together, finding a rhythm which filled each other with ecstasy, rocking slowly, at first, then faster, and faster, until their bodies reached a pulsating, simultaneous climax. Michael's body convulsed, and he cried out in pleasure.

They lay together, still, as their hearts beat loudly, and Ratna could feel Michael's hot breath on the side of her face. She kissed him, tenderly, and then held him tightly as their breathing returned to normal She stroked his head, brushing aside the yellow-bleached strands of hair which covered his brow. Michael responded, kissing her gently, then moved to her side.

'Tell me you will never leave me, Michael,' she pleaded softly, her eyes still dreamy with the moment. He moved his arms around her, tenderly.

'I love you, Ratna,' was all he said, and kissed her again.

* * * * * *

Jakarta — the Presidential Palace

'..and it is therefore my great pleasure to announce that the three-day peace summit will be held on the seventeenth of January, in Bali.' The speaker was immediately inundated with questions, as journalists jostled each other for advantage.

'How will Xanana Soares travel to Indonesia?' one journalist called.

'*Bapak Presiden* has kindly consented for Mister Soares to be present at the Bali Summit conditional on his undertaking that, under no circumstances will he participate in any discussions outside the agreed agenda, and that he will not attend any rally of any kind during his stay. It is my understanding that Mister Soares will first attend discussions in New Delhi, following which he will accompany the Indian Prime Minister and South African President on their flight to Indonesia.' The journalists held their recorders higher to catch the Palace spokesman's words.

'Can you confirm who will attend the Summit?' another asked, pushing back angrily as someone behind shoved.

'As I have already mentioned, Xanana Soares will attend, his presence sponsored by the South African Government. The Indian and South African leaders will, of course, attend. We have confirmation that the Australian Prime Minister will be present, as will the ASEAN Heads of State.'

'Will the President also be present for discussions?' the Singapore Straits Times journalist asked, hoping his cameraman was catching it all for the SBS early evening news.

'*Bapak Presiden* will attend the formal opening ceremony, and will remain only until the official reception on the first day. *Bapak* has advised that Vice President, *Bapak Sujono,* will arrive early on the second day of the Summit, and will represent Indonesia during ongoing discussions. The *Istana* wishes to emphasize that the Indonesian leadership places great store in bringing its neighbouring nations together for the Bali Peace Summit, and sincerely prays that the meeting will result in an accord satisfactory to all.'

JAKARTA

'With the *Istana's* acceptance of Xanana Soares' participation in these talks, does this signal a rapprochement between his government-in-exile and Jakarta?' David Murdoch from the International Herald Tribune asked, his tall frame dwarfing his colleagues.

'The Government of Indonesia does not recognize claims over *Tim-Tim* by refugee East Timorese who abandoned their own country and migrated to Australia. The *Istana* wishes to make this point quite clear; there is no East Timor delegation to the Bali Summit. Mr Soares' presence has been agreed to primarily on the basis that the South African President has sponsored his attendance. The Palace therefore hopes that this clearly demonstrates its willingness to resolve the issues which have contributed to regional tension, and its sincerity in offering its neighbouring countries the opportunity to settle their differences peacefully.'

'In view that the United Nations has already voted on the East Timor issue, and Indonesia's refusal to withdraw from the colony, won't Xanana's presence overshadow other issues such as accessibility to your country's sea-lanes?' Murdoch asked.

'Mr Soares' presence is not an issue,' was all the *Istana* spokesman was willing to add. He then ignored Murdoch's raised hand, annoyed by his aggressive line of questions.

'Will the visiting Heads of State be invited to attend the inauguration ceremony for the Mt Muria reactor?' someone down the back of the room called. The spokesman was pleased with the opportunity to mention the project during the press conference.

'No,' he said. 'However, the Vice President will officiate at the plant's final commissioning ceremony, and this will coincide with the second day of the Bali Summit. Unfortunately, due to security considerations, the press will be not be permitted to attend. The Palace public relations office would be pleased to provide photographs after the event. *Terima kasih*,' he said, smilingly, indicating that the conference had come to a close.

He had fielded enough questions and was relieved that he had successfully avoided the more sensitive issues. Taking up his notes, the *Istana* spokesman then stepped away from the podium leaving more than fifty journalists to file their stories. He reported personally to *Bapak Sujono*, confirming that the press conference had gone well.

The following day most international newspapers carried the

story on their front pages, with headlines which ranged from 'Indonesia Extends Its Hand in Peace' to 'Xanana Soares Scores Political Victory' and 'Indonesia Takes Soft Stance', declaring the Bali Summit would provide Asia with the long-awaited opportunity to resolve regional issues and restore peace.

Nowhere, in any of the stories, was the inauguration of Indonesia's powerful Fast Breeder Nuclear Plant even mentioned.

Chapter 22

The Oval Office

Secretary for State, William James Deakin, shuffled restlessly around the President's office listening, as the CIA Director concluded the Central Intelligence Agency's Asian situation report. This had followed similar submissions by General V. 'Sonny' Davis of the Joint Chiefs of Staff, and the three-star Defense Intelligence Agency's director. There was a moment of silence as those in attendance waited for the President's response. There was not a man present who envied the American leader at that moment. Without exception, they sensed that they were participating in what future historians might even identify as the turning point in American-Sino relations, or worse.

'What do you think, Bill?' the President asked Deakin, who immediately ceased pacing and addressed his superior.

'You know my position, Mr President,' he answered formally. They had been close friends since college. Had it not been for that relationship, Deakin would have refused the offer to become the country's Secretary for State. William J Deakin would have been quite content to remain where he was, with General Motors. 'I have never been supportive of military action other than to defend these shores.' He looked across at the four men sitting, facing their President.

'We are dealing with some fairly nebulous conclusions here, I would say,' this was directed at the CIA Chief. Deakin found it difficult to accommodate the clandestine operations as an integral component of State's activities, although he accepted that the intelligence gathering activities were essential to their national security. Deakin's primary objection was to CIA and DIA covert operations which often undermined the State's own solution-seeking efforts on the world stage.

'I don't believe we have sufficient intelligence information to take an informed position. My recommendation is that we wait for a while and see how it all develops. Then, if we feel that action is still required, our decisions would be based on intelligence which, in the future, would justify what they're proposing.' Deakin indicated with his left hand just whom he was referring to in the room.

'Well, Sonny, how do you respond to that?' The President asked his country's most senior military officer. Victor 'Sonny' Davis' star had been on the ascent ever since the American press had practically deified him and many other US Army field officers involved in *Desert Storm* more than a decade before. Since then, apart from Bosnia and a few minor skirmishes in Africa, the United States Military had been given few opportunities to provide American troops with battle-field experience.

'The Joint Chiefs are all in concurrence, Mr President,' he replied, knowing just how much weight they carried in such decisions. The general was not too happy with the Secretary for State's obvious influence over the President and the knowledge that Deakin had never so much as served one day in any of the US forces.

'All intelligence points to the Indians mobilising their Navy. If, for the moment, we can put political issues aside and concentrate solely on the military aspects of a major naval expedition, we would have to agree that, considering India's naval strength, in the absence of a successful retaliatory or pre-emptive enemy missile attack, they would be successful.' The general moved his large, beefy hands through the air as he spoke.

'The Indian Navy is third only to the United States in strength. Unless they were also contemplating taking the Malay Peninsula, which would then afford an excellent opportunity for ground forces to sweep down through Bangladesh, Burma and Thailand, then we do not see any real long-term benefit for India in the scenario suggested by the CIA. However, we do agree that a military expedition by India's forces is imminent. It is, in our opinion, most unlikely however that the Chinese would sit back and let the Indians go; that is,' he added, looking directly at the Secretary for State, 'unless they are acting in concert and intend conducting a joint expedition.' This statement was immediately met with surprised glances from both Deakin and the CIA director.

'No, I can't accept that the Chinese would ever entertain such an alliance,' Deakin stated, shaking his head in emphasis, 'and there is nothing to support such conjecture.'

'Is there?' the President pressed, conscious that there was an air of antagonism developing, and he didn't like it at all.

'No, Mr President,' General Davis answered, 'but the Joint Chiefs are most concerned with the spread of China's Southern Fleet across the South China Sea from Natuna Island off Malaysia, right though to Hong Kong. One would have to ask the obvious question regarding what they might do, should they perceive the Indian Navy consolidating its own position in nearby waters as a potential threat. We have initiated a number of war-game scenarios Mr. President, which all seem to indicate that, without Chinese accord, the Indians would be most unlikely to move further east than Singapore.' The thought of the South East Asian financial centre, Singapore, falling to India, whilst China dominated Hong Kong, startled others in the room.

The President put his fingertips together in thought. General Davis' statement provided substance to the suggestion that India might consider annexing the entire peninsula. There was virtually no other viable area in which they could expand; China blocked India in the east, and there was little to be gained by moving into the arid areas of Pakistan and Afghanistan. On the other hand, any overland expedition into the fertile plains of Thailand and Malaysia would require access though Bangladesh and Burma.

The President was all too aware of his country's weakened military position in Asia. Having given Vietnam back to the communists in 1975, the United States had been unable to sustain its credibility amongst the Asian nations. Then, when the Philippines evicted the US Navy from its base in Subic Bay, he had not been surprised when the Japanese voted to send American ships sailing from the majority of their bases as well.

He had been against the reduction of American forces in Asia. Singapore was one of the few countries outside Taiwan which still welcomed American ships. New Zealand's historic ban on nuclear ships had come as no surprise, back then, to the American people, but what had shocked them most was Indonesia's recent insistence that US submarines, which had enjoyed undetected passage through their waters since 1965, were no longer permitted to transit below the surface.

The President had always expected the West to experience a downside to supporting the Indonesians' claim over international sea-routes through their waters. As American influence waned in Asia, so too did trading with those nations become more one-sided. He had been pressured into granting Most Favoured Nation status to just about every goddamn country in that part of the world. He was painfully aware that the United States needed the heavily populated markets of China and Indonesia to continue to stimulate its own domestic growth, a growth which, during his Administration, had slowed dangerously.

He had always believed that the United States would be unable to sustain the growth it enjoyed over the previous fifty years. Even with the implementation of the NAFTA agreements which had been expanded to provide his country access to most of the Americas, industrial growth had slowed. Having already recovered from near economic collapse less than a decade before, he was convinced that if the Asian power-houses continued their amazing advances, their success would be achieved at the expense of the West which, in his mind, meant the United States of America.

His initial reluctance to extend MFN status to these Third World countries had been viewed by his colleagues on Capitol Hill as a clear indictment of his inability to understand the commercial realities of global politics in the twenty-first century. But he knew that they were wrong. A blunt edged sword it might be, but he firmly believed that Most Favoured Nation status should be raised whenever the situation demanded his government bring pressure to bear on some of the more recalcitrant Asian leaders.

'How are the Australians positioned?' the President asked his old friend, Deakin.

'Well, understandably, they're not too happy with us either. Historically, they have always suffered from the 'yellow-peril' syndrome Down Under. Relations between Indonesia and Australia are on the mend, but there is still considerable tension between the two countries over what is happening with East Timor. In hindsight, I believe that we should never have pressured..,' he hesitated, searching for the man's name, '...ah, yes, Whitlam, I believe it was, that we should not have prevented the Australians from going into East Timor at that time.'

Deakin was objective enough to understand how the US Administration in 1975 had been swayed by the CIA to prevent the Australians from occupying the former colony, even though initial requests had originated from both the Timorese and the Indonesian President, Soeharto. He remembered how paranoid his government had been at the time. The Australian Government was led by a team of left-wing socialists, and there was just no way that the United States could accept a government sympathetic to America's enemies, gaining a foothold in what was obviously to be another socialist state.

Upon his appointment to State, which provided access to sensitive information buried by past Administrations over the years, Deakin was not surprised to discover how his country had influenced the outcome in Timor, and understood American fears. In the course of that one year, they had lost Vietnam to the communists; New Guinea had become independent, Pol Pot had started on his path of genocide, Indira Ghandi had declared a state of emergency in her country, and Indonesia had been encouraged to invade East Timor. It was obvious to Deakin, as he read the confidential memos of that time, that his government feared Soviet intervention as far south as Dili. He agreed that the premise was probable; look at how the Russians had poured into Vietnam filling the vacuum created by the American withdrawal!

As Australia was considered pro-socialist, his predecessors had decided that it would be in American interests to have Soeharto's Indonesia take over the small colony, rather than have another Cuban-styled missile crisis develop in the centre of one of the world's richest oil and gas deposits. These thoughts passed through his mind before he replied to the President's question.

'I fear that the Australians believe that we would never honour our undertakings to come to their assistance in the event of hostilities threatening their shores. In short, they believe that we would simply walk away from our obligations under the ANZUS Treaty, should conflict erupt between them and, say, Indonesia.' General Davis interrupted him immediately.

'That may very well be so, but it was the Kiwis who first weakened that Treaty by banning visiting American warships!'

The DIA director nodded in agreement. 'The Aussies don't seem to understand exactly where they're going with their regional alliances. First they sign an enduring defense agreement with Indonesia, which states that each would come to the aid of the other in the event of external forces threatening regional stability, and then they embark on a programme of destabilising their relationships by permitting this fellow...' the DIA director referred to his notes, '..Xanana Soares to establish his own anti-Indonesian platform right on Jakarta's doorstep. The Australians have brought a great deal of what has happened recently on their own heads. Before you know it, they'll have dragged us into open conflict with the Indonesians, and that might just be the end of American influence in Asia.' The President looked at the director and then over to Deakin.

'Is there no way we can diffuse the situation then?' he asked. Deakin was about to answer when General Davis spoke.

'The Joint Chiefs recommend that we demonstrate to our allies that we are still very much committed to an American presence in the area by positioning the Seventh Fleet in Singapore on a more permanent basis. This would also send a clear signal to India and China that we are prepared to prevent further territorial expansion, and might mollify the Indonesians and Australians.' Deakin glanced over at the general, and nodded his support for the suggestion, particularly having considered the alternatives.

Positioning an American fleet in Darwin would, he believed, only antagonise the Indonesians further, and would not necessarily discourage the Indian Navy from moving across towards the Malay Peninsula; nor might it prevent further acquisitions by China, in the South China Sea. He had seen a copy of the Sultan of Brunei's written appeal to London, requesting British forces to be sent to the area, in answer to China's provocative annexation of the nearby islands.

Deakin had anticipated his associates' reaction to having any British forces back in the area. It had taken decades to displace the Commonwealth's influence, and the United States was not keen to have them restore any military presence in Asia.

'I would support the Joint Chiefs' suggestion, Mr President,' Deakin offered. 'I'm certain that the Singaporeans would welcome the idea.'

'I'm not so certain,' the DIA director challenged 'They would want to appear neutral.'

'Not so,' Deakin argued, 'we have sent the US Navy in before, and they were only too happy to have our fleet stationed there.' The director knew that the Secretary for State was referring to an earlier American plan to invade Indonesia through Sumatra, back in the chaotic 'fifties', during the times when most of his fellow countrymen still believed their government's propaganda that communists lurked behind every closed door.

'Yes, but the Singaporeans were under threat from the Indonesians then. Regional politics have changed dramatically, as you would well know,' the director added, knowing that his snide barb would not go unnoticed, 'and most Singaporeans would not entertain antagonising the Chinese either. What makes you believe that the Indonesians would not feel as threatened with our ships sitting in Singapore as they would if we positioned the Seventh Fleet in Darwin?'

'Because Indonesia has a substantial stake in Singapore, and they are politically astute enough to understand that any threat to Singapore would result in an immediate response from the British and American forces.' Deakin looked across the room at the man who would make the final decision for them all. 'Mr President, I reaffirm my support for moving our fleet into Singapore.' The President seemed pleased that the Joint Chiefs and State had taken similar positions. He looked at the others and raised his eyebrows.

'Gentlemen?' he asked the two directors.

'I'd go with that, Mr President,' the DIA Director said. He was closely allied to the Joint Chiefs and would follow his superiors' recommendations. The President nodded, satisfied that the decision had already been made for him. He then looked for the CIA's response, hoping for unanimity from his advisers.

'I would agree providing we keep other options open, Mr President.' The others all glanced in his direction. They knew what he meant. The CIA would want to maintain all of its covert actions, regardless of where the Seventh might be based. The President's face broke into a partial smile indicating that he was pleased his most senior advisers had reached consensus.

'Well, that's it then, gentlemen,' he said, rising from his chair and moving around to the front of the historic desk. 'All we have to do now is convince the Singaporeans that it is not our intention to stay forever,' he half-joked, but the others present knew that this would not be an easy task. They were a sophisticated people with a history of strong leadership, and would do only what was best for Singapore.

He held his hand up motioning for Allan Cox to remain. It was apparent from his earlier reaction that something else was troubling the intelligence chief, and the President thought a few minutes alone might clear the air. The other advisers shook their leader's hand and departed, leaving the CIA director alone with the President.

'Well, Allan, you had very little to say - weren't you happy with the decision?'

'Mr President, it's only a short-term solution,' he replied.

'What's on your mind, then?' The President propped himself up against the desk and crossed his legs, the palms of his hands resting on the structure behind.

'I still don't agree with the Joint Chiefs' appraisal. My money is still on India making a major move, one that will firmly ensconce them in the heart of things territorially speaking. I believe that they will go to war in support of territorial expansion and I do not believe reports that their army has not been mobilised.' The President thought about what the director suggested, and waited for him to continue. General Davis had not mentioned this possibility. *Was it an oversight?*

'Whatever they're up to, its real, and it's going to happen soon. As for the Chinese acting in concert with the Indians, we would be foolish not to prepare for such an eventuality, or at least work towards disrupting their developing alliance in other ways than via State.' He looked at the President feeling that he might have gone too far, but they had enjoyed a number of frank discussions in the past, and he knew that his leader valued his opinions.

'I think we have lost the plot, Mr President,' he said, not wishing to alarm, but sensing that what he was about to say might just do that. 'I think the Indian Government is most definitely preparing to go to war.' For a moment the director thought he could hear distant traffic outside, but he knew that this was not possible. Double-glazed bullet-proof windows and other security measures made this room a cocoon.

'We don't have anything to support that; you heard the others,

JAKARTA

Allan.'

'Yes, sir, I did. But I'm not convinced that the Chinese are not acting in concert with India.

'Do you have anything which the others have not had access to?' the President asked, knowing that this would be so. Having being appointed to office, he had learnt to accept the idiosyncrasies of government, dealing with the jealously guarded power-bases which permeated all levels of each Administration, although he had been surprised to discover the competitiveness which existed between the intelligence agencies. The President waited.

'I do, Sir, but it's not directly related to today's discussions. There is something brewing on the Indonesian front, which has only just come to our attention.' The President accepted this would most likely be untrue; the CIA would have squatted on any new information until an opportunity to reveal whatever it was presented itself. 'I have not briefed the other departments as we still have no confirmation that the source, or the information, is reliable.' The President became impatient with the evasive ploy.

'Allan?' he insisted, and the director knew he would have to reveal his information prematurely. He hesitated, collecting his thoughts.

'I would hope that the President understands that this information has not, in any way, been circulated to the other agencies, including the Joint Chiefs.' It was meant as a question and the President nodded in affirmation.

'Go on.' he ordered, sensing that he might later regret his decision to push the director to reveal all. He had learned early in his political career that knowledge was not always power, that there was much that was better left unsaid. He waited, his impatience growing.

The director sighed, knowing what impact his words would have. He looked directly into the politician's eyes and said, 'I believe that Indonesia is less than a year away from having sufficient material to produce its own nuclear device.' He paused, expelling a heavy sigh, before continuing. 'If I am able to substantiate the information we have received, then the world will have its newest member in the Nuclear Club ready to go, possibly even before the end of this year. The President came upright from his relaxed position, stunned by the alarming news.

'Are you sure?' he demanded, shocked at the implications.

'Reasonably certain. We'll know more in a few weeks,' he said, in a tired voice. The President moved back behind his table and sat, his face creased with worry.

'Sonofabitch!' he said, glaring at the bearer of bad news. He crossed his arms and leaned back into the heavy, leather-covered chair. 'Sonofabitch!' he said again, as if the other man was no longer there. The director stood, uncomfortably, wishing he had not been pressed for the information until he was absolutely certain of its validity. He remained standing, waiting for the further response. 'And how do they intend delivering this weapon which they may or may not have in the near future?'

'With an Indonesian missile,' he answered, quietly. He watched the look of disbelief grow as the President's mouth fell open.

'The hell you say!' he exploded, jumping to his feet as the blood pumped from his face. 'You confirmed that goddamn project had been discontinued!' he accused, loudly, almost losing control. 'For chrissakes, Allan, are you now telling me that the Indons have resurrected that project alone, without the Japs, and without our knowledge?' he asked in disbelief.

'Indications are...' Director Cox started.

'To hell with your goddamn indications,' the President roared, 'just talk straight!'

'Mr President, I have already given this the highest priority. One of the reasons we believe that China is lining up with India is because they, too, are aware of Indonesia's Bandung project. Beijing would not wish to see them armed with any rocket capacity, let alone ICBMs.'

'ICBMs! How did they manage to acquire the technology once the Japs withdrew? I thought we had put an end to all that?' the President asked, openly furious.

'This is why I believe the Chinese might be tempted to take advantage of any move the Indians have planned. The ICBM technology has been handed to them by our old friends in Iraq,' Allan Cox admitted.

'What!'

'Iraq was given the technology for the Chinese *Long March* series when Beijing was desperate to avoid disruption to its Middle East oil supplies. It obviously worked. Iraq has developed its rocket industry well beyond that of its *Scud* capabilities as we discovered during *Desert Storm*.'

'How did Jakarta access the technology?' spluttered the President.

'Not difficult, when you consider the religious affiliations. We shouldn't lose sight of the fact that Indonesia is the world's largest Moslem society. The two countries are not just tied together because of their oil reserves.'

'Why would the Iraqis inform the Chinese?' the President asked, already aware of the answer. 'Why would they do that?'

'We don't know, sir,' the CIA director responded, lamely.

'And how far advanced are the Indonesians with this project?'

'We expect to have confirmation within two weeks. This I can promise you, Mr President. Whatever the Indonesians have hidden away in their Bandung Research center will not be secret for long. We have men on the ground as we speak, and they are doing everything possible to infiltrate their security.

'Why didn't you come to me before, Allan?' the President asked, sharply. The intelligence chief gathered his thoughts before responding.

'There seemed little point in coming to you with something the Agency couldn't substantiate. You would most probably have ordered us to determine the veracity of our intelligence, which is what we are doing, now, as we speak.' He drew in a deep breath, then continued.

'Give me the two weeks I need to establish beyond doubt that we have something to really concern us, before throwing it open for general discussion. I'm not even convinced that the credibility of our sources in Indonesia has not been tainted by earlier misinformation.'

He watched the President's blood pressure ease slowly, as he lowered himself back into his chair. The President fell silent, his mood deliberative as he considered what he had just learned. If the information was correct, this would change his country's entire perspective in relation to America's position in Asia. He needed to think. And he needed to take time alone to decide what action would be necessary should Indonesia's nuclear capabilities be confirmed.

He swore under his breath. The United States was expected to play the role of International Policeman again! When the Japanese had withdrawn from their earlier commitments to the Indonesians, the Presidential advisers had all agreed that the development of Indonesia's future delivery systems had been successfully frustrated.

Angry to the pit of his stomach, he dismissed the director, having instructed him to mobilise all efforts to determine the accuracy of his intelligence. The President then called his Chief of White House Staff to cancel all appointments for the coming days. He would go to Camp David, alone. He had some thinking to do. Once there was evidence confirming or repudiating the world's largest Moslem nation's entry into the Nuclear Club, there was the possibility that the world might soon see a joint Sino-Indian effort to dismantle the Indonesian Republic.

* * * * * *

Federal Reserve Offices

James remained still like some unsmiling Buddha as he listened to the Federal Reserve Bank official's critical comments. James had never enjoyed visiting the Capital; he had found Washington to be cold, and most of the people unreceptive. Most, that is, with the exception of his powerful friends on Capitol Hill.

He glanced sideways at his brother, pleased that Denny, too, was not showing signs of distress under pressure. After years of dealing with government officials, he was not at all concerned with the summons to appear before this officer for preliminary discussions regarding the Lims' offshore banking activities. Had the veiled threat been delivered whilst the former President still occupied the White House, James knew that the official sitting across from him at that moment, would never have been permitted to summon them to Washington D.C.

James Salima remained undisturbed by the innuendo and veiled threats, believing that this further attempt by the Federal Reserve Bank officials to solicit access to records of their dealings in China would simply disappear once he had spoken to the White House aide.

During the meeting, James suggested that the government officer speak directly to the bank's lawyers, insisting that neither he nor his brother, Denny, had committed any offence, that their relationship with the Chinese shipping line and its principals was entirely legal.

The investigator in charge did not react well, visibly annoyed by James's reference to the Lims' powerful connections. The meeting lasted less than fifteen minutes, after which James and Denny Salima departed, leaving the frustrated officer to inform his superiors that he had been unsuccessful in his attempt to pressure the Lim brothers into disclosing more information than the United States Government was, in fact, entitled to. A copy of the official's report was forwarded to the Director, Central Intelligence Agency, where this was added to the substantial file maintained on the Lims' activities in America, and their growing role in providing conduits for the flow of Western technology into Communist China.

Kerry B. Collison

Chapter 23

General Kumar — India

The army's Protocol Officer informed General Rahul Kumar, Chief of Staff of India's Armed Forces, that the Prime Minister had been taken to hospital and that his condition was considered most serious. Army security had phoned from the hospital, only minutes before. Kumar had wasted no time covering the short distance to where the Prime Minister lay dying, his staff car ploughing dangerously through the congested streets between army headquarters and the hospital in record time. Upon arrival, he had marched directly into the building where he was expected, and taken immediately to the Prime Minister's side.

'He doesn't have long, General,' the doctor advised, in a hushed tone, hurrying alongside the country's most senior military officer, whose strides caused him almost to run to keep pace. They approached the intensive care unit where Vijay rested, security officers standing guard on both sides of the door leading into the room, their faces reflecting the seriousness of the situation.

The doctor signalled for the nurses to permit Kumar a few moments with the failing leader. He was heavily sedated and there was nothing more they could do to make Vijay's last moments any more comfortable. The sister in charge bowed her head sadly, fighting back the tears.

'General,' was all she said, acknowledging the army officer, then moving away from where Vijay lay drifting in and out of consciousness.

The general looked down at the Prime Minister. He moved closer and nodded at the second nurse as she moved from her bedside seat, leaving the two great men alone. The doctor followed the women outside and stood, waiting, between the guards.

Kumar placed his left arm on the bed, and rested his hand on the dying man's arm. Vijay's eyelids fluttered, then suddenly opened. Then, as if nothing out of the ordinary had taken place, the Indian Prime Minister smiled, totally at peace with the world. He had little time left, but at least he was no longer in pain.

'Oh, you're here,' the dying leader said, feeling the other man's hand on his arm. He felt the warmth and, with great difficulty, smiled. 'I didn't think I would see you again.'

'You should just lie there and rest,' Kumar said, stricken by the moment. He had never been close to the Prime Minister; they had never been friends. Their lives had caused them to follow different paths, often bringing them into conflict with each other. To Kumar, this person who lay dying before him was not just Vijay Rakesh, but India's Prime Minister and, although he personally had little affinity with the man, he respected him for the office he represented.

'Come closer,' the man in the bed whispered hoarsely. Kumar leaned forward, his hand still on Vijay's arm, feeling bone through the thin hospital gown. 'You must not tell Kumar,' the Prime Minister said, his voice barely audible as he fought to breathe.

Rahul Kumar frowned, then moved his hand slightly. The man was bordering on delirium, the general could tell. He looked over his shoulder but the nurse and doctor stood with their backs to the glass-panelled door.

'It's all right, I'm here,' he said, softly. Vijay's arm moved slightly, and found the general's hand. He squeezed, but there was little strength left in his fingers. Kumar heard him wheeze, and leaned ever closer in order to hear the dying man. He felt Vijay's feeble attempt to squeeze his hand again and he waited, patiently, knowing that the end must be near.

'The.. army.. must..not.. be involved, Imran,' he whispered. Kumar looked at the frail man lying before him. He was puzzled by what he thought he'd heard.

'It's all right, Vijay,' he said, kindly, but curious as to what the man had meant. *Had he said not to tell Kumar?*

'Imran,' the voice called, even more faintly then before. Kumar knew there was little time left. He listened closely as Vijay spoke, his words forming slowly as he struggled to give his dear friend his last instructions. The doctor peered through the door to see if he was needed, and observed that General Rahul Kumar was still with the dying man. He felt a sense of pride as he quietly observed two of India's most powerful men together. One dying, one comforting the other. The nurse caught his eye and the doctor merely shook his head sadly. It would be all over, soon. Several other senior officials hurried in, but the doctor raised his hands and indicated that they were too late. He gestured for them to wait, quietly, for a few moments longer.

The corridor outside where Vijay lay dying became hushed, as those present felt the terrible loss which was about to descend upon them and their country. He may not have been cherished by all, but those who waited outside his room knew that, with Vijay's passing, the man who had worked so tirelessly for the country he loved would be greatly missed.

Kumar remained still, his head close to the Prime Minister's as he listened to the incoherent words trip slowly from Vijay's lips. He was stunned by what he heard, tempted to discount what the man had said in his sedated state. Finally, he heard a soft rattle in the throat and Vijay's spirit departed this world. Kumar rose slowly from the bedside. He looked down at the man's peaceful face. Then he turned, his face grim, and marched determinedly away from the smell of death.

* * * * * *

Centre for Strategic Studies, New Delhi

General Rahul Kumar stepped out of the BMW and moved to climb the steps into the building which housed the Centre. As he attempted to do so, his path was blocked by a row of beggars crowding the steps.

'Get away with you all, or I will give you a bloody hiding,' he challenged officiously, while rocking his head from side to side in the habitual manner of his people. He was in a particularly foul mood, and the beggars must have sensed this, scurrying away quickly, missing limbs and other handicaps in no way impeding their escape. Kumar looked up, sharply, as the portal guards appeared and saluted their unexpected visitor.

India's army Chief of Staff arrogantly touched the brim of his cap with the tip of his baton and stormed through, as the guards jumped forward to open the glass doors obstructing his entry. The general marched further into the building, ignoring startled looks as he continued through the maze of corridors, making his way up to the executive offices on the second level. He continued down the hallway to the door marked 'Officer-in-Charge' and, without hesitating to knock, turned the knob angrily and barged in.

Dr Imran Malhotra looked up in surprise, but made no attempt to rise. He had occupied the Centre's senior chair for more than eight years and had seen such intimidating displays before.

'Good morning, General,' Malhotra said, his voice in no way betraying how he resented the man's arrogance. 'Please take a seat if you wish, or will you not be staying?' he said.

'I will not be bloody staying,' the officer responded, tempted to whack the man sitting before him with the swagger-stick, just to teach him some respect. His eyes narrowed as he struggled to control his temper.

'Doctor, I demand to know why your recommendations regarding India's forward strategy were not first cleared through me!' Imran Malhotra was taken aback. *Could Kumar be possibly referring to the East Indonesian strategy?* Caught off-guard, he struggled for a response. He looked at the volatile man standing before him and knew, immediately, that Kumar had discovered something concerning the navy's proposed expedition to Timor.

Malhotra guessed from the general's presence, and his reaction, that he was obviously not aware of the overall strategy, otherwise he would be banging his stick on the Prime Minister's desk, and not his. He decided to be evasive until he learned just how much Kumar knew.

'The answer is quite simple, General, because the Prime Minister insisted that all communications and reports go directly to him before being viewed by others.' He looked at the intimidating figure before him. Had the situation not been as serious, Imran Malhotra would have enjoyed the general's discomfort. His face clouded, as if he were about to suffer an apoplectic fit.

'You have not made any friends in the military today, Doctor,' Kumar barked, his voice carrying through the thinly partitioned walls, where anxious staff wondered whom they might call should the general become violent. 'I am here to warn you that if you persist in keeping the Armed Forces ignorant of what transpires between this Centre and the Prime Minister's office, then you will find that your future will be very cloudy, indeed!' he warned. Dr Malhotra sighed.

'General, do not threaten me. I am the appointed Head of this Centre. I will do as I am instructed by the Prime Minister. I do not take orders from you, neither do I take orders from others in India's military. If you have not noticed, General, I am a civilian. Please now leave, I find your behaviour totally inappropriate and unacceptable.' Imran Malhotra remained seated as the army Chief of Staff glared furiously. He worried that he might have gone too far. The tall man had removed the baton from under his arm, and was tapping his empty hand with the end of the rod.

General Kumar was most surprised that Imran Malhotra was unaware of what had transpired over the past hour. *My God, he thought suddenly, Malhotra doesn't even know that Vijay is dead!*

He knew of their relationship, which only added to his surprise. No doubt efforts had been made to contact Malhotra but, for one reason or another, he had not been informed of the seriousness of the Prime Minister's condition. Kumar knew that official notification of Vijay's death would not be made public for some hours. The military would need to position itself first, in anticipation of civil unrest. He decided to let the man before him discover the news for himself.

'We are all in this together,' Kumar said. 'You would do well to remember that it will be the army, not the bureaucrats, who will be called upon to make the most sacrifices.' The doctor became concerned. *How much did Kumar know?*

'I believe that you mean, the Armed Forces, General, of which the army is but one component,' Malhotra argued, intent on not permitting the man bully him any further. 'As for service to one's country, I as have many others in similar civilian positions, have devoted my life to serving India. So please do not talk about who has made sacrifices and who has not.'

The general's temper was dangerously close to spilling over. Malhotra could not recall ever having seen such a display by an officer before. Suddenly, there was a blur of movement as Kumar's hand whipped through the air, slamming his baton down furiously on the desk.

'Damn you!' the general yelled, 'damn you to hell!' with which, he turned and stormed out of the Centre. Malhotra's staff heard the general leave, and waited until the sounds of his boots had disappeared before one of them crept cautiously into their chief's office. Imran Malhotra waved the man away, telling him to close the door. For a while he sat deep in thought. Concerned that he had not heard the end of General Rahul Kumar, Imran picked up his phone and asked to be connected to the Prime Minister's personal assistant. It was then he discovered that the lines from his office were out of order, for the fifth time in that week. Frustrated by his country's deteriorating infrastructure, Imran knew that it would be best for him to visit his old friend's office personally, and some minutes later, followed the general out of the Centre.

When Dr Imran Malhotra discovered that India's Prime Minister, Vijay Rakesh, had passed away hours before, and that General Kumar had been in attendance, he panicked, guessing then, how Kumar came to know of their secret Timor strategy. *How much did the general know?* he worried. Imran called Admiral Gopal, and together they went in search of the Deputy Prime Minister.

* * * * * *

United States Embassy, New Delhi

'What do you think?' The question was asked by Ralph Davidson, the Defense Liaison Officer for the DIA. He chewed on the end of his ball-point, a habit which had only developed since joining the Agency.

'I think that Kumar is a very dangerous man, that's what I think,' the CIA station chief replied. Davidson glanced at the other man and wished he could read his thoughts. He had never been comfortable sharing intelligence with these agents; as far as he was concerned, it was too much of a one-way street.

'Did you recommend that we run with him?' he asked. The intelligence chief removed his feet from the Defence Liaison Officer's desk, flicked the toothpick he had been playing with into the waste basket, and stretched.

'I don't see that we have much choice.' He yawned. The briefing had continued through the night. He checked his watch and

JAKARTA

saw that he had missed breakfast in the embassy canteen.

'Let's face it,' he said, 'there aren't too many pro-American leaders in this neck of the woods.' Davidson observed that the other man had already conceded that General Rahul Kumar was likely to become India's next Prime Minister, or President, or whatever. He had never really understood how a country could have both, each elected, and often from different political leanings.

'They'll call it a *coup*,' Davidson suggested. He too felt tired from the marathon discussions. The Ambassador had chaired the meeting, replaying the taped session with General Kumar, India's army Chief of Staff.

'The general says if he calls a State of Emergency, this would give him time to prepare for an election. Where have we heard *that* before?' he asked, with an appropriate sarcasm. The phone rang and Davidson answered.

'Let's go,' he said, wearily, rising to his feet, 'the Ambassador wants us all back, now.' The station chief seemed surprised. He too rose slowly to his feet and tugged at the knot in his tie. 'Seems he has a response already.' The men wandered out of Davidson's office, down the hall though the security gates, and into the East Wing. They were ushered into the Ambassador's office, where they joined the other senior advisers. Davidson looked around at the small group, noticing how exhausted they all appeared.

'We have a response from State, gentlemen,' the Ambassador began, raising the communication he held for all to see. 'The Secretary has advised that, after due consultation with the President and his advisers, we are to make ourselves available to General Rahul Kumar when the time arrives. We are, under no circumstances, to openly support any action which may be interpreted by others as an American commitment to provide for the General's successful attempt to seize power.'

The Ambassador finished reading Washington's response, and remained discussing the situation with his advisers. At noon, he left the Embassy to attend a luncheon being held in honour of the acting Prime Minister, knowing that he would most probably be required to repeat the performance for his successor in the not too distant future.

Chapter 24

Washington — CIA and Michael

Michael returned the file marked '*Indonesia - Rama Nuclear Power Plants*' to Central Registry, checked that the receiving clerk had signed his name off correctly, then went up to the Director's office as instructed.

'Well, what do you think they're up to?' the director asked. He believed he already knew. It was confirmation that he now required.

'They obviously have the capacity to produce sufficient material. It would be difficult for them to disguise what they're doing, though. I read that two of the NPPs will remain under American management, so I don't see any difficulty there. As for the other two enterprises, they are also subject to IAEA inspection. Assuming that the inspectors are doing their jobs, and management teams have not been compromised, then it would be extremely difficult for the Indonesians to remove sufficient quantities of fuel without raising suspicions.'

'What about the Fast Breeder Reactor, *Rama II* ?' Michael was prepared for this question.

'Well, access for inspection has been denied. That's sufficient justification for us to believe that they are most definitely planning to remove fuel. Let's see,' Michael said, referring to notes, '*Rama II*'s reactor would have commenced operations with just under five thousand kilos of uranium. The fast breeder process would produce around three hundred and fifty kilos of surplus Plutonium-239 within eight months.' He looked at the director to ensure that his superior understood. Satisfied, he then continued.

'It would be most unlikely that they would play with their fuel and commence extracting plutonium within, say, a month. Operational staff would realize what was going on immediately. Also, this would be terribly inefficient. The three hundred plus kilos of 'surplus' plutonium would be distributed throughout the core and, to extract it, you must remove, dissolve and process the entire core. It would make more sense to have some of the plant supervisors orchestrate the removal as a normal part of core operations; that way, the plutonium could be siphoned off during processing. They could simply claim processing inefficiencies to account for missing a few kilos at a time.

'Normally, plutonium is accounted for in gram increments, so you can easily see just how difficult it would be to disguise the removal of the required amount. There are many other ways they could camouflage their activities, such as doctoring instrument readings to show that neutron flux was lower than expected, therefore producing less plutonium than anticipated. The International Atomic Energy Agency has identified most of the covert practices rogue operators could employ.'

'As you say, access has already been denied by the Indonesian operators. How much would they need to produce, if that is their intention?'

'Not much,' Michael replied, 'they would probably need about thirty kilos to make a decent weapon. It would not be in the megaton range, but sufficient to destroy a city.'

'How would they hide thirty kilos?' the director asked.

'The density of plutonium for this configuration is such, the entire mass would only be about two litres in size.' Michael saw the surprise and smiled. 'Not that I would recommend it, but you could just about carry it around in a container the size of a shoe box.' The director thought about this.

'Satellites could identify such a supply without too much difficulty,' he stated.

'Sure, but they would be unlikely to leave it lying around. My bet is, if they are producing, there would be an underground storage facility to prevent prying eyes from discovering its existence.' The director understood. The Agency had suspected that Japan might also be disguising its own surplus production, but had been unable to identify where the plutonium might be stored. The IAEA had free access to all of the Japanese Fast Breeder Plants and had not once identified any violations to the International Code.

'Then there is nothing for it but to press for access to *Rama II*

JAKARTA

and take a peek inside their plant. I'm surprised that our friends have been unable to penetrate the Indonesian operation. Having a *friendly* inside the plant would certainly remove any doubt.' Michael knew that he was referring to the CIA. He had never understood how two such similar agencies, both with their own national interests at heart, had managed to generate so much antagonism towards each other.

'We will have to come up with something, soon. Your suggestion to visit is appropriate, Michael. We'll send you over with IAEA credentials. I want you to build your visit around the two American operated plants. In the meantime, we'll twist a few more arms about visiting *Rama II*.' Michael nodded, and rose to leave.

'I'll set up a schedule for your approval,' he said, 'while I'm sifting through the rest of the files relevant to Indonesia.' He then left and returned to Central Registry where he withdrew the first of thirty-seven folders, all related to his brief, and settled down in one of the reading rooms for the day. Each time he finished a file, Michael would return this and withdraw another, continuing the process until he had read more than a dozen. It was approaching early evening when he suddenly sat up, and whistled.

'You crafty old devil!' he said, aloud. The file he had opened was entitled *Indonesia - Rama V - Corporate Details*. Michael sat there staring at the photographs of the principal shareholders and directors of the *Nasihat Corporation*. Memories of his childhood flooded back as the familiar, boyish face stared back at him, almost mockingly. He slapped his leg and laughed, remembering how this man had taken him sailing around the bay during his infrequent visits and, during other opportunities, had taught him how to handle himself on the tennis courts.

Michael was carried back in time to when the loneliness of life without a father would immediately be forgotten whenever this man arrived. He often stayed with Michael and his mother when visiting Melbourne, and always brought with him an atmosphere of bonhomie and excitement.

He looked at the photograph again, then read the biographical data which followed. Michael was surprised to see cross-references to data banks he had not come across before, and noted these for later. Then he settled down and slowly examined the rest of the relevant information. Twenty minutes passed, after which Michael closed the file, deep in thought. He would seek this man's assistance to visit the *Rama II* plant. It was obvious from the file that his mother's old friend had a peripheral relationship with the Indonesian Nuclear Power Plant operators, being a senior director of the *Nasihat Corporation*, which operated *Rama V*. Convinced that he might now have found a way to penetrate the inaccessible plant, Michael took the file back to Central Registry, then returned to his office where he placed a call to Murray Stephenson, in Indonesia.

* * * * * *

Visakhapatnam Naval Base, East Coast of India

In the week following Vijay Rakesh's death, Admiral Krishna Gopal returned to his Eastern Command Headquarters, in Visakhapatnam, and continued with his preparations to take the Indian Navy on its scheduled exercises in the Indian Ocean, which would precede the goodwill visit to New Guinea. He, and the other senior officials, had reached an accommodation with General Kumar. They expected that the acting Prime Minister would be confirmed in his position before the end of that week, after which he would take Vijay's place at the Bali Summit.

Admiral Gopal was indeed proud of the role he had been selected to play in India's future. He had been deeply saddened by the loss of his dear friend, Vijay, but his concerns following the Prime Minister's death had been directed towards the implementation of the strategies formulated under Vijay's leadership.

Once he had received the acting Prime Minister's assurance that he would support the daring move as vigorously as his predecessor, Admiral Gopal had wasted little time returning to his operational command on India's eastern seaboard.

He had personally co-ordinated the selection of ships to accompany his armada. Gopal had ordered two *Rajput* class destroyers from his Western Command bases in Lakshadweep and Karwar, and another from Goa, to join his convoy where they would gather, off the Maldives. The admiral had also decided to increase the number of frigates to twelve, including the three *Godavari* class FFHs, as these were equipped with Sea King helicopters.

He drew these from the Southern Command where five corvettes had already been stationed in preparation for the naval exercise. He had considered increasing the submarine fleet's complement to twelve, but finally elected to leave three of the older *Kursura* class SSs behind in the Visakhapatnam base. Gopal's armada would further consist of two aircraft carriers, including the pride of his fleet, the *INS Indira Gandhi*.

Admiral Gopal smiled as he considered the naval staffing levels. India's Navy had been boosted to almost one hundred thousand, which included ten thousand fleet air arm and marine personnel. During the previous years, his navy had seen considerable growth in its numbers and equipment, and could now boast some of the most sophisticated weaponry available. American, British and Russian equipment adorned the decks of his ships. Ten years before, the United States had sold his government two squadrons of Seahawks, complete with missile capability, and he was confident that these would be put to good use during the second phase of the exercise.

The smaller of his carriers was equipped mainly with Russian MiG 29s and, although these were becoming increasingly difficult to maintain due to the shortage of spare-parts, he believed that their helicopter and VTOL squadrons would provide the support required for the initial phase of the task force's assault. Then, of course, the eighty-thousand tonne aircraft carrier *INS Indira Gandhi*, pride of the Indian Navy, would stand by with its arsenal of modern aircraft, should these become necessary.

Admiral Gopal believed that the Indonesians would walk away from Timor once they realized that the Indian Navy had acted, albeit unilaterally, with world opinion supporting their action. The United Nations had voted in favour of an Indonesian withdrawal, and had been effectively ignored. He believed that the overall strategy would be successful, providing his country with an opportunity to expand its sphere of influence without too much resistance from its neighbours.

Krishna Gopal's mind turned to the army as he considered India's ultimate goal, the rich, fertile land of the under-populated Malay Peninsula. He was no longer concerned that General Kumar might obstruct their plans. It would not have been wise for the acting Prime Minister to consider replacing the army Chief of Staff, as they believed that Kumar's support within the army was far too strong for such a move. The confrontation which had followed Vijay's death-bed disclosure had been bitter indeed, resulting in a stand-off between the government supporters and General Kumar. The army Chief had intimated that he was of a mind to reveal Vijay's plan to the general public, but when he realised that few would believe that he had not, in any way, been involved in the planning, Kumar had rethought his position. Gopal was relieved that at least Kumar had given his assurance that he would not interfere.

They had agreed that, as the army was not to participate in the initial phase of the Timor strategy, then no blame could be attached to Kumar should the ambitious move fail. When they had discussed inviting the Chief of Air Staff to share their confidence, both Malhotra and the acting Prime Minister had opposed such a move, insisting that Air Marshall Gurege not be informed until the navy's mission could be considered a successful *fait accompli*. He would be briefed, finally, once Gopal's armada was positioned off Timor, and Xanana Soares had been safely placed in power.

The admiral was confident that with this initial success his faction would have little difficulty in encouraging others to follow. He believed that their support base would grow quickly, and loyalties would change. Malhotra had suggested that they be patient until this moment arrived, and only then consider removing the obstinate and pro-American Kumar, replacing him with one who would support the final phase of their strategy. They knew that their success in Timor could not be ignored by the army, who, together with India's impressive airforce of over one thousand aircraft, would be encouraged to occupy and control the northern corridors leading into the Malay Peninsula.

When the new borders were redrawn, India would have succeeded in occupying all the rich, fertile rice bowls of Western Malaysia. China would find little resistance when taking the resource rich areas of Eastern Malaysia and Brunei. Indonesia would no longer be in a position to prevent international shipping from passing through its sea lanes as long as the Indian Navy maintained its presence in East Timor and China controlled the South China Sea. Between the two nations, they would control all shipping though Asia, including that of Japan and Australia.

* * * * * *

JAKARTA

Washington, the United States

The National Security Agency Director sat quietly as his driver turned into the White House gates and stopped. Guards moved across, checked through the windows, smiled, then saluted. As he was driven under the building, he could not help but think that the information he held in his hands alone, would be sufficient to silence critics of his agency's substantial, and undisclosed budget. But he knew that the sensitive documents would never be released for public consumption, as these would be destroyed once the President had read and understood their contents.

Through its supervision of the Defence Advanced Research Projects Agency (DARPA), the NSA has been able to create and install a sophisticated global communications system of computers, satellites, telecommunications devices and the latest surveillance technology. Every second of every day, twenty four hours a day, the NSA beats along, as its massive computer network hums almost silently, collecting, correlating, deciphering, analysing spy-satellite imagery and other data, sifting through incredible volumes of wiretap and sensor material, as the never-ending flow continues from the most unlikely sources. This most secret premier cryptographic agency, derived huge financial and computer allocations directly from US military budgets.

The director arrived and was escorted directly to where the President waited. The American leader read through the classified material and handed these back to the NSA Chief.

You really believe that the Chinese are preparing to move?' he asked, still not convinced that the increased signal traffic identified by the NSA's world-wide listening network had proven anything other than a substantial increase in telecommunication activity between the two nations.

'It's mainly military traffic, and our analysts believe that the Indian Navy is keeping the Chinese fully informed of whatever they're doing.'

'Wouldn't it just be possible that they don't wish to ruffle Chinese feathers?' the President asked, wishing it could really be as simple as he suggested.

'The Chinese don't play war games, Mr President,' he suggested. 'Communication traffic between the Chinese Southern, Eastern and

Northern Naval Commands has reached unprecedented levels. Satellite tracking has identified a concentration of activity running from Shanghai down to their ships stationed in the South China Sea. There has not, however, been any real change in their army's status. Our analysts agree that it is unlikely for China to make any further moves territorially, without mobilising its land forces. This is why we believe that we should expect to see such movement at any moment.'

'How much time do we have?' the President asked. The NSA Director had anticipated this question also.

'If what they have in mind is purely a naval action, then not much time at all. At best, probably a week to ten days for them to prepare. It would depend on what targets they had in mind.' The President thought about this, his concern causing the deep lines in his brow to deepen.

'And this would be Taiwan?' he asked, fearing the answer. The director shook his head.

'That would not account for the increased traffic between India and China. Beijing would not need to inform anyone if they intended moving against Taiwan; they would simply charge in and hope that we remained away from the conflict. There has been nothing to indicate any specific targets, or at least, not yet,' he answered, also concerned with his analysts' failure to interpret what the heavy COMINT traffic really meant.

The President remained silent, thinking through the possible scenarios developing on the other side of the world. He knew that there was little that could be done until further intelligence confirmed whatever the two governments were plotting together. He finished discussing the developments with the NSA Director who then left, promising to keep the White House informed as the situation changed. Then the President summoned William Deakin, his Secretary for State.

* * * * * *

Jakarta, Indonesia

The Vice President ate sparingly in the *Bapak's* presence. It had become a tradition for the President to preside over Saturday dinners with all of his family in attendance. Even though Major General (retired) Sujono Diryo knew how the President doted on his favourite daughter, he felt ill at ease sitting alongside his wife at this command performance.

'Jono, you're not eating,' his mother-in-law scolded, playfully. He smiled and said nothing.

'Maybe he has been eating too well outside,' one of the President's sons quipped, bringing a scowl from his sister. There had been great consternation within the First Family when Sujono had unwisely become entangled in an extra-marital relationship involving a vivacious and well known Indonesian actress. The Capital had been a buzz with the gossip, as the most public affair continued. Those closest to Sujono had appealed for him to consider his position, while the beautiful starlet's friends applauded her audacious fling. Then, without warning, all levels of Jakarta's society were rocked when the girl had been discovered, murdered, on the back seat of her car.

Everyone believed they knew who was responsible for the star's death, but none even dared whisper, except in the privacy of their homes, that a jealous wife had issued the order. The President had been shielded from the sordid affair. The *Bapak* rarely read newspapers anymore, never listened to the news, and was almost entirely dependent on those around him to keep him informed as to what was happening in the capital and the world in general.

When gossip relating to the affair first broke, none dared mention such defamatory stories in the Indonesian press. In private, Indonesians jokingly referred to the torrid affair as *kumpul kerbo*, and were not overly critical of the Vice President, nor his reprehensible behaviour. The Australian press, however, had not been as reluctant to run the story. Editors exposed the affair in their tabloids, nation-wide.

The President's daughter had moved quickly, summoning the Commander of the Jakarta Garrison and soliciting his services. That evening, her husband's lover, one of Indonesia's more familiar screen idols, was stabbed to death and dumped unceremoniously on the back-seat of the car which the President's son-in-law had given to her just weeks before. The city's inhabitants mourned her death, but none dared come forward to identify her killers, or even suggest that an investigation take place to bring those responsible to trial. To do so would have been suicidal. The President's daughter glared at her brother for having made the remark.

'*Be careful of your mouth!*' Sujono's wife warned, waving her fork menacingly in her brother's direction. Her father had no idea whatsoever of his son-in-law's infidelity, and his daughter used this to keep Sujono in line. Although Indonesian Muslims were still entitled to take up to four wives, very few amongst the educated class continued to practice this right. When Sujono had learned of his lover's demise, he had known immediately who had been responsible. He accepted his loss quietly, relieved only that his wife had not discovered his other marital misdemeanours.

The President smiled at his family, pleased that they had all gathered together in his home again.

'*Sujono?*' he started, watching his daughter fill his son-in-law's plate with more *rendang* and *nasi*. He waved for her to stop, and she added another spoonful and smiled caringly. The servants were never permitted to serve the food on these occasions.

'*Sujono, is everything now in order with Bali?*' asked the *Bapak*. Sujono swallowed slowly. The President was referring to the Summit. For weeks there had been diplomatic wrangling over the dates, who should or should not attend, who would have seniority during the discussions, where they were going to stay, and so on. His hours were filled with endless messages and calls for which he, as Vice President, had become responsible. Then, having selected several dates for the venue, they had discovered that the Balinese calendar would clash with the Summit, and that *Hari Nyepi* would occur during the three-day conference.

Sujono knew that it would be unthinkable to expect the international leaders to be present in Bali while everything ground to a halt to celebrate the *Quiet* Day according to Balinese custom. He knew just how seriously the Balinese practised their customs, remembering that village police paraded around on that day, making sure tradition was observed by all. In the more isolated pockets of the tourist haven, Sujono knew that even generators were turned off for the day, cutting power in observance of the custom.

'*They have agreed to the dates as you requested, Pak,*' he answered. It had been decided that the Indian Prime Minister would preside over what the world press had hailed as the Bali Peace Summit, and South Africa, Australia and what was left of the ASEAN membership, had all agreed to the agenda.

The conference was being promoted as essential to restoring regional stability, although few outside Asia believed this would contribute in any significant way. A virtual trade war had broken out between Australia and its northern neighbours and, although the Indonesian sea lanes were strictly monitored by Indonesian warships, oil shipments continued to pass through the archipelago finding their way easily into China. The Japanese continued to enjoy unhindered passage of their vessels, their trade relationships with the Indonesians not at all diminished in importance in spite of the failed nuclear power plant co-operation agreement.

The Timor Shelf oil and gas concessions continued to feature as one of the stumbling blocks between Australia and its giant neighbour, and Indonesia's insistence that East Timor remain an integral part of the Republic was rapidly losing political support. Both Sujono and the President agreed that they had to at least appear responsive to their neighbouring nation's requests. ASEAN was in danger of losing more of its members, and the Palace knew that they needed more time to reposition themselves as a regional military power, believing that their Fast Breeder Plant and their secret installations in Bandung, once fully developed, would realize their dream for the Indonesian people.

'And Rama II?' the President asked. Sujono knew that the plant was on-line already, and the commissioning process complete. The President insisted that the plant's official inauguration should coincide with the Bali Summit. It made little difference to the plant's operation, one day being as acceptable as the next. The Vice President had been a regular visitor to the high-security operation; the plant's operation, although under Russian supervision, had fallen directly under his control.

The operating team had included a small number of Eastern Bloc technicians whose responsibility for training Indonesian engineers had all but been concluded. Sujono had to accept that there were not enough skilled Indonesian technicians to manage the facility effectively without the remaining Russian support. Sujono believed that he would require those foreign experts for no more than another year, after which the plant's operation would be totally under Indonesian management.

The one thousand hectare site had the finest security money

could buy. The troops employed had been specially trained for this duty and were paid handsomely, well in excess of their standard army pay. These soldiers had been hand-picked by officers loyal to him, officers who had been, in many cases, more senior when he had first caught the President's daughter's eye. Sujono glanced across the table at his wife, visualising how she would present in the following years. She was not an attractive woman. He had known many others whose temperament and beauty far exceeded the homely girl he had married, but none of these could give him the key to the power that would now most surely be his. He realized that his often, indiscreet and flirtatious behaviour could easily endanger his position, and that he should be far more circumspect in these liaisons if he wished to succeed.

* * * * * *

Sujono expected to be the next President of Indonesia. His father-in-law had all but served his two, five-year terms after challenging and winning leadership, then governing the country as Acting President for a number of years, before calling elections to legitimise his position in power.

When Sujono had been appointed to replace his ailing predecessor, he realized that the President was merely ensuring continuity of his own rule, expecting to govern in some defacto manner once his son-in-law had been elected. There was little doubt in his mind that this would be so, for Sujono had already secured the support of *Golkar*, the ruling party in government. There would be only minor opposition to his appointment, he knew. The President had seen to that, with the incarceration of most political opponents over the years, and a controlled press, there was rarely any visible dissent directed against the country's leadership.

Sujono accepted that his fortunes had changed primarily due to General Seda's demise. The powerful man's death had further exacerbated existing tensions between Australia and Indonesia, and had contributed to a breakdown in negotiations concerning the disputed Timor Shelf oil and gas concessions. There was little doubt in Sujono's mind that his circumstances could have been radically different had the powerful Seda not fallen victim to the incredible Canberra bombing. Seda had been mooted to fill the position of

Vice President; Sujono considered how fate had presented him with the opportunity, and how he had not hesitated to grasp the golden ring. Earlier in his career, his experience with the Japanese and knowledge of weaponry had made him an obvious choice, at least to General Seda, to control security at the Bandung Research center.

Sujono had become aware of the late general's association with the Japanese Military only during his tour as Defense Attaché in Tokyo. He had not realized, then, that Seda was grooming him to carry out Indonesia's secret research and development programme in conjunction with the Japanese. At the appropriate time, and prior to his appointment as Ambassador to Australia, Seda had Sujono recalled to Indonesia, where he had been appointed by Seda as Officer in Charge of the H-3B's joint development, under the auspices of what had formerly been known as the Habibie Aerospace Centre.

He had reported to Seda that it would be impossible to maintain secrecy regarding their project unless a dedicated location be built specifically for this purpose. Seda had not taken long to decide that the construction of a dual-purpose facility would be more appropriate, and that this should be located within reasonable access to Bandung. They had spent considerable time examining possible sites, finally agreeing that the most suitable location was that of an old Dutch gold mining concession, thirty kilometers from the provincial capital.

The secret installation demanded the most stringent security, and Sujono had successfully implemented procedures which had ensured that none outside a limited number of technicians and military personnel, would ever become aware of what really transpired in the research centre. Within months of his return from Japan, he had been promoted to Major General, and the President had been most pleased with his son-in-law's advancement.

* * * * * *

'You will both be in attendance for the inauguration?' he heard the President ask.

'Most certainly, Bapak,' he replied, dutifully. World attention would be focused on the Bali Summit, and the Palace had orchestrated for the *Rama II* commissioning ceremony to take place

during the formal gathering of world leaders. Sujono knew that the President had considered attending the plant's inauguration, but had accepted that protocol demanded his presence in Bali. Sujono understood that his leader had not been keen to go, annoyed at having been pressured into permitting the East Timorese refugee into Indonesia to attend the conference.

Sujono listened to the President's argument, that he had only agreed to Xanana's presence once he had been assured that his acquiescence would not be construed as acknowledgement of the legitimacy of the so-called government-in-exile.

'It will be a proud day for us all, Jono,' the President suggested, and Sujono understood precisely what was going through the *Bapak's* mind. While he was in Bali as Head of State, his daughter would be officiating alongside her husband, the Vice President, demonstrating the powerful grip the First Family maintained over the land. And Sujono knew that he was an integral part of that power, as long as he remained in favour. He looked across at his wife and, conscious that the President was watching them both closely, Sujono smiled lovingly at the President's daughter.

* * * * * *

Washington — the Oval Office

Secretary for State William Deakin remained expressionless, thinking, while opposite him the President waited, impatiently, tapping the desk with the *keris* shaped letter-opener, a gift from the Malaysian Ambassador to the First Lady some months before.

'I'm afraid it's time to decide just how far we wish to go,' Deakin finally said, referring to their earlier discussion. 'We seem to be rapidly running out of options.' He looked at his old friend and sympathised with his dilemma. The United States President would have to decide within days on one of two options. He could commit his country's forces to the Asian theatre and risk jeopardising American interests, or do nothing, thereby creating a military vacuum which would undeniably be filled by either India or China. It was imperative that the United States not lose access to the Ombar-Wetar Straits for its own national security and, they both believed, their Australian allies.

'Can we be certain that this General Kumar will not be in a position to gain control without the Indian Navy?' the President asked, fearing he already knew the answer. Deakin nodded, confirming his fears.

'Krishna Gopal is a dedicated naval officer, totally loyal to the new Prime Minister. It appears that it was Admiral Gopal who acted as Vijay Rakesh's emissary to China, before Vijay died. There is no love lost between Gopal and the Army, particularly Rahul Kumar. If the General is to be successful, he will need to have Gopal's ships return to their Indian bases where Kumar can seize control. Without the navy, he would be defeated.'

They had been caught by surprise when satellite intelligence from the NSA had alerted them to the Indian Navy's move. Throughout the week, as the armada had taken shape, the President's advisers had urged him to press the Singapore Government to accept the American Seventh Fleet's presence in their harbour. Diplomatic overtures had all but stalled; the Singaporeans were not convinced that the United States naval presence would please Jakarta, and had vacillated over the American request.

'How far south of Indonesia could they be at the time of the Summit?' The President had asked the question earlier when the Joint Chiefs had been present. It wasn't that he had forgotten, he merely required confirmation that the Indian Navy would still be sailing in international waters.

'Ten hour's steaming,' Deakin answered, 'less if they wished to split their convoy.' The President rested his chin on one hand, deep in thought. Within two weeks the Bali Summit would take place. India's goodwill naval visit to Papua New Guinea could not have been more poorly timed. It appeared that Port Moresby had been miffed when not included in the Bali forum.

The New Guinea Prime Minister had been easily persuaded to host the visit, expecting to distract world attention away from the Bali Summit. India's clever use of the opportunity to move its navy through international waters during such a sensitive period was, to say the least, provocative. The Americans had suggested to General Kumar that he take pre-emptive action, immediately, but he had refused to accelerate his original plan to move against the Indian leadership until the now confirmed Prime Minister was away, attending the Bali Summit.

'Do you agree with the NSA assessment?' the American leader asked. The President had insisted that all intelligence departments and the Joint Chiefs attend the earlier briefing. The Oval Office had been filled with his advisers from the CIA, NSA, DIA, the Joint Chiefs and Deakin, from State.

'We can't afford to ignore the intelligence. China obviously understands the opportunity created by India. They might just use the moment to swing across, while our attention has been distracted, and hit Taiwan,' he said, disappointed that the State Department had missed all the apparent signs over the past weeks. There had almost been a sense of apathy in relation to the Taiwan-China question. They accepted that it would only be a matter of time before China used force to occupy the island, even though earlier tactics of intimidation had failed.

Taiwan's economy continued to outstrip its neighbour's, sending the Taiwanese reserves to a record high of one hundred and seventy billion dollars which, ironically, presented the industrialised nation as an even greater prize than before.

The President remained deep in thought, depressed by events which had worsened over past weeks, threatening Asia's stability and America's markets. Then there was the problem of Australian security, and the ANZUS pact. China, he knew, might consider the under-populated country and its abundant resources as imperative to her future survival. Australia and the United States continued to enjoy more than adequate mineral reserves well beyond that of their envious Asian neighbours.

A world dominated in the East entirely by China and India occupied his thoughts, and the President wished he could escape, once again, to deliberate more on the question in the comfort of Camp David. Time constraints, he knew, would not permit such luxury. He had to sanction the Joint Chief's recommendations or find an alternative solution to sending American troops back into Asia.

He recalled the last occasion when an American President had entertained such a commitment. The United States had lost fifty thousand lives, and the communists had swallowed all of Vietnam. No, he would not send American men and women to the defense of another corrupt Asian government. There would have to be another solution. He looked across at his friend and was comforted by the knowledge that Deakin would remain loyal, regardless of the decisions he might take. He rubbed his weary face and sighed.

'I don't think I could support the Joint Chiefs' option,' was all he said. Deakin looked at the President, understanding his reasons for taking this decision. They were alike, and the Secretary knew how difficult it must have been for the man not to take the easier option. He smiled sadly and rose slowly to his feet.

'I'll leave it to you to let him know,' Deakin said, feeling that they had all failed. He would not be involved in whatever followed. Those were the unspoken rules. He turned and left the Oval Office, his shoulders bent in disappointment. For a long moment, the President of the United States sat alone, his eyes closed in silent prayer, as he asked his God for forgiveness. Then, with the calm of one whose conscience was clear, he sanctioned the executive action as proposed by Allan Cox, the Director of the Central Intelligence Agency.

* * * * * *

They had spent the day lazing around in his Washington apartment, watching television, half-undressed, snacking when the need arose. Both knew that the discussion which had ended abruptly the evening before, was far from finished. Michael offered Ratna one of the snacks but she ignored the offering.

'Well, Michael, are we going together or not?' she asked, turning away, busying herself with some invisible spot on her naked knee. She picked away at nothing, waiting for his response.

'I'll be tied up the whole time, Ratna, and you'll only become even more annoyed,' he answered. He did not want to leave her behind, angry; but he also could not afford to have her tied to his coat-tails the entire time he was in Indonesia. Due to increased political tensions in the Asian theatre, it had become more imperative that he somehow arrange to visit the *Rama II* plant.

Michael had spent some time with his Director being briefed on what was happening in the region. He had been surprised to learn that the White House had placed the highest priority on all activity related to missions involving South East Asia, until he learned of the intensified communication traffic between China and India. As one of the more respected Asian analysts, even he had been caught off-guard by the recent and intriguing developments. Then there was the interesting question of Murray Stephenson's cross-referenced files. When he had attempted to access these, he had found that it was the CIA which had prevented his delving further in Murray's past. He had raised this problem with his superiors but was quietly told that the information held by the Central Intelligence Agency would not be released to him, and that it would be best if he just dropped any further enquiries into the Australian's past.

'I'm going, anyway,' Ratna said, defiantly, turning her hand to inspect her nails. She was furious with Michael. He had announced that he would be gone for several weeks and, when pressed, he had revealed that he would be visiting Jakarta, and perhaps even Bali. Ratna could not understand his reluctance to have her accompany him, especially as it would have meant an opportunity for them to spend some time with her family in Jakarta.

'Look, Ratna,' he said, wearily, 'it's not that I don't want you to come with me, you should know better than that. It's just that I'm going to be up to my ears in meetings with dull engineers, and going to dull functions with their dull wives, and I know you would be bored to death. Why don't we compromise? We could fly out together, and you could remain with your family in Jakarta while I go on my inspection visits without you.' Ratna considered this, then looked coyly over her shoulder from where she sat, her knees under her chin.

'Okay,' she smiled, a little too mischievously, and he sensed he'd made a mistake. She had given in too readily. He leaned over and placed his strong hands on both sides of her light brown, sun-tanned neck, and rubbed gently. Moments later she placed her hands on his, and he stopped. 'You will have time to come and meet Aunty?' she asked, almost childishly.

'Of course!' he laughed, pleased now that they would be travelling together, at least, to Jakarta. Ratna turned and faced him, still on her knees. She stretched up and kissed him warmly, and then held him tightly, as if he might escape.

'And then you will take me on to Bali?' she asked, knowing that he would say yes. Michael sighed, and broke away, holding Ratna at arms' length.

'Okay,' he said, suddenly realizing that he had already lost the argument before it had begun. It seemed that their discussions inevitably ended with Ratna winning her point, or having her way. He admired her strong-willed personality, but admitted that sometimes Ratna could be a little difficult to get along with. They were deeply in love, and Michael realized that he might soon be required to make another life decision, one that he had put off years before. He looked over at the woman who had so totally captured his heart, and was pained that he had lost those years with her, to another, when they could just as easily have been his.

One week before the Bali Summit was scheduled to commence, Michael Bradshaw and Ratna Sari boarded the flight which would take them into Asia and Indonesia. Before their flight had even left American airspace, Admiral Krishna Gopal's fleet had already assembled at the designated rendezvous point, and begun steaming in an easterly direction, south of Java.

* * * * * *

Virginia

In Langley, Virginia, the CIA Director checked his desk one final time before moving down the hallway to the room which housed the shredders. He extracted the loose pages from the blank cover file, and fed these, one by one, through the efficient machine. Satisfied that he had destroyed all record of the damaging evidence relating to his covert activities, the Director then returned to his office and continued with his duties, as if nothing of any real import had transpired.

On the other side of the globe, in what was once American-friendly territory, two men moved under the cover of darkness, grunting as they lifted the stores they would require, and loaded these into the steel-hulled ship.

'Shit!' the bearded man cussed, drawing his hand back quickly from under the box. He waved to the other man to place his end down for the moment, while he placed the injured finger in his mouth. The salty taste of blood did not alarm the ship's captain. He could tell that the wound was relatively minor compared to those he had suffered in the past. He wiped his hand against the side of his filthy trousers, then nodded to Mohammed Fuad that he was ready to continue. Silently, and without further event, they loaded their deadly cargo. Less than an hour later, when they had finished, the two men crawled into the forward bunks and immediately went to sleep.

As the early morning sun captured the tranquil setting, Filipino villagers wandering down to the sandy shore across the wide, deep, tropical lagoon ignored the ship's silhouette as it glided, silently, away from the idyllic setting. On board, Captain Dave Bartlett accepted the hot, steaming, black coffee from Fuad, and settled down for the first leg of a long voyage, which would end in Bali, the Island of Gods.

Chapter 25

Ratna and Michael in Jakarta

Ruswita hoped she had not been too obvious. She had found it extremely difficult to sit opposite the beautiful and vibrant young woman, knowing that she was her daughter, without demonstrating a mother's pleasure. As she viewed Michael Bradshaw with critical eyes, Ruswita was forced to admit, silently, that Ratna Sari had done very well in her selection of companions.

Their guest had been escorted into the main lounge, Ruswita's eyes twinkling as she observed Michael's reaction to the Van Gogh and other collector's items which were placed, inconspicuously, around the already overcrowded room. They had talked for hours together, after which she had insisted that he remain for dinner. It had already been arranged; Ruswita had wished to examine her daughter's beau before issuing the invitation. Over the years she had had the opportunity to meet many foreigners, and found their indifference to local customs or arrogance towards Asians most offensive. She was most pleased with the cultured man whom, she hoped, would make Ratna finally settle down and have children.

There was something about Michael which reminded her of another, but Ruswita put this down to the fact that so many of his race looked familiar, especially to her failing eyes. They had spoken about Indonesia and Asia in general, and Ruswita had been delighted with Michael's obvious knowledge of regional affairs.

The afternoon meeting had gone well, so well in fact that Ruswita had felt no desire to escape and take her customary afternoon break, alone, upstairs. Lani had also been introduced to Ratna's beau, and Ruswita was pleased that the woman had remained reasonably silent during Michael's visit. Ruswita had grown increasingly concerned about her old friend's ability to communicate, and about

Lani's moody silences. Recently, she had noticed, Lani would remain silent for days on end, never so much as uttering a single word. She knew that Lani missed Ratna; but there again, so did she. Their home had not been the same since the children had all married and established their own homes, leaving the two ageing women alone.

Denny and James remained in the United States, and called only when business demanded that they communicate with Ruswita. Although Benny and his family were domiciled in Jakarta and still visited regularly, this had been of little interest to Lani who often remained, a recluse in her own small domain at the rear of the Lim mansion.

* * * * * *

'Michael, have some more *laksa*, she insisted, surprising the attending servants. None of them had ever seen *Ibu Ruswita* in this mood before. The *pembantu* hurried towards the table at Ruswita's direction.

'Thank you, thank you,' Michael protested, holding his hands up to prevent the woman from refilling his large, empty bowl. Delicious as it was, the curried soup had already sent messages to his delicate stomach, warning him not to over-indulge. He looked on in dismay as his bowl was replenished, wondering if he would offend by not finishing the spicy noodle and prawn dish. Michael glanced across at his hostess and smiled diplomatically, wondering how the women managed to remain so slim in this country.

From the moment he had set foot in the warm, hospitable environment, he had enjoyed the company of the magnificent woman he had heard so much about through Ratna. Upon his arrival, Michael had been ushered into *Ibu Ruswita's* home and doted upon, almost embarrassingly, like some long-lost child.

Michael was astonished to see the incredible wealth displayed casually around the guest lounge room. He was positive that the painting he had seen leaning against the wall near one corner was a Chagall.

* * * * * *

JAKARTA

They had flown into Jakarta's Soekarno-Hatta Airport that morning. Michael had been pleased to finally leave Kuala Lumpur and the toxic haze which covered the unfortunate city. He had found the polluted air impossible to breathe, and understood the extent of the problem once they were airborne, heading for Singapore.

Indonesia's forest fires in Borneo and Sumatra had thrown a blanket of smoke across most of the Malay Peninsula and the South China Sea. Asia's financial centre, Singapore, had not avoided the pollution. As they drove around sight-seeing, Michael observed that the brown cloud had settled dangerously over the entire magnificent city, its density so thick in places that even the many skyscrapers were hidden from view. They spent two days at the Raffles Hotel before continuing their journey to Indonesia, saddened that their time in Singapore had been spoiled by the smoky conditions.

Upon arrival at Jakarta's international airport, Michael followed Ratna through the formalities, smiling at how quickly officials moved to assist the beautiful Eurasian woman and her friend. He had not known at the time that he was witnessing a touch of the Salima power at work. Ruswita's personal assistant had made just one call, and the officials were prepared for Ratna's arrival.

Outside the terminal, a white-uniformed driver jumped from a metallic blue Mercedes 600 and barked orders for the porters to load their luggage, then drove his *tamu* at dangerous speeds into the city. Several times Michael was tempted to ask the driver to slow down. Each time he moved to speak, though, it seemed that the driver's hand would hit the horn, and so he gave up and remained in anxious silence until they arrived at their destination.

Michael watched as the servants strained to lift her baggage from the luggage compartment. Then the security guard took hold of Michael's cases.

'No, please leave those there,' Michael said, surprising them all. He felt uncomfortable being placed in this situation, having expected to go on to his hotel after dropping Ratna at her home.

'Michael?' Ratna frowned, wondering what was going on. She removed her sunglasses and placed one hand on her hip, then suddenly removed this when she remembered where she was, and how offensive the gesture would be considered in Indonesia.

'I'm sorry, Ratna, I had no idea that you expected me to stay with your family. You knew that I'd booked a room at the Grand Hyatt,' he said, observing from her reaction that she was annoyed with him. She strolled around the car, took his hands in hers, then looked directly up, into his eyes.

'Michael, don't do this, please!' she whispered, but loudly enough so the servants could hear, further embarrassing him.

'Ratna, I have to stay at the hotel. That's where I will be contacted by the government agencies. Be reasonable!' he pleaded, irritated that he had been placed in this predicament. When the Mercedes had pulled up at the home and servants had descended upon the car, Michael immediately guessed what was happening. He could not permit Ratna to take charge; that would severely impede his ability to remain mobile and unencumbered.

They continued arguing for several minutes, Ratna still insisting that they stay together, at her family's home. Michael remaining adamant, determined that he be taken to his hotel.

'It will only be for a few days, Michael,' Ratna had come close to stamping her foot, tempted to tell him how angry she really was but, at that moment, *Ibu Ruswita* ventured out, and introduced herself. She had been listening with a certain amount of pleasure as the two stood arguing in her driveway. They both became silent as she spoke.

'Ratna, Michael has already arranged to stay somewhere else and you should accept that,' she quietly admonished. Michael was relieved by her intervention, and promised to ring once he had checked in and unpacked. Offended, Ratna turned in a huff, crossed her arms in one of her familiar tantrums, and ignored Michael's wave as the Mercedes drove away. Ruswita clucked happily as she placed her arm around her beautiful daughter and they entered the Lim home.

* * * * * *

Michael had welcomed the invitation to dine with the Salima family. He had been delightfully surprised to discover that the invitation had included *Ibu Lani,* and that he was to be entertained in their home. Slightly concerned that his earlier refusal to stay might have offended, Michael returned to the Lim mansion with three freshly cut bouquets of tiger orchids, one for each of the ladies.

JAKARTA

His concerns were soon allayed, as he was warmly welcomed and treated as if he had enjoyed a long association with the family. Before his evening visit, he had really no comprehension as to the enormous wealth Ratna's aunt had gathered. He was embarrassed, and knew from Ratna's coy expression that she enjoyed her lover's surprise when he discovered who Aunt Ruswita actually was with respect to the international financial community.

The thought had crossed his mind that he could have so easily used his department's resources to search for information relating to the family. As he listened to Madame Ruswita Salima outline her group's activities, Michael experienced a sense of inadequacy in the face of such wealth and position, which far exceeded anything he had known.

Not once during his visit had he observed any visible sign that the expensive paintings and other *object d'art* were of any great importance to their owner. Michael had spent more than three hours being entertained by the pleasant Aunt Ruswita, before he understood that she was, in fact, the matriarch of such a formidable corporate powerhouse, known internationally as the Salima Group. He had read of the conglomerate's wealth and power, and now felt more than a little ridiculous, considering his intelligence analysis background, that he had not associated Ratna's Aunt Ruswita with the powerful Indonesian conglomerate.

'Ratna,' Ruswita said, smiling happily across the table, 'you should take Michael up to visit our mountain resort.'

'I will, Aunty, I will,' she promised, enjoying the attention. Michael observed Ratna's mother, Lani, from the corner of his eye and wondered why she played such an inconspicuous role in the proceedings. 'Michael will be …' Ratna was cut off by Michael.

'Thank you, Mrs Salima,' he interjected. He did not wish to lose control of his itinerary, and he suspected this could easily happen with these hospitable people. 'I would really enjoy that, but I don't think I'll have the time this visit.' He noticed Ratna pout, and Madame Salima smile. *Was she enjoying the sight of the strong-willed young woman being put in her place?*

'You will be visiting the *Rama II* plant?' Madame Ruswita asked innocently, with which Michael almost dropped his spoon in surprise. He was startled by Madame Ruswita's directness. From her influential position, she would surely have been aware of the secrecy surrounding the former Japanese-controlled plant, and that IAEA inspections had been forbidden.

'I have not received approval for an inspection, Madame,' he answered. Michael had read the historical background on the tender process associated with the first five *Rama* plants. Old Lim had been very clever, not revealing his company's position until the plants neared completion. It seemed that, by disguising their ownership in this manner, Salima was able to avoid accusations of cronyism. When Salima's controlling position had been revealed, it had been disclosed in such a manner as to suggest that the acquisition had been a recent undertaking to assist with budgetary overruns. The market had reacted favourably at the time, driving the family fortunes to even greater heights.

Michael was not entirely comfortable knowing that his lover was this close to Indonesia's most powerful family. He knew there were three boys, the heirs, who assisted Madame Salima with her empire. He sensed there was a bond between Ratna and her aunt, one which appeared stronger than her relationship with her mother, Lani. Michael put this down to the fact that her Aunt Ruswita had no daughter of her own.

He glanced over at Lani, thinking how different she was to her sister. One was a power-house of energy, while the other a reluctant participant in the proceedings before her. He found himself staring as Lani caught his eye. Immediately he remembered that this was considered rude in the Orient, and glanced away to hide his embarrassment.

'Perhaps once the plant has been officially opened, they will approve a visit,' Ruswita suggested.

'Let's hope that this is so,' was all he said, not wishing to reveal too much to his astute hostess. It was apparent to Michael that she would most definitely have the power to arrange for such a visit. But as an offer of assistance had not been forthcoming; he did not press. During these few hours, Michael's understanding of where he was had become much clearer, and he decided to proceed cautiously.

'Do you have any other friends here, in Indonesia, Michael?' Ruswita asked.

'Not really,' he answered, not wishing to associate himself openly with Murray Stephenson; such a relationship might be misconstrued by others. He had to avoid being seen associating with any specific interest groups for the duration of his inspection tour, at least until securing an opportunity to visit Rama II. He knew that it would be inconceivable for Murray and this powerful woman to not have met; Jakarta was a throbbing commercial hub, and as the two parties had common interests, Michael was absolutely certain that somehow Murray had played a role in the Lim's acquisition of the *Rama V* nuclear power plant. After all, Murray's name, along with that of his Singaporean partner, Peter Wong, were registered as the two largest shareholders in the *Nasihat Corporation*, the foreign partners in the *Rama V* joint venture, and now it belonged entirely to the Salima Group.

Michael's experience warned him to be careful. He was moving in unfamiliar territory filled by wealthy and very powerful people, with Ratna's aunt amongst those who enjoyed the most influence. Michael glanced across the table and saw that *Madame Ruswita* was observing him closely. In that moment he experienced a strange sense of foreboding, almost as if old Lim Swee Giok had been standing behind his chair, watching over Michael's shoulder to ensure that he brought this family no harm.

* * * * * *

As the late evening breeze brushed dark monsoonal clouds aside revealing the brilliance of a rare January moon, Ratna awoke suddenly and sat up, startled, her heart pumping in fear.

'*Who is it?*' she called, terrified, her fingers searching desperately for the familiar switch.

'*Na, Na, don't be afraid,*' Lani replied, '*it's only me. Don't be frightened!*'

'*What is it?*' Ratna asked her mother, finally locating the light switch, and illuminating the room. She was surprised to see Lani sitting at the end of her bed. She checked the bedside clock. It was not even two o'clock.

'*Is something the matter, 'Bu?*' she asked, concerned that she might be ill. Lani moved to her side and wrapped her arms around Ratna, then placed her head alongside that of the younger woman's, resting gently against the soft pillow.

'*No, Na, there's nothing wrong. I have just missed you so much, that's all,'* she said, sadly, holding her tightly. Ratna squeezed Lani in response, then yawned. She had stayed up late, talking with her aunt, once Michael had returned to his hotel.

'Are you going to marry this one, too?' Lani asked, not wishing to leave.

'He hasn't asked me,' Ratna replied, with a hint of remorse in her voice. She wondered if he had gone directly back to the Grand Hyatt, or if he had decided to take in the sights of Jakarta City without her.

'Don't get married again, Na,' Lani said, squeezing as she did so for emphasis. *'Why don't you stay here with me? I'll take good care of you.'* Ratna knew that she was in danger of being hooked into one of her mother's tireless conversations, and did not answer. She looked down at Lani but could only see the top of her head. Too tired to encourage further discussion, Ratna switched the light off and lay completely still, willing herself to sleep.

In the darkness of the room, Lani rested alongside the beautiful woman she considered her daughter, listening to her breathe, wishing that she would wake, and talk to her, as Ratna had with Ruswita earlier. She was saddened that Ratna no longer cared for her, that there was no longer any room in her heart for the woman who had mothered and taken care of her from the day she was born.

Bitter from years filled with endless hours sitting quietly alone in her quarters, Lani uttered a silent prayer to her God, begging that Ratna and she could stay together as they were then, forever.

* * * * * *

Java Sea

Twenty-three nautical miles North-north-east of what local fisherman called the *Java Hook*, where Gods and spirits connived to spoil one's catch or even boil the ocean with a fearful turbulence capable of capsizing the sturdiest of vessels, the small fleet prepared to return to shore. As they pulled their machine-woven nets over the side of their unstable boats, the crews remained silent. Their poor harvest had thrown a blanket of despondency over the fleet.

JAKARTA

These were simple but suspicious people. They understood the weather, and watched the skies and birds for indications of where they should cast nets. They listened to their Gods and, surrounded by Petromax lights, still chanted around village fires when evening fell. They feared angering the powerful elements which controlled the currents, the wind. The invisible spirits of their *nenek-moyang* - their ancestral spirits which lurked in the darkness beyond - had to be placated.

Further out to sea, and deep in the earth's crust where basalt converts into still denser rocks, the subterranean structure covering the earth's molten mass grunted and heaved. As lateral slip faulting occurred, the two mighty masses wrestled momentarily until one surrendered. The interplay of these colliding plates instantly dispatched shock waves both vertically and horizontally through the earth's crust. The oceans above wobbled, absorbing much of the initial shock. Then the two plates began to slip against each other again.

One hundred kilometers to the south, and along the Sumatra-Bali Ridge, twenty-one active volcanoes coughed up plumes of black soot and molten rock. Then, for a moment, it was as if the Gods were content with their display of force.

A deafening silence fell over the sea, followed by a sudden, total absence of wind. The older men turned their faces to the open sea. Many had heard the stories; only a few of their number had actually witnessed what was sure to follow. The fishing fleet's headman screamed for all to turn their vessels towards the open sea, standing on the open deck of his boat and waving furiously for the others to follow his small, diesel-driven craft. Many among the younger fishermen did not understand his wild gesticulations. Bewildered, some even imagined their fishing-fleet commander had been affected by the sea's spirits, while others thought he was merely venting his disappointment at the poor catch.

The weather-withered Javanese head-man stood, gripping the boat's upper-structure. He had lived to tell the tale of a similar experience. Even then, he remembered, few had believed what he had witnessed. Fear gripped him as the first, and ever so soft, puff of wind brushed gently across his bare torso. He screamed once more to all within distance, but few understood his call; some even laughed at the irrational behaviour as he clung desperately to the timber ship's stern's upright deck-beams. They listened to the old man's ravings and shook their heads; he was old, and becoming senile.

Suddenly, distracted by an unfamiliar sound, several of the men cocked their ears and looked around the fleet to see who else might have started their diesels. They looked out to sea and listened, trying to identify the source of the low murmur flowing across the waves. A long, wailing cry startled those closest to the mothership, and those on board the commander's vessel were shocked as their head-man slid to the deck and started to pray. The sea groaned under the now-terrified fishermen. Without further warning, the wind screamed across the water, whipping the waves into mountainous foam which towered over the decks of the vessels.

The fishermen clung desperately to whatever was within reach, terrified they would be washed away. When the first shock passed through their flimsy wooden craft, the full force of the sea rose before them in the darkness, and they screamed, as the tidal wave roared in upon them. They all knew that they were about to die.

* * * * * *

The Indonesian Urban Disaster Mitigation Centre at the Bandung Institute of Technology registered the major shudder on one of its continuous analogue seismographs as the Great Indian-Australian mantle grated against its counterpart, the Eurasian Plate, releasing pressures which had taken scores of millenniums to build.

As the sapphire stylus left its long, spiral trace around the seismograph's drum, Wiranto Arismudari, the Indonesian representative for the Asian Urban Disaster Programme, watched, full of apprehension, at the magnitude of the subterranean earthquake. The energy released registered 7.6 on the Richter Scale. He glanced nervously across at Widiadnyana Jegillos, his assistant, who immediately allayed his fears with an incandescent smile and a reassuring wave of the hand.

* * * * * *

Bandung Research and Development Centre

Several technicians grabbed at their benches frantically as the earth supporting the underground facility shook, frighteningly.

Many of the other team members looked up, as if expecting the thousands of tons of earth above to come crumbling down upon them.

A solitary light-globe had been strung across under the fluorescent fixtures to enhance visibility in one corner. It was swinging silently, indicating that the powerful tremor had shaken the secret facility's foundations. Minutes were to pass before the staff returned to work, all more conscious of their dangerous location than they had been before, some even resolving to submit their resignations upon receipt of their next pay.

* * * * * *

Mount Muria, Java — Rama II

Engineer First Class Mochtar Pribadi strutted along the interconnecting catwalk, dressed in his freshly washed white overalls. He was the midnight-to-dawn, assistant shift supervisor. His initial training had taken place in Japan and, subsequent to the Japanese withdrawal from their project, Mochtar had been sent to the Cernavoda project in Romania to learn more of Russian design and operational procedures. He was deeply proud to have been appointed to assist Vladimir Kruchinsky, first supervisor for the plant's operations. Mochtar was dedicated to his work, and grateful for the opportunity which had been provided for him and his young family.

When the tremor first struck, he was startled by the sudden rocking of the steel walkway under his feet, and he grabbed at the handrail to steady himself. It was all over within seconds. Mochtar peered over the steel-latticed enclosure, and observed that none of the others below had noticed the slight jolt. Accustomed to many such geological shakes since early childhood, he continued his inspection duties, not giving the tremor another thought.

The nuclear plant had been built partially on floating foundations. The Japanese had insisted that standards be similar to those employed in Japan, an area notorious for its sudden volcanic and other geological disturbances. The shell of the overall installation was constructed with concrete, suitably strengthened with steel reinforcing bars, giving the protective cover, or containment shield, strength to withstand geological shocks.

When the Japanese construction had been taken over by the President's family, using Russian techniques and Indonesian practices, quality control had slipped to unacceptable levels. Graeme Robson's *kongsi* won the ongoing contract to provide materials to the site. These included cement and Vietnamese reinforcing steel.

High above Mochtar's head, at the point where two concrete sections had been sealed together completing the containment cover's dome, a hair-line crack appeared, tracing the inferior join.

* * * * * *

Jakarta

Graeme Robson observed the two men, and conceded that they were disturbingly similar in their mannerisms, and even appearance. Had he not known otherwise, Robson would have assumed that they were brothers. He looked around for another towel and gestured to one of the attendants to bring him another bourbon and coke.

'Make that three,' he called to the slight Sundanese houseboy, while watching Murray and Michael stroll back in his direction. Considering Stephenson's age, he was still in fine condition, he thought enviously, conscious of the flab of his own body. Robson could see that the younger man was obviously still in his prime. He had surprised them all with his skill on the courts earlier in the afternoon. Robson was unsure whether he liked Michael Bradshaw, with his ivy league manner. He watched the women surrounding the pool-side barbecue flirt openly with Bradshaw and he didn't like it at all.

Graeme was unaccustomed to not being the centre of attention and expected it, particularly when he was paying for the service. He watched his wife move amongst the other women, her slender shape and delicate features lost to a life of over-indulgence. John Georgio came to mind, and Graeme wondered if his wife knew of the arrangement he had with the professional pimp. Robson had never permitted Georgio to phone him at home; neither would he consider having the man anywhere around his residence in Jakarta.

Apart from the fact that John Georgio oozed from the pores at the slightest sign of a beautiful woman, the man had a total lack of class. Robson made a mental note to explore other avenues of supply for his secret interludes. He was becoming bored with Georgio's behaviour.

'When are you off to Bali, then?' he asked Michael, as his guests flopped casually down. The humidity was unusually high for that time of the day, and the men were still dehydrated from their tennis workout.

'I've had to rearrange my schedule, Graeme,' Michael responded, accepting the drink which appeared, magically, the moment he sat down. 'This Summit has screwed things around a bit, but at this stage I still expect to be in Bali from the sixteenth through to the middle of the week.' Michael then paused and took a long swallow from the tall glass before adding, 'but this could change if I'm able to swing a visit to the Mt Muria plant.' Graeme looked across at Murray, then fluttered his eyelids. It was an affectation that had grown into habit over the years, and made him appear quite ridiculous.

'The Vice President will attend that plant's commissioning ceremony during the Summit,' he said, a bit officiously. 'My sources have informed me that only a handful of Palace players have been invited.' Michael smiled. Robson was obviously miffed at not having been invited.

'Well, if I can't make it this trip....' He didn't finish, opening his hands in resigned acceptance that he would not be given the opportunity to see inside *Rama II's* operations.

'I might be able to swing something after the official opening, Michael,' Robson suddenly inferred, surprising Murray, who cocked an eyebrow at the suggestion. 'My company has been involved in the facility's construction. If you were to come along with me as my guest, it might just be possible. We still have an ongoing relationship with the operators, and there is still a considerable amount of ancillary work to be done around the site.' His eyelids flickered several times like butterfly wings, then stopped.

'I have an idea,' he said, leaning over and slapping Michael's well tanned leg, 'why don't you come down with us on the Lear Jet, and after we've had a few days resting up in my villa, I'll take you directly over to the *Rama II* site?' He paused, then added, 'I'll fly you over myself.' Robson was pleased to see that he had scored. Michael was obviously interested. Looks weren't everything, he mused, resisting the smirk hiding behind his mask of generosity.

Murray looked at Graeme Robson, wondering why he continually persisted in bragging about his executive jet and his pilot's licence. Murray knew that there were at least fifty such private aircraft owned by Jakarta entrepreneurs, most of which remained standing at one of the three airports, primarily as status symbols.

'Well, if the offer is to join you guys after my Bali inspection, I'm in,' Michael said. 'Not before?' Robson asked, surprised that someone would refuse an opportunity to fly down to Bali in a private jet and spend time at *'Puri Kauh'*, undisputedly one of the finest private villas to be found amongst the island's lushly vegetated mountains.

'Thanks, Graeme,' Michael offered, not wishing to offend this man, particularly if he really could orchestrate a visit to the fast breeder plant in Java, 'but I have already committed to spending some quiet time with my lady. She has her heart set on some place along the beach and, to tell you the truth, I'm looking forward to just lying around doing nothing for a few days once I finish the local inspection.'

'Perhaps we could get together while I'm down there and discuss the next step?' he suggested. Robson's weak smile indicated that he might have been offended.

'Sure, let's do that,' Robson said, obviously peeved. The conversation then drifted onto other matters while Michael continued to observe the other two men closely, trying to determine what their relationship might really be. He suspected that the intricate Jakarta expatriate network would have thrown Murray and Robson together in business at some stage. It was apparent that some synergy between the two did exist, considering that both had considerable involvement with the *Rama* energy plants.

As he listened to them discussing matters of little relevance to either the Summit or the nuclear power plants, subjects which had occupied most other conversations during his brief stay, Michael believed that these men had deliberately steered their conversation away from these topics while he was present. And he couldn't help but wonder why.

* * * * * *

JAKARTA

'You look a bit strung out,' Murray suggested. He had remained after Michael had returned to his hotel. Graeme crossed his arms and straightened his back, bored with sitting.

'Having problems with the bankers,' he admitted. Murray was one of the few people he still trusted with such confidences.

'Anything I can do?' Stephenson asked.

'Well, that little bastard Benny Salima has really stuck it to me this time,' Robson said, leaning forward and stretching. One of the servants observed the movement and hurried in his *tuan's* direction, only to be waved away.

'What's the problem, Graeme?' Murray asked. He didn't particularly like the man any more, persevering with their relationship only because of their cross-business ties.

'Asian Pacific has indicated that they might not roll my notes over,' he said, grimly. Murray was surprised. The APC Bank was, he knew, the Lim flagship. Robson must have done something to upset them, he thought. Either that, or Graeme's company was in financial difficulties.

'Move the notes elsewhere,' he suggested, interested now in the other man's predicament.

'I've already tried, Murray,' he replied. 'The Lims have their noses out of joint because they couldn't get their cement and steel into the *Rama II* project. And,' he added, 'the Bandung Research and Development center.' Murray thought about this; it made sense to him. He guessed that the Salima group would have financed Robson initially, hoping that this would give them some leverage over the man's access to materials supply.

'How long do you have?' Murray asked. Graeme didn't have to think before replying; this had been foremost on his mind, lately.

'Three months,' he said, then asked, 'do you think Peter might be interested?'

Murray knew that the old Chinese sitting in Singapore would not be keen on taking over any debt, particularly if this was being transferred from the Lims. They rarely left any meat on a bone, and any suggestion that they were not interested in maintaining a client would only indicate that there was something suspicious with the deal in the first instance.

'No, I don't think so, Graeme. Peter is winding down most of his activities,' he lied. This didn't bother Murray in the least;

everyone lied in business, otherwise how could they survive? Graeme Robson rose from his pool-side chair and stretched again.

'Maybe we can talk about it more in Bali,' he suggested. Murray nodded, realizing that it was time for him to leave.

'Sure, Graeme,' he said, knowing that they would not, 'let's do that.'

Later that day Murray Stephenson filed the information suggesting that Robson's *kongsi* was experiencing financial difficulties. Before Graeme Robson retired for the day, having made one discreet call to John Georgio to establish that arrangements were in place for their Bali escape, his financial dilemma was already known to Peter Wong in Singapore. Before noon the following day, Wong's indiscreet enquiries had been recorded by at least five lending institutions, most of which referred the information search back to the Lims' bank in Jakarta. Word was then circulated that Madame Ruswita would be unhappy if the loan was to be picked up by any other institution.

Within twenty-four hours, Benny Salima sat smiling confidently, knowing that Robson would be unable to meet the notes when these fell due.

Chapter 26

Xanana and the Chinese Fleet

Xanana Soares accepted the hot towel from the Lauda Air stewardess and wiped his face. His attention was diverted from the attractive girl as the captain's voice announced that they had just left the coast of Western Australia, and that their flight was back on schedule. Xanana smiled as another stewardess opened the armrest and re-stashed his tray. He re-adjusted the in-flight monitor, and continued watching the movie. As the figures on the tiny mercury screen danced, his thoughts returned to what lay ahead.

It did not bother Xanana that he had left Australia, perhaps forever. Within a few days he would travel from New Delhi to Bali with the Indian and South African delegations. They had guaranteed his safety. Everything had been arranged. He was to travel, for the purposes of the Summit, on an Indian diplomatic passport, and remain with the Prime Minister only for as long as was required. Then, when everyone's attention was focused on the Summit, he would leave, quietly, with Admiral Gopal.

The thought of remaining in Indonesia for even one day concerned him. He did not trust the Indonesians. He feared that they might attempt to arrest or at least intimidate him in some way. It had been agreed that he was to play no public role during the discussions. His presence in Bali was to add credibility to the agenda, and provide India with the opportunity it had worked so long to achieve.

Xanana felt greatly indebted to the people of India. Through their generosity, he would be taken back to East Timor aboard the magnificent aircraft carrier, *INS Indira Gandhi*, and reclaim his country in the name of the East Timorese people. The will of the United Nations would finally be expressed through India's unilateral action, supported by the might of their navy and marines. Xanana had been assured that the Indonesian troops would have little choice but to withdraw once they witnessed the strength of the Indian forces. He would then be taken ashore and ensconced as the country's legitimate President, after which India would continue to provide a military umbrella to the fledgling country.

He closed his eyes and tried to visualize how things would be in an independent, free and democratic East Timor. Memories of the bitter struggle flashed though his mind, and the many faces of those who had given their lives in the fight for freedom. He remembered the brave, poorly-armed men who had fled into the mountains and continued their struggle through the turn of the century and into the next. He drifted, his mind wandering as he envisaged the prosperity he would bring to his people from East Timor's natural resources, and the pride his countrymen would finally feel once they had achieved their long-awaited freedom.

Finally, his stomach full of the rich in-flight food, Xanana fell into a troubled sleep, until the First Class attendant woke him with instructions to prepare for the landing.

* * * * * *

Lombok Straits

Fuad adjusted his sunglasses against the brilliant glare reflected up from the calm ocean, as the *M.V. Rager* glided through the warm, tropical waters. He cast his eyes around the horizon in search of weather, but could see only the light, pale-blue heavens, the flat sea and some distant coral islands.

When dawn had broken some hours earlier, their world had been blanketed by a deep, thick, sea-mist, causing them to reduce speed. Bartlett had called to him earlier, instructing Fuad to look for small fishing vessels which would not show-up on their radar.

An hour passed, and Fuad became nervous when, in the still, ghostly conditions, the *Rager* suddenly lifted and rocked several times before settling down once again in what had been perfectly calm conditions. His first fear was that the wave had been caused by some distant tanker passing through the mist; but then he could not recall hearing any other shipping in the area. Fuad was not to know that this small swell had been a result of the same undersea movement which had devastated the fishing fleet hours before, and which continued to send out shock waves.

The morning sun finally pierced the fog, and a soft breeze swept the remaining mist away. A pod of dolphins swam alongside, diving playfully for some minutes, before leaving in search of a more responsive audience. Fuad stretched, yawned more out of boredom than fatigue, and continued to search the horizon for other shipping. Fuad knew, without having to look over his shoulder, that the only other man on the vessel would be watching him from the bridge. Fuad didn't like Dave Bartlett. He had the smell of evil about him. Fuad knew that he didn't need to stare into the bearded sailor's cold, lifeless, green eyes to know that he had killed.

They rarely spoke and the long silences didn't bother either man. They were only interested in their mission - and remaining alive to enjoy their rewards. Fuad thought about the money he'd been promised. It was a great deal, even for one who had made and lost a small fortune trading drugs and arms with the Filipino Muslim separatists. Then there was the promise of a green card for entry and residence in the United States. That had been the clincher. All those years of dreaming how he could return to America and remain would soon become reality.

They had promised that this would be his last mission, and he trusted them. His last venture into the Moslem-held Filipino islands near Mindanao had almost cost him his life. And that of Bartlett's. He wondered how the New Zealander earned the almost invisible scar buried behind his reddish-brown beard. Fuad assumed that the rust-bucket which carried them deep into Indonesian waters was Bartlett's. He seemed to pay too much attention to the ship's detail, not to have lived aboard for many years. The single-screw, seventy-foot steel-hulled work-boat had seen better days. When he had been briefed, Fuad was not too keen on the idea of steaming such a distance in the old ship but decided that, if Bartlett was to captain the vessel, they would most probably make it back to home port.

Images of Bartlett standing coolly pumping the twelve-gauge shotgun almost point-blank at the intruders flashed through his mind. The Filipino pirates had erred badly, and their assumption that the *Rager's* crew might be unarmed had cost them their lives. Fuad had watched in fear, as Bartlett had blown five of them back over the side of his ship, then calmly extracted a magnum from his belt and shot several more dead as they scrambled to hide on the smaller boat's deck. From that moment, he had been most careful not to cross the man, sensing that it would take little to attract his wrath.

Fuad wondered if the New Zealander's reward for this mission would be similar to his own. One hundred thousand dollars didn't go far these days, and Fuad knew he would need every penny of that to establish himself once in the States. He considered this, then decided that Bartlett's share would be more, perhaps even a quarter of a million.

His attention then turned to the stores hidden below. It had been the New Zealander's responsibility to clear the ship through customs when they passed into Indonesian waters. They had dropped anchor outside Ujung Pandang, the old Makassar Port, and waited. As darkness fell, a small boat powered by Yamaha outboards brought the Harbour Master alongside, where he recognized Bartlett and accepted the carton of cigarettes containing one thousand dollars. Fuad had been ready, below, armed with a machine pistol in the event the official had become curious and insisted on inspecting the ship's stores. He had not heard Bartlett conversing in the local language and, even if he had, Fuad would have thought little of this. He had discovered that the often sullen captain had little difficulty communicating wherever he travelled.

Fuad thought about the two *Stingers* sitting in their packing cases. He had argued for three, and reluctantly accepted what was stored below. Given that there was only one target, he had been told, even carrying two of the hand-held missiles was considered excessive for such a mission. Fuad reflected on the battle-field proven *Stinger*. Howard Hughes had not survived to witness the incredible destructive power of these man-portable, shoulder-fired rockets, designed and manufactured by the Hughes Missiles System Company.

During the most recent Pakistani-Indian war, Fuad had used the vehicle-mounted version more commonly known as a SVML. He had fired the MANPADs, or man-portable versions only once, but was confident that he would not miss his target when the time arrived, as the infra-red, heat-seeking guided missile was designed specifically for the application they had in mind for their Bali mission.

Once at sea, and far from their port of embarkation, both he and Bartlett had opened the well fortified cases in the ship's hold and examined their deadly caché. With a little support from Bartlett, Fuad had easily lifted one of the two *Stingers* to his shoulder, refamiliarising himself with the sixteen-kilo assembly which consisted of an individual missile, a disposable launch tube with its detachable grip-stock, and the integral range-finder (IFF) system. Although it was some time since Fuad had attended missile training courses in the Pakistani ground forces, he had not lost his respect for the formidable weapon.

He also remembered that the *Stinger* was unique in possessing an in-built TAG guidance technique, which biases missile orientation towards vulnerable portions of its targets, assuring maximised lethality. Fuad had little reason to doubt the reported combat success rate of the weapon in the Afghanistan-Soviet war, during which the *Stinger*, travelling at a speed nearing Mach Two, reportedly downed almost three hundred Soviet aircraft, helping to stop air assault operations and precipitate the Soviet withdrawal from the Moslem-dominated territory.

At first, Fuad had attempted to lift the one and a half metre missile assembly onto his shoulder alone and, although he managed to do so, both men agreed that on a cramped and moving deck, common sense dictated that Bartlett assist. They rehearsed this procedure several times, then repacked the cases. They would not reopen these until they had already positioned the ship in preparation for their strike. With a range of only four kilometers, Bartlett had decided not to move the ship into the strike zone until absolutely necessary.

There would be few preparations required. The *Stingers* would only require minutes to unpack, and they would be ready. Prior to that, he planned to leave the *Rager* moored off-shore, not too distant from Benoa Harbour as to attract attention, but far enough to deter others from visiting the disguised dive-cruise ship.

Fuad had wondered about the other cargo they carried, until Bartlett had explained the reasoning behind the incompatible equipment. The other weapons had consisted of machine-pistols of

Chinese manufacture, and additional life-rafts and flares which had identification tags indicating that these had been part of a Chinese submarine's inventory. A used HN-5B Beijing equivalent to the American *Stinger* had been included in the shipment. The idea of laying the blame for the air disaster at China's door somehow appealed to Fuad, although he wished that he could, one day, claim credit for having destroyed India's Prime Minister.

They had taken on bunker fuel the previous day, and would now not require further diesel until they returned to the Philippines. The ten two hundred-litre drums stowed below would see them through the remainder of the mission.

He heard Bartlett call and he turned, then followed the man's outstretched finger pointing to the West. Fuad removed his sunglasses and peered through the 8x30DIF Nikon binoculars, making a minor adjustment which brought the distant ship clearly into focus. After some moments Fuad turned and shook his head, but then continued to watch the huge tanker just in case. Bartlett had warned him that the Lombok Straits were dangerous; larger ships passed through here, one of Indonesia's busiest sea lanes. He wandered lazily back to where the other man stood, his left hand on the ship's wheel.

'How much longer?' Fuad asked, watching Bartlett extract a cigarette from its packet, using his teeth. He had been on four missions with the surly sailor, and had not once seen him remove the well-worn baseball cap, not even to scratch his head.

'We'll be sitting off Benoa Harbour at first light,' Bartlett answered. 'Then I'm going ashore.' Fuad frowned, thinking that this would be foolish. He said nothing, though, realizing that Bartlett would do as he liked, anyway. He walked back up forward and leaned on the ship's rail, wondering why the other man would take such unnecessary risks. Fuad knew that they would have to moor away from the other shipping until the time arrived, in order to remain as inconspicuous as possible. He turned slowly and glanced guardedly towards the bridge, and immediately wished he hadn't. Bartlett was smiling; and the expression sent a cold shiver through his spine.

* * * * * *

JAKARTA

He looked down at the man he would later have to kill, and his eyes narrowed, wondering if perhaps Fuad had been given similar instructions. Dave Bartlett unconsciously scratched his face with his free hand, pondering this thought.

He had been betrayed before. More than once. He recognized that with age he had lost some of his edge, but Bartlett still considered himself capable of being able to defend himself, particularly against the likes of the Pakistani drug dealer forced upon him for this mission. They had worked together several times in the past, but Bartlett had never had much confidence in the other man. He'd seen him panic in situations which might have cost them both their lives.

Fuad disappeared below and, choosing that moment, the bearded captain raised his cap then dragged the palm of his hand across his head, recognising how thin the hair on his scalp had become over the past few years. Resisting the temptation to touch the scar, he adjusted his sun-glasses, then gazed out across the calm, blue sea. A flock of gulls swooped together, then veered away. In the distance, he could see the volcano's outline, and knew that this would be the majestic Gunung Agung, its smouldering rim evident above the clouds. For a brief moment, the scene triggered painful memories and he resisted the temptation to indulge in what might have been.

More than thirty years had passed, yet he could still clearly recall the image of the woman he had loved, Louise, standing on the dimly-lit foreshore, her golden hair nestled against his face, as villagers danced in rhythm to the ancient *gamelan* sounds. The irony that he was soon to take the lives of others, who would also die in the air, was not lost on Bartlett as he continued to stare at the island, and the point from where Louise had taken her fateful flight.

Bartlett touched his head again and accepted that he was lucky to have anything there at all. The force of the bullet which had struck the side of his head as it penetrated the skin above his upper jaw, had come within a millimetre of killing him. The bullet had turned against the shattered bone and travelled upwards, before exiting more than eight centimetres above his right ear. He had been shown Polaroid shots taken of his black, swollen face which looked like some badly inflated and severely bruised melon. Dave Bartlett, formerly known as Stephen Coleman, knew he was indeed most fortunate to have survived yet another attempt on his life, those years before in Canberra.

His unconscious body had been taken directly to a safe-house maintained by the United States Government, in the small border town of Queanbeyan, not twenty kilometers from where he had been shot. There, at the request of the Station CIA Chief, he had been secretly cared for by the Embassy doctor. When he recovered consciousness, two days after his near fatal shooting, the questions had started. During the first, groggy hours, his memory of the incident totally lost, Coleman had no comprehension whatsoever, of whom, or where he was. His amnesia had lasted for several months, and even now, he admitted, there were still major gaps which related to the time leading up to his near-death experience. He could still, however, clearly remember the man Anderson who had betrayed him.

When he had expressed concern that his disappearance would attract attention the CIA Station Chief, Harold Goldstein, had assured him that Chalmers had returned to the scene and removed the car in which Coleman had been shot. It would later be assumed that the vehicle had been stolen and his body dumped. During the course of that evening, the Canberra and Queanbeyan hospitals had been in turmoil as a result of the devastating blast which had occurred at the Indonesian Embassy. Coleman's credentials were thrown amongst others that had been collected by the authorities, who were unable to identify many of the bomb-blast victims. The Americans believed Anderson would come to accept that Coleman's body had been discovered and sent to one of the hospitals, where confusion had led staff to believe he had been one of the bomb casualties.

While sitting on the ship's deck steaming between Port Moresby and Guam, pieces of the annoying puzzle moved into place inside his head, but never enough to create a full picture of the events which had led to his attempted execution. He had remained under American care for almost one year, before they too decided that there was little left of any substance for them to glean from his memory. In their ongoing watch over the Australian security services, Coleman could be of no further use.

When they released him, Coleman became apolitical. In his anger, he also refused to acknowledge that he had any debt, or ties, or owed any loyalty to his country of birth, or to those who lived there. Unable to make contact with his bankers for fear this would reactivate interest in his death, Coleman knew that the funds he had squirreled away would eventually be sent to Australia, along with a number of letters containing detailed reports of his earlier activities. He was confident that these would find their way to Wanti's estate, and her daughter Seruni. These, he hoped, would bring an end to Director Anderson's rule over the Australian Secret Service.

It was then that Stephen Coleman moved into an even darker world, accepting assignments from those who had saved his life. He became a willing, well-paid, American mercenary.

They provided him with a new identity. His new name, Bartlett, was given as a result of intensive computer research which provided the basis for his new character. Coleman had grown a beard to cover the permanent scar tissue, and wore a cap to hide the damage the exiting bullet had caused above his hairline. Satisfied with his new persona, Stephen Coleman had remained in Guam for several years before moving to the Philippines, at his new masters' insistence.

There, while maintaining as low a profile as his activities permitted, he grew into his new identity as the owner of a small, inter-island ship, named the *M.V. Rager,* an ageing vessel that suited his purposes perfectly. He accepted missions which took him occasionally across into Vietnamese waters, where he traded in smuggled goods, and down into Mindanao where Moslem separatists paid handsomely for the weapons he carried.

He sailed to ports throughout the region, from Puerto Princessa on Palawan, to Davao and up to Tacloban, and even as far north as Taiwan and across to Hong Kong, and any other destinations which provided him with irregular but handsome earnings.

Coleman had not hesitated when required to kill. Nor was he concerned about the morality of his actions. Now, in this new life, he lived for survival, and developed no ties other than those with the Americans, whose generous flow of funds guaranteed him some security for advancing years. He knew he would not be able to continue working the ship alone too much longer. When he had been offered the contract to sail into Bali, Coleman had been reluctant to accept the mission, knowing that it would entail taking Fuad along on the voyage.

Once it had been revealed that Fuad's usefulness had been outlived, only then did Stephen Coleman agree to sail into Bali and was briefed on the mission's purpose. He had been indifferent to the fact that his instructions would require him to execute Fuad once they had left Indonesian waters. As for the passengers who would die on flight *India One*, he had no feelings, one way or another regarding their planned demise.

* * * * * *

China — Xianggang (Hong Kong)

Admiral Tung-Pi Chen's South Sea Fleet's territorial command extended from deep in the South China Sea to the north, touching the border of Fujian Province, and across to the southern-most tip of Taiwan, the so-called Republic of China.

The Admiral stood on the modified *Luda* class destroyer's bridge, wishing his country had built, or at least acquired, a number of aircraft carriers. He believed that Beijing had made a grave tactical error years before, in not committing to the construction of at least two heli-carriers to be added to the Chinese fleet. Tung-Pi Chen thought about the imminent action, concerned that Vice Admiral Lieu, who commanded the Eastern Fleet, might enjoy most of the glory. Taiwan lay within the Vice Admiral's fleet's territorial control, and was less than one hundred and fifty nautical miles from his mainland bases.

The action would commence within days, and Admiral Chen was one of the few senior-ranking Chinese officers aware that this would coincide with the Indian Navy taking a permanent position in East Timor. It was likely that the associated turmoil arising from the simultaneous operations would, most probably, occur without either nation so much as engaging their enemies in any real action. And there would be rich prizes for both countries.

The Chinese would demonstrate their naval superiority in the Far East, as they carried out naval-military exercises in both the South and East China Sea. Strategic Rocket Units based on the mainland would commence the exercise by launching a number of

DF-15 rockets into zones near Keelung in the north of the island, and Kaoshiung, Taiwan's southerly port. Further launches would be conducted, at two hourly intervals, throughout a three-day period of intimidation.

Seventy-five *Hunagfeng* class missile craft would then join the joint fleet exercise. They would steam to within ten miles of the Taiwanese coastline, accompanied by ten destroyers and twelve *Jianghu* class frigates. More than two hundred amphibious and other craft would leave China's coast, and sail towards Taiwan. Chinese intelligence was aware of the United States Seventh Fleet's presence to the south-east of the Philippines, led by the US Navy's only remaining forward deployed aircraft carrier, the *Kitty Hawk*. The Admiral was not concerned by the Americans' close proximity to Taiwan, because the Seventh was steaming somewhere near the Caroline Islands group, and he anticipated that they would turn immediately to the south once they discovered that the Indian fleet had turned north, towards Timor. But they would be too late. China's leaders in Beijing believed that the combined movements of both nations' navies, the threat of Chinese retaliation with its improved version of the *Dong Feng 31* Intercontinental Ballistic Missiles and America's need to maintain its commercial interests in Asia would force the United States to finally concede Taiwan to China.

The American public, now aware of Beijing's ability to deliver nuclear warheads with great accuracy to parts of the United States would, the Admiral believed, turn the tide. The lethal power of his country's forces had been greatly enhanced by supercomputers, innocently provided by the United States to China's military-industrial complex over the past years. China was most indebted to the former American Secretary of Defense, William Perry, who was instrumental in revising the legal limit on the export of super-computers, making it possible to acquire powerful machines.

Then, of course, there were his navy's improved *Xia* class Nuclear Ballistic Submarines. Official notification that two of these SSBN's were steaming towards the Chinese-controlled Long Beach Naval Base had already been served on the American authorities and Admiral Chen admired the strategy of positioning two Chinese nuclear submarines in American waters to coincide with the overall operation. He had no doubt that the American press would create sufficient alarm over the presence of the deadly vessels, as they steamed arrogantly into the United States' own backyard.

Chapter 27

The Bali summit day one

The Grand Bali Hyatt suddenly fell quiet as Indonesia's ageing President shuffled forward and, watched by millions via satellite, hit the brass *gong* slowly, three times, in ceremonial style. As the deep, musical tone reverberated through the hall, the guests broke into loud applause. The Bali Summit had commenced.

Murray Stephenson returned to his seat alongside Graeme Robson and settled down to listen to the South African President address the assembled guests. Murray knew that once the formal addresses had been given, the visiting Heads of State would adjourn and commence their discussions in private. More than one thousand guests had been invited to the official ceremony, but only a few would participate in the three-day summit. Applause followed the President's speech and, after a polite pause, the floor was handed over to the Australian Prime Minister.

'*Bapak-bapak, dan ibu-ibu,*' the Australian leader commenced, then paused, permitting the thunderous applause to continue as the guests warmly welcomed his conciliatory opening words in the host country's language. He then continued in English, first addressing the Indonesian President, then the other visiting Heads of State.

'The Australian people welcome this opportunity to…' Murray looked around at the huge gathering and identified familiar faces he had not seen for some time. There was little doubt that the *creme de la creme* of Asian society had been invited, and Murray spotted a number of high-profile merchant bankers dressed in suits, sitting with Benny Salima across the hall. He wondered if Ruswita had attended the ceremony. '……and, with the deepest sincerity, I wish to state that the Australian people wish only to be your friends.

Terima kasih,' the Prime Minister finished his brief address.

As the visiting leaders each spoke in turn, they were greeted warmly by the guests who, without exception, understood the significance of this great occasion. Regional differences might now be resolved, and prosperity would continue to grow in their respective countries. The general consensus amongst those present was that the leaders could not be presented with a more opportune moment for open dialogue to seek whatever solutions were necessary to avoid a further escalation in disputes over territorial waters, sea lanes and borders. The general mood was one of hopeful anticipation that this summit would achieve an acceptable reconciliation for all, and restore regional stability. Without China's participation, however, many believed that Indonesia's position had been weakened, as there was little that could be discussed in relation to the Chinese seizure of Natuna Island without China's presence at the forum.

In their opening addresses, the Heads of State from Malaysia, Brunei, Vietnam and the Philippines all publicly criticised China for its aggressive actions, and called upon the Summit participants to support further action through the United Nations.

Murray noticed that Xanana Soares was not present on the podium. He thought about the Timorese exile. His absence was probably not a bad thing; after all what could he possibly contribute? It appeared that he was not going to be given the public stage at any time during his visit. Murray knew that the Indonesians would have insisted that Xanana's presence be played down, and that he would have no official recognition during his stay. Murray guessed that the self-appointed President of East Timor's government-in-exile would be experiencing doubts about his safety at that moment.

He conceded that once again the world was witnessing the perfect Indonesian compromise in their handling of the sensitive and highly emotional issues relating to their annexation of the former Portuguese colony. He joined the others, applauding, as the last of the formal addresses was delivered by the Sultan of Brunei. The guests rose to their feet as the leaders dispersed and followed the official party down to the informal luncheon, which had been prepared in the garden setting overlooking the beach. Murray followed Robson out of the hall and down to the swimming pool area, where hundreds of white-clad waiters prepared to serve the guests.

The atmosphere was most relaxed, and Murray could not help but marvel at the ease with which the foreign Heads-of-State moved amongst the other guests, stopping to talk to those who offered their sincere wishes for the Summit's success and waving back at others who had caught their attention.

The buffet commenced, and the guests settled down to enjoy the magnificent feast provided by the hotel catering staff. Roast suckling pigs turned slowly on spits while chicken, turtle, beef and goat *satés* were cooked to perfection across a bed of smouldering charcoal. Carved pineapples and watermelons, decorated with hibiscus and frangipani flowers, had been strategically placed around the tables. Exotic dishes with mysterious herbs tempted the brave, and foolish, while mounds of rice, white, yellow and fried, were dished out freely. Champagne flowed and the luncheon soon developed a carnival atmosphere which belied the seriousness of the occasion. Later, once the guests had retired to their rooms, Murray and Graeme were to return to Robson's villa, *Puri Kauh*, leaving the delegates to commence their three days of discussions.

Murray waited patiently until the crowded buffet area thinned before approaching the line of waiters serving the guests. He thought it clever that the Indonesian security had all been dressed in *batik* shirts to play down their presence. Further out, through the tall coconut trees which separated the hotel's finely manicured lawn from the sandy beach, he observed a number of well-armed patrols maintaining vigilance. He knew that the entire area would be under the strictest surveillance during the Summit, and hoped that the guards would not be called upon to protect the VIPs from any armed threat.

1245 Hours

Ratna giggled childishly as Michael rubbed the oil into the back of her thighs, while taunting her playfully. She was deliriously content, and wished they could remain on the island forever.

'Don't rub me there!' she laughed, as Michael's hands wandered, then she slapped his hand with hers, as his fingers found a sensitive area. Ratna rolled over on the beach towel and smiled lovingly, delighted that they would have the entire day to themselves before Michael's visit to the nuclear plant the following morning. She accepted the tropical fruit drink from a waiter and sipped slowly, enjoying the cold tingling sensation.

'Let's eat!' Michael suggested, with which Ratna shook her head. 'Why don't you order something light, then we can have an early dinner over at the *Puri Selera*?' She knew this would appeal. They had dined in this romantic setting the evening before and she could see from Michael's response that he had been captivated by the romantic, tropical ambience. Later, they had strolled along the soft, cool sand, admiring the moonlit night, and had lain together at the palm-fringed water's edge, listening to the outgoing tide and the gentle, lapping waves.

As the sea-breeze became cooler, she had shivered, and Michael had picked her up in his arms and carried her back into the hotel grounds, past smiling security guards, into their pool-side cabin. Their love-making had been sensual, soft, and loving. As they lay together, the warmth of their passion still evident, Michael had held her closely as she cried, filled with blissful contentment.

And now, as they lay around the pool, resting, Ratna wished their time together in Bali would never end. She looked over at Michael, and repeated her suggestion. He seemed to be dozing in the warmth of the tropical sunshine but he eventually raised himself to glance down at his wristwatch.

'That's a great idea,' Michael said. Then he yawned, and rose lazily to his feet. 'I'll order a plate of those tasty sticks of *saté babi* after I make a quick call.' He leaned over and kissed her forehead before strolling away in the direction of their cabin. Ratna wondered whom he could possibly wish to phone on such a magnificent day.

1322 Hours — Bali Harbour

Fuad looked over and observed his ship-mate staring across the water, apparently at nothing. They were bored, and he recognized the danger of their being so. Suddenly, Bartlett went into the makeshift cabin-cum-galley immediately behind the bridge, and reappeared wearing jeans, T-shirt and his tiresome baseball cap.

'I'm going ashore,' was all he said. Fuad watched as the New Zealander moved to the stern and prepared the rubber Zodiac to take him to the island. Minutes passed before he heard the twenty-five horse-power Evinrude outboard cough, then hum into life, as Bartlett pointed the dingy towards shore and opened the throttle wide.

1348 Hours — Java

Sujono and his wife arrived at the refurbished government guest-house and immediately rested from the arduous helicopter flight. That evening, they would be entertained by the local Governor and his family. The advance party had prepared their accommodations, and light refreshments for their arrival. While his wife rested, Sujono walked through the adjoining tea plantation, never out of view of his two armed security guards for more than a few moments.

He thought about the following day's programme, and considered the significance of the occasion. Vice President Sujono Diryo turned and faced the north, shading his eyes from the mid-afternoon sun, while he attempted to identify the distant buildings of *Rama II*. Scattered cumulus clouds moved across the sky gathering for the typical, monsoonal, late-afternoon thunderstorm. He searched the scene below and, at that moment, a break in the clouds permitted sunshine to strike the dome-like containment structure which covered the nuclear reactor.

Sujono breathed the fresh, sweet-scented mountain air, and his face broke into a knowing smile. He was reminded of the plant's dark secrets, and how these would soon place him at the helm of the Indonesian Republic. He then strolled back to the guest-house, intent on taking a brief nap, in preparation for the formal, evening dinner.

1540 Hours — Indian expeditionary Force, South of Java (Longitude 114 degrees East, Latitude 11 degrees South)

Admiral Rajesh Gopal was filled with a swelling sense of pride, greater than he had experienced at any other time in his distinguished naval career. He looked out and across the massive floating structure and considered his naval forces.

Since the establishment of the navy's three commands, India

had not once needed to deploy its ships in battle. His Western Command, with its headquarters in Bombay, was now the second largest naval base in the whole of Asia. He was most proud of his country's achievements. India had built a naval-air wing in Goa, at Lakshdweep, and now commanded the entire north-west of the Indian Ocean. Gopal's Eastern Command with its headquarters in Vishakhapatnam was well supported by its other naval bases in Port Blair and Calcutta. He smiled, recalling how efficient the crews of India's twenty-eight submarines had appeared during exercises out of their home port, Vishakhapatnam.

Gopal had supported the drive to increase his country's naval capabilities. When the *INS Vikrant*, India's first aircraft carrier, was decommissioned before the turn of the twentieth century, there had been only one other aircraft-carrier capable of leading India's navy. The *INS Viraat*, acquired from the British in 1987, was already showing its age. Less than thirty-thousand tonnes, it had been an embarrassment until the government had acquired the seventy-eight thousand tonne *INS Indira Gandhi* to lead the navy into the new millennium. His fleet had already steamed past Christmas Island, through the Java Trench and into the North Australian Basin, and he knew that they were currently maintaining their easterly heading, ostensibly for Port Moresby.

Gopal looked out again from the Group Battle Commander's bridge, directly above that of the captain's, and wished Vijay could have lived to see this day. Below, on the fifteen thousand square meters of flight deck, he watched as another of the F/A-18E Super Hornets was catapulted out, over the ocean, before climbing away to join the others. His flagship carried forty combat aircraft, including the two squadrons of Super Hornet advanced strike fighters, which had been wisely equipped with the smokeless F414 engines.

Gopal enjoyed being at sea, especially on this ship, which accommodated five thousand personnel and could cover seven hundred miles each day. Below, when you took one of the four aircraft elevators to lower levels, lay an entire city. There, one would find F-14 Tomcats, CH-53 transporters, many more Hornets and, deep inside the ships bowels, two nuclear reactors, which drove the massive bulk through the ocean at more than thirty knots. From keel to mast, Gopal knew that his ship stood more than twenty stories, and was three times the length of a football field. It was only fitting, the admiral thought, that such a magnificent structure should lead India into a new era, one which would see his country expand its territory for the first time since the time of the British Raj.

As he stood on the bridge overlooking the flight deck, Gopal considered the historic moment which would soon take place, while the Indian Navy was under his command. Once the armada had arrived at the point where Australia's territorial limits ended, his ships would turn sharply to the north and steam directly for Dili, around the point off Tutuala. The fleet would position itself between Dili and *Pulau Kambing*, utilising the island's airstrip to further consolidate the Indian force. There, Indian marines would be ferried ashore under cover of darkness, where they would wait until day broke across the island.

The fleet air-arm would then take control of the skies around Dili, alerting the Timorese of their President's return, while other propaganda material would be dropped across all major population centres, encouraging the people to take to the streets, as they had been liberated by the Indian Government. India's naval aircraft would control the sky, providing confidence to the people whose country had been occupied by one foreign government or another through four centuries.

Gopal believed that the Indonesian occupying forces would surrender under the might of the Indian Expeditionary Force, after which they would be given the opportunity to retreat, in an orderly fashion across their own lines, back into Western Timor. Gopal's orders were to threaten the Indonesians on all fronts, as India was not even prepared to concede Oe-Cusse, the small Portuguese enclave formerly locked and isolated inside Indonesian territory. India would then, by its actions, have succeeded where others had failed. East Timor would have its independence; an independence supported by the United Nations resolution. India, in turn, would have achieved the pivotal position it so desperately needed. An advance defence point for further expansion into the oil-rich and fertile basins of the Malay Peninsula.

Gopal was one of the few to understand that it had never been his belated friend's plans to invade Indonesia. East Timor was to be a bargaining strength from which the Indian's second phase would been implemented. With China in the north and east, and only arid terrain in the north-west, India had no choice but to consider the fertile peninsula which ran from Singapore, through Malaysia and Thailand, to the northern borders of Myanmar.

World opinion, he knew, would be against them. In a climate where China could successfully annex the oil and gas-rich fields north of Indonesia without foreign military intervention, Gopal believed that they had made the correct decision. *Who would possibly move against their supporting the reinstatement of a United Nation's recognized government?* Their tactics were clear. The Americans would be beside themselves over the Indian action, and call for a United Nations Security Council sanction to be imposed. He believed that this would not eventuate. China, as a member of the Security Council, would veto any action requested by other members of the United Nations Security Council. In turn, India would support China's annexation of Taiwan.

Admiral Gopal then thought about Xanana. It had been imperative that Xanana's presence on board be hidden from the world. Knowing just how difficult maintaining the integrity of such an exercise could be, he had decided that Xanana should not be taken aboard until after the Bali Summit had commenced, using the fleet's proximity and his own presence to disguise their intentions. Xanana would accompany him on the return flight to his flagship. Xanana Soares' presence on board the occupying force would then provide legitimacy to the armada's entering what would otherwise be deemed foreign territory.

Admiral Gopal was not entirely convinced that Soares had the strength of character to lead his country, even under the auspices of India's expeditionary forces. Once India had occupied the former Portuguese Colony, world recognition for Xanana's government would, he believed, soon follow. Admiral Krishna Gopal agreed with Dr Malhotra and his new Prime Minister that it was unlikely that nations which had earlier pledged their support for an Indonesian withdrawal from East Timor would renege on their earlier commitment, once India had ensconced its forces there, in support of a free and independent state. But it might become necessary for them to identify someone to fill Xanana's shoes if he did prove to be unsatisfactory.

He looked out from the Battle Commander's bridge, towering

more than a hundred feet above the sea, and watched the waves grow in height, some white-capping, licking the powerful carrier's sides as she steamed ahead. The admiral checked his chronometer, nodded to the Commodore who had been appointed Battle Commander, then left the bridge to prepare for his bumpy ride to Bali in the AH-64E Apache helicopter.

1549 Hours — Bali

John Georgio splashed water over the girls' heads as he kicked in their direction, swimming away from the small group standing in the shallow end of the beautiful pool.

'Come on, girls, get wet!' he yelled, back-stroking his way through the water.

'Johnny, no!' several cried, struggling to wade away from the splashing before their hair had been ruined. None of them could swim, and all of them disliked the idea of standing around half-naked under the hot, baking Balinese sun. They moved away from the man who had organized their paid excursion to the island, wishing he had remained behind. Not one of the young women was to receive less than five hundred dollars for the part they would play in entertaining the wealthy visitors.

'Grae! Grae!' one of the young prostitutes called, happily, as Graeme Robson returned and strolled down to the pool-side. 'Hey, Johnny, its Graeme!' she called again, moving as quickly as she could through the water, close to where he stood, and away from the offensive Georgio.

'How did it go?' John called, standing on tip-toe and wiping excess water from his face. He didn't care that he was not included in the arrangements to attend the opening, preferring to accompany the girls.

'Not bad,' Graeme replied, stripping down to reveal all as he spoke. 'Murray remained behind, says he'll join us later.' He eased himself gently into the pool, then slowly immersed his head under the crystal clear water. Moments later he found himself gripped playfully by one of the girls. He lifted her out of the water, then let her fall. She sprang back, terrified, her hair wet from the dunking. The pretty *Dayak* girl pouted, then turned on her friends, splashing them furiously as they squealed for her to stop.

'What have you got arranged for tonight, John?' Robson had given Georgio a permanent retainer to provide a constant flow of young, beautiful models for his extra-marital activities. When Peter Wong's shrivelled body and weakened libido had reduced his sexual appetite and activities, John Georgio's services had no longer been required. Graeme Robson had then engaged the American, knowing that John's access to the discreet amateur circuit was legendary around Singapore circles. He had been surprised to discover the daughters and sons of some of the more influential families on John's list.

'What, not satisfied with this lot?' Georgio answered, flinging something across the other side of the pool. Robson laughed; having already slept with two of the four dazzling creatures, he was already becoming bored with the Indonesian girls.

'No, I meant what have we organized for later in the evening.' He slipped his arm around the closest girl and untied the knot securing her costume. She did not resist, permitting Robson to remove the top of her two piece bathers. She lowered her body further, not wishing to catch too much sun. Then she felt his hands move to her thighs, and she assisted him to remove the lower half of her bikini. A servant appeared, moving silently around the pool and retrieving the drink coaster Georgio had flicked, unsuccessfully, at one of the girls. The servant then moved back inside the main building.

The servant had learned from earlier visits never to remain outside when the *tuans* were playing, remembering that the more these men drank, the greater was their abuse. What the prostitutes did inside the bedrooms was, to her, their own affair. Everyone had to eat, and although she would never consider selling herself to any man, she was not critical of others who did.

Her main concern was to watch these young women to guard against their sticky little fingers which, invariably, removed considerably more from the villa as they left than the *tuan* believed, often accusing his own staff for missing items instead. She watched and listened, as the two men talked, but did not understand.

'Well, if you and Murray are in the mood, we can go down to the new cabaret in Kuta.' He waited for Robson to stop fooling around and respond. John was careful how he handled this man's private assignations, knowing that his volatile temper had cost others before him their opportunity to remain in the wealthy playboy's employ, and John desperately needed the income generated from these excursions.

'Sounds good to me, let's take Murray, but we'll leave these behind,' he suggested, tilting his head in the direction of the four girls. John understood what was required of him. He would have to leave beforehand and see what he could arrange for Robson at the new Kuta Beach Club Cabaret. He thought about this and decided that it would be wise to make a few advance calls and have one of his contacts position a few ladies at the club, just in case. He waded to the side of the pool and climbed out.

'I'll make the arrangements now,' he said, snapping a towel off a table, drying his bald head while he walked back into the villa.

1804 Hours — Bali, Ngurah Rai Airport

The Indonesian President climbed the steps to his aircraft slowly, and turned to wave at those who were watching from the observation deck. Within minutes, *AURI One* was in the air, heading for the capital, Jakarta. The President's flight plan took him directly over Mt Muria but, by the time he was overhead, it was dark, and the presidential flight had already reached twenty-two thousand feet, making visibility below impossible.

As his aircraft bumped in response to the turbulent air currents flying over the rough terrain below, back in Bali, Admiral Gopal's helicopter set down on the designated area marked with a large white cross, located between the main hotel building and the beach. The pilot needed to refuel his machine at Ngurah Rai before the return flight, and maintained the engine's revolutions with the rotor-blades continuing to chop through the thick, humid air as the admiral ran, in a half-crouched position, towards those who waited for him in the magnificent hotel grounds. The Prime Minister's aide immediately escorted India's Admiral of the Fleet through a throng of surprised dignitaries who had gathered for cocktails, and led the way through the rows of security, into the main building, and upstairs to the Indian Prime Minister's suite.

* * * * * *

'Welcome, Krishna, welcome!,' the recently-appointed leader grinned profusely as he embraced his colleague. 'Welcome to the Islands of Gods,' he paused, 'and India's destiny', he added, gripping the Admiral's shoulders warmly in a gesture of camaraderie.

'Is all in order?' he asked, 'are we ready?'

Admiral Gopal stepped back from his Prime Minister, his face beaming with pride.

'Yes, Prime Minister,' he said. 'We are most certainly ready.'

* * * * * *

Java — Mt Muria (overlooking Rama II)

Vice President Sujono was wakened by the gentle knocking, and he called out to the housekeeper, acknowledging the call. He rolled to one side and observed that his wife had already slipped out quietly, leaving him undisturbed. Checking the bedside clock, Sujono knew that he had plenty of time to bathe and prepare for the Governor's dinner. He swung his legs over the side of the bed, found his slippers, then rose slowly and shuffled to the bathroom to take a *mandi*, hoping that the water would be warmer than it had been earlier.

Outside, standing alone admiring the beauty of Java's mountainous views, his wife stood contentedly, breathing in the cool, fresh, lightly-scented air. Terraced rice fields fell away below, their careful configuration a result of thousands of years of farming and irrigation. She looked out across the western slopes where the tea plantation encircled a small village, and wondered what it would be like to be raised in such an isolated, primitive environment.

Sujono entered her mind as she thought about preparing for the evening function, wondering if he would be as happy as she was at that moment, knowing that after the years of trying, his seed had finally found fertile ground. She then rubbed her stomach, excited by her secret. She would tell him tonight, before they went to sleep. Then she would wait until returning to Jakarta before informing the President that she was finally with child.

2147 Hours — Bali

JAKARTA

Candlelight danced through the diamond-shaped holes cut into the hollowed pineapple, touching Ratna's face and accentuating her aquiline features. Michael reached across and touched the side of her soft face, then smiled.

'I could easily grow accustomed to this,' he whispered, captivated by the balmy, tropical ambience and his partner's beauty. Ratna raised her hand and placed it over his, then nestled her face against them both. Somewhere out in the kitchen the cook called out angrily for the staff to hurry, and she giggled, understanding precisely what the man had said.

Tantalising aromas drifted through the restaurant, teasing their palates as *saté penyu*, *gado-gado*, *rendang* and even *ikan pepes* were carried in by waitresses clad in traditional attire. Toothless members of the *gamelan* orchestra smiled happily as they played their timeless instruments, the bamboo xylophone tones prominent above the others. Then, when Michael believed the atmosphere was already perfect, a young Balinese girl sprang out onto the small stage and commenced dancing to the exotic music. At that moment, Ratna moved their joined hands closer to her lips, and she kissed Michael's softly, lovingly, and whispered across the table that she loved him.

2205 Hours — Rama II, Java

Their room flashed alive with a brilliance only lightning could deliver, and she flinched, anticipating the inevitable thunder-clap. The evening storm had brought their function to an early end, cutting power to the mountain guest-house as loose, dangerous cables whipped around the building's exterior, flicked about by the wind.

The Vice President and his wife had returned to their room with the help of candles carried by an army of servants. As the couple made their way up darkened stairs to their suite, Sujono thought it ironic that they were without electricity, practically within sight of one of the world's largest energy plants. They had changed quickly and climbed into bed, the silence between them interrupted only by the terrifying clashes overhead. He moved closer, knowing that she would be frightened.

'No, Jono,' she protested, '*I'm very tired.*' She was angry with her husband and his flirtatious, roaming eyes. The Governor had invited his senior Military staff with their wives to join his family in entertaining the Vice Presidential couple. The reception had barely begun when Sujono started flirting with the Governor's daughter, obviously basking in the excessive flattery of the younger woman. Later, when they had retired, the Vice President's wife had decided against telling her husband about her pregnancy. She would tell the President first, and then see how Sujono reacted when he discovered that she had informed everyone else in the Palace before him.

Sujono understood her mood. She was not unlike any other Indonesian woman he had known, and was expected to show some signs of jealousy. He ran his fingers along her spine, knowing how she enjoyed his touch.

'I said no, Jono!' she snapped, unable to reach his wandering hands. But she could not resist. Minutes later she lay on her back, urging him to continue. He thrust against her, groping to remove the rest of her bedclothes when, suddenly, he cried out in pleasure, as the warmth of his body flowed prematurely into hers. Disappointed, she lay quietly under the light quilt, her eyes filled with tears.

2350 Hours — Bali

They strolled into the club reception, arms around each other's waist. Michael broke away to pay the cover charge, then reached out for Ratna's hand and escorted her inside the Kuta Beach Cabaret. Two overdressed doormen bowed as they opened the club's main doors. The cabaret show was under way as they entered.

'My God!' Ratna cried, deafened by the band's excessively loud amplifiers.

'What?' Michael shouted, bending his head closer to hear what she had said. Ratna shook her head and leaned closer, on tip toe.

'Let's not stay,' she shouted, the music so loud she could feel the pulsating rhythm vibrating through her chest.

'Just one drink over there,' Michael insisted, leading her by the hand through the packed night club. They made their way to the bar and stood while Michael screamed his order to the busy barman.

'Michael, I'll be back in a moment,' Ratna shouted, pointing to the red exit signs down past the end of the long, saloon-styled bar. Just then, the floor show came to an end. The club erupted with drunken cheering and whistles, as the Filipino dance group all turned their bottoms towards the guests and displayed what little they were wearing. Ratna made her way through the unruly crowd of drinkers packed around the bar to the toilets.

When she had finished, Ratna exited the dimly lit area and was startled as an arm slipped around her waist and lifted her bodily off the floor. She yelled, but her cry was lost in the cacophony around her. She felt a hand grab her right breast, and struggled, jabbing her elbow at whoever held her tightly from behind. Pain flashed through her lower arm as she struck her assailant's face, managing to struggle free. As her feet touched the floor, Ratna turned and kicked John Georgio directly in the left shin, glaring at the drunken American.

'You bitch,' he screamed. The tip of her shoe had struck bone. He lifted his fist to strike her, but before he could deliver the blow another guest sprang into action and blocked Georgio's attack.

'Cool it John!' the man yelled, holding Georgio firmly.

'For chrissakes, Murray!' he yelled at the older man. 'The bitch kicked me!' Ratna stood glaring at her attacker, shaking with rage.

'Are you all right?' Murray asked, leaning close and placing his hand under her elbow. His breath smelled heavily of alcohol, and Ratna immediately pulled away, then turned and pushed through the packed crowd. She found Michael, sipping his drink, standing at the bar.

'Are you okay?' he asked, concerned by her distressed appearance.

'It's all right, Michael,' she lied, 'can we just get out of here?' He placed his drink back on the bar, withdrew ten dollars and permitted Ratna to take his hand, leading him away.

'What happened in there?' he asked, as they sat inside the taxi, heading back to their hotel.

'Nothing, Michael, let it be. I'm just not feeling well, that's all.' Ratna was concerned that if she explained, Michael would most probably go back inside the club and beat the living daylights out of the obnoxious drunk.

'Are you sure?' he insisted, but Ratna ignored the question.

As they drove the short distance to Nusa Dua, Michael knew clearly that there was something wrong. Back in their cabin, when he had attempted to hold her comfortably, she had feigned tiredness, undressed hurriedly, and gone straight to sleep.

Back in the Kuta Beach Cabaret Club, John Georgio called for more bourbon as the music grew even louder. Murray Stephenson simply shook his head in amazement at the noise generated by the revellers as they continued to have a great time. He checked his watch, and patted Graeme Robson on the shoulder.

'That's enough for me!' he shouted, rising to leave. Robson checked the time also.

'Too early!' he yelled, as he attempted to grope one of the Filipino dance group John had managed to drag back to their table.

Murray just shook his head. *I'm too old for this*, he thought as he left the others to play on. He walked out to the waiting driver and climbed into Robson's waiting Mercedes 600, where he promptly fell asleep for the whole of the drive back up to their mountain resort.

As the smooth German machine glided through the foothills, the driver felt his steering wobble briefly, and slowed noticeably for a few minutes. The sensation did not reoccur, and he increased his speed, satisfied that his imagination had been playing tricks again.

Chapter 28

Bali — the countdown
0040 hours, day two

John Georgio fell drunkenly to the dance floor as the revellers tripped over each other, oblivious to the cause for their sudden loss of balance. The jolt had shaken the night-club, but most inside were past being able to recognize the sensation for what it had been. They picked themselves up and continued to dance to the screaming sounds of the heavy metal band.

In their hotel room, Ratna awoke and looked across at Michael. In a few short hours she knew that he would have to rise and leave for his visit to *Rama I*. She reached over and stroked his hair tenderly, then went back to sleep.

* * * * * *

Rama II — Java

Engineer First Class Mochtar Pribadi felt the slight shake and immediately looked up at the control room instrument panel. He watched the indicators for several minutes, then returned to reading the smuggled Playboy magazine which one of the men had brought onto the site during the earlier shift. Boredom was the only danger he could see threatening the *Rama II* plant, only boredom.

The structural crack along the top of the containment building moved infinitesimally, and from the broken section precariously held by inferior re-enforcing steel came a faint groan.

There was no shift supervisor awake to note the seismic disturbance at the Bandung Institute; the automatic seismic measuring devices recorded that the epicentre of this most recent movement was somewhere off the Island of Madura, to the east of Java. The tremor registered only 4.2 on the Richter Scale, falling into the category of more common shocks felt around the unstable island chain and, as such, did not represent any real danger.

Shift engineers at the other plants ran the mandatory checks described in their operators on-line procedural handbook and noted that there had been no change in their instrumentation as a result of the light tremor.

Two hundred and twelve nautical miles south of Java, the tremor's weakened shock waves were not felt by any of the Indian Navy ships sailing in group formation with the aircraft carrier, *INS Indira Ghandi*, as they continued on their course for Timor.

0732 Hours — Bali

Some seven hours later, the Indian Prime Minister grabbed both sides of his chair as the breakfast laid out in front of him suddenly jumped and skipped noisily across to the edge of the coffee table, where it fell onto the thick, plush, royal blue carpet. He looked up in surprise trying to determine what had happened and was struck by the sight of the white face of his friend, Admiral Gopal, opposite him. The tremor continued for several moments until the Prime Minister noticed that the water in his fine crystal glass had finally stopped shaking. He looked at Gopal and shrugged.

'We shall not be staying too long,' he joked. Gopal clenched his fists under the table, concerned with the possibility of tidal effects generated by the tremor. He looked up at the Prime Minister and smiled weakly.

'That was a most severe shake,' was all he said, trying to appear less alarmed than he was.

Across the hallway, the South African President watched with curiosity as the bath-water sloshed around uncontrollably, and he pulled himself upright to avoid swallowing the thick layer of bubbly foam.

In an adjacent suite, Xanana Soares lost his balance when the tremor struck, falling to the carpeted floor, and two armed Indian security officers came to his assistance.

The Bandung Institute recorded the earthquake at 7.9 on the Richter Scale, just as the first staff arrived to clean and prepare the offices for the day.

JAKARTA

* * * * * *

Rama I — Bali

Michael leaned forward as his driver eased the vehicle slowly around the corner, then veered off the main highway onto the secondary road which led up to the power plant's armed entrance. The security guards approached the vehicle and Michael displayed his official IAEA identification, to the more senior of the men.

'*Tuan* Michael, please wait, and I will inform the plant manager, and he will send someone down to accompany you to his office.' He thanked the officer and sat back to wait for his escort to arrive. He experienced the sudden movement as if something large had shaken his car, and Michael looked up, startled, but was surprised to see that there was no one remotely near the vehicle. *Not enough sleep*, he thought, before returning his attention to the file he had opened to read while waiting.

* * * * * *

Rama II — Java

The morning-shift first engineer checked the previous night's log book, then placed this back in numbered sequence, noting that there had been nothing annotated in the events column. He felt the jolt, and watched as the building around him absorbed the impact, moving ever so slightly, before returning to normal.

In the upper-most section of the containment chamber, the fine crack widened, permitting sunlight to penetrate. A shower of small concrete lumps broke away from the inferior cladding and fell down through the containment area, striking piping and machinery before fragmenting into tiny pieces.

Instrumentation continued to indicate that the plant remained on-line, and the structural anomaly continued to go undetected. Then, within minutes, the affected area experienced an aftershock which tripped the plant's turbines off-line. The shift engineer was startled by the shut-down, and sat mesmerised by the instrumentation for fully two minutes before hitting the red alert button on the monitoring console.

He moved across to check the auto-start, emergency, stand-by, diesel generator flow gauges, then hesitated, knowing that this machinery had not yet been fully commissioned and could not, therefore, provide alternative power.

The crack in the containment shelter widened under the additional pressures, throwing even more rubble into the plant below. The reactor's coolant pumps ceased functioning, due to the sudden loss of electrical power. Further away, in Java, nuclear power plants *Rama III, IV,* and *V* were kept under close observation by engineering crews as the second tremor was registered, without any incident being noted. But at *Rama II*, things were quite different.

Within the passage of a few, brief moments, the nuclear power plant attempted to *scram*, or shutdown automatically. Instructions to close the reactor down flowed through to the control panels from fail-safe protection circuitry which was designed to cut power to the latches holding all the important control rods in place.

* * * * * *

Mt Muria, overlooking Rama II

Sujono listened as his wife continued to throw up in the bathroom, and scowled when he saw that they were in danger of being late for the *Rama II* inauguration ceremony. Moments later she appeared, her face ashen from the morning sickness.

'I'm sorry, Jono, but I don't think I can make it,' she pleaded. Sujono could see that she was quite ill. He thought that the winding trip down to the plant would only make her worse, but was tempted, anyway, to insist. The President would not be pleased, and this was foremost in Sujono's mind.

'What if we wait a few minutes?' he enquired, but this was answered with further proof that this would be most unlikely. He cursed her under his breath and checked his watch again. He was going to be late! Moments passed and his wife appeared, her face a ghostly white. She shook her head, unable to go with him.

'Then remain here,' he said, turning to leave. *'After all, its only a formality anyway. The plant is already operational and doesn't even need*

our presence. I'll go down as planned, cut the ribbon, then return as soon as the photographs have been taken and Bapak has spoken by phone.' Relieved, she nodded, and then hurried back into the bathroom. Sujono left the guest house, and his convoy drove the short distance to *Rama II*.

0734 Hours — Rama I, Bali

The Bali plant's turbines were also tripped off-line with the full force of the earlier tremor.

'Activate the emergency diesel generator,' the chief engineer ordered, noticing that the generators had not automatically cut in as they were designed to do. Several minutes passed before the shift supervisor knew that he had further problems.

'Anything yet?' he asked, anxiously.

'Nothing,' the other man answered, shaking his head.

'What's happened to those emergency generators?' the chief demanded, anxiously. He followed established procedures, checking the instrumentation as valuable minutes passed. Still there was nothing. He grabbed for the internal phone and punched three buttons.

'Answer the phone!' he muttered desperately as the intermittent buzzing tone continued, unanswered. He tried again, but still no one answered. *What in the hell was going on out there?*

'Hamid, get over there and see what is holding them up, quickly!' he ordered.

He watched as the shift engineer hurried away to check. All staff had been well-trained to follow established procedures, but none had actually been exposed to any serious drama during the limited time the nuclear plant had been operating. Hamid disappeared to check why alternative power had not been supplied by the emergency diesel generators. When he arrived at the generator station, he found two other engineers arguing about the cause of the problem.

'No way!' the first man yelled, angry that his judgement had been questioned.

'It has to be!' the other responded. Hamid stepped in quickly.

'What happened?' he demanded, outranking both men.

'The engine fired, ran for less than a minute, then choked,' one said.

'It has to be contaminated fuel,' the other man claimed.

'Then let's check the fuel,' Hamid ordered, *'and quickly!'*

Both the men immediately went about checking the generator's diesel fuel supply to determine if this had been responsible for the machine's malfunction. Indonesian fuel supplies were, they all knew, notorious for causing such breakdowns.

While the men busied themselves, they were unaware that the reactor's coolant pumps had also ceased functioning, and had gone off-line as well at the time the engineers hurried to investigate why the stand-by power had failed.

The *Rama I* reactor tried to *scram* automatically, failing to shut-down as the control rods refused to budge. The rods were precisely machined to slide easily into place during a reactor *scram*, even after expanding when the core heated up to its normal operating temperature.

During reactor plant operations, though, the control rods are bombarded by neutrons, causing them to swell even further, but the design engineer had neglected to make these critical allowances prior to installation. The additional expansion of control rod volume caused the rods to stick, further confusing the inexperienced and poorly-trained operating staff.

0735 Hours — Rama II, Java

As a result of the tremor, a small piece of concrete which had worked its way loose finally fell from above into the reactor vessel area, damaging the hydraulic control valves. These valves were essential to the *scram* shut-down system, and this damage would later jam the valves when they were activated.

The incident went unnoticed by the staff, who were busily checking each others' appearance in preparation for the Vice Presidential visit. What had been a hairline crack in the containment structure just hours before had opened even more, revealing now cloudy skies. Further cracks occurred threatening to dislodge large sections of concrete.

0736 Hours

The rods were held in place by latches which, during a reactor *scram* or a loss of electrical power, are opened by powerful hydraulics. At the ends of the rods are strong *scram* springs designed to drive the rods into the core within a fraction of one second and thereby shut the reactor down. On *Rama II*, these failed to move. Immediately, the valve jammed, preventing the *scram*, or shutdown, from taking place. The shift engineer searched for his supervisor, but he was standing outside talking to security and others in preparation for the Vice President's visit. The engineer grabbed for the phone and punched frantically at the buttons. He listened to the slow, double buzzing tones.

'Come on, answer!' he yelled angrily at the handset, as it continued to hum.

'Shift controller,' a bored voice answered.

'What time will Vladimir arrive?' he asked the shift controller, who immediately identified the concern in the engineer's voice.

'He won't be here until later,' the man replied, stifling a yawn.

'Sialan!' the engineer cursed.

'What's wrong over there?' the other man asked, placing his cup of coffee down.

'The turbines have tripped off-line and we can't shut the reactor down!'

'What?' the shift supervisor yelled, jumping to his feet.

'We've lost power!' the engineer almost stammered, then waited, wondering why the other man remained silent. The shift controller thought quickly.

'What has the supervisor done?' he asked.

'I think he is out of the building. Can you come over?' The shift controller was not, in fact, rostered for duty that day. His presence had been mandatory, along with all other Indonesian personnel, due to the Vice President's visit and the official inauguration ceremony scheduled for just an hour from then. He had planned to return to his quarters once the VIPs had all departed. Now, this was out of the question, and he had no choice but to get over there, and quickly.

'Coming now!' he yelled, replacing the handset abruptly. He looked down at where he had spilt coffee over himself and wondered if the stain on his white coveralls would be noticed. He left the building and hurried over towards the main reactor centre. There he joined the shift supervisor whom he spotted hurrying also, returning from one of the auxiliary buildings which housed the stand-by generators.

'Problems?' he asked, walking quickly alongside the supervisor. *'It will still be days before they've finished installing the stand-by generators. Who called you?'* he asked, as they passed through the reception area and the additional security placed on duty for the ceremony. There were dozens of flower arrangements everywhere, sent by well-wishers, foreign legations and contractors.

Minutes later the shift supervisor stood alongside the command console, scratching his head, and wishing that the Russian was there to advise. Even during assimilation trials he had not had the opportunity to personally witness the sequence of events which now confronted them all.

'Follow me!' he ordered, and the shift controller nodded. They climbed the first steel stairway and moved along that level checking for something they could not see, as neither knew what it was they were supposed to be looking for.

They could not know that the hydraulic valves which would normally have been thrust into action by extremely powerful springs had simply been jammed, by the falling concrete. These springs were designed to open upon loss of electrical power, allowing hydraulics to open the control rod latches. The shutdown *scram* springs alone, could not force the fuel rods down, because the latches could only be released by hydraulic pressure. These latches were designed to hold the rods up, and the *Scram* springs had been engineered to drive them into the core. Without hydraulics, the latches could not be released, preventing an automatic shutdown.

Then the reactor's temperature started to climb.

* * * * * *

0737 Hours — Rama I, Bali

Michael checked his watch and shook his head at the obvious bureaucratic response to the main-gate security's call. He knew that he was expected. Apart from the numerous communications that had exchanged hands between the *Rama I* management and the International Atomic Energy Agency concerning his impending visit, Michael had also made several direct calls to the management, informing them when he had arrived in Jakarta and later, upon arrival in Bali. He flicked another page open and continued to read on, resenting having to wait.

Inside the plant, less than a kilometre from where Michael Bradshaw waited, because of the sudden loss of coolant to the core, the temperatures and pressure inside the nuclear reactor began to rise.

Engineering design had anticipated such a malfunction, and an established mechanical set of procedures were automatically initiated by computer control. The primary relief valve opened, causing a reduction in pressure, and then closed again as it was designed to do. Two employees from the engineering team scrambled outside and hurried to the building where the stand-by generators were located, panic beginning to overwhelm the well-trained, but inexperienced team.

* * * * * *

0754 Hours — Rama II, Java

Vice President Sujono Diryo returned the officer's salute as he stepped from the black Mercedes and walked towards the reactor's main entrance. The Governor's party followed at a discreet distance, smiling broadly whenever the Palace photographer pointed his camera in their direction.

In all, the guests numbered twenty, including the Vice President's aides. Sujono's chest swelled with pride as he climbed the steps, admiring the huge welcome banner strung across the building's upper structure. Inside, the plant's General Manager stood nervously waiting to greet the VIPs dressed, as were others in his team, in a white dust-coat.

Sujono strolled majestically across the highly-polished ceramic floor and shook the newly-appointed controller's hand. He then commenced his official tour of the facility.

The Vice President had visited the site on a number of previous occasions, and was comfortable with his limited knowledge of how the plant actually functioned. Sujono checked his watch, noting that there was ample time before the ceremony and the President's call. He knew that the *Bapak* would be disappointed by his daughter's absence. Sujono anticipated this problem, and reminded his aide to instruct the official photographer to include a selection of the photographs taken during the Governor's dinner party in the final press release.

Over in the control centre, an engineer continued to monitor the rapid rise in the reactor's temperature. His associate's worried face reflected his own alarm.

They were nervous at having been left alone with the dangerous situation and were afraid that they might be held responsible for any further mishap.

'I'm going to get the senior supervisor,' one of them suddenly called, hurrying away buttoning his long, white jacket as he climbed the steel steps, two at a time. He found the supervisor on the third level, fifteen metres up, deep in discussion with his assistant.

'The temperatures are rising too quickly!' the engineer called, hurrying towards the men. The supervisor could see that anxiety had taken hold of the man, and knew this would not help matters.

Why hadn't the hydraulic scram valves closed? he worried. He could not understand why the reactor had not automatically shut down. Unable to identify what was causing the malfunction, he started to lose focus, and felt an over-riding panic taking charge. Just then, the station communication's red light flashed, and he moved to the end of the steel-latticed walkway and lifted the phone.

'The Vice President's here!' the operator informed him. The supervisor cursed all things Russian and scrambled down the steep steps, down through the second and first levels, reaching the ground platform in record time. He hurried out to speak to the General Manager.

Sujono was discussing the plant's desalination benefits with the Governor, when he noticed one of the white-clad staff enter into a huddle with the General Manager. Seconds later, they moved quickly in his direction.

'Bapak Sujono, I'm afraid we have a problem,' the senior man said, his face concerned.

'What is it?' the Vice President demanded.

'We might have to close the plant down,' the engineer hesitated, *'temporarily, that is.'*

Sujono's face clouded over.

'What's the problem?' he asked, sternly. The supervisor was totally intimidated. He understood what normally happened to the

messenger carrying bad tidings.

'*Well?*' Sujono insisted, speaking to the general manager, but turning his head to the engineer.

'*We have a malfunction, Bapak Sujono. We have lost our turbine power and have no auxiliary stand-by generator on-line to correct the problem.*' He could see that the Vice President did not understand. The engineer wished the earth would open and swallow him. He would be held responsible for disrupting the auspicious occasion.

'*Can you fix this problem?*' Sujono asked, lowering his voice so others around could not hear.

'*Not without closing the entire operation down, sir,*' the supervisor advised. He could see Sujono thinking this through.

'*How much time do we have,*' Sujono asked, his concern growing rapidly that the ceremony would be delayed.

'*I don't know. If there was some way of providing alternate power, we might manage.*' The engineer really did not know what to do next. There had been no simulated training for such an unthinkable sequence of events. He scratched his head nervously; he would be blamed, that was sure.

He realized that there was little point attempting to explain, even with the use of simple terminology, what was happening inside as the nuclear reactor core's temperature climbed to uncontrollable levels. The mechanical failure which had occurred was most probably the result of inferior Russian equipment and installation procedures. He was at a loss to know what he might do and was breaking into a sweat.

Vice President Sujono frowned as the official photographer lifted his video camera and started rolling. He was merely testing his equipment again, in preparation for the brief televised broadcast which would soon go to air live, simultaneous with the President's call. It was essential that the timing of the ribbon-cutting ceremony not be delayed. Tens of millions of Indonesians and foreign viewers would be watching via satellite, and Sujono knew that the President was counting on the event's publicity to attract world attention to his country's achievements, while international interest was still focused on the Bali Summit.

Sujono feared that cancellation of the event might prejudice world opinion. After all, they had proudly established that the plant was operational, and that management had been passed to

Indonesian technicians. The possibility that some may laugh at the outcome struck home, and Sujono knew what he must do.

'Do whatever you can to keep this quiet; and don't panic the guests,' he ordered, leaning close. The unhappy supervisor could not believe that he was hearing these words.

'You may close it down as soon as the satellite feed has been disconnected.' The engineer nodded unhappily and left. He calculated what it would take, to do as instructed, and keep the plant operational for at least another thirty minutes. He cursed those responsible for the decision that prevented the Russian technicians from being present. The supervisor knew that he was lost without their guidance, and that the senior technician, Vladimir Kruchinsky, would not return to the complex until later in the morning after the ceremony had been concluded.

As the reactor's temperature continued to rise, a poor-quality weld finally cracked due to the plant's earlier movement, and the steam generator tube failed, allowing high pressure and high-temperature steam and water to enter the primary system. The heat and turbulence generated by the sodium-water reaction then extended into the reactor vessel.

* * * * * *

0810 Hours — Rama I, Bali

The moment Michael's driver opened his door, he knew there was a problem. Security escorted him into the main building, where he was met by the plant's manager.

'What happened?' Michael asked the manager. His question was met with a cautious smile.

'We had a minor malfunction as a result of the earth-tremor earlier. We're attending to the problem as we speak,' the man seemed unruffled by the event. Michael shook his head.

'Seems I could have picked a better time to visit, then,' he suggested, and the manager nodded. Michael noticed some of the staff hurry past; their worry was obvious.

'Why don't you wait inside, in my office, Mr Bradshaw?' the manager suggested, coolly. Michael followed the man, noticing that he was being led away from the main reactor building. Then he spotted several more white-clad staff running towards what he expected would be the auxiliary plant buildings.

'What happened exactly?' he asked, shortening his stride alongside the other man.

'I'll let you know, inside,' the officious administrator answered, hoping that the plant's engineering teams would have rectified the problem before the inspection commenced. He had expected Bradshaw's visit, but had honestly forgotten all about it in the turmoil which had occurred not minutes before. When he had been advised of Michael's arrival, he had deliberately kept him waiting at the main gate, hoping that the technicians would rectify things before the inspection commenced. After fifteen minutes, however, he had no pretext to delay meeting the inspector further.

They both knew that whatever had occurred in the plant's operation would eventually be disclosed anyway, as the IAEA required that all incidents be fully documented and passed to the Agency for review. As they entered the administration building, the automatic glass doors remained open after they passed inside, and Michael observed that the overhead wind curtain, designed to keep the cooler air locked inside, was not functioning. The entrance area was stuffy, and for a brief moment he concluded that the local staff might have turned the power off, knowing that they often did this when the air-conditioning became too cold for them. Minutes later, he knew that this could not be so, as the entire area was in semi-darkness.

'Coffee?' Michael shook his head, anxious to start.

'Are you going to tell me what the hell's going on here?' Michael asked, irritated by the man's complacent attitude. He watched the manager drop his eyes before looking up with a forced smile.

'The tremor knocked our turbines off-line,' the manager announced, his voice lowered as if those in the adjoining rooms might overhear. Michael raised his eyebrows in surprise.

'And?' he asked, annoyed with the deliberate attempt to downplay the significance of the event.

'They're still off-line,' the manager answered, fumbling with documents lying loosely spread across his desk. Michael jumped to his feet.

'Jesus!' he exploded, frightening the smaller man, 'how long have they been off-line?' he demanded, turning to leave the room as he spoke. The manager checked his watch, then answered.

'Twenty-one minutes.'

'What happened to the auxiliary power?' Michael demanded, standing in the now open doorway.

'The stand-by generators kicked in, then lost power before running more than a few minutes. The engineers are over at the power-plant now, trying to rectify the problem. All we have on line is the local power supply, and that could go out at any time. If that goes, we will also lose power to monitor through the control centre.'

'Jesus Christ!' Michael exploded. 'Take me over there. Now!'

'Certainly, Mr Bradshaw,' the manger responded, leading Michael out of the administrative offices, across a smaller car-park, which Michael assumed was for senior management, past buildings with signs indicating that these were data processing and storage areas, and over to the building where mechanical engineers were working desperately to clean the adulterated fuel from the diesel's lines.

Michael knew that inside the main reactor building, temperatures would be on the rise, and that they would not have much time to restore power before a major accident would occur.

The chief engineer monitored the temperatures with growing concern as they continued to climb and the system's relief valve, as designed to do, opened, then shut, in accordance with the escalation in core heat. He watched, as the cycle continued to repeat itself, without the desired result. Unbeknown to him, and those in attendance, this failure resulted in a steam bubble forming in the reactor's fuel core. This would inevitably accelerate the rise in local core temperatures because steam cannot carry-away heat as efficiently as water. In the adjacent building, Michael arrived on the scene to find mechanics yelling abuse at each other, panic threatening to exacerbate the dangerous situation.

'Where are we up to?' Michael asked the supervisor standing over the two mechanics as they wrestled with the fuel line assembly.

'We are trying to establish what's wrong with the fuel supply. The diesel may be tainted,' the supervising engineer replied.

'How long before you can have the generator back on-line?' Michael asked, trying to keep his voice level. The engineer looked up at the tall foreigner and shrugged his shoulders. Michael wanted

JAKARTA

to tell this man in less than twenty words that if he didn't hurry they could get their asses blown off; but he remained patient, waiting for the engineer's response.

'Depends on what we find. If it's what I think, then we might need another hour,' he said. Michael knew that they could not afford this much time. He took the manager aside and explained what he knew would be taking place inside the main reactor building, as they spoke. Less than a minute later, having encouraged the engineers to work faster, they both hurried over to the containment building to investigate what was happening there.

The moment they set foot inside Michael could see that panic had already set in. He asked to be taken in to speak with the senior technician on duty, and minutes later he found himself facing one very frightened plant supervisor.

'Temperatures are already well up,' the man explained, leading Michael around the terminal. Michael looked up through the overhead plant assembly, then calmly removed his coat, and his tie, and climbed the steel staircase to level one.

0820 Hours

'*Aduh!*' one of the mechanics cried loudly in pain, stripping skin from his knuckles as the wrench slipped forward.

'*Hurry,*' the other man cried, having learned from the senior engineer that the plant could self-destruct if electrical power was not soon restored. And they both clearly understood what that meant!

As the technicians at the Bali nuclear plant worked to clear the adulterated fuel from the lines while others went in search of alternative diesel fuel, those inside the main structure which housed the nuclear core and fuel watched the temperature rise to dangerous levels.

Lessons learned from the United States' Three Mile Islands accident meant that the American-designed plant's operational configuration allowed for make-up water, in the event of such an emergency, to be added directly to the pressuriser to minimise thermal stresses on the core.

Michael knew that the pressuriser would act as a buffer for the cold water which flowed through the heat exchange system. He also knew, from experience, that the pressures would drop immediately, as the added water would be considerably cooler.

When he checked the instrumentation again, Michael could see that there was some problem with this emergency procedure as well. He cursed the government which had permitted the plant's commissioning before staff were fully trained to handle such emergencies, although he recognized that, in most cases, only hard experience would have assisted identify the problems they then faced at *Rama I*.

Inside the reactor plant, technicians scrambled to learn why this was not happening. Michael wiped the sweat which threatened to run into his eyes as the ambient temperature became unbearably uncomfortable. He checked the monitoring station, desperate for a lead on what had happened to the fail-safe system.

When he finally identified the cause, he moved quickly to rectify the oversight, hurrying from the main station building with one of the engineers, showing him the way into the secondary structure. There, he checked the pump station responsible for directing the emergency reservoir of heated water which would be flushed from the pressuriser into the reactor's core.

The engineer responsible for ensuring this would occur had left his post to assist the others. He had never been called upon in the past to activate the pumps as an emergency procedure, for the unfamiliar sequence now taking place remained a mystery to him, as it did to most of the other inexperienced technicians at the plant.

Michael knew it was one thing to train people in procedures, and quite another to expect them to react according to the guidelines once placed under extreme pressure, especially if danger was present. He instructed the engineer who had accompanied him to engage the pumps immediately and, satisfied that this had been done, raced back to the reactor building.

His eyes darted across the maze of instruments. Indonesian technicians nervously watched the large digital clock above the console.

'My God!' an engineer exclaimed, pointing to the temperature reading.

'Let's get the hell out of here!' another called, turning to run.

'Wait!' Michael called, 'wait!' and the engineer stood transfixed.

'What's happening with that goddamn stand-by power?'

JAKARTA

Michael yelled at the supervisor who had just hurried into the area. Michael could see that the other staff were dangerously close to abandoning the plant. He knew he had to contain the panic.

'The fuel lines have been cleared,' the supervisor answered quickly, as his eyes darted across the console. 'They're testing the alternate fuel tanks for water. If they're okay, we should have the stand-by back on-line within ten minutes.' Michael took him by the arm and pulled.

'Let's go!' he called, and the smaller man's feet fought to keep balance as Michael hurried back to inspect what was happening for himself. The remaining engineer watched the control console gauges in trepidation, as temperatures and pressure continued to rise. He looked at the double-doors, contemplating escape then, masking his panic, he waited while his co-engineers worked frantically to overcome the fuel problem.

When the reactor's core temperature reached a volatile twelve hundred degrees Celsius, the engineer prayed; he was sick to his stomach with fear, his eyes darting continuously from the temperature readings on the console, to the door, and back again. He wished they hadn't left him alone in there!

Less than a minute later, the stand-by power fuel system was declared clear, and diesel flowed into the huge generator as an engineer, perspiration stinging his eyes, leaned on the over-ride starter. Michael stood stoically in line with the others, as the familiar grunting mechanical noises rose from the machine, and they waited, willing the huge machine to start.

He closed his eyes, counting, listening to the compressed air turning the reluctant machinery slowly, a choking sound, a pause, then a groan. Suddenly, with an incredible roar, the generator clamoured into life.

Without exception, the engineers yelled, and even before the operator had attempted to place any load on the delinquent generator, they had left the building, running back towards the Control Center to establish whether they had sufficient time remaining to prevent the core from melting down.

0832 Hours

Michael's heart pounded as he ran back into the Control Center, his long athletic strides leaving the other engineers well behind. Over on the main console, he was staggered to see that temperatures had climbed to fifteen hundred degrees.

Moments later, he was joined by the others, panting as they gathered around the instrumentation to watch. Michael placed his hand on the shoulder of the engineer who had remained alone at the console.

'Good work,' he intoned. The man looked up at the foreigner, and forced a weak smile.

'Did we make it in time?' he asked, and Michael could see that the man had done well to contain his apparent fear.

'We should leave!' one called out, overcome with fear, turning to run.

'Let's get the hell out of here, now!' another cried, watching the gauge hovering around the fifteen hundred degree mark.

'Wait!' Michael yelled, holding his hands out, pointing back to the gauge. It had slipped slightly, as the cooler water had taken effect. In the deafening silence which followed, the team stood transfixed, watching. Then the temperature fell again. Suddenly, they all burst into cheers, grabbing each other's shoulders in excitement, as emergency power was finally restored. Michael remained standing at the console, his eyes glued to the instruments.

Below, as the steam in the core attempted to reach the same temperature as the core fuel, the pressure relief valve lifted, as if it were operating on some gigantic, domestic pressure-cooker. As the cooler water flowed into the system, the temperature dropped dramatically, collapsing the steam bubble which had formed inside.

Slowly, the nuclear core began to cool.

Michael waited at the control station until certain that the system had been restored, and that heated water was being redirected in a controlled manner to avoid cooling the fuel elements too quickly. He muttered a silent prayer, hoping that these would not shatter from the incredible thermal stress they would be subjected to as the temperature differential came into force. He didn't need to ask the engineers to check radioactivity levels.

Michael observed from the instrumentation that the additional release would be of little concern to them all. Still, he would insist that they continue to monitor the levels within the plant, just to be certain.

JAKARTA

Michael looked across at the Indonesian supervisor and nodded. The man's face broke into a wide grin.

They had all done well.

They had trained for emergencies and, although there had been confusion during the incident, he believed that they had handled the situation in a most professional manner. He shook the hands of those around him, noticing that he had not seen the plant's manager since they had discovered the extent of the danger.

Michael's remaining concern then was whether they had managed to prevent irreparable damage to the plant, knowing that intense examination would be required to determine the extent of repair required to bring *Rama I* back to an acceptable operating standard. He glanced at the monitor clock, and was surprised to discover that the entire emergency had occupied less than an hour of his life. He found an empty chair and threw himself down heavily, mentally exhausted.

* * * * * *

0844 Hours — Rama II, Java

Vice President Sujono resisted looking at his wrist-watch again. It was only minutes since he had last checked. He forced a smile in the cameraman's direction, hoping the perspiration which threatened to soak his safari jacket would not be obvious.

Sujono preferred to dress in the same manner as Indonesia's founding President, Soekarno, believing that he had a great deal in common with the charismatic leader. He wished he knew what was happening with repairs, and how much danger there might really be. The agitated faces of the engineers around the control centre did nothing to calm his nerves.

Sujono walked towards the two brass poles which were several meters apart and supported the crimson coloured ribbon he would cut to officially inaugurate the plant. Unable to resist any longer, Sujono glanced nervously at his watch. It seemed as if time had suddenly stopped.

He turned around to view the guests, and was surprised that they did not seem to be at all uncomfortable with the sudden rise in heat. He breathed deeply, then waved for his aide to move to his side. It was almost time.

'Gentlemen and ladies,' the aide called, and the other guests immediately moved closer to where Sujono stood, eager for the ceremony to commence. They took their positions, the ladies straightening their colourful *kebayas*, tugging gently at their blouses. Additional lighting flooded the area to accommodate the television cameras.

The Vice President moved to centre stage where an ominous, red telephone had been placed in readiness for the President's call. The cameras whirred softly, and Sujono was given the signal to lift the telephone receiver, as satellite viewers stood by.

The guests were totally oblivious to the dangerous situation which had developed as they waited for the ceremony to commence.

While the sodium-water reaction continued unabated, unbeknown to the inexperienced engineers, it was also producing hydrogen gas. As the reactor's core temperatures rose, due to the ferocity of the sodium-water reaction, water disassociated with the temperature increase, further compounding the already volatile situation. The energy released by the reacting sodium and water pushed temperatures and pressures towards the point at which the pressure vessel would rupture.

'Bapak Presiden,' Sujono said into the hands-free telecommunications module, knowing that the Indonesian leader would be watching the proceedings via satellite, while speaking directly to the small assembly. In Jakarta, sitting comfortably in the *Istana*, the President frowned. *Where was his daughter?*

The President glanced at the members of his Development Cabinet, then turned back to the screen and proceeded to give *Rama II* his blessing.

'May Allah smile upon his people and bless this, the harvest of their toil, so that the world may see His children come of age.' The President then smiled, and nodded to his representative to proceed.

Hundreds of kilometers to the east of Jakarta, Vice President Sujono bowed his head in acknowledgement, then moved to cut the ribbon. As the cameraman panned across the guests' faces amidst the polite applause which followed, he captured the frightened figure of an engineer running towards the gathering, waving his arms frantically.

JAKARTA

An aide stepped directly in front of the terrified supervisor, and blocked his entry. The man struggled as he was held, his shout of alarm suffocated by the powerful colonel's hand before he could warn those present of the imminent disaster.

'On behalf of the people of Indonesia, I declare this facility, Rama II, to be officially on-line' Sujono cut the ribbon and turned to face the cameras, his forced smile evident for only the briefest of seconds, as television screens around the world suddenly lost their coverage of the momentous event when the nuclear plant erupted, the rapidly expanding force ripping easily through the fractured containment structure, instantly spewing hot, steam-driven, deadly radioactive spume into the morning sky.

As both are pyrophoric, the uranium and plutonium, now exposed and incredibly hot, ignited, causing a highly exothermic reaction to occur instantly, and a lethal combination of water, heat and graphite burned with an intense, almost flame-less, heat.

At the same moment that the resulting hydrogen explosion ripped through the containment building, throwing shattered pieces of the deadly core into the heavens, Vice President Sujono Diryo died.

Radioactive particles from fuel rods, and spent fuel stored nearby, were also sent soaring more than a mile into the sky, where the prevailing wind carried it, mostly towards the east, in the direction of Bali, the other eastern islands of the archipelago, and northern Australia.

* * * * * *

0931 Hours — Bali Harbour

Fuad shook his head in disgust, as Bartlett prepared to head ashore for his second reconnoitre of the Kuta Beach's bars. He was annoyed with Bartlett. Fuad had remained on watch throughout the captain's absence, and when Bartlett had returned in the early morning drunk he wanted only to sleep. And now, having recuperated from his previous night's drinking spree, it was obvious that Bartlett was going ashore again. When the captain had seen the discomfort on Fuad's face, his lips had curled into a cruel smile.

'Watch the ship,' he ordered, mockingly, lowering himself into the Zodiac, once again, leaving Fuad alone. *Damn the man!* Fuad fumed. He felt so close to completing his last mission, the one which would take him to America with his pot of gold, he was on edge.

Fuad calculated that, with other payments he had secreted away since his arrival in the Philippines, this final mission would see him with almost four hundred thousand dollars to his name. He cursed Bartlett then moved out of the sun into the galley, where he opened a can of cold *halal* meat.

* * * * * *

Rama II — Java

Vladimir Kruchinsky, the Russian training supervisor, arrived at the high security area and knew, immediately, that something was wrong. As all foreign personnel had been instructed to vacate the area during the Vice President's visit and commissioning ceremony, he had taken the time to drive to Jogyakarta, knowing that he might not have the opportunity once his services were terminated.

The main security gates to the one thousand hectare site hung crookedly on their hinges. There were no security personnel in sight. Even the military guards had vanished. As Kruchinsky drove down the wide concrete road leading to the nuclear plant, it was as if he had entered a ghost city.

Unbeknown to the Russian, when the meltdown had occurred, only an hour before, survivors had panicked and fled the area. They had not needed to be reminded by the wailing, warning sirens that they should flee. The shrill sounds had pierced the morning air, and could be easily heard high up into the mountains, as far as the government guest-house where the President's daughter remained resting, waiting for her husband to return.

Twenty minutes after the explosion had ripped through the plant, *Rama II* was totally deserted.

The banner which Kruchinsky had seen the Indonesians erecting before he had left lay in tatters on the ground hundreds of meters from the main buildings. A puff of wind picked up one end, and the long, thin announcement lifted lazily for a moment before

JAKARTA

settling back among the debris.

To the Russian, it was reminiscent of a scene he had visited in his past; he knew immediately that something was terribly wrong. His heart beat faster as fear gripped his insides and Kruchinsky drove on, faster, towards the main plant, tapping the radiation detector inside his jeep. It continued to read zero. The meter was malfunctioning due to the intensity of the high radiation field.

Kruchinsky swerved to avoid a large piece of concrete which had been deposited several hundred meters from the seat of the explosion. He braked, avoiding a smaller block lying on the other side of the road. The engine stalled, and he looked up at the main plant, and what he saw caused the Russian to cry out aloud. The entire side and cover to the containment structure had been destroyed.

He spun the wheel of his pickup, re-started the engine and drove the gas-pedal hard to the floor. Kruchinsky switched off the air-conditioner and cursed himself for having left it on while inside the plant's perimeter. *This place would be hot as hell!*

* * * * * *

After the initial explosion, the few brave men who had entered the damaged containment building to offer help to others quickly discovered that there was little that could be done there.

Poorly trained, and totally unprepared for such an emergency, their ignorance would cost them their lives.

In the days that followed, nearly two thousand men and a handful of women would receive deadly doses and suffer acute radiation sickness. Some would meet their end within hours through extreme damage to the brain and other vital organs. Others would die, painfully, within weeks from damage to bone marrow and severe burns.

As the communication centre had been quickly abandoned, those who had fled the scene carried news of the disaster to the closest military garrison. There, the officer-in-charge of security alerted his superiors in Jakarta. Until then, nothing had been known of the blast outside the area. Although thousands had watched as the televised opening had suddenly lost transmission, no one guessed at the momentous event which had caused the black-out.

Following his report, the officer then phoned his family to reassure them.

News of the catastrophe immediately flooded the capital, where announcements were immediately leaked to both radio and television, and picked up by the international electronic media.

And if as the people of Indonesia had not already suffered enough, another earth tremor rocked the island chain.

1112 Hours — Jakarta, the Stock Exchange

Indonesia's tallest building shuddered as the tremor struck its floating foundations, signalling that the geological upheaval which had threatened the islands of Java and Bali during recent months would continue to intensify.

Trading on the Jakarta Stock Exchange came to an abrupt standstill as confused news of the *Rama* nuclear plant disaster flashed across the overhead bulletin board. As information was scant, speculation about the extent of the meltdown grew, in the absence of any real evidence confirming the extent of the catastrophe.

As the news release scrolled across the electronic information board high above their heads, looks of disbelief swept over the traders' faces. Then pandemonium exploded across the floor as the extent of the Salima Group's exposure struck home.

'*Sell Salima!*' The cry went up immediately, as the panic-driven traders scrambled to off-load the blue-chip stocks, driving the shares' trading value for both Salima Jaya and Salima Energy through the floor. In the subsequent thirty minutes of trading, the Jakarta Stock Exchange shed thirty percent across the board. As news flowed to other financial centres, these too abandoned Indonesian shares as quickly as their own markets could absorb the collapsing stocks.

Kuala Lumpur and Bangkok Exchanges closed, unable to sustain any further losses in their own markets. In Singapore and Hong Kong, *taipans* shook their heads in despair, wondering how such a calamity could occur so close to Chinese New Year.

* * * * * *

JAKARTA

1147 Hours

The Indonesian President listened to his aide's report in silence. The First Lady entered as the verbal report ended, and the aide slipped away unobtrusively.

'*How bad is it, Bapak?*' she asked, having only just learned what had occurred. The older man looked at his wife, sadly, and shook his head.

'*The information is very scant. There has been a nuclear accident and the damage is significant. There have been casualties but, as it seems that the plant has been abandoned by remaining staff and security, we won't know until a team arrives from Bandung to assess the situation.*' The First Lady was stunned. She scanned her husband's face for a sign that he was not hiding the worst from her.

'*There is no other news as to who has been injured. There has been no word from Sujono,*' he added. He sat rigidly still, but his wife of so many years sensed the turmoil in his heart.

'*What would you have me do, Bapak?*' she asked, resigned to the possibility that their daughter might be amongst the casualties. The President looked at his wife, fighting back tears, and blessed her for her strength. '*Should we go there?*' she asked, her voice near to breaking, but he shook his head.

'*No. We will wait for the first damage assessment report. General Suharman is on his way to the site at this very moment. He has undertaken to report directly to me once he has arrived at Rama II.*' The President paused, out of breath, containing the pain he felt inside.

'*How long must we wait?*' she asked, fighting back her tears. She knew that she must now be strong; especially for him.

'*It might be some hours,*' he said, softly. He had been determined to demonstrate to the world that Indonesia had entered a golden age of technological development, and had shed its shackles of economic dependency on the West.

Instead, he had brought his country to the brink of a nuclear Armageddon, and this may have cost him his daughter's life.

* * * * * *

Kerry B. Collison

1205 Hours — Bali

International news broadcasts revealed that the Indonesian nuclear power plant in East Java, only minutes by air from the popular holiday destination of Bali, had suffered an explosion, resulting in the plant known as *Rama II* being destroyed. Within minutes, Indonesia's telecommunication's systems were overloaded as family and friends of those visiting Bali attempted to phone through to the tourist destination.

As news continued to sweep the island, fear of Bali's proximity to the nuclear disaster and the possibility of radioactive clouds caused mass panic. The words Chernobyl and nuclear holocaust were on everyone's lips.

Tourists packed their luggage and fled to Ngurah Rai Airport. There, crowds had already swamped the ticketing counters. Many waved hundred dollar bills in their outstretched hands to secure seats, and airport security struggled to control the unruly mob. Taxis sped to and from the airport terminal, delivering more panic-driven tourists to add to the congestion. The Australian Prime Minister requested Qantas and Ansett Airlines to redirect as many aircraft as possible to the scene, conscious of the large number of his countrymen spending their New Year school holidays in the tropical paradise. Singapore, Malaysian, Cathay and Thai Airways immediately ordered additional flights into Bali to assist with the urgent repatriation of their citizens from the disaster zone.

* * * * * *

Ratna had learned of the meltdown from her cousin, Benny, who had remained in Bali to hold side-talks with the Indian delegation regarding Salima's banking investments in their country. He had suggested that she remain indoors and wait. Bored, and a little frightened, Ratna followed Benny Salima's suggestion and waited impatiently in the cabin for Michael to return. He had promised to be back before lunch. She checked her watch again, anxiously. He was late.

* * * * * *

JAKARTA

Rama I, Bali

Michael dropped the receiver heavily back into its cradle and shook his head.

'The lines are still out,' he said to nobody in particular before leaving the administration block and walking over to the plant's canteen. There, he discovered, the scene was almost one of celebration, as staff and other employees grinned at each other while recounting who was doing what when the reactor almost melted down.

'Over here,' he heard a voice call, and Michael turned to see the senior supervisor standing, beckoning for him to join his table, around which most of those who had been directly involved in the panic-driven moments of some hours earlier sat with dazed expressions. As Michael approached, he could see that someone had smuggled a bottle of local Bintang beer into the compound, and had opened this to help them celebrate. Normally this would have been a dry station, so Michael understood the necessity for turning a blind eye to what he had seen and accepted a chair which had been pulled across from one of the adjacent tables.

'We all want to say, *terima kasih*, to you Mister Michael,' the now inebriated supervisor advised. Michael knew that these people would not normally drink, and that the one bottle had obviously gone a long way to destabilising all four of the men around the table.

Then he understood; looking around, he spotted another of the brown bottles, then another, unopened, protruding from the engineer's overnight bag.

'Tuan Michael!' one of them called, his voice slightly slurred. He turned and accepted the froth-filled plastic mug, and thanked the men in return.

'*Terima kasih,*' he responded, and they all clapped warmly.

* * * * * *

1435 Hours — Rama II, Java

General Suharman and his immediate team, dressed in protective clothing, entered the disaster area. They were astonished to see the extent of the meltdown and its associated explosion, and could only wonder how it might have happened. An assessment was made of the general area, but Suharman already knew that they were too late to prevent the radioactive clouds from showering their deadly dust over the surrounding villages and beyond.

General Suharman had climbed through the rubble in search of the President's daughter and her husband. One of his team had called him over to inspect the half-hidden, broken body, lying crushed under a large slab of concrete, its legs twisted in grotesque fashion.

It was Sujono Diryo.

Later, the general spoke directly with the President by phone, informing him of the Vice President's death and the devastation which he had encountered at *Rama II*. His team then moved to the facility's perimeter, and sealed the entire area off, pending arrival of reinforcements.

* * * * * *

The Vice President's wife had been awakened by the guest-house security and informed of the explosion. Terrified for her husband, she demanded to be taken to the plant, but was finally convinced that this would only endanger her own life. Overcome, she had burst into tears, demanding that the staff phone the nuclear power plant.

Their attempts to reach anyone there were unsuccessful. It was then that she phoned her father in Jakarta and learned of Sujono's demise. She collapsed, and was immediately evacuated by helicopter.

* * * * * *

1450 Hours — Bali, Puri Kauh Villa

Experience told the servants that it would be inadvisable for them to wake the sleeping *tuans*. They, too, were tired from waiting on the three foreigners and their entourage, for the *tuans* and their women had frolicked and played through the early morning hours, oblivious to the rest of the world.

JAKARTA

Exhausted from the evening's entertainment and having continued with the merry-making upon their return from the cabaret, the occupants of *Puri Kauh* slept through the morning and into the early afternoon.

Murray had been the first to rise, and although he had been first to return to the villa, he still did not feel all that well. He ventured out of the luxuriously appointed bedroom, leaving his delightful companion for the evening lying naked on her side. He wandered down to the pool, spread a towel out under the sun, and lay down. Murray was asleep, pool-side in the deck-chair, when Graeme Robson emerged and instructed the servants to bring coffee for them both. They remained there recovering from the excesses of the evening before, and were finally joined by Georgio sometime after three.

As the afternoon sun diminished in strength, and began to dip behind a thick copse of coconut trees, a soft, late-afternoon breeze blew gently across the hillside, from the East, and from the direction of the disastrous meltdown at Mt Muria.

* * * * * *

1512 Hours — Kuta Beach

Dave Bartlett rolled over and looked at the girl he had picked up sometime mid-morning. They had demolished a bottle of Myers Rum before lunch and had crashed together, on her bed. He sucked in several deep breaths, and immediately felt giddy which caused the bile to rise in his throat. He coughed, and the Canadian tourist turned her body towards him, exposing the breasts which had lured him back to her room in the budget mini-hotel.

Dehydrated by the alcoholic binge, Bartlett climbed out of bed and looked around for something to drink. He cursed, knowing that he would have to go outside to one of the roadside stalls for a can of soda, for not even the foul, furry taste inside his mouth could tempt him to drink from the bathroom tap. He had learned that lesson years before, and had paid the penalty for the oversight.

He staggered over to the mirror and checked himself out, wondering if he might have banged the plate in the side of his head which would, he believed, account for the ferocious headache he now suffered. Bartlett checked his wallet and observed that he had already paid the tourist her fifty dollars. He checked again to see that she had not taken more while he had slept off his alcoholic state.

He dressed slowly, covering his head with the baseball cap, then wandered outside. The afternoon sun flickered through the tall coconut palms, making him squint painfully. Bartlett made his way across the road, where a small roadside *warung* advertised cold beer. He sat down and sipped the *Bintang* beer.

'Can't get a flight?' Bartlett looked up at the tourist who had rushed in to buy a packet of *kretek*, the local clove cigarettes, and addressed him. He ignored the man, returning to his drink.

The tourist looked at him and shrugged his shoulders. 'Yeah, I'm in the same boat,' he said, with a hint of remorse, 'last time I'll bloody well buy one of those cheap tickets!' Bartlett glanced at the man, disinterested.

'Reckon the next best thing to do is remain indoors then,' the tourist suggested, then hurried away. Bartlett sighed, finished his beer and waved for the check, deciding to find something a little more up-market.

He dimly recollected that there was a bar somewhere around the corner, so he strolled slowly in that direction, totally unaware of the panic which had cleared most tourists from the Kuta Beach streets during the past few hours. He found the place he'd remembered, but it was closed. Bartlett checked his Rolex Oyster, then looked inside the bar. It was empty. Annoyed with the owner's tardiness, he turned around and went in search of another location where he could sit down and rest in reasonable comfort. He looked down at his hands and saw that they were shaking.

He knew he was getting too old for this business. He had already decided that this contract would be his last. Once he'd returned to Manila, he would change identities again and head for Rio.

As he wandered around, Bartlett thought it unusual that the narrow streets were so quiet. He found another place and walked up to the bamboo bar. The neglected television set there was showing the Cable News Network, and Bartlett, while waiting for the bartender to appear, began to watch the broadcast. Suddenly he was riveted to the spot. Now he understood why the streets had been so empty. Minutes later, swearing profusely, he went on a frantic hunt for transportation to get him back to the harbour. And his ship. Bartlett was furious with himself, but not because he feared any possible radioactive fallout. He was no man's fool and guessed correctly that the alarming news would undoubtedly affect the Bali Summit, throwing their meticulously planned operation into jeopardy.

At last Bartlett found a local driver who was only too willing to accept the excessive one hundred dollar offer for the drive over to Benoa Harbour.

* * * * * *

1520 Hours — Rama I, Bali

Michael shook hands with the group of smiling engineers and technicians before climbing back into his vehicle, waving as he was driven away. He was dog tired.

He looked at his clothes and decided that he badly needed a bath. He wondered why he had been unable to communicate in any way with Ratna since departing early that morning.

Michael considered the reports which had been received regarding the *Rama II* meltdown in Java, and shook his head, knowing that this disastrous accident would most probably precipitate widespread panic and fear, not just amongst the local Indonesians who would have nowhere to escape, but also among the hundreds of thousands of foreign tourists currently enjoying their holidays on Bali and the surrounding islands.

Then, as the driver passed through the first major town between Negara and Denpasar, Michael realized that his worst fears had been correct. A massive traffic jam had been created as trucks, buses and other vehicles blocked the wrong side of the highway. It had been caused by a collision between two tourist mini-buses racing to the airport, still more than an hour away.

Michael had stepped out of his own sedan and walked down through the amazing mess more than half a kilometre before locating the problem. He jogged back to his own car, and instructed the driver to meet him back at the hotel, once the traffic had been sorted out by the local police and he was finally able to proceed. Then he walked back to where the front vehicles were slowly moving away, and found himself a lift by waving a fifty dollar note in the air.

* * * * * *

Bali Harbour

Fuad spotted the Zodiac speeding towards the ship. He swore, angry that the other man's self-indulgence might have threatened the success of their operation. As the outboard engine's motor died, Fuad scanned the immediate area, concerned that Bartlett's hurried return might have attracted unwarranted attention. He listened as the New Zealander loaded the dinghy, then walked towards the ship's stern.

'Now it's my turn for a break,' Fuad said, deciding not to engage in any conversation. It would, he knew, most probably result in a fight as he could see that Bartlett had been hitting the bottle hard. 'I'm going to catch up on some sleep.'

'No you're bloody well not!' the bearded sailor spat, 'We're getting under way. Now!' Fuad looked at him with a quizzical expression then, believing the man to be drunk, his anger rose. He could smell the hard liquor on the other man's breath and knew, immediately, that Bartlett would be dangerous in this condition.

'I'm tired, and you've left me alone onboard for ages,' Fuad said, wishing the other man wasn't wearing sunglasses so that he could see his eyes.

'The sleep can wait,' Bartlett snapped, taking a step towards Fuad.

'Why?' Fuad asked, stepping back from Bartlett, shifting his feet into a better stance. If the other man swung, he would be ready.

'There has been a change in plan, Fuad,' he hissed. 'We'll get under way now!' Bartlett removed his sunglasses suddenly, and glared at Fuad. Fuad glared back and the cold, green eyes convinced him that Bartlett was indeed serious.

'What's happened?' Fuad asked, but Bartlett brushed past him as if he wasn't even there.

'The Summit's been cancelled. For all I know, the bastards have probably already left. Now let's get going for chrissakes!' Fuad cursed but moved quickly, as ordered, visions of the lost opportunity clouding his mind. He signalled to Bartlett back on the bridge as the anchor noisily rose and was locked into place. Minutes later, they were under way, steaming the few kilometers to their destination where they would wait, listening to the Ngurah Rai air-traffic control tower's communications.

* * * * * *

1620 Hours — Nusa Dua

'My God, Michael, where have you been?' Ratna cried, distressed. He had returned and gone directly to their cabin. Michael was confronted with a barrage of questions. He stepped forward, expecting that her reaction had most probably been precipitated by fear, and held his arms out to her, forgetting how he looked.

'We had no idea until just two hours ago, Ratna. I tried to phone but everything's overloaded to hell. The Negara exchange could not get through. Besides, there's no longer any danger here,' he said, attempting to comfort her.

'My God, Michael, what have you been doing?' she exclaimed, stepping back, surprised.

'There were major problems at the *Rama I* plant as well, Ratna. I had to stay on when everything came back on-line, just to be sure.'

'Were you exposed to any radiation?' she asked, fear in her eyes.

'No, Ratna,' he said, wishing he could take her in his arms and comfort her as he could see that she was visibly distressed. 'The Bali plant did not release anything which would be of concern to me, or those working there. As for the Java accident, there's likely to be far more people killed and injured from panic than there would from any radioactive fallout this far away.' He tried to reason with her, but the fear of nuclear holocaust had struck deep into the hearts of those even remotely within the critical fallout path.

'We must leave, immediately!' she insisted. He noticed that their luggage had been packed and left standing beside the door.

'Look, Ratna, this is silly,' he tried again, hoping that she would listen to common sense. 'If we remain indoors, there will be practically no effect at all. Hell,' he said, controlling his temper, having been through a very demanding day, 'there's probably a higher reading here than outside right now,' he said, pointing to where the television stood. Ratna looked at Michael, unsure. She sat down on the bed and looked at the floor.

'I'm going, please yourself,' she said, standing again, and reaching for her handbag. Michael moaned silently. He yearned for a long, hot, bath, then a few quiet drinks in the lobby bar.

There was no doubt in his mind that he would be expected to report back in Washington, immediately, as a result of the disastrous accident. There would be little point remaining alone there in Bali; he sighed heavily, resigned to the new problem which then confronted him.

'I'm serious, Michael, I'm leaving.'

'But Ratna, listen to what I'm saying. You will be perfectly safe here, for chrissakes!' He looked at his filthy clothes and started to remove his shirt.

'Goodbye, Michael,' she said, stepping to one side, then turning.

'My god, Ratna, don't do this, please. I'm tired, I've had one hell of a day, and I really don't need any of this right now. Okay?' Ratna hesitated, then looked challengingly, directly into his eyes.

'I'm really going, Michael. If you love me, then you will understand. Please, Michael, please!' she pleaded. Realising that there would never be any peace between them unless he agreed, Michael reluctantly gave in to Ratna, then shook his head, more out of disappointment for his own decision than anything else.

He phoned downstairs to reception. Then he remembered the traffic problems he had encountered on his way back from the Bali plant.

'This is most probably going to be a total waste of time, Ratna,' he said, exasperated by her behaviour. The lobby had been a beehive of activity when he arrived. A large number of guests were huddled together in the foyer, desperation on their faces.

Unable to obtain confirmation of seats, many had refused to return to their rooms, hoping that their situation might improve by waiting close by reception, not caring that their presence only hindered others.

'We might not even be able to find a cab. Have you any idea what's happening on the roads? It's chaos, Ratna, pure chaos.'

'I don't care what you say, Michael, I'm going to the airport,' with which, she opened the door and left for the lobby, leaving him behind to organize their luggage. She hoped he would follow.

JAKARTA

Michael fumed, angered by her behaviour, and was tempted to let her go, alone. By the time he arrived at reception, their account had been prepared, and Ratna had secured transport.

Michael shook his head, thinking he should have known that she would have her way. Several minutes later their driver fought his way through a maze of buses and other vehicles, and they headed for the airport.

Although Ngurah Rai Airport was not of any great distance, their driver could do little more than creep slowly along, his hand firmly on the horn as he made way through the incredible mass of people heading for the same destination. Occasionally, those stranded along the half-blocked highway threw rocks, while others banged their fists against the side of the vehicle, venting their frustration at having been left behind. Ratna gripped Michael's hand, refusing to look at those less fortunate outside.

'Michael, I'm scared,' she admitted, as more stragglers angrily pounded their car.

'It'll be okay, Ratna,' he said, hoping that his voice was reassuring. Michael too was worried. He knew what mob anger could do and in no way wished to be the object of their misdirected rage.

'Is it much further?' she asked, but there was no way he could tell. Michael had never been to Bali before and, even had there not been a crowd surrounding the vehicle, he still would not have known where they were.

'Not long now,' he answered, hoping that this was true. Finally, having suffered the abuse of the roadside throng as they drove slowly on, the driver turned and spoke.

'Can't go any further,' he announced. Michael looked outside but could not understand what was preventing them from proceeding.

'Go on!' he ordered, but the driver merely shook his head and pointed to his front. There, amongst the crowd, Michael could see a line of soldiers ahead, blocking the road.

'Police no let you pass here,' the driver said, agitated, holding his hand out for the promised fare. Michael swore and turned to Ratna.

'Now we really have a problem,' he growled. They had been stopped from passing through the well-guarded airport entrance, and forced to leave their taxi at the airport perimeter fence. There was not a porter to be seen anywhere. Instead, they were horrified by the sea of white faces clambering over each other, fighting for access into the airport terminal. Michael knew that it would be futile to attempt to carry luggage through the mass of humanity, even if they were permitted through the gates.

'Do you still want to do this?' he demanded. 'We'll never get through!'

'Let's leave the baggage, Michael,' Ratna decided. He looked at the crowd ahead of them and was unsure. When he observed that she was determined to proceed, with or without him, Michael extracted his passport folder and, together with Ratna's papers, placed these inside his jacket pocket. Michael then wrote down the taxi's number, handed over fifty dollars, and instructed the driver to take their cases back to the hotel.

* * * * * *

1625 Hours

The Indonesian President declared a state of emergency following telephone discussions with each of the Heads-of-State still gathered in Bali. They had all decided to return to their countries immediately, and continue the discussions at a more appropriate time.

The President's announcement was followed by a similar call from the Australian Prime Minister. Both leaders were stricken by the catastrophic loss of life in Indonesia, and the people of both nations prayed for those still trapped in the path of the deadly, radioactive clouds.

Presidential advisers had informed their ageing leader that the imminent radiation spill from the country's East Java *Rama II* plant would spare few within the immediate area, and that heavily contaminated clouds of radioactive dust would most surely affect Bali.

Contamination would also, unquestionably, reach far into northern Australia. Forecasts were that the radioactive plume would be carried by prevailing winds across the Timor Sea and penetrate deep into the Australian hinterland. The projected fallout was then expected to spread, affecting population centres as far as central Queensland.

JAKARTA

In Canberra, Cabinet's advisers tried to tell the country's leader that the Australian death toll in Darwin would be more likely to be caused by panicking Territorians hitting kangaroos as they fled the northern city than any radioactive poisoning which might reach their isolated city.

In East Java, Bali and major centres of East Nusa Tenggara through to New Guinea, the figures indicated that more than seven million Indonesians would be affected in some way as a result of the *Rama II* meltdown.

Fortunately for those who resided in the national capitals of Jakarta and Canberra, their population centres would not be affected, due to the direction of Indonesia's prevailing winds.

* * * * * *

1642 Hours — Bali

The Indian Prime Minister had finished conveying his confirmation to the South African President that they would depart as soon as was practicable. The Boeing 777, designated *India One*, was being prepared for their early departure, and would be ready within the hour. The African agreed, anxious to leave the island before their lives were, in any way, endangered by radioactive fallout. Aides scrambled to advise security, drivers, and the many others who would be involved in overseeing the revised arrangements.

Most roads leading into Den Pasar had already been cleared by the Bali Garrison Commander. The protocol highway leading to Ngurah Rai airport had remained partially blocked for hours, as traffic congestion choked the vital arterial road. Thousands upon thousands of tourists had vacated their hotels and stormed the airport, fighting for a place on any aircraft which might take them away from the dangers of radiation poisoning. They had refused to listen as broadcast information bulletins assured them that they were not in danger, that the only real risk to their lives would come from panic-related accidents, and that they should remain calm, preferably inside their resort hotels. But very few of the panic-stricken tourists believed this to be true.

Exaggerated forecasts had been irresponsibly made on satellite news broadcasts and, fuelled by confirmation that the Bali reactor had also experienced some mishap earlier in the day, the visitors wished only to leave as quickly as possible. By mid-afternoon, more than one hundred thousand tourists had inundated the airport. As buses plied continuously between hotels and Ngurah Rai, taxis raced at breakneck speeds over the mountains, bringing tourists from the more isolated districts.

* * * * * *

1705 Hours

Admiral Gopal entered the Prime Minister's suite, accompanied by Xanana Soares. There was a brief discussion, an exchange of warm handshakes, and smiles all around. The Summit's delayed discussions could only work in their favour, distracting attention from the Indian Fleet's mission.

'Good luck, Krishna,' the Indian leader said, with the deepest sincerity, smiling at Admiral Gopal. Turning to Xanana Soares, he said, 'and good luck to you also, *Mr President*.' Xanana beamed at the man who would liberate his people, shook his hand warmly then left with the Admiral. They hurried to their respective quarters to prepare for their imminent departure.

* * * * * *

1710 Hours

Murray felt like turning around and smacking Graeme Robson on the side of his head. He hadn't shut up once in more than thirty minutes, ever since they discovered what had happened. While others around the island were already making arrangements to leave, Robson and his guests had slept, and played, without their having the slightest inkling of what was transpiring outside the luxurious and isolated setting of *Puri Kauh*.

'You're a bunch of useless bastards!' Robson had screamed at the servants. 'Christ, John, and you!' he yelled at Georgio. 'You're supposed to know what the hell is going on, for chrissakes! Isn't that what you're paid for?' Robson continued to whine and curse, distressed with the knowledge that they had been lying around in the open for several hours before discovering that the area had, most probably, already been subjected to radioactive fallout from Java. Immediately they had learned of the danger they were in, Robson had grabbed for the phone, desperate for further information regarding the extent of the disaster. He phoned his office in the capital.

'There's nothing much getting through,' Robson's private secretary in Jakarta had advised.

'What do you want us to do?' his senior management had asked, anxiously. They had been unable to raise their chief executive throughout the entire day because the Balinese servants, following the instructions which had been explicitly given to them by Georgio, the evening before, refused to wake the *tuans*.

'What happened to the market?' Robson asked nervously. He heard the director at the other end of the phone cough nervously. When he finally learned how his own company's shares had tumbled, following Salima's, the air resounded with expletives which might have embarrassed a seasoned soldier.

'What is it?' Murray asked, concerned. Robson turned to him, his face white with shock.

'The market's collapsed,' he said, his voice suddenly running out of steam. Then, with the grim realization that their lives might be in danger, fear generated panic, and Robson screamed for Georgio to get the car ready while he attempted to contact his pilot and crew. Again, contact could only be effected via their mobile phones. To their relief, the forward thinking pilot had already summoned his engineer the moment news had filtered in about the disaster. Robson ignored what little luggage he had, yelling for the others to leave theirs as well while he made several more calls before hurrying out to the waiting sedan.

Their group numbered ten, including the additional girls from the cabaret. Robson and Murray climbed into the back of one of the Mercedes, squeezing two of the girls into the front, while the other vehicle, a wagon, carried the remaining troupe.

'John, can you take us by our hotel first?' the Filipino girls asked, only to be ignored.

'John, what about our clothes and passports?' another complained.

'Look, girls, it's like this. We're not going anywhere but the airport. Okay?'

'But John,...' one started, then cried out in pain as Georgio slapped her hard across the face.

'Shut up, bitch!' he screamed, 'or you'll stay behind!' The other girls put their arms around the shocked dancer, terrified that they might be dumped in the middle of nowhere. By then, they all understood quite clearly what was happening. They too had watched the CNN broadcast with the men and, like them, had sat shocked, disbelieving that all of this had happened while they slept.

Georgio had wanted to leave the women behind from the start, and Robson had been inclined to agree. It was only at Murray's insistence that Robson had finally acquiesced, and stormed out to the waiting cars while screaming for Georgio to take charge of the other vehicle. As an angry Robson sped away from the isolated *Puri Kauh* villa, the others were left behind and, although Georgio persisted in yelling at the driver to go faster, the winding, mountain roads surrounding Ubud only added to their frustration, causing the driver to drive even more cautiously because of the additional passengers he carried.

When the two vehicles hit their first traffic snarl upon arriving in Denpasar, Robson lost control, screaming at the driver. Finally, a traffic officer waved them through, and Robson seized the opportunity. He wound the window down and called the policeman over to the car.

Five minutes later, his entourage sped down the highway, wailing police sirens clearing a path for their vehicles as the white traffic jeep's driver leaned on his horn for additional affect. His sergeant winked, then laughed, patting the five hundred dollars he had pocketed, a gift from the bad-mouthed foreigner.

Behind, at the check-point, three disillusioned Filipino dancers placed their hands on their hips and screamed abuse at the departing vehicles, having been abandoned alongside the road and ordered to make their own way back to their club's hostel. Had it not been for the fact that the dancer's accommodations lay in a different direction to that of the airport, Murray would have objected.

* * * * * *

Jakarta

1735 Hours — Jakarta

Ruswita turned anxiously to the woman who had entered and coughed politely.

'Any news, Sumi?' she asked her personal assistant. Sumi looked helplessly at the woman she so admired, and shook her head.

'I'm sorry. We still have been unable to locate her.'

'Have they left the hotel?' Ruswita asked, hopefully.

'Yes. They have already checked out,' Sumi replied softly. She too had difficulty keeping the tears back. The day had been disastrous for the Salima Group of companies, she knew. But that was only secondary in their minds at that moment as concern for both Ratna and Michael's safety grew by the hour.

'Have you been able to locate Benny?' Ruswita asked, wishing that neither of her children had gone to Bali at this time.

'He has left a message for you,' her assistant replied. *'Benny did not want to interrupt the meeting. The message says that he is all right, that he has spoken to Ratna, and that he will accompany the Indian Prime Minister's team back to New Delhi.'*

Ruswita turned back to gaze through the window and watched the small pedestrian dots barely moving along the footpaths below. She turned back to face her personal assistant and forced a smile.

'Go home. Sumi, there's nothing you can do here,' she ordered, kindly. Sumi took several steps towards Ruswita and shook her head slowly.

'I'll stay,' was all she said, and then reached for Ruswita to comfort her. She placed her arms around the older woman and spoke softly. *'Ratna will be all right, Rus,'* she said, hoping that this would be true.

Chapter 29

Bali and Rama

Fuad watched his associate's face for a sign, deeply concerned that they had missed their opportunity. It seemed that the airport was in chaos as additional flights arrived to evacuate tourists, throwing established aviation procedures into total confusion. Tempers ran short, and ill-equipped personnel attempted to handle the overload.

'Anything?' Fuad asked, agitated by the lack of information.

'Shut up!' Bartlett hissed, concentrating on the communication exchange taking place between pilots and the control tower. Then he heard what he had been listening for, and his face cracked into a grim smile.

'Bali tower, this is *India One*, do you copy?' He heard the pilot ask.

'*India One*, Bali tower, what is your ETD?' Bartlett listened for the pilot's confirmation of his departure time, then looked at Fuad.

'Bali Tower, this is *India One*, anticipate rolling at Zulu 1035,' the voice of the captain responded.

'Copy *India One*, contact the tower for final taxiing instructions.'

'Copy that, tower,' he heard the captain say, before the air traffic controllers switched to another aircraft. Bartlett turned to Fuad, his expressionless eyes never more frightening.

'You've got about thirty minutes,' was all he said. *India One* had not yet departed and Fuad, breathing a sigh of relief, went about his own preparations. He immediately climbed down into the ship's hold, where they had stored their weapons and additional cargo. He crouched, then lifted the *Stinger* assembly carefully, looking up for Bartlett's assistance to lift the deadly missiles.

'Easy!' Fuad heard Bartlett hiss, as he handed up the weapon.

The man above then laid it down carefully on the deck.

'Ready?' Bartlett called, wondering what was keeping the other man. Fuad was sweating, and consciously warned himself to slow down.

'Fuad?' he heard Bartlett call, before his silhouette appeared above, and the sailor leaned down to receive the missile. Minutes later, having placed the *Stinger* inside the bridge, the captain called down once more, then lifted the second missile, taking this away also and stowing it safely alongside the first. Bartlett checked his diver's watch, then called to Fuad.

'Get the rest of the gear up, quickly!' he ordered, and Fuad complied, lifting the end of the Chinese inflatable upwards for Bartlett to drag onto the deck. This was followed with an assortment of supplies and equipment, all stamped with Chinese points of origin. He threw the PRC 7.62-mm sub-machine-gun and silencer into the dinghy, and placed a well-used Chinese Communist Type 54 pistol alongside, for good measure.

'Five minutes!' he heard Bartlett call. Fuad scrambled quickly back out of the hold, and prepared the launcher, retrieving one of the missiles from where Bartlett had carefully placed it, beside the bench aft of the ship's wheel.

He looked up into the heavens, away from the fading light. Then, having checked his equipment one more time, he glanced over towards the bridge and raised his thumb to indicate his readiness. He could see that Bartlett was engrossed, listening to the air traffic controllers struggle with the heavy aircraft traffic. Satisfied that he had done all that was necessary, Fuad then settled down to wait, watching the golden sun settle behind the island.

* * * * * *

Michael held Ratna roughly by the hand as they pushed their way through the multitude of hopeful tourists who crowded the airport's entrance in the hope of securing a flight away from the troubled destination. They almost felt like giving up at one point. Ahead, Michael could see little but a mass of passengers kicking, shoving and screaming as they surged towards the building's entrance. Then, airport security fired several shots above the foreigners heads; the effect was immediate, and restored some semblance of authority over the disorderly gathering.

Michael heard sirens approaching from behind, and attempted to move Ratna out of harm's way, but only succeeded in getting them both pushed back into the oncoming vehicles' path. The driver of the white police-jeep had never seen anything like it before. Indonesian crowd control exercises were one thing; driving his vehicle through a mass of foreign tourists which refused to budge was something he had not been trained to do. The vehicle following the police car contained Murray Stephenson and Graeme Robson. Murray opened his window and shouted at the pair standing amongst the crowd, then yelled for his driver to stop.

'Michael! Michael!' he yelled loudly, relieved when the man's face suddenly broke into a smile of recognition at hearing his name called. 'Get yourself in here!' Murray called.

'Jesus, Murray, what the hell are you doing?' Robson shouted, attempting to lean over to close the window, but Murray had his hand on the operating switch.

'That's Michael!' he snarled, pushing the door open against the swelling crowd. He stood in the doorway, above the mob, and screamed threateningly until they moved aside. By then, the police escort had stopped, its red lights still flashing. Foreigners amongst the crowd pulled back in fear, away from the armed men; Indonesia's riot-control police had earned their vicious international reputation on the country's bloody city streets. Foreigners closest to the police struggled, pushing back in desperation as they resisted those shoving from behind, fearing that they might antagonise the well-armed police who stood menacingly only meters to their front.

'Ratna, get in!' Michael ordered, lifting her bodily, and shoving her into the rear seat with the others.

'There's no room!' she shrieked, banging her head. Murray pushed with all his strength, forcing Robson across the seat. Then Michael climbed in, dragging his long legs after him as he squeezed, finally closing the door behind him.

'Tell those bastards to move!' Robson yelled to the driver, who immediately blew his horn at the escort in front. The forward jeep began to advance, police siren screaming.

'Who the hell are you?' an angry tourist screamed, his face dangerously close to the off-side rear window. Another kicked the door of the lead car in frustration, while others banged whatever part of the Mercedes was in reach, with their fists and drink-cans, while screaming abuse. As their car forced through the angry crowd, someone spat on the window. Ratna looked wildly at Michael. The crowd surged forward, blocking their path, and Robson's driver hit the horn again, hard, flashing his lights alerting the police to their difficulty. The escort police jumped from their jeep, brandishing their batons, threatening the tourists blocking their access.

Suddenly, the sound of automatic fire filled the air, as one of the airport police, not fifty meters away, opened fire, scattering the crowd. Terrified, those tourists closest to the entrance immediately jumped back, only to be pushed forward again by the crowd behind. The sergeant in charge of the unit withdrew his sidearm and also fired, twice, into the air. The response was instant. The area directly between the vehicles and the airport entrance cleared instantly, providing a path for them all to scramble through. They raced towards the terminal.

'Let's go!' Robson yelled, first out of the lead car.

'For chrissakes, move!' Murray screamed, and Michael tumbled from the vehicle.

'Ratna!' he called, waiting with his hand extended.

'Wait, Michael! Wait!' she screamed. She banged her knee and bit her lip in her haste. Then she grasped Michael's hand and they dashed for safety towards the waiting airport police.

'Leave the luggage!' Georgio yelled from behind, leading the way into the heavily congested area. Airport police moved forward and raised their arms to prevent them entering the building, but Robson's pilot was on hand to assist, yelling from the safety of the building's main doors as he alerted the police that this was his group of VIPs.

'The door's open!' someone cried, and the mob roared.

'They're taking more passengers!' another yelled, and immediately the crowd surged forward again, pushing from behind. Ratna was catapulted forward.

'Michael!' she screamed, and Michael dragged her back to her feet even before she had hit the ground. The crowd continued to push up against the airport police until another burst of automatic fire drove them away. People yelled and screamed, throwing whatever was in their hands at that moment, in sheer frustration, at watching these privileged few enter the building ahead of the queue. Murray cried out in pain, as a rock glanced off the side of his head, and he gritted his teeth, lunging forward towards the entrance.

'Murray?' Michael called, but he could do little more than push with the others, protecting Ratna as best he could. Crowded together, under a hail of abuse, they finally reached safety behind airport police lines, and rushed inside the terminal.

Their group was ushered through the impatient crowd inside the building, and Robson's two-man crew arrogantly pushed other passengers aside. Bruised from their ordeal, they finally made it to the passenger holding area, and paused for breath. Inside, through the glass doors separating departing passengers from immigration and customs, officials had long since thrown their hands into the air, permitting the heavy flow of departing tourists to board their flights without further checks. Robson's pilot banged on the locked partitions, displaying his permit to the soldier armed with a machine pistol. Moments later, they were all inside the waiting hall.

'What flight are you on?' Murray shouted, bending closer to Michael as he did so.

'Flight?' he yelled back, 'none, Murray,' he shook his head and looked at the impossible numbers cramped inside this section of the building. Murray leaned forward again and gripped his arm. Michael pulled Ratna closer to him.

'Come with us, there's room,' he yelled again, his throat becoming hoarse from the effort. 'Besides, you were supposed to be on this flight anyway, remember?' he grinned, but not convincingly. Michael nodded, remembering how their circumstances had changed in the course of just a few hours. He had been offered the opportunity to visit *Rama II* with Robson on his return journey.

'That's great, Murray, thanks,' he said, turning to Ratna. 'Seems we have lucked out after all.' Ratna didn't feel like smiling, she was feeling faint with the heat. She looked across at the others in the group, identifying that the women accompanying the other men were obviously professional hookers, what her mother would have referred to as *panggilan*. Immediately she was concerned that people might think she was one of them.

'Michael,' she said, tugging at his arm. He turned as she pinched the flesh around his waistline to gain his attention, causing him to jerk away in pain. She leaned closer, and stood on tiptoe.

'Michael, those women are all prostitutes!'

'For chrissakes Ratna, don't be so goddamned childish!' he snapped, holding her right arm tightly with his strong hands, 'who cares who the hell they are. It's a lift out of the stinking place. Isn't that what you dragged us out here for?' She pulled away, angrily. He had hurt her arm. She glared back at him, then turned away.

The noise outside was deafening. Here, amongst the fortunate few who would leave over the next hours, the cramped passengers were far more subdued. Michael could see that Ratna was close to tears, and stepped after her, throwing his arm around her shoulders to comfort her.

'*Ratna?*' a voice called, '*Ratna, over here!*' She turned instantly to follow the voice, but she couldn't identify who had called her name.

'*Ratna, here!*' someone yelled again, but amongst the thousands cramped together, packing the hall, she couldn't see who it might be. Then, she saw him, his face breaking into a wide grin as he managed to force his way through to her.

'*Benny!*' she squealed, and immediately pushed through the crowd until she reached her cousin, throwing her arms around him.

'*Benny, I thought you would be gone by now!*' she exclaimed, excitedly. They spoke together for a moment, and Michael watched. He saw her nod, then embrace Benny again. Michael pushed through the crowd, making his way over to where they stood.

'Michael, this is my cousin, Benny. He is *Ibu Ruswita's* youngest son,' she added. Benny extended his hand to Michael. His grip was limp.

'Seems that we're all stuck here together,' Michael said, raising his voice above the noisy, babble. Benny smiled.

'No, I'm not stuck,' he said, 'just waiting for the Prime Minister and South African President to arrive so we can board.' Michael looked confused. 'I'm returning on their flight, as I still have some business to attend to in India,' he added, pointing in the general direction of the waiting Boeing 777. Benny looked at Ratna.

'*Sure you won't join me, 'Na?*' he asked her, in their own language so as not to offend the foreigner. She responded by squeezing his hand.

'*Oh yes, Benny, please!*' she accepted, gratefully. Benny waited for her to ask if Michael could come too and was surprised when she didn't. Embarrassed, but not wishing to intrude on their arrangements, he checked his watch and decided it was time for them to leave. He held his hand out to Michael, in farewell.

'I'll see that Ratna gets back to Jakarta all right,' he said. 'I will speak to the Prime Minister's security. I'm sure, considering the circumstances, there'll be no difficulty. The Salima Group has committed a substantial amount of foreign exchange to the new banking systems to be introduced in India, and I'm certain they won't object.'

Michael was dumbfounded.

'You're dumping me to go on a separate flight?' he asked Ratna incredulously.

'Yes,' she said, and moved away with Benny, who led her through the crowd and out through the glass doors which connected with the VIP lounge. Michael stood stunned, speechless with what had just taken place. He watched as Ratna disappeared amongst the throng.

'Michael,' he heard his name called, and raised his hand in acknowledgement. Murray stood waiting, his impatience showing. Michael looked back in Ratna's direction, but she was nowhere to be seen.

'Son-of-a-bitch!' he cursed to himself, filled with anger. He then followed Murray and the others as they were led out through the double-glazed, plate glass doors which opened onto the hard-standing area where aircraft crews were hurriedly loading passengers.

There was no ticket control inspection required for their private flight. Security gave them a cursory check, then permitted the group to leave the terminal. As he stepped outside, the heat slapped him in the face and Michael covered his ears to shield them from the incredible noise.

'John, throw those bloody women aboard so we can get the hell out of here!' Robson shouted, his voice almost drowned out by the screams of aircraft turbines as they whined into readiness for departure. He saw Georgio yelling at the group of young, attractive girls, hobbling hurriedly across the busy concrete apron, trying desperately to avoid speeding service vehicles, their red warning-beacons flashing ominously as they raced to and fro.

Murray also tried to hurry, but his ageing legs were suffering from the past few days, what with dancing late into the night and frolicking in the pool with girls a third of his age. As he walked stiffly onto the parking apron, he looked, almost with awe, at the number of aircraft that had managed to squeeze into the area.

A dozen aircraft ranging from small private jets to jumbos lined up waiting for departure instructions. Murray wondered how there hadn't already been an accident. As jet engines continued to scream, pushing their gargantuan loads into readiness for take-off, Murray turned to see what had happened to Michael.

* * * * * *

Ratna walked slowly across the concrete apron, turning her head to avoid the hot, kerosene-filled air as another aircraft moved across her path. She hesitated, looking across in the other direction, away from the suffocating, acrid smell of burning fuel. She saw Michael, alone, standing not fifty metres to her left, watching as she headed for her aircraft. He waved, and in that moment, Ratna was overcome with regret for the way she had behaved.

She turned, looking for Benny, and saw that he was waiting for her. She looked back at Michael, then across at Benny Salima again. Suddenly, she knew what she must do.

'Michael!' She ran towards Michael, calling his name, narrowly missing a speeding power-unit as it passed dangerously close.

'Christ, Ratna,' he yelled loudly, 'be careful!' He stepped towards the woman as another vehicle threatened to bowl her over. He leaped forward and reached out, barely in time to pull her from harm's way.

'Michael, Michael!' she cried, falling into his outstretched arms, clinging to him tightly. He wrapped his arms around her.

'Well?' was all he could say. Ratna reached up, and there, standing on the concrete apron amidst the chaos of the moment, she kissed him firmly.

'I'm so sorry, Michael,' she shouted, 'I was scared, and reacted poorly. Will you forgive me?' He reached for her, pulling her close to his body.

'Of course,' he shouted back, then glanced after the others.

'Will you come with me?' Michael looked directly at Ratna, and she nodded.

'Okay,' she surrendered, agreeing to accompany him on board

the Lear Jet. Michael looked at her sternly and she smiled. Realizing just how ridiculous their situation was, they both suddenly broke into laughter and hurried to board Robson's jet together. Ratna waved at Benny, but he did not understand. He remained standing, watching as she entered the executive jet not one hundred meters across from where *India One* was parked, towering over the smaller planes.

They hurried aboard and found that the others were already strapping themselves into their seats. Murray twisted around, looked back and waved.

'Glad you could make it,' he called, as Michael ushered Ratna into one of the remaining seats. The engineer closed then locked the cabin exit door, and moved forward to join the captain who, at that moment, was absorbed with his pre-flight instrument check.

'Let's get this bird moving,' Robson called forward to the open cockpit door. The pilot obeyed his employer's command, and called the tower for instructions. Several minutes passed before the overworked air traffic controllers responded, and the captain spoke briefly.

'We're seventh in line,' he called back to those in the cabin. 'The tower has told us to wait for taxiing instructions.'

'Christ almighty!' Robson cursed, angered by the delay. He knew that this could easily compound, with priority being given to military and senior government officials. This, added to everything else, only raised his ire more. In their haste to depart, he had not had time to fully consider the devastating ramifications of the Jakarta market's collapse. He knew that his position would be precarious; his bankers would be anxious for an explanation of how he intended repaying the enormous debt he had acquired. He snapped back at the pilot.

'Call the bloody tower and get us some priority!' he ordered unreasonably. The captain responded with a nod, but did nothing, knowing that they would just have to wait their turn. He motioned with his head for his fellow crewman to distract the passengers. The engineer moved from the cockpit and stood where the passengers could see him clearly. He commenced with his rehearsed air safety demonstration.

'Not this goddamn bullshit again,' a voice complained, somewhere up front. 'Hey, Graeme,' Georgio then called, 'why don't

I just get him to pass out some drinks?' with which, he unbuckled and rose from his seat, moving into the aisle with some difficulty.

'Jesus, John,' Murray called out, 'leave it till we get airborne.'

'Move, goddamn it!' Georgio cursed, stomping over the girl strapped alongside. He dragged himself into the narrow aisle, then stood and faced the others, smiling at Robson. Georgio had already been drinking.

'Hey, Graeme, come on,' he said, flashing a bottle of bourbon from out of nowhere. At the rear of the small cabin, Michael felt Ratna's nails bite into his wrist. In that instant of recognition, her face clouded as the recent memory flashed through her mind.

'Michael, that's him!' she said, angrily, unbuckling her safety belt.

'What are you doing?' Michael asked, surprised. He too unstrapped, and squeezed out into the aisle behind her. Robson turned in his seat, craning his neck to see what was happening.

'What in hell is going on back there?' Robson yelled, his anger causing an ugly vein on the side of his neck to protrude. Murray also turned to see what the commotion was all about.

'Michael, I'm getting off,' Ratna announced. She called to the engineer. 'Open the hatch,' she insisted, moving to the rear of the stationary plane. The engineer looked bewildered by what was happening. Ratna turned to see that the crewman had remained standing next to the cockpit. She snapped at him in Indonesian. *'Open the door or I will do it myself!'*

'Jesus bloody Christ! What in the hell is going on?' Robson unbuckled, then flew out of his seat, furious with them all. He glared at the beautiful Eurasian woman causing the disturbance. One of the amateur hookers offered some snide remark which went unheard by all except Ratna, who immediately reached for the exit lock and turned the handle, releasing the door. The engineer hurried to her assistance.

'Who is this dumb bitch?' Robson snarled, moving away from his seat.

'Hold it, Graeme!' Murray barked, moving to block the aisle which his larger frame.

'Michael, that's the one who assaulted me at the club!' she called loudly, as noise exploded into the cabin through the now open doorway. Michael shook his head, raised his hands in surrender, and followed.

'Shit, not again!' he muttered angrily, having no idea whatsoever, what Ratna was talking about. Ratna sent Georgio a smouldering look and clattered down the steps to the apron. Michael followed her.

'Once you're out, you're out!' Robson yelled, motioning for the engineer to close and lock the hatch. He turned around and saw Georgio standing, still holding the bourbon. He snatched the bottle and took a long pull on the contents before offering the bottle to Murray, who shook his head, and refused. It was only then that Murray vaguely remembered something of the incident between John and some woman in the club. *My God*, he thought, *was that only last night?*

Outside, Michael caught up easily with Ratna as she stormed away from the aircraft.

'What in the devil's got into you?' he yelled, grabbing her arm, spinning her around to face him. They stood, facing each other angrily, both shouting to make themselves heard above the incredible noise.

'That man was the one who tried to assault me in the nightclub, Michael,' she shouted, then stamped her foot in childish frustration. Then she remembered that she hadn't told him what had happened inside the cabaret. Instead, she had behaved selfishly, recalling that she had taken it out on Michael, insisting that they return to their hotel. Ratna looked up at Michael.

'Oh Michael,' she cried, competing against the impossible noise, 'I'm sorry. I'm really, really sorry,' she said, reaching up to cling to him. 'I'll explain later.' Michael placed his arm around her and looked around the noisy, confused scene. He knew they should move off the concrete apron, quickly. They waited for several speeding vehicles to pass, then started walking back towards the terminal building.

'*Ratna!*' someone yelled, his voice barely audible as the thunderous roar of huge Rolls Royce aircraft engines signalled another aircraft's departure. They both turned.

'Michael, its Benny!' she shouted, taking control, and leading him towards the short, stocky banker.

'*Do you still want that lift?*' Benny yelled. He had watched her climb aboard the smaller aircraft and wasn't sure what was happening until the cabin door closed. He assumed she had changed her mind. Fortunately, as he walked slowly back to his own flight, he had glanced back, and witnessed Ratna hurrying away from the executive jet.

'Both of us?' she asked, holding onto Michael's arm tightly.

'Let's ask,' Benny shouted, indicating that they should follow. The three bent forward, hands in front, shielding their faces from a hot exhaust blasting across the busy apron as an aircraft bumped across the uneven concrete and came to rest where instructed. Michael could see from the arriving plane's cabin lights that the huge jet was empty, guessing correctly that this would be another evacuation flight that had just landed at the busy airport.

They made it to the foot of the mobile passenger-stairway together.

'Wait here,' Benny instructed them. 'I'll just go up and clear your travel with the Prime Minister's personal assistant.' Michael stood holding Ratna's hand under the scrutiny of more than a dozen heavily armed Indian soldiers. The *palace guard*, he thought, then looked down at the woman beside him.

'Okay?' he asked, holding her hand tightly.

'Okay,' she responded, but he could see that she was still distressed.

Moments later, Benny reappeared, and waved down for them to come aboard. They climbed the tall passenger steps, Michael impressed with the Salima family influence. They were met by security and physically checked before being permitted to enter the aircraft. Sirens sounded as they stepped inside the wide-bodied jet, alerting security that the Prime Minister's entourage had arrived. Michael and Ratna were ushered inside hurriedly, and escorted to seats in the forward compartment allocated to the accompanying Indian press contingent.

Minutes later they stood, awkwardly, holding onto the seats in front of their own, waiting while the VIPs all boarded the elegantly decorated Boeing. As the Prime Minister passed, followed by the South African President, the members of the press clapped politely, and remained standing until the two leaders and others of their group had all filed by into the VIP compartment. Their door was then locked from the inside. Four heavily armed Indian soldiers boarded the flight, taking positions in seats to either side of the

JAKARTA

VIP compartment's access door.

'Well, we're on our way,' Benny Salima smiled, accepting a glass of juice from the dark-skinned stewardess, and both Michael and Ratna thanked him again for what he'd done.

* * * * * *

Bali

Xanana had never been aboard a helicopter before.

He followed the Admiral's example, bending his head as the powerful rotor-blades chopped noisily through the heavy, humid air. He watched as Admiral Gopal strapped himself in and copied the procedure. Then they sat, waiting, while the pilot attempted, unsuccessfully, to contact the Ngurah Rai tower.

'Admiral,' the pilot said, looking back over his shoulder at the Navy's most senior officer, 'Bali tower communications are not responding. The hotel structure may be the problem,' he said, indicating the eight-hundred room complex surrounding the ocean at that point. In fact, this had not been the reason for the airport tower's refusal to acknowledge.

As air traffic controllers battled with incoming aircraft, stacked waiting for permission to land, they had not been able to communicate with the helicopter, knowing that the pilot must wait. The Indian Navy pilot glanced over his shoulder at the Admiral and waited for a response.

Gopal nodded and the pilot leaned forward, looking for the hotel ground engineer's signal that they were clear. Satisfied, the experienced airman pushed the cyclic control forward as he manipulated the collective, lifting the heavy machine off the ground a few metres. The helicopter wobbled unsteadily, and Xanana suffered momentary panic as the helicopter's nose turned to face into the sea-breeze.

Conscious of the congested traffic overhead, the pilot selected a course for the *INS Indira Gandhi*, deciding to maintain an altitude which would keep them above any incidental pleasure craft as they passed along the shallow, dangerous coast.

* * * * * *

The captain of *India One* waited, patiently, for his final clearance.

'*India One*, you are cleared to roll,' the air traffic controller's voice finally announced, instructing the Boeing's crew to depart.

'Roger, tower,' the captain responded, immediately pushing the controls forward, pumping aviation fuel rapidly through the system, where it converted into pure thrust. The Rolls Royce engines whirred then whined, the crescendo building to an impossible scream as the two hundred and fifty thousand kilogram aircraft strained under the captain's brake.

Out at sea aboard the *M.V. Rager*, Bartlett listened to the air traffic control clearance instructions carefully, then removed the headphones and flung these, carelessly, on top of the receiver. He turned to Fuad and nodded.

'They're up next. Get ready,' he ordered. Fuad moved to the port side of the ship and positioned himself firmly, bracing his feet, while Bartlett helped raise the deadly missile until it rested comfortably on Fuad's shoulder. He felt the *Rager* move slightly when a light breeze pushed the steel hull gently, and he compensated, adjusting his stance, ready to fire.

* * * * * *

Brakes released, the aircraft moved forward, slowly at first, then gathering momentum as engines screamed, thrusting the aircraft forward, along the well-lit runway. The passengers looked out through the windows as the jet continued to accelerate, the light rocking sensation signalling that they would soon lift off, and be safe.

Navigation lights continued to blink furiously as the jet's engines' high-pitched whine pierced the early evening air, changing pitch as the aircraft became airborne, and the undercarriage retracted. They were on their way.

* * * * * *

Fuad grasped the awkward launcher firmly and stared down through the sights, waiting for his target to come into view. It would be soon. Above, the sky was alive with blinking navigation lights as departing and arriving aircraft flew along their designated courses, guided by the over-worked Bali air traffic control tower.

Fuad wiped the perspiration from his brow, and breathed deeply. As darkness had descended he had become increasingly worried by the amount of air traffic, and he knew that he would have to strike the aircraft before it reached any real altitude. Suddenly, he cocked his head and listened, as haunting, familiar and unmistakable sounds approached through the darkness. He spun around in surprise, recognising the heavy, chopping sounds emanating from somewhere to his right. There! He spotted it, and knew immediately that he had been right as his eyes focused on the slow-moving navigation lights traveling just above sea-level.

Memories of helicopter gun-ship attacks flashed through his mind. They had been discovered, he knew, his eyes darting in panic from the flashing helicopter's lights to the end of the runway, then back again, his mind visualising the gunner's actions as he prepared to bring his thirty millimetre automatic cannons into line and fire.

Bartlett remained at the wheel, not meters from where Fuad stood, unable to see the fear which washed across the man's face as he listened in terror to the familiar sounds beating through the air, heading for their ship. At that moment, navigation lights blinked just above the runway's darkened horizon. Fuad froze, terrified to fire within view of the helicopter.

'Shoot! Fuad, shoot for chrissakes!' Bartlett bellowed, and Fuad swung the missile back instinctively, concentrating his line of sight slightly above the runway's end, barely catching the faint silhouette of the approaching aircraft as it left the airstrip behind. To his trained eyes, the target seemed to be low. But in that second, in one well-rehearsed motion he raised the launcher a fraction, aiming the missile directly to the left of the port navigation lights, then squeezed the trigger.

The *Stinger* leapt from its launcher leaving a light trail as it tore through the dimly-lit sky towards its target. Bartlett watched in fascination as the deadly rocket locked onto the fully-fuelled aircraft and, almost in that same moment, impacted with a blinding flash, creating an enormous fireball which lit the early evening sky.

In the distance, the seasoned helicopter pilot reacted spontaneously and, as trained, twisted the collective around expertly and pointed his gun-ship in the direction from where he had seen the missile fired. He armed the two cannons attached to the lower sides of the AH-64 Apache, then bore down on the floating target, prepared to open fire. It was only then, for the first time, that Bartlett recognized the approaching threat.

'Jesus Christ!' he yelled, knowing what must be done. He lifted the second missile assembly and rushed outside to assist Fuad before it was too late. Fuad had barely sufficient time to shoulder the *Stinger* before the gun-ship was upon them. Without further hesitation, he lifted the launcher and fired into the whirling blades as the helicopter bore down on them no more than a hundred meters from their ship.

For an infinitesimal moment, there was nothing. Then their world erupted all around, smashing them both brutally back onto the ship's deck.

The explosion filled the sky with a roar as the helicopter's long-range fuel tanks ruptured, then ignited under impact, killing all on board. As the last pieces of shrapnel fell into the sea, Bartlett was already on his feet and moving.

'Let's get the hell out of here!' Bartlett yelled. While he weighed anchor, Fuad rushed to throw the evidence into the sea. Within minutes, they were under way. By the time the first Search and Rescue teams finally arrived to search for survivors, Bartlett's *Rager* had already disappeared from the scene, steaming through the Lombok Straits on course for the Philippines.

* * * * * *

Less than a few minutes before, the *India One* aircraft captain swore loudly as the Lear Jet cut across the concrete hard-standing surface and entered the runway, just as the VIP flight had commenced to roll. The experienced pilot braked and looked at his crew in disbelief.

'What the…!' the startled officer exploded, just as the air traffic controller's voice flooded the airwaves.

'Bravo Delta Foxtrot,' the tired officer screamed, 'you are not cleared, do you read me, you are not cleared!' Others in the tall tower overlooking the airfield rose to their feet to see what was happening.

JAKARTA

'Bravo Delta Fox-trot,' someone growled, 'get the hell out of there!' The executive jet pilot ignored the instructions, turned, then lined up on the runway directly ahead of the huge jumbo and started rolling.

'Bali tower, this is Bravo Delta Fox-trot, we're rolling,' Robson announced arrogantly, as he pushed the throttle forward and smiled. In the cabin, John Georgio returned to his seat, still laughing at Robson's dangerous manoeuvre.

'Oooh weee!' he shouted. The smaller jet barely missed touching the 777's wing as they pushed recklessly past and jumped the long queue of waiting aircraft. The girls on board all screamed, believing that they would hit the other plane.

'Bravo Delta Fox-trot,' the frustrated controller called, 'you are endangering the lives of others. You are instructed to return to the terminal!' He knew now that this was most unlikely to happen as one of the other controllers yelled, 'He's going!'

Robson pulled a face and corrected the aircraft's line as it rolled on down the runway, gathering speed, knowing that he had the influence to have the matter settled later, when the complaint was lodged by the air traffic controllers. He looked across at his captain's concerned expression, and laughed.

'Don't worry, *Mas*,' he said, 'it's my licence they'll be after, not yours!' The captain glanced at his engineer, frightened. He could still smell the alcohol on Robson's breath, and had protested when the man had taken control of the aircraft. The seasoned captain sat strapped into his seat, carefully observing his employer's handling of the controls. He breathed deeply and watched the runway lights start to merge into one as the jet gathered speed and started to lift. He heard the engine pitch change, and glanced at Robson, who turned, caught his eye, and winked. Just as the missile struck.

* * * * * *

Most of the air traffic controllers caught the fireball out of the corner of their eyes, returning immediately to their screens to see what had happened. None in the tower sighted the second, low-level missile impact, the flash associated with this only confusing them more. The helicopter had only been identified on their screens during the last of those chaotic moments, which led to what they believed to be, a mid-air collision. Air investigators would later conclude that the helicopter had somehow strayed across the Lear Jet's path.

'*Get the Indian Prime Minister's flight away, immediately!*' the senior traffic controller barked, realizing the security implications should the VIP flight be delayed, not to mention the compounding problem of stacked aircraft waiting to land. The officer responsible for directing the Indian Prime Minister's aircraft obeyed.

* * * * * *

None of the passengers aboard *India One* flight had seen either of the two explosions, although a few of their number had heard something which they believed to be thunder. The captain had seen it, however, and communicated what he had witnessed to the tower. He discovered that several of the officers had watched the Lear Jet's departure with great concern, warning other flights to avoid the irresponsible pilot's flight-path. He had obviously collided with the Indian Navy helicopter which had appeared only moments before on their screens.

The explosion had occurred over the sea. Search and sea rescue teams were alerted immediately, but it would be some time before crews could be encouraged to don their uniforms and proceed in search of survivors. The traffic controllers then turned their attention to moving as many aircraft as quickly as possible, commencing with the VIP flight which had been paused, waiting for clearance when the accident had occurred. Satisfied that there would be no further danger, the tower gave clearance for them to leave.

'You may proceed, *India One*,' the tower advised, and the captain uttered a silent and practiced prayer as he repeated his procedure once gain. The passengers all remained silent, noticing that the cabin lights had been dimmed for their takeoff. As the engines thrust their aircraft forward, they leaned back, listening to the tyres bouncing along the uneven concrete runway. An overhead locker-door crashed open as the Boeing developed sufficient momentum to lift, wobbling slightly, before heading out over the dark ocean.

As their aircraft climbed, Michael looked out the window in time to catch the distant setting sun's last light, a thousand kilometers to the west. He turned to Ratna and smiled. They leaned closer, and embraced.

'I love you, Michael,' she said. He ran the back of his hand across her lips, then the soft skin of her face.

'I love you, too,' he said, and they kissed. Suddenly, witnessing the exchange, the cabin broke into thunderous applause, as the journalists, led by Benny, clapped and cheered enthusiastically.

KERRY B.COLLISON

Chapter 30

India

General Rahul Kumar sat behind the desk in the opulent office and signed the State of Emergency Decree, not dissimilar to the order imposed in 1975 by Prime Minister Indira Gandhi. Unconcerned with what might happen at the airport upon *India One*'s return, Kumar went about removing files and personal effects from the building, while the unsuspecting Prime Minister slept on board his flight. Upon his arrival, another crew would fly the South African President on to his own country, and the Prime Minister would be placed under arrest. Only hours before, the General had ordered his troops into New Delhi to support his imminent military rule.

Dr Imran Malhotra had already been arrested and incarcerated behind the walls of the Northern Command's military prison where he would, Kumar expected, spend the remaining days of his life. Politics being what they were in his country, the General would ensure that, with the first sign of any mass support for the late Vijay Rajesh's co-conspirator, Imran would undoubtedly be found dead in the detention centre before his popularity could further grow.

As he waited for confirmation that *India One* had landed, Rahul Kumar, dictator-to-be, read through the highly sensitive documents once again, wondering if the Americans might not consider supporting the original concept conceived by his predecessors. He took the folders and locked them away in his personal case for further consideration at a later, and more appropriate, occasion. Now it was time for his announcement. He checked the clock, then rose, brushed his uniform with one hand and marched proudly across the wide, marble floor of the room from which he would rule all of India. He paused momentarily, as if reminded of something, and turned, but could see nothing there. Then he opened the tall, white and gold double doors, moved into the adjacent chamber, and took his position in front of the television cameras. Kumar's aide closed the doors gently on the empty room, unmindful of the long, highly-polished Canadian Oak table standing majestically at the centre of the Premier's office. A solitary reminder of democratic rule — Viceroy Mountbatten's gift to a new nation.

* * * * * *

India's naval expeditionary force approaching Timor

In Admiral Krishna Gopal's absence, a worried commodore hesitated, wondering what to do. The Admiral was more than six hours overdue, and the Battle Group Commander was most reluctant to send SAR further into Indonesian waters, concerned that this might jeopardise their mission. Leaving instructions to be woken immediately if there was any news of Admiral Gopal, the Commodore retired, exhausted by the long hours spent on the flag bridge.

He made his way aft through the non-watertight door which had been latched open, brushing the dark, navy-blue curtains aside as he entered that section which led to his quarters.

At 0455 hours he was woken by an excited aide, who advised that his presence was urgently required back on the ship's bridge. The Commodore dressed hurriedly, hoping there would be news of Krishna Gopal. Instead, when he entered the Captain's navigation bridge, he was handed a decoded signal which he read, then immediately crushed into a ball, his anger apparent to the other officers.

The order had been for the fleet to return immediately, as a State of Emergency had been declared throughout his country. The brief, but succinct instruction had been signed by General Rahul Kumar. The Battle Group Commander scowled, confused as to what he should do. There had been no mention of the Prime Minister.

In Gopal's absence, he stood on the carrier's bridge, conscious that the Indian armada was still steaming on its original course. *Should he ignore the impertinent General and attempt to contact the Prime Minister for his advice, or should he discontinue the mission?*

JAKARTA

What had happened to Admiral Gopal?

He looked out towards the horizon and observed a flock of birds flying mockingly alongside the massive, floating platform. As the first morning light cast grey shadows across the sky, his decision was made for him.

'Commodore?' the alarmed Captain came up to the senior officer, his face white, another signal in his extended hand. The Battle Group Commander accepted the communiqué, and read the message. Minutes later, he ordered the armada to turn around, and instructed the Captain to have his officers plot a new course for their home port. And to ensure that they complied with the demands contained in the signal, two United States SSN-21s surfaced within view, demonstrating that the American President was indeed prepared to support his request, if necessary with force.

* * * * * *

East China Sea, off Taiwan

China's Fleet Battle Group Commanders acknowledged that their attempts to intimidate Taiwan into submission by engaging in nuclear blackmail had failed miserably. Beijing's campaign to dominate the nations of East Asia and the South China Sea had been countered by the United States Seventh Fleet forward forces, and in the absence of the Indian armada's confirmation that they had arrived at their destination off Timor's shores, the planned assault had been considerably delayed, resulting in a dramatic and sudden change in Chinese tactics.

As Chinese DF-15 rockets fired from Fujian Province impacted at sea less than twenty miles to the north and south of Taiwan, the first of the Seventh Fleet's forward deployment entered the waters to the island's east. Before noon, led by the aircraft carrier, *USS Kitty Hawk*, the full American fleet's composition became known to the Chinese commanders and the confrontation ended.

And in the East Pacific, both Chinese *Xia* class SSBNs were surprised at the activity surrounding their ships when the submarines surfaced two hundred miles off the California coast and were immediately instructed to turn about. In the presence of four American SSN-21s, they willingly complied, plotting a course which would take them back into the North Pacific and away from the hostile American reception.

******

Philippines, Celebes Sea

A hundred miles to the south-east of Zamboanga, Captain Dave Bartlett, swung the wheel of the *M.V. Rager* to port, then corrected his course heading for the small coastal Filipino village deep in the Moro Gulf. Satisfied that there was no shipping ahead, he left the wheel-house and moved forward to where Fuad sat, crouched on the deck eating meat from a freshly opened can.

'Fuad,' he called. The other man hesitated, turned, then dropped what he was eating as he sprang to his feet.

'What are you doing?' he asked, fear twisting his bowels. Bartlett was holding the Winchester shotgun directly at Fuad's head. His lips trembled and his knees went to jelly as he recognized the look in his killer's eyes. He had seen this expression before and knew, with certainty, that he was going to die. In the instant Fuad's mouth moved to beg for mercy, the blast removed most of his head, throwing him bodily over the ship's railing and into the sea. Bartlett watched as the body disappeared in the *Rager's* wake, then returned to the wheel-house and locked the weapon away.

He gazed out to sea as a flock of seagulls winged their way overhead, his mind preoccupied with what he would be required to do on arrival at his destination. He had decided to sell the ship, although he knew he would be lucky to see more than fifty thousand dollars in the exchange. Then he would see to whatever outstanding commitments there were, including settling up with the Americans before disappearing once more. With this thought in mind, he considered what name he might use for his new identity. A sardonic grin pulled at one side of his face as he recalled how difficult it had been adjusting to being known as Bartlett. On more than one occasion, he remembered inadvertently signing himself away as Stephen Coleman, and that it had virtually taken years for him not to respond whenever someone called 'Stephen' in his presence.

He removed the dirty baseball cap and rubbed the side of his face. He examined the torn brim, ruefully, then flung the faded cap out through the open cabin doorway, into the sea, deciding that it was time he bought himself one of those hair-pieces he had seen in Manila.

His recent killing of Fuad already washed from his mind, Stephen Coleman stood happily, gazing at the distant mountains, humming an old tune he remembered from his hazy past.

* * * * * *

Bali

Soft swells running in from the Indian Ocean lifted pieces of wreckage, burying some under timeless sand, while other metal fragments were pushed gradually towards the shore. Here, they would undoubtedly be found and turned into trinkets by the local craftsmen.

The force of the explosion had ripped through the helicopter with such ferocity the few remains recovered of those who had been aboard were not identifiable. Admiral Gopal, Admiral of the Indian Fleet, and Xanana Soares, President-to-be of an Independent East Timor, were cremated together in the traditional Balinese manner. When their ashes had been gathered, these were taken down to the beach overlooking the place where they had met their final destiny, together.

There, their remains were scattered with great ceremony, providing an escape for their spirits from the worry of earthly concerns, forever.

* * * * * *

The radiation released by the *Rama II* accident represented the equivalent of one twentieth of all that resulting from post-World War II atmospheric atomic weapons tests. As Java lies just below the Equator, Indonesia's northern neighbours of Singapore, Malaysia and Brunei were spared. Had the meltdown occurred in Northern Sumatra or even Indonesian Borneo where bush-fires would continue to rage out of control for a number of years, the death toll would have been considerable in those neighbouring

ASEAN nations.

Those most affected were the farm workers and peasants who lived within the immediate disaster area. Radioactive clouds were carried across to the east of Indonesia, over Bali, Nusa Tenggara, Timor and across the Timor Sea to Darwin. The levels of contamination varied according to the distance these deadly clouds travelled. In Java, some fifty million people were exposed, in one form or another, to contaminated air, water and crops.

Although the initial death toll was less than two thousand, a further six hundred thousand families were affected. Among these, another eighty-three thousand would develop radiation related diseases, and within six months from when the meltdown occurred. In spite of the massive evacuation undertaken by the Indonesian authorities, many of the evacuees were peasants, deeply bound to the land. Within weeks, they drifted back to where they had spent all of their lives, and started again. As levels of contamination decreased with time and weather, the farmers recommenced that timeless cycle of rice production, planting the first of their new crops just one year later.

The entire area surrounding *Rama II* was declared a no-go zone, and no attempts were made to restore the project in any form whatsoever. Before Indonesia was permitted further uranium imports, the International Atomic Energy Agency successfully extracted an agreement for open inspection on its remaining plants, thereby circumventing any future misuse of excess fuel generated in these nuclear plants. The threat of Indonesia developing its own delivery system for ICBMs, or becoming a member of the Nuclear Club in the immediate future, disappeared. The Bandung Research and Development Center remained idle, waiting for the day when some future leader might look enviously at neighbouring shores and decide to resurrect the project.

Tourism in Bali saw a dramatic fall in the number of visiting tourists to the island. Exaggerated fears of contaminated food and water sent many of the smaller operators to the wall.

In Australia, an attempt to restrict products originating from Northern Queensland and the Northern Territory was, sensibly, aborted.

* * * * * *

In the months that followed, a further and overwhelmingly supported South African-sponsored resolution was passed, calling for the United Nations to implement a plebiscite in East Timor, one which would guarantee the people the opportunity to vote, without fear, to remain as part of Indonesia, or elect their own independent government.

Surprisingly, Indonesia agreed. When the Act of Free Choice was conducted under United Nation's supervision, the people domiciled in the former Portuguese Colony voted, by a clear majority, to remain as Indonesia's twenty-seventh province. In the preceding months leading up to the plebiscite, Indonesia redirected a substantial number of its transmigrants from other programmes, settling these in areas surrounding Dili and other major population centres throughout the Timor province still referred to as *Tim-Tim*.

The United States signed a defense co-operation agreement with Indonesia, and moved its Seventh Fleet to its new home port, in Timor.

China continued on its belligerent path, threatening regional stability, poking and prodding at Taiwan. The following year, just months after the paramount leader passed away and was succeeded by a younger but more aggressive tyrant, China and Taiwan signed a friendship treaty, finally committing their two countries to union within the decade.

Lim Swee Giok's flagship, the Asian Pacific Commercial Bank, continued to flourish under the astute management of the Salima brothers. Their investments in China in no way suffered from the 'incident' between the two Chinas, and both Denny and James were invited to the American Presidential Inauguration Ball the following year. Benny maintained his position in Indonesia, but after two years of fighting Indian bureaucracy, withdrew his banking operations from the sub-continent.

Epilogue

Ruswita leaned back into the soft, cushioned settee, and immediately felt her energy drain away. As she lay there, thinking about that morning's events, she experienced a sensation of wholeness, of togetherness, and she smiled contentedly, thinking of her children and friends. Tomorrow, she knew, would be a most special day.

It had been Siti's first birthday in Indonesia, and Ruswita had thrown a most lavish party for her granddaughter. Michael and Ratna had returned to Jakarta, as promised, so that Aunt Ruswita could see their child for the first time. They had married in India, with a quiet, civil ceremony. Then after a whirlwind honeymoon visiting exotic places such as the Taj Mahal and the Pyramids of Egypt, Ratna had finally settled down with her husband, in Ohio, where Michael had taken up teaching at the State University, lecturing primarily in radiation safety procedures.

He was not at all unhappy with his decision to leave Washington, and the Defense Intelligence Agency. When their first child had arrived, they returned to Indonesia to fulfil a promise Ratna had given her aunt many years before.

* * * * * *

Lani had not attended the granddaughter's party.

For weeks, Ruswita had been preparing her old, dear friend, for a most special moment in their lives. Ruswita had decided to reveal her secret to Ratna, as she had already included her name with her other heirs in a revised will. The two grey-haired women, had spoken in depth as to how Ruswita would break this news to the one Lani had loved, cared for and cherished as her own child, since birth.

As Ruswita lay quietly, her body bordering on sleep, her thoughts turned to the woman who had been her dearest friend since her first days in Jakarta, and she prayed that Lani would understand her need, to now openly call Ratna her own.

* * * * * *

Lani had been deeply shocked by Ruswita's announcement, and still could not believe that she would proceed with her cruel and selfish disclosure. Distressed and bitter, she had feigned a severe migraine, refusing to attend the lavish lunch-time celebrations.

As was her custom, Lani prepared the tray of Chinese tea and cookies.

For several, long moments she stood, thinking, almost as if she had forgotten something. Then she lifted the tray supporting the Chinese porcelain service, and walked through the garden and into the main house.

During recent months, she noticed that the stairs had become even more difficult to manage and Lani rested, half-way, placing the tray alongside while recovering her breath. Looking down at the refreshments, Lani suddenly smiled at the countless number of times she had carried afternoon tea upstairs, in readiness for when Ruswita would wake from her customary nap. She had never once failed to have the lukewarm tea and biscuits sitting there, ready for her dear old friend.

She sighed deeply, recalling the burdensome memory of an earlier attempt at preventing Ruswita from distancing Ratna from her, and how it had failed. At that time, Lani had been deeply hurt, and desperately wanted to punish Ruswita. She glanced at the two biscuits sitting innocently, positioned, as she had done so many times before, to one side of the Chinese tea.

The prolific and highly toxic fungus grew in parts of their garden. The hot, humid tropical conditions were ideal for such mushrooms. The hallucinogenic jamur had been easily disguised in the cookies she'd prepared, and she had placed these on the tray knowing that Ruswita would not be able to resist the freshly baked biscuits.

JAKARTA

On that fateful day, years before, and totally out of character, Lim Swee Giok had woken and consumed the biscuits prepared for Ruswita. The small amount of *jamur* that she had used at that time would only have made Ruswita violently ill, but was apparently far too toxic for her ailing husband. It was fortunate that Lani had noticed these missing, and had later removed the service. After the doctor had returned for Lim's body, Lani had informed Ruswita that she had seen the housekeeper talking to someone at the front gates. She had never understood why Ruswita had not called the police.

Refreshed by her brief rest, Lani rose and continued upstairs, not at all surprised to find Ruswita asleep on the lounge, nestled amongst the pillows Lani had made during the many long and lonely hours she had spent alone in her room at the rear of the house.

She placed the cookies, tea, and miniature cups on the glass-topped, carved coffee table, and stood admiring Ruswita's magnificent rings as her left arm hung listlessly at her side. Lani leaned over, and kissed Ruswita softly on her face. Then she left her alone, confident that Ratna would never, never discover the secret of her birth.

Author's Note

Whilst reflecting on another manuscript which had occupied much of my time when living in Asia, I came across a section which related to the period of my life when I was required to spend considerable time in Thailand. Memories of Bangkok came flooding back to mind, amongst which was the occasion when, by chance, I shared a car and driver with Sahid, who was in town undergoing treatment for wounds to his arm and shoulder.

Sahid was Mohammed Gadafi's brother, and had been caught during the American aerial attack aimed at removing Gadafi from the world stage; instead, the Libyan leader survived, but sadly his adopted daughter died in the bombing. Sahid had then slunk off to Bangkok where, having discovered his identity, I thought him to be either extremely naïve or a little too daring considering the number of American agents stationed in Thailand.

Reagan, as President, would have approved this attempted assassination attempt. The point of this inclusion is relative to my story, Jakarta. American Presidents have, throughout history, sanctioned the execution of foreign Presidents, Heads-of-State and other world leaders.

During the Eisenhower Administration, CIA attempts against the life of President Soekarno of Indonesia were sanctioned on a number of occasions. It is most probable that this executive order carried over into the Kennedy era as further attempts, financed by the CIA, were also made against the Indonesian Republic's founding father. Needless to say, *Bung Karno* survived all six attempts, although many who were present were not as fortunate, including the six young children whose distressing deaths resulted from the grenade attack aimed at their President during the official opening of the Cikini Hospital in Jakarta.

We have also learned that Lyndon Johnson and Richard Nixon both, understandably, considering the politics of that era, placed a price on Ho Chi Minh's head. And then, of course, there was John Kennedy and Fidel Castro, George Bush and Saddam Hussein, and a host of South American leaders who were perceived in the United

States as dangerous to the security of the world's largest democracy. It is, therefore, not without reason that I have suggested the possibility of an American President sanctioning executive action to remove another country's leader as an integral part of the storyline in my novel.

* * * * * *

There has been considerable concern in the United States in relation to the Communist-owned China Ocean Shipping Company (COSCO), which is a six hundred ship global corporation supervised by the People's Liberation Army (PLA). In documents registered with the United States Government, the employer of record for this organisation's interests in America is a notorious arms dealer who has, on occasion, been sighted taking coffee with the President in the White House.

COSCO's acquisition of the former United States Navy shipyard at Long Beach was cited as one of three questionable deals. The first of these was the twenty year, US$14.5 million per annum lease of the Long Beach facility, which was closed down earlier this decade as a result of American defense cut backs. The City of Long Beach, under the terms of the agreement, is obliged to pay approximately $235 million to modernise the facility for the Chinese; COSCO's annual lease payments of $14.5 million would require 16 years to repay the initial costs. A penalty clause in the agreement provided for COSCO to receive $32 million dollars worth of dock-side cranes as reimbursement if the contract turned sour. The second arrangement was the $138 million taxpayer-subsidized loan guarantee to a COSCO subsidiary to build four container ships in an Alabama shipyard.

The third, and most contentious of the three deals, was a recent agreement reached between a Hong Kong based COSCO subsidiary and the Panamanian Government to lease "anchor-ports" to the Panama Canal, a move which grants Communist China a strategic toe-hold in the Western Hemisphere. It is true that China, through this shipping company, has acquired control over the Pacific port of Balboa and the Atlantic port of Cristobal, both of which flank the Panama Canal. According to Panama's leading newspapers, COSCO's lease arrangements were effected through

JAKARTA

Hutchinson Corporation in Hong Kong. It is a fact also, that 2,000 AK-47 rifles were seized in Oakland, America, from one of the COSCO ships, and General Chi of the PLA made the statement that Communist China had already developed the technology to deliver nuclear warheads to America's West Coast. (Sections of the preceding paragraph have been quoted with permission from 'The New American' Internet pages titled 'China Takes Over Former U.S. Navy Shipyard')

And the Japanese Government has already developed a missile titled H-2A, and is currently considering its conversion to military use.

* * * * * *

In the course of the past year, we have seen a series of calamities strike South East Asian nations, most of which, as in the case of the oil spills off Singapore and the Asian currency raids, were manmade. Then we had drought, and the disastrous fires which raged for many months across the islands of Sumatra, Borneo and Java. The fires undoubtedly resulted from the slash and burn tactics used to further enhance the pockets of the incredibly rich in Indonesia; we know that these most destructive fires could easily have been avoided, but graft and corruption are difficult masters to control, particularly when there are hundreds of millions of dollars involved. Even so, none of these events could, in any way, ever compete with the devastation which frequently accompanies a volcanic eruption or an earthquake.

Having lived in Asia for more than thirty years, I still believe that there is nothing more frightening than to be caught on the upper levels of a skyscraper when a tremor strikes. I recall attending dinner in the Hotel Sahid Jaya supper club one evening, to farewell a couple who had become dear to my family over the years.

This well-appointed restaurant was located on the eighteenth floor of the building. When the tremor struck, the lights failed and the building started to sway, terrifying the guests, as the restaurant's windows extended from ceiling to floor, providing a view directly down to Jalan Jenderal Sudirman and the footpaths below. Tables danced around the room and we clung to our chairs, waiting for the whipping motion of the tall building to cease. The memory of those minutes will remain with me forever, and the feeling of total helplessness I experienced still haunts me whenever I enter skyscrapers, even today.

Tremors are not an unusual occurrence in Indonesia, which boasts some sixty active volcanoes. Once, while dining in our villa in the mountain resort area of Cimacan, I witnessed a tremor with such incredible force that it bounced the four hundred kilo teak dining table across the room leaving startled guests with their mouths hanging open in surprise. Moments later, I recall, we then watched as an aftershock emptied the swimming pool. The point I wish to make here is that Indonesia would not be the safest of places to be considering the introduction of nuclear power plants.

As for Bali, I sometimes wonder just how many of the island's tourists have any idea as to the extent of the calamity caused when Gunung Agung erupted, spewing poisonous gases from its crater before spilling down the mountain's side killing thousands of one of God's most delightful races. The final death toll resulting from lava flow, gas and the eruption itself, which threw boulders the size of motor cars kilometers into the air, exceeded eight thousand.

It is fact that the Indonesian Parliament passed a bill on the twenty seventh of February, 1997, that cleared the way for the construction of up to twelve nuclear power plants on the geologically volatile islands to Australia's north. The first of these was to be built at the foot of the dormant volcano, Mount Muria, which lies some four hundred kilometers to the east of Jakarta, in one of the most densely populated areas known to mankind. Dr Habibie, Indonesia's Minister for Science and Technology, quite nonchalantly stated that his country must *'pasang pajung sebelum hujan'* which literally translates as, *prepare the umbrella before it rains*. He was, of course, referring to Indonesia's enormous power problems, and his desire to push for the accelerated development of nuclear power plants. Within six months, public pressure and world opinion caused Habibie to declare that Indonesia was no longer considering the use of nuclear power.

As an experienced Asia-phile, I would insist that it would be naïve of any to believe that, with the promise of billions of dollars in construction contracts in the offing, and given yet another opportunity to siphon large amounts of infrastructure funds away, those responsible for the final decision may not necessarily spend

JAKARTA

too much of their time worrying about the consequences of building a national power grid, driven by nuclear power, over the geologically unstable islands. Over the past forty years, the world's populations have had the misfortune to experience the following nuclear accidents:

- Windscale, England (October 7, 1957) A fire broke out at this plutonium production plant, releasing significant amounts of radioactive material.

- Idaho, USA. The SL-1 plant (January 3, 1961) Three workers were killed when a control rod was ejected from the core while being manually moved by one of the workers.

- Enrico Fermi, Michigan, USA. (October 5, 1966) A partial meltdown occurred, when a component broke loose and blocked the flow of coolant.

- Browns Ferry plant, Alabama, USA. (March 22, 1975) A fire erupted in the control room when a candle flame was used to check for air leaks.

- Three Mile Island, Pennsylvania, USA. (March 28, 1979) As a result of equipment failures and human error, the water level in the reactor core decreased to the point that the fuel was no longer submerged in water. Without the cooling normally provided, the cladding and some of the fuel pellets melted. Large quantities of radioactive material were released into the containment building which, thankfully, performed as designed.

- Chernobyl, former Soviet Union. (April 26, 1986) Failure to follow established procedures and poor design resulted in this, the world's worst nuclear accident. The design of the Chernobyl reactor resulted in a very rapid increase in heat after the water used to cool the core was lost.
  Thirty-one people, all of whom were on-site emergency response personnel, died as a result of the accident. Two workers were killed by an associated explosion. Twenty-nine were killed by acute affects of radiation exposure; two hundred and three were

hospitalised with radiation sickness; more than thirty-six hours elapsed after the accident before the more than one hundred thousand local inhabitants living within a thirty mile radius were told to evacuate.

My reasons for writing this story were triggered by the concerns that I have regarding the possibility that Indonesia may, in the future, decide to resurrect the Nuclear Power Plant programme. Although I sincerely believe that technology developed in the United States and Japan severely reduces the risk of nuclear accidents occurring, particularly those resulting from structural damage caused by such geological disasters, I cannot resist wondering what might occur if a nuclear plant were constructed, as the Indonesians had originally planned, on such an unstable location as Mount Muria in Java, one of the most densely populated rural areas in the world. Coupled with the presence of those two old Indonesian warlords, Graft and Corruption, I, for one, would be most concerned.

* * * * * *

The story 'Jakarta' is a work of fiction, based on my own imagination and personal experiences whilst living in Indonesia and other parts of Asia; although I have based the story-line on some historic fact which is easily identified. The rest, I leave to the reader's imagination. However, there are some disturbing facts which should be mentioned here. India's population grows by some twenty-five millions each year and, according to United Nations projections, it could well be that we will see India become a net importer of food within the next two decades, about the same time as its population exceeds that of China's. Both India and Pakistan have nuclear technology, and are likely to use this in the event of another major altercation between the two nations.

Oil, gas and uranium will most surely run out before the close of the next century, leaving us with another hundred years of coal before the disappearance of all known fuels.

* * * * * *

Jakarta

It is imperative to stress, here, that I admire the Indonesian people for their culture, their kindness and their resilience. I was born in Australia but my adopted country, Indonesia, will always hold a very special place in my heart. I trust that my readers understand that in no way has it been my intention to denigrate the people of Asia. I wish merely to provide entertaining reading whilst, in some small way, affording those who may not have had the opportunity to enjoy the beauty of Asia and its colourful cultures, a small glimpse into what these might be.

Kerry B Collison
Melbourne

Glossary

ABRI	Indonesian Armed Forces
Aduh	exclamation, a cry
a.k.a.	also known as
AKABRI	Indonesian Armed Forces Academy
ALRI	Indonesian Navy
ANZUS	Australian, New Zealand, US Treaty
ASEAN	Association of South East Asian nations
ASIO	Australian Security Intelligence Organization (Australian domestic spy-service)
AURI	Indonesian Airforce
Antara	Indonesian News Agency
APCB	Asian Pacific Commercial Bank
APODETI	early East Timorese political party
arisan	office-run guaranteed lottery
ASAP	as soon as possible
ASIS	Australian Secret Intelligence Service Australian Overseas Spy Service
bahasa	language
BAKIN	Badan Kordinasi Intelijen: Indonesian CIA
bangsat	arse-hole, bastard
bapak	sir, respected male, often used to refer to the Indonesian President
Bapak-bapak dan Ibu-ibu	Gentlemen, and Ladies
BATAN	Indonesian Atomic Energy Authority
batik	Indonesian/Malay traditional cloth design.
becak	three-wheeled pedicab
bonsai	Japanese miniature trees
BOT	Build, Operate then Transfer, of projects
BWR	Boiling Water Reactor
bubur	porridge
bulé	derogatory name for white people

capung	dragonfly
CIA	Central Intelligence Agency
COMINT	Communication Intelligence
COSCO	China Shipping Company
DARPA	Defence Advanced Research Projects Agency
DIA	Defence Intelligence Agency
Diet	Japanese Parliament
Dili	former capital of East Timor
dim sum	Chinese breakfast individual serves
Dong Feng 31	Chinese ICBM
dukun	medicine man, spell-caster
durian	delicate tasting but foul smelling fruit
El Niño	climatic influence
FBR	Fast Breeder Reactor
Fretelin	Front for the Liberation of East Timor
gado-gado	mixed, cold vegetable dish, covered with peanut sauce
gaji	wages
gamelan	Balinese orchestra (bamboo xylophone)
GOLKAR	ruling political party in Indonesia (called a functional group)
gudang	store room
Gudang Garam	popular cigarette brand
halal	unadulterated Moslem-prepared style in food
Hankam	Indonesian Department of Defense
har gao	Chinese steamed dim sum dish
Hari Nyepi	religious 'quiet day' in Bali.
H-2A	Japanese rocket programme
H-3B	Japanese rocket programme
HN-5B	Communist Chinese man-portable surface-to-air missile
Ibu	older woman, mother
IAEA	International Atomic Energy Agency
ICBM	Intercontinental Ballistic Missile
ikan pepes	BBQ'd spiced fish wrapped in banana leaf
IFF	range finder for Stinger
IRBM	Intermediary Range Ballistic Missile
Istana	the palace, often used figuratively
jamur racun	poisonous mushroom (amanita muscaria)

JAKARTA

JB	Johore Bahru: Malaysia's causeway city
kain-kebaya	traditional ladies blouse and sarong
kali	river or stream, canal
Kalimantan	Indonesian Borneo
Kalki	mythical Hindu god of destruction
Kakadu	Northern Australian National Park
kampung	village
kecil	small
kelereng	a game of marbles
kemasukan	to be posessed by a spirit
kongsi	partnership, commercial enterprise
korupsi	corruption
kretek	clove cigarette
kumpul-kerbau	literally a gathering of buffaloes but used by Indonesians to mean living together, having an affair
laksa	spicy Malay-Chinese curry noodle soup
LCC	famous early seventies Jakarta night-club
LE-7A	Japanese rocket engine
LE-9	future Japanese rocket engine
LMFBR	Liquid Metal Fast Breeder Reactor
Long March	Chinese ICBM
lurah	village head, chief
losmen	boarding house
Mach two	approximately 2,000 kph
mandi	to bathe
MANPAD	Man Operated Stinger Missile unit
MW	megawatt
'Na	abbreviated name form for Ratna
NAFTA	North American Free Trade Agreement
nasi	cooked rice
nenek-mcyang	ancestors
NPP	nuclear power plant
NSA	National Security Agency
NSC	National Security Council (India)
nyonin kinzei	Japanese for 'women forbidden'
nyonya	Madame, Mrs
Oe-Cusse	former Portuguese enclave in West Timor
Ombar-Wetar	deep submarine trench off East Timor

Operasi Komodo	Indonesian Fifth Column activities in former Portuguese Timor
Ora Et Labora	a school in Jakarta
Pak	abbreviated form of Bapak (Mr, sir)
PALAPA	Indonesia's satellite system
Pedoman	leader
pembantu	servant
panggilan	whore
PEPELIN	Perusahan Pembangkit Listrik Nuklir (Indonesian Nuclear Power Company)
peranakan	of mixed extraction
PERTAMINA	Indonesian State-owned oil company
pici	small black cap worn by men
pisang	banana
pisang goreng	fried banana
PLA	Peoples Liberation Army (China)
Presiden	President
pribumi	indigenous person
PWR	Pressurized Water Reactor
Pulau Kambing	an island in East Timor
pungli	pungutan liar: demands for corrupt payment
P.T.	Perusahan Terbatas: limited liability company
Puri Kauh	Balinese name for Robson's villa
Puri Selera	Balinese restaurant
Rama	a king from the Ramayana Epic
Rama I to V	Indonesian Nuclear Power Plants
rendang	Indonesian spicy beef stew (goulash)
RCTI	Indonesian commercial TV station (owned by one of Soeharto's sons)
SAR	Search and Rescue
saté	skewered meat cooked over a charcoal BBQ
saté babi	pork ditto
saté kambing	goat ditto
saté penyu	turtle ditto
saudara	brother, friend, relative
SBS	Singapore Broadcasting Service

scram	terminology explaining a reactor shutdown procedure
Selamat datang	welcome
Selamat pagi	good morning
Selamat siang	good morning, good day
Selamat sore	good afternoon
Selamat malam	good evening
sialan!	exclamation, similar to goddamn
siao mai	dim sum dish
SS	submarine
SSN	nuclear submarine
SSN-21	twenty-first century nuclear submarine
SSBN	nuclear ballistic missile-armed submarine
Stinger	American manufactured, man-portable surface-to-air missile
SUBUD	Susila Budi Dharma religious cult
SVML	vehicle mounted Stinger rocket
TAG	Stinger guidance system
tai chi	Asian martial art
Taipan	powerful wealthy entrepreneur
telepon	telephone
terima kasih	thank you
tikar	woven mat
Tim Tim	acronym for East Timor (Timor-Timur)
tuan	sir, usually for foreigners
totok	pure Chinese immigrant to Indonesia
TPP	Thermal Power Plant
rezeki	luck, fortunes
sarong	wrap around dress
selendang	shoulder scarf, shawl
VTOL	Vertical Take-off and Landing aircraft

Places in India:	Places in Japan:	Places in China:
Goa	Shikoku	Shanghai
Lakshdweep	Hamaoka	Guangzhou
Vishakhapatnam	Kyushu	Chongging
Port Blair	Hokkaido	Xianggang
New Delhi		(Hong Kong)
Calcutta		Beijing
Bombay		

Chinese Navy Ships:
Jianghu	class of frigate
Huangfeng	class of missile ship
Han	class of nuclear submarine
Anshan	Soviet destroyers
Luda	ex Soviet destroyers

Indian Navy Ships:
SSGN Chakra	submarine
INS Viraat	aircraft carrier
INS Indira Gandhi	aircraft carrier
Rajputs	destroyers
Godavari	frigates
Vijay Durg	corvettes
Vidyut	missile craft

JAKARTA

New Authors Welcome!

New Authors are invited to submit their manuscripts to our offices in the United States of America, or Australia. For further details regarding manuscript submission contact our offices of visit our web page on:

http://www.sidharta.com.au
email: karam.1@osu.edu

Sid Harta Publishers
P.O. Box 1102
Hartwell Victoria 3125
Australia
Phone: (61) 3 9560 9920 or mobile: (61) 0414958623
Fax: (61) 3 9560 9921
email: author@sidharta.com.au